THE SOULSEER CHRONICLES BOOK ONE

SUE TINGEY

MARKED

Jo Fletcher

New York • London

Jo Fletcher Books
An imprint of Quercus
New York • London

ISBN 978-1-62365-920-2

Library of Congress Control Number: 2015946253

Distributed in the United States and Canada by
Hachette Book Group
1290 Avenue of the Americas
New York, NY 10104

Manufactured in the United States

10 9 8 7 6 5 4 3 2

www.quercus.com

To Howard

One

The school's entrance hall was smaller than I remembered, but then, the last time I had been there, more than fifteen years ago, I'd been only ten and easily intimidated—I had changed since. But even so, I wasn't looking forward to this visit.

My heels announced my progress as I walked across the tiled expanse of the lobby toward the woman waiting to greet me.

Miss Mitchell was everything one would expect of the headmistress of an all-girls' private school: tall and buxom with a ruddy complexion and short, wild, wavy hair. The expression "jolly hockey sticks" could have been made for her, although from the tightness at the corners of her mouth I could see that any jollity she had this afternoon was forced.

"Miss de Salle," she said, crossing the lobby to greet me, her hand extended, "I have heard so much about you."

"Lucky, please," I said.

"Then you must call me Lydia," she replied, briskly shaking my hand. "Can I offer you a cup of tea or coffee?"

"I think I'd rather get on with it," I told her.

"Of course." She gave me an odd, twisted smile, as though she was embarrassed. "I really appreciate you coming. I would have understood if you hadn't wanted to assist."

"Water under the bridge." My eyes shifted upward and I shivered. "But I'm not sure I can help you." I couldn't see any point in playing games.

"I was told that if anyone could, it would be you."

I'd read that this woman had been headmistress for only three years, so she didn't know me—not Lucky de Salle the person. She almost certainly knew of me as Lucinda de Salle, the disgraced ex-pupil; she might have even heard of Lucky de Salle, a very minor celebrity, but she didn't know *me*. And I liked to tell things as they were.

"Look," I said, as we approached the stairs I had hoped I would never have to climb again, "last time I was here I tried to help and was scared half to death and then expelled for my trouble. I couldn't help then and I'm not sure I can help now. The only reason I agreed to come here at all is because of the Ouija board. If your three boarders were playing with it and didn't perform the final ritual, you could well end up with a problem far worse than the spirits of two young girls."

"What do you mean?" she asked, glancing my way.

"The twins are nasty, vindictive little things, but there are far more vicious creatures out there." Which was true: I myself had faced some deeply malevolent spirits. But fifteen years ago the twins had frightened me more than any spirit had before or since, and today I was confronting my demons. It didn't help that my best friend Kayla had refused point-blank to come with me. Kayla was never scared of anything, so if she was scared of whatever was up in the attic, I was pretty certain I had good reason to be.

Lydia walked with me through the silent corridors and up the first two flights of stairs, but when we reached the third she hesitated. This last climb led up to the sixth form common room and the attic beyond.

"It's okay," I said. "You don't have to come."

She managed a small smile. "Thank you."

I returned her smile, but I had to force the corners of my mouth to curl upward. I took the first step up, and that's when the girls began to call to me.

"Lucky, Lucky," they whispered. "Lucky's coming; Lucky, Lucky, Lucky."

I hesitated. My legs felt leaden, but I gripped the banister and forced my feet to move upward, slowly, one step at a time.

By the time I reached the common room I was shivering. The last time I'd been there I had been running through it, running to get help, running to get away.

I crossed the room, the sound of my heels cushioned by the carpeted floor. When I reached the door at the other end I lifted my hand to grip the doorknob, but before my fingers even brushed the cold brass the door swung open. Shocked, I stepped backward.

"Lucky, Lucky, come and play, come and play our games."

"I don't like your games," I said as I stepped through the door and onto the first step up to the attic. "And if you don't promise to play nicely I won't play at all."

The door slammed shut behind me. I grimaced and continued up. They were children, for Christ's sake, dead children at that, and although they were vicious, they couldn't hurt me. Spirits have very little physical power.

The door at the top of the stairs opened as I climbed the last step. Were they stronger than before? Or had I just forgotten what tricks they could play?

The attic wasn't in total darkness. A dirty skylight halfway along the roof let in enough of the gray afternoon light for me to see piled-up desks and chairs at the far end. There were a few boxes stacked next to them, their dark bulk reminiscent of a beast ready to pounce. There was a lot of storage space up there, and very little stored. I guessed it had been a long time since this room had been used for that purpose.

The abandoned Ouija board was lying on the floor in the middle of the long room, just below the skylight. The planchette was upside down a few feet away. I took a pace forward and then another, the floorboards creaking at each step.

"Lucky's come to see us. Lucky's come to play." Their whispers filled my head. "Where's Kayla? We want to play with Kayla."

"Kayla doesn't want to play with you," I said.

"We want Kayla, we want Kayla, we want *Kayla*!"

Their chanting was loud and strident, aggressive, even: not a good sign. I wasn't sure whether only I could hear the voices or not, but if others could, I was pretty certain they would hear the words reverberating through the school's long corridors.

I walked across the room and reached down to pick up the board. My fingers had barely skimmed the surface when it was snatched away and sent skidding across the floor to crash into the wall. I followed it across the room. Could the twins have become this powerful? I frowned. Something wasn't right.

Once more I reached for it, and once more it skidded away.

"*KAYLA.*" This time the word came out as a deep growl. Not the voice of children at all. The hairs at the nape of my neck bristled.

I spun around. Dark gloom surrounded me.

"Who are you?" I asked, my voice coming out as a shaky whisper. Silence.

I went to retrieve the board again. I bent down and picked it up, gripping it tight—and it was wrenched from my grasp with such force I stumbled forward and fell to one knee.

I stayed there for a moment, my eyes scanning the shadows. My ragged breathing was forming small clouds of mist in the air and I was shivering. It had suddenly become very cold. Goosebumps pimpled my arms and legs, but I wasn't sure the chill had anything to do with that. I clambered to my feet, my eyes still searching the darkness.

"Lucky, help us." Soft whispers floated across the room. "Please"—a tremulous cry—"help us."

I turned toward the stacked furniture and there they were: two girls in long, white nightgowns. Today they were huddled together, crouched down between the old desks and the stacked boxes, making themselves small.

I swallowed hard. Last time we had met they had been reaching out toward me, their greedy eyes glowing with malicious glee. Now they were just frightened little girls. Fear bloomed in my chest. It wasn't the girls who had been called forth by the Ouija board, nor had they been the ones calling out to me. It was something far worse.

They looked up at me and even in the dark I could see the fear on their sad, little faces.

"Help us and we promise to be good. We promise. Make him go away. Please make him go away."

"Who?" I whispered.

Their eyes grew wide and they turned their heads, burying their faces against each other's necks. I stood stock-still.

There was definitely something else in the room.

My breath was now white smoke and the air around me could have been made of syrup, it felt so thick. I tried to turn but it was hard, like I was swimming against the tide. Slowly I forced my body around.

It was dark—too dark for the time of day. I took a couple of steps backward until I was standing beneath the skylight and the pale autumn light formed a rectangular patch on the dusty floor around me. Darkness so dense I could no longer see the door rose up to fill the other end of the room. It blocked my way out. I took another step back and heard whimpering behind me.

The darkness began to swirl in thick, soupy swathes, drawing in on itself, pulling together, solidifying and taking shape.

The girls behind me were crying. I could hear their hiccoughing little sobs, and it was then I realized they had never really been evil, they were just children, acting up the way kids sometimes do. Now they were afraid themselves and unfortunately I had the feeling they had good reason to be. I caught a sudden waft of a familiar sweet smell that reminded me of old ladies, but then it was gone as quickly as it had come.

Gradually the figure of a man grew out of the blackness. At first I thought he was exceptionally tall, then I noticed the high gray hat perched at an angle on top of his head. His close-fitting coat and breeches were also gray and his waistcoat and cravat a pale primrose. He wore white stockings, black shoes and looked very much like an eighteenth-century gentleman caught out of time. He even had a beauty spot near his top lip. I was surprised; he didn't look at all frightening—but then his mouth curled into a cruel, supercilious smile.

"Well, hello," he said.

I remained silent. It's never wise to engage those from the other side in conversation unless you know what you're dealing with; some delight in telling lies, twisting everything you say and generally playing with your head.

He took a step toward me and it took all of my self-control not to take a step back. The girls whimpered. I glanced around, trying to locate the Ouija board. He followed my eyes and chuckled—a low, menacing sound.

"Aren't you going to ask me why I'm here? Aren't you going to ask me what I want . . . Miss de Salle?"

"Why don't you tell me?"

He moved a step closer. Three more and he would be within touching distance. I really didn't want him that close.

He smiled again, and this time he was near enough for me to see his very white, pointed teeth. I had been right to be afraid.

"You have something we want."

"Kayla, he wants Kayla," the girls whispered from behind me.

His face twisted into an expression as close to madness as I would ever want to see. His lips pulled back into a snarl, exposing more of those vicious teeth.

"Be quiet, you little wretches. Hell will be too good a place for you if you do not hold your tongues."

I risked glancing over my shoulder. The two girls were still wrapped together in a small, quivering ball. When I turned back he had closed the distance to an arm's length. Too close. I needed to get to that Ouija board.

He plucked at the lace cuffs of his shirt that flounced out from beneath the sleeves of his jacket, drawing my attention to long ivory fingernails that would have been more at home on a big cat. He noticed the direction of my gaze and the smile returned to his face. He looked solid, almost human, but it was obviously nothing more than a veneer; malevolence oozed from his pores, tainting the air. I was finding it very hard to breathe.

"Where is Kayla?" he asked at last.

"Who wants to know?"

He raised an aristocratic eyebrow at me, then chuckled. "Forgive me," he said, sweeping into a low bow. "I am Henri le Dent."

French name, terribly English accent. He was lying, but then, they usually did. This one was a comedian: le Dent—the Tooth. I didn't find it particularly amusing.

"Well, Henri, I would like you to leave now. *Goodbye*."

He chuckled again. "Come now, Miss de Salle—you're far too experienced to expect that to work."

I gritted my teeth. It had been worth a try, though I'd begun to realize I wasn't dealing with a spiteful, restless spirit this time. Henri was something else altogether. Miss Mitchell's three students had managed to call up a demon.

"Okay, Henri, so what do you want?"

He flashed those pointy teeth again. "I have a message for your friend."

He took a step closer and this time I couldn't help but recoil. His smile grew broader. He knew I was afraid of him.

"Tell Kayla you have a message for her from the other side."

He moved so fast I didn't have time to react. In an instant he was beside me and his slender fingers were closing around my throat. I clawed at his very solid hand, but it was futile. He lifted me up so my toes were barely touching the floor and pulled my face so close to his we were eye to eye.

He grinned. His teeth seemed to fill his face and I was quite sure I was about to die.

He saw the realization dawn in my eyes and laughed out loud. "Yes, Miss de Salle—or may I call you Lucky?" He contemplated my face for a moment and then very slowly licked his lips. "I think so. Death is such an intimate thing. Yes, *Lucky*, you are going to die—but not today, for you have a message to deliver. Tell Kayla she has been away far too long and we want her back."

He leaned even closer and breathed in, closing his eyes for a moment as though savoring the bouquet of a fine wine, but when they sprang open they were black coals. His tongue flicked out and he licked the side of my face, tracing its pointed tip down from the corner of my eye and across my cheek. I tried to turn my head away, but his fingers were locked beneath my jaw. He was obviously enjoying himself, enjoying my fear. I caught a waft of his breath and the sickly-sweet scent I had smelled earlier returned full force. This time I knew what it smelled like: Parma violets.

"I'm hoping she will resist," he murmured, "for if she defies us, I will visit again, and when I do I will get to take another taste of you." He stroked my hair with his free hand. "I can hardly wait. I know you will be so sweet, like nectar. Oh yes, Miss Lucky de Salle, I am very much looking forward to meeting you again. I might even make a special visit—or two."

I couldn't breathe and my eyes were beginning to water. A tear overflowed and trickled down the side of my face.

He caught the teardrop on the tip of one of his viciously sharp nails and raised it up as if to study it. His nostrils flared as he took a flamboyant sniff, then with a reptilian flick of the tongue, he tasted it.

"A woman's tears, so fragrant, so delicious, so—endearing."

He let go of me and I fell to the floor, gasping. When I looked up he was stepping into the thick black shadow cloaking the door.

He glanced back at me. "Au revoir, Miss de Salle. I shall be seeing you again very soon. In fact, I will be keeping a close eye on you."

The darkness wrapped itself around him until all that remained was a black stain in front of the door, and then it was gone and the room was once again full of autumn gloom.

Somehow I managed to pull myself up onto my knees, though I was shaking so hard I had to clench my mouth shut to stop my teeth from chattering.

"You must close the door or he'll be back," a voice said from beside me, making me jump.

I looked around. The girls were standing there. The Ouija board slithered shakily across the floor and came to a faltering stop in front of me. The planchette followed. I reached out toward the board and then stopped, my fingers outstretched, but not quite touching it. I had a feeling it was too late for any of this.

"What about you two?" I asked. "Don't you want to move on to where you belong?"

They glided around to stand in front of me, on the other side of the board.

"We belong here."

"It's been almost two hundred years. You need to leave this place," I said.

"Why?"

"You've been frightening the girls."

They both smiled, the sweet, sunny smiles of children. "We haven't, not for a long, long time."

I frowned at them. I knew spirits didn't have the same sense of time as we did, but even so, barely a few days had passed since their last escapade. "What about the three girls the other day?"

It was their turn to frown. "That wasn't us," one said with a pout. "It was him, and when they'd gone he started being mean to us."

"Did they call him with the board?"

They both nodded, their faces solemn.

With a sigh I dug in my pocket and pulled out a sealed plastic bag. I emptied the contents—a candle and matches—onto the floor, then set the candle upright. My fingers were trembling so badly that I managed to spill half the matches onto the floor, then had trouble picking them up. Eventually I managed to grasp one between shaking fingers, but I didn't have the strength to light it.

I closed my eyes and took several deep breaths, then tried again, and this time a small flame flickered, faltered, almost went out, then bloomed. The girls watched me as I lit the candle.

I picked up the planchette, placed it on the board and pushed it to where it read "Goodbye."

"Goodbye," I said as firmly as I could.

I lifted the planchette and passed it through the candle flame, then did the same with the board, then, murmuring the Lord's Prayer, I whacked it three times on the floor.

The girls drifted away.

"Wait!" I said, and they turned back to me. "Remember, you promised to be good."

"We will," they whispered, and then they were gone.

Still shaking, I gathered the candle and matches together and dropped them back in the plastic bag. I didn't imagine for one minute that they would keep their promise—although if this was the first time the school had experienced any trouble in the fifteen years since I'd left, they hadn't exactly been going out of their way to be nasty to the pupils. I would suggest to Lydia Mitchell that she arrange for the door to the attic be locked and bolted. It wouldn't keep the two little spirits confined, though they had never really strayed far from the attic room, probably because it was where they had died. It would, however, keep her pupils out and hopefully away from this sort of mischief.

I climbed to my feet and started toward the door, but after a few steps I hesitated. There was no thick darkness blocking my exit now, but even so I was wary. I took another step, and another, then scampered across the room as fast as my heels would let me, threw open the door and bounded down the stairs into the upper sixth common room.

Any relief I might have felt immediately washed away when I looked back up the stairs. The doorframe at the top was filled with solid black darkness.

"Remember my message," a voice whispered with a hint of laughter, then the door slammed shut with enough force to shake the doorframe and rattle the coffee mugs littered around the common room.

By the time I reached the entrance lobby I had managed to control the shaking, but my throat felt raw and bruised. I could have done with a hot drink, or preferably something stronger, but if I tried to hold a cup or glass, I thought my trembling fingers would give away my fear.

It was very tempting to leave without seeing the headmistress, but I had to warn her to get that damn room locked up tight. If it had been up to me, I'd relocate the common room too. I would suggest it, but it was up to her; she might not want to risk upsetting the girls—and more importantly the parents—anymore than they were already.

I hesitated outside her door, then knocked. A voice called out for me to enter. Lydia was not alone; she was sitting at a rectangular coffee table with a man who, upon seeing me, put down his cup and stood, offering me his hand.

"Lucky," Lydia said, with a worried glance toward the man, "this is Philip Conrad. It was he who sent the car for you this afternoon."

I took his outstretched hand. "Thank you," I said, when all I wanted to do was tell the headmistress her problem hadn't gone away and get the hell out of there. I wasn't in the mood for small talk; I needed to have a much more pressing conversation with my friend Kayla, waiting outside in Philip's car.

"Your hand is icy," he said, holding onto it for a bit too long.

I withdrew it from his grasp as delicately as I could. "No heating in the attic," I said, and then wondered if my visit up there was something I should be sharing with him.

Philip gestured for me to sit as though he was now the one in charge and the headmistress had been relegated to the sidelines. He sat down so that he was facing me, then leaned back and deliberately put an arm along the back of the sofa and crossed his ankles. The creases in his elegant charcoal-gray pants could have cut cheese. His suit alone probably cost more than Lydia earned in a month. His shirt was a very pale blue, his silk tie charcoal and sapphire stripes. His skin was lightly tanned and his black hair was professionally tousled. His smile looked speculative to me, and his dark eyes were alert. I was instantly on my guard. All my senses told me that he was another problem I didn't want to be dealing with.

"Was your trip . . . successful?" he asked.

I looked at the headmistress. Her eyes were on him and there was certain grimness to her expression which gave me the distinct impression she didn't much want him there either.

"Not very," I said.

"I thought you could make it go away?" Lydia said.

"I'm a psychic, not an exorcist. I can help someone to move on, but I can't force them to go."

"This is terrible," she said.

"It's actually far worse than either of us thought," I admitted. "Your girls managed to conjure up something very dangerous. I doubt he'll be coming back here, but I suggest you lock that room up tight. It won't keep the spirits in, necessarily, but it would be a very good idea to keep your pupils out. As for the sixth form common room . . ."

Her fingers tapped a rapid tattoo on the arm of her chair. "Yes, yes, of course. We've never had a problem with them before—at least since I've been here."

"It was the room where they died," I said. "Most spirits either hang around the place they spent their last moments, or somewhere that held a special or emotional meaning for them."

"They died in the attic?" Philip asked.

After I'd been expelled I'd researched the history of the building. "Before this was a school it was an orphanage," I said, "and apparently not a very nice one. The twins had been locked in the attic for the night as a punishment and there was a fire. The orphanage tried to cover it up—they said the girls hadn't been locked in, that they'd just been overcome by the fumes and died in their sleep."

"But they didn't?" Lydia asked, reading my expression.

"Sadly, no—they couldn't get out. When their bodies were found they were huddled together by the door."

"Oh my," she said.

"The scandal closed the orphanage and after the building had been repaired it became a school."

"Miss de Salle, you said my pupils had 'conjured' something up—what was that?" Philip flashed perfect white teeth that were horribly reminiscent of the dreadful Henri: two sharks, two different ponds. He didn't sound at all worried, just curious.

"A demon, Mr. Conrad." I waited for the curl of the lips, the derisive sneer, but he surprised me.

"Is this common?" he asked.

"No," I said. "I've heard it can happen and I've read documented cases, but I've never before had the misfortune for it to happen to me."

"But then, you're a professional," he said.

"I'd hardly say that."

"Come now: you're quite well known within the"—he made quotation marks signs with his fingers—"circle."

"What 'circle'?" I said.

"Psychics, clairvoyants, experts in the paranormal—they all know of you."

I gave a rueful smile. "In which case, Mr. Conrad, you'll also know that most of them hate me with a passion."

"Only the charlatans."

I studied him for a moment. He had certainly taken the trouble to research me. "That would be most of them, I'm afraid," I said. "True psychics are few and far between."

"But there are some out there?"

"Most of those with a real ability try to hide it. To some it's almost a curse."

"But not you?"

"Mr. Conrad, if you knew anything about me beyond my reputation you'd know my ability almost destroyed my life. My mother abandoned me; I was expelled from this school, and I was constantly bullied everywhere I went afterward."

"You've turned your life around."

"I've had help."

His knowing smile suggested he knew something I didn't, or something he shouldn't. I wasn't sure which it was, but I was pretty certain I would soon be finding out.

Two

Philip, as he had invited me to call him, wasn't about to let me go so easily. When I stood to leave he told me he would be joining me in the car. I could hardly complain; it was, after all his.

His driver opened the door for me and I slid inside. Kayla was curled up on the far side of the back seat, her knees drawn up to her chin. She was defensive, and I had the distinct impression she knew there had been something in the school other than the spirits of two mischievous children. While Philip was walking around to the other door I made the most of the few seconds I had with her.

"I have a message for you," I hissed, "from someone very unpleasant with teeth like a piranha."

Before she had a chance to respond the other door opened and she had to scramble across the seat to sit next to me while Philip climbed in.

"Would you like to go somewhere to eat?" he asked.

For a moment I was completely thrown. I hadn't seen that coming.

"A very kind offer, but I'm feeling a little tired."

"Of course you are—but I really would like to hear more about this demon."

Kayla glanced at me, her eyes wide. I ignored her. "There's nothing much to say other than that he's dangerous and I really wouldn't want to meet him again."

"It was a 'him'? Not some creature?"

"He was in human form. I think he'd styled himself on an eighteenth-century gentleman by the way he was dressed, but my history isn't particularly good."

"Did he have a name?"

"I doubt the one he gave me was his."

"Which was?"

"Why are you so interested? Why do you even care?"

He stared at me for a moment then turned away to look out of the window at the passing scenery, but not before I saw his face cloud over.

Kayla shifted in her seat and reached out to put her hand on his shoulder, but then drew back. "He's in pain," she said. "His life has been touched by something from the other world."

"What happened, Philip?" I asked.

He was silent for a very long time. He gave a shiver and glanced across at me, his expression bleak. "Come to dinner with me and I'll tell you."

Kayla twisted around to look at me. Two sets of eyes waited for my answer: one pair filled with hope, the other with an expression I couldn't quite define. Kayla and I had been friends for a very long time, but for the last few minutes I had started to wonder whether I knew her at all.

"All right, I'll have dinner with you tomorrow night."

He gave me a sad smile and in it there was an air of vulnerability I would never have expected from a man like him—but then, a sharp suit and expensive tastes didn't mean he had no feelings, did it? Just that someone like Philip probably knew how to hide them.

He dropped us off at my cottage and walked me to the door. "I'll see you tomorrow," he said. "About eight?"

"That's good for me."

He raised a hand and strode off down the path, stopping to give me a parting smile as he closed the gate behind him.

I watched the car pull away, then started rummaging for my keys.

"He's troubled," Kayla said, as I let us in.

"Not as troubled as you're going to be if you don't tell me what this is all about."

"Don't be like that."

"Kayla, this demon had teeth that would make Dracula look like a pussycat and he was drooling over me like I was his packed lunch, so I think I'm entitled to be a little pissed off."

"That's not my fault."

"Really?" I said, as I threw my jacket down on the sofa and slumped down beside it. "Well, he said to give you a message."

She sat down on the chair opposite me, knees together and hands clenched as if praying. Maybe she was. She looked at me from beneath lowered lashes.

"What did he say?"

"He said: 'Tell Kayla'—that's you, I believe—'that I have a message for her from the other side.' He said, 'Tell her she's been away far too long and we want her back.'"

"Oh," she said.

"Is that all you've got to say? What does he mean?"

"I have no idea."

"He seemed to think you would."

"So, you're going out to dinner with this Philip guy?" she said, changing the subject.

It was clear that she didn't want to continue our previous conversation and I knew better than to push her, she often just disappeared if she wasn't getting her own way. I gritted my teeth and counted to ten. As frustrating as it was I was going to have to tease it out of her.

"I'm not sure I want to, but he is in pain, as you yourself pointed out. Either that or he's a very good actor, because he didn't appear to be hurting much when I first met him."

"I think what you saw inside the school was probably the act."

"Any insights?" I asked her.

"He was very interested in your demon."

I shuddered. "The reason that demon was there is all down to you—at least, that's what he said."

Her forehead wrinkled and she drew a little closer to me. "Did he threaten you?"

"Oh yes."

"Tell me."

"I don't want to talk about it," I said with a shudder my hand rising to my cheek as I remembered his tongue trailing across my skin.

"If he threatened to harm you, I want to know."

She wasn't the only one who could be difficult. "It'll have to keep," I said playing her at her own game and checking my watch. "It's getting late and I really need to go for a run before supper."

"It's dark outside."

"I'm not afraid of the dark."

"If you've been threatened by a demon you should be."

"I got the impression the time of day or night wouldn't really matter much to him."

"What name did he give?"

"I told you, it wasn't his name; it was a joke."

Her lips pursed and she gave me one of her old-fashioned "just tell me, why don't you?" looks.

"Okay, okay, it was Henri, Henri le Dent. It was a demon joke, I think, because he had very white, very sharp teeth."

"I'll come with you," she said, and it was then that I realized the situation was worse than I'd thought. One of the few activities Kayla refused to join in with was my daily run, so if she really was willing to accompany me, it must be because I was right about old Henri Toothy Pegs being some seriously scary dude.

I ran for just under an hour, not for the exercise, although I suppose it was good for me, but because running gave me time to let my mind drift without any other distractions. Curiously enough, I had never come across a restless spirit while running. Like Kayla, it appeared they had an aversion to it.

Kayla lagged along behind, but after the first few minutes I cranked up my iPod and forgot all about her. It had stopped raining and it wasn't cold, just damp. I kept to the main roads; even I wasn't crazy enough to risk the bridle paths I might use on a bright summer evening. Even though I'd said explanations could keep, the afternoon at the school had seriously spooked me. *Henri* had spooked me.

By the time I reached my gate I was ready for a shower and a glass of wine. Kayla caught up with me as I opened the front door.

"I still can't understand why you do this running stuff," she said. "You just get all hot and sweaty for your trouble."

I switched off my iPod and dumped it on the small table in the hall. "Do I have to keep repeating myself? It gives me time to think."

"Time away from me, you mean."

"I didn't say that. You know you're welcome to join me anytime you like." Though this wasn't strictly true; it was nice to get away from her sometimes. "I'm hitting the shower." Then I hesitated on the bottom step and sniffed. "Can you smell something odd?"

She shook her head and I took another long sniff, but I must have been imagining it, because there was nothing there. Henri must have rattled me even more than I'd thought. But for a moment I was sure I could smell Parma violets.

I took my time in the shower—my wine and TV dinner would still be waiting for me at the end of it—and had just pulled on a pair of clean tracksuit bottoms and a T-shirt when Kayla appeared at the door.

"You expecting someone?" she asked, knowing full well I wasn't.

"No, why?"

"Well, there's some man walking up the path."

And there was a rap on my door.

"What now?" I muttered to myself. My cottage was at the end of an unlit lane and a ten-minute walk from the village, so I didn't usually get unwanted callers.

I padded down the stairs and had a quick look through the peep-hole. A youngish guy was standing a few feet back from my doorstep, his face angled away from me, then he turned, giving me a distorted view of his face. He was wearing a gray hoodie and I caught a glimpse of blond curls escaping onto his forehead. His brow was crinkled into a frown and he was chewing on his lower lip. He was clearly anxious, maybe worried there wouldn't be an answer—or maybe worried there would be. Of course there was no way I could ever be sure from a quick glimpse through a peephole, but he didn't look particularly dangerous to me.

"Know him?" Kayla asked.

"Nope," I said, as I reached out to open the door.

"Are you sure you should?" she asked.

"If he turns out to be trouble you can scare the crap out of him," I said.

"Goody." Her face lit up into a smile: she had a very wicked sense of humor at times, and a variety of ways of getting rid of unwanted guests, all of them interesting.

As I pulled the door open, the young man immediately drew himself up to his full height and pushed his hood back. His lips curled into a smile that was more like a grimace.

"I'm sorry to call so late," he said. "Are you Lucky de Salle?"

"That's me."

"I wonder if I could have a few moments of your time?" he asked, and I noticed a slight quaver to his voice. He was very nervous and I wasn't sure whether this was a good sign or not.

"Depends what you want."

"I've been told you might be able to help me."

I waited, one hand resting against the door in case I needed to slam it shut.

"Please, I need your help," he said again, and there was more than a hint of anxiety in his voice. "*Please.*"

I glanced at Kayla. "I don't know—he looks vaguely familiar," she said, her forehead creasing into a frown, "but"—she tapped her forefinger against her lips—"I'm not sure."

I gestured for him to come inside and stood back to let him pass. "This way," I said, pointing him in the direction of my sitting room.

He walked in, stopped in the middle of the room and turned to face me. "I'm sorry to barge in on you at this time of night but I really couldn't—I just couldn't wait any longer."

"Okay," I said and gestured for him to sit. "What's this all about?"

He perched on the edge of my sofa as though he was getting ready to run at any moment. His hands, resting on his knees, curled into tight fists, his knuckles white as bone.

"I really don't know where to begin," he said.

I waited, and Kayla sat down beside me on the arm of my chair, strangely quiet.

"Look," he said, "at the risk of sounding flip, I can't think of any other way of saying this." He took a deep breath. "I see dead people."

Kayla muttered, "Oh, *puh-lease*." We had both seen the Bruce Willis film and that part cracked us up every time. I found myself struggling to stop my lips twitching, although it really wasn't that funny, especially as he was visibly distressed.

"So," I said, as soon as I was sure I could speak without laughing, then, "Sorry, what's your name?"

"Jamie," he said. "Jamie Banks."

"So, Jamie, you think you see the dead?"

"I don't *think*, Miss de Salle, I *do*."

"And you've come to see me because . . . ?" I winced. It had come out all wrong: haughty and condescending. It was the tone I used on all those so-called mediums, and he hadn't deserved it.

His cheeks flushed and he jumped to his feet. "I was told you might be able to help, but clearly I'm wasting my time."

"Sit down," I said, and he hesitated, then slumped back down on the sofa. "Now, tell me why you think I can help you."

He sat staring at his clenched fists. His cheeks were still burning, but from his lowered eyes and the way he was pinching his lower lip between his teeth, I would have bet money on him being more embarrassed than angry.

"I was desperate, so I went to see a medium," he said at last.

"Her name?" I asked. I couldn't think of one psychic who would volunteer me as a recommended source of information.

"Constance Selby." He said it like he knew I wouldn't like the answer; he was right.

Kayla gave a snort. "That was money well spent."

"Paul the Octopus had more psychic ability than that woman," I said.

"I thought she was quite good," he said, with a frown.

Kayla threw up her hands. "Hell's bells, this guy is *not* for real."

I ignored her. "Jamie, it's really easy to make someone believe you're giving them messages from the other side. You just have to be able to read body language and pick up on the things people say. To start with, nine times out of ten, if a person consults a psychic it's because they've lost someone, so right away they have a starting point."

"She *knew* things—"

"You appear to know things about me: like where I live, for instance." *And how did he know that?*

"After she mentioned you I read your book," he said seeing my frown. "When I decided I wanted to meet you it wasn't that difficult to find out where you live."

That was slightly alarming—I would have to check how available my personal data actually was.

"He obviously didn't read beyond Chapter One," Kayla said.

"Did you read all of it?" I asked, and when he nodded, I pointed out, "I spent several chapters explaining how so-called mediums can make a person believe that they're getting messages from loved ones."

He stared at me for a moment then gave a small laugh. "I've been conned, haven't I?"

"Sorry," I said. "Though, I must admit, I can't believe she recommended that you come to see me."

He looked down at his shoes and when he raised his eyes back to mine a flush had crept back across his cheeks.

"She didn't, did she?"

"No, not exactly. I didn't have a one-to-one consultation. I wanted to check her out, so I went to see her show at the local hall in Bromley, just up the road from where I live. Later, when I read your book, I could see how she had been manipulating the audience all along—the things you talked about, they were all there—but that was the first time I'd been to one of these things and she was really convincing, and then, at the end of the evening, I don't know, it got even more . . . well, incredibly *real*."

"What do you mean?"

"There was a question and answer session and someone asked what she thought of Lucky de Salle."

"Oh my, I'd have just loved to hear what she had to say about you," Kayla said.

"And?" I asked, ignoring her.

"Well, she got all sort of huffy and said something like 'that woman . . .'—but then she stopped midsentence and her face kind of went all slack. The whole audience could see something odd was happening. She was silent for so long that people began to whisper, then she started to smile, it was a really weird—actually quite scary—smile. She looked—well, insane, really. Then she started to talk in this strange voice, you know, real *Evil Dead* creepy." He paused for a moment and shuddered. "It gives me goosebumps just thinking about it."

"So what did she say?" I asked.

"It was really peculiar stuff, you know, something like, 'Lucky the spawn of Hell,' and she was chanting it in this sort of singsong cackle, then her voice got deeper and she said, 'guided by a demon child.'"

I inadvertently glanced at Kayla, who looked far from happy.

"Well, credit where it's due, that's a new approach."

"You still think it was a con?"

I laughed. "I think it was a rather pathetic attempt to discredit me."

He gave a wry smile. "I didn't believe the demon thing; that would be nuts. But I bought your book anyway and what you said in it made sense, so I hoped you might be able to help me."

"What do you want from me?" I asked.

"I want you to make it stop. Can you make it stop?"

I tucked my hair behind my ear. "If you really do see spirits I can't do anything to make them leave you alone. Maybe I can help you deal with it, but that's all."

He lowered his head, eyes focusing on his knees. Then he looked up and the fear in his eyes brought a lump to my throat.

"Whatever you can do will be better than nothing," he said. "I'm too scared to sleep and I'm too scared to stay awake. On my way here I was tempted to leap off the platform in front of a train just to make it all go away."

"You don't want to be getting involved in this," Kayla said.

"Jamie, how long has this been going on for?"

He ran his hand through his hair in a jittery motion. "Ten months, two weeks and five days."

"Very precise," I said.

"It's a day I won't forget."

"What happened? It was obviously memorable."

He took a deep breath. His hands were back on his knees. "It was the day I died," he said.

This time I couldn't help it: I looked at Kayla. She was frowning, and was obviously concentrating, because she'd got her forefinger pressed against her bottom lip—it was her tell.

"What are you looking at?" Jamie asked.

"You died?" I repeated "So what happened?"

He was staring at Kayla—at least, he was staring at where she was sitting next to me, perched on the arm of the chair. His brow furrowed, he squinted, then pinched the bridge of his nose between finger and thumb. Then his eyes opened wide and shot to mine.

"Who's she?" he said, pointing at Kayla. His hand was trembling.

"What can you see?" I asked. I wasn't feeling so good about this myself: even people who actually had some psychic power never acknowledged Kayla.

"A woman, sitting next to you: fair hair, slender, dark eyes."

"Her name's Kayla," I said.

"Lucky," Kayla hissed.

"If he can see you he can see you. No big deal."

"Maybe not for you," she said with a pout. "Will you stop staring," she added, glaring at Jamie. "Hasn't anyone ever told you it's rude?"

"You really do have a spirit guide," Jamie said.

"Not so much a guide as a pain in the backside," I said, "but she does sometimes have her uses."

"Thanks a million," Kayla said. "Can you hear me as well as see me, 'I can see dead people' boy?"

His eyes flicked from her to me then back again. "Yes," he said.

"So, Jamie"—I clicked my fingers to get his attention—"back to business. How did you die?"

"And why aren't you dead now?" Kayla added.

He was still staring at Kayla. For someone who was apparently seeing dead people on a regular basis she was sure making him uncomfortable. He dragged his eyes away from her with some effort. "I was at Victoria Tube Station the day of the bombing," he said at last, in a low whisper.

I winced. "Shit," I said.

He swallowed hard. "We'd just come down the stairs into the entrance hall when the bomb went off."

"We?"

He looked up at me with glittering eyes, then back at his tightly clenched hands. "Sara, my girlfriend. We were going to town for the day. It was like a big adventure—she'd never been to London before." The last words were almost a sob.

I gave him a few moments before asking, "You lost Sara that day?"

He took several deep breaths, then started again. "She was slightly ahead of me, trying to push through the crowd—it was packed solid down there."

I had read the newspaper reports and seen the aftermath of the devastation on the TV and I had promised myself I would never again visit the place as long as I lived, not because I was afraid of another terrorist bombing, but because if ever there was a place that would be haunted by lost souls, it would be there.

"I can't remember the blast, just Sara, glancing back at me, smiling, her mouth opening to say something. Then it went black and the next thing I know, I'm looking down into what I thought was Hell. There was smoke, lots of smoke, and then as it started to clear, I could see bodies, piles of broken bodies, some almost unrecognizable as people."

He stopped and took another deep breath. "It was the silence that was weird. And then I saw them."

"Saw what?" I asked.

"People—people rising up and drifting past me. I searched their faces for Sara, but she wasn't there, so I searched the bodies, but I couldn't find her. Though I did find my body. My eyes were closed." He screwed his shut as if trying to remember. "I was sprawled out on top of some people on the bottom steps leading into the station. I guess I must have been thrown backward. I reached out to touch my face and then everything faded away." He stopped.

I could feel my own eyes prickling and I had to fight back the tears. Poor, poor boy. "Then what?" I asked, when I was sure my voice wouldn't break.

"I think I might have woken up in the ambulance, but the next thing I really remember is the hospital, and that was a total nightmare—too many injured, too many dead and dying. Apparently I'd stopped breathing, not just once but several times, and they'd kept bringing me back—but I couldn't bear to stay in that place any longer than I had to. Being among the horribly injured was bad enough, but the dead—they were scared and confused and some of them couldn't understand what had happened to them. Then, somehow, they realized I could see them and they crowded around me asking me to help them, and I couldn't. I just *couldn't*." He dropped his head into his hands.

I got up and moved across the room to sit beside him and put my arm across his shaking shoulders.

"I would have been overwhelmed too. It's not your fault you couldn't do anything to help them. Most of them will find their way eventually."

"But what of those who didn't?" he asked, looking up at me with red-rimmed eyes. "What happens to them? Are they like the ones I keep seeing? Can they never find peace?"

I squeezed his shoulder. "Jamie, don't torture yourself. It's taken me almost my whole life to get where I am today. I asked myself exactly those same questions again and again as I was growing up."

"How did you survive?"

"I had help," I said, looking across at Kayla. "Look, why don't I make us something to eat? We can talk some more, see what I can tell you to help make it easier. I can't promise I'll be able to solve all your problems, but I can tell you how I dealt with mine."

He gave a sniff and muttered a muffled, "Yes, please."

I patted his shoulder, got up and made for the kitchen. "Would you like a beer? A glass of wine?" I called over my shoulder.

"A beer would be great, thanks."

Kayla trailed me into the kitchen. "Do you really need a stray hanging around here?"

"Like you, you mean?"

"Not nice," Kayla said.

"Nor are you when you say things like that. He's hurting."

"I guess."

"He was talking about jumping in front of a train."

Kayla gave a snort. "Not a pleasant way to end it all, I'd say, particularly for the poor train driver. If you've got to do it, why burden other people with your shit?"

"I don't think people who do that sort of thing are thinking rationally. It's probably more of a spur-of-the-moment thing."

I found a beer for Jamie and poured a large glass of white wine for me, switched the oven on and strolled back into the lounge with the two glasses.

"Here," I said, handing him the beer. "It's pizza and garlic bread for dinner, I'm afraid."

"I don't want to be any trouble," he said.

"Too late for that," Kayla mumbled under her breath.

Why she was choosing to be such a bitch I had no idea. I'd have thought she'd be pleased to have someone else who could see her— someone else to talk to—or at least torment.

Three

We ate around the kitchen table, with Kayla wafting around us; she always did that when there was something going on she couldn't join in with. Jamie couldn't keep his eyes off her; he was trying to look like he wasn't staring, but he was.

"Why are you so interested in Kayla?" I asked. "If you see spirits all the time now, she can't be anything new."

He finished his mouthful, then said, "I've never seen one quite like her." He took a swig of beer, then added, "All the ones I've come across are scared and needy or angry and aggressive, but she's none of those things."

He was right: most spirits hung around either because they didn't understand what had happened to them or they had some last message for a loved one, or some other unfinished business. Occasionally you'd get one all bitter and twisted, wanting to take vengeance on the living for some imagined slight or there were those, like the twins I'd dealt with earlier that day, who just wanted to hang around their school and be naughty—they might be a little malicious but they caused no real harm; they just enjoyed scaring the crap out of people.

"Kayla is one of a kind," I admitted.

"How did she die?"

"I am here, you know," Kayla said.

"Sorry," Jamie said, his cheeks glowing.

Kayla gave a morose grunt and sat on the worktop opposite us. "I didn't die," she said. "At least as far as I know."

"Have you been together long?" he asked.

"As long as I can remember," I said.

"From when you were a kid?"

"I sometimes wonder if we were born together. It certainly looks that way."

"We grew up together," Kayla added.

"Is that usual?"

"Usual for what?" I asked.

"Spirit guides?"

I hesitated a moment, thinking about his question. "I don't know, I've never met a true psychic who's had one."

"In your book you're quite opinionated about people who claim to speak to the dead."

I took a slurp of wine. I could talk about this all evening—in fact, I had, on numerous occasions: seminars, after-dinner speeches, interviews, pubs . . . After my book was published I did the usual publicity rounds and I think I probably went onto the psychic circuit's "Most Hated" list. I'd even had some loony sticking pins into a wax effigy of me on a TV show. Kayla thought it was hilarious. "People who claim to speak to the loved ones of the vulnerable are leeches. It doesn't matter what excuses they use, taking money for lying to people is just plain wrong."

"You're right," Jamie said. "I'd give anything not to be able to see the dead, and I bet those fake psychics would too if they really could."

"Did you see Sara?" I asked.

He stopped midbite and dropped the pizza back onto his plate. He screwed his eyes shut, breathed deeply, then shook his head.

"I'm sorry," I said.

"No, it's okay," he said, giving me a lopsided smile, "it's just that if I'd ever wanted to see a spirit it would have been hers. But I never have."

"Didn't you ever try to call to her?" Kayla said.

His head jerked up. "Is that possible?" he asked.

I glared at Kayla.

"It's not a good idea," she said, albeit rather half-heartedly. "I just wondered, that's all."

He turned to me. "Is it possible?" he repeated.

"If she's gone, she's gone. To try and call her back would be a mistake."

"But it is possible?"

"Don't you think you'd have seen her by now if it was?"

He frowned.

This was something I really didn't want to get into with him. The problems he had already would pale into insignificance if he started trying to call up his lost girlfriend. It was time to change the subject. "Have you got somewhere to stay tonight?"

"I've got a room at the local pub."

"Oh," I said.

"Are you going to tell him or shall I?" Kayla whispered, loud enough that he could hear her.

I gave her a killer glare, which she ignored.

"Tell me what?" he said, looking from me to Kayla and back again.

Kayla grinned in my direction, leaving it to me to break the bad news.

I sighed. "The pub is haunted by a former landlord. A rather unpleasant old man who broke his neck falling down the cellar stairs. He keeps out of my way because he's scared of Kayla, but he'll make your stay a misery if he thinks he can."

"That's all I need," Jamie muttered. "Can anyone else see him?"

"Every now and then some perceptive guest will catch a glimpse of him, but the present landlord and his wife are about as receptive as brick walls so they never have, which is probably just as well—the place changed hands so many times over the past five years it was beginning to look unsellable. They've been there two years now and can't understand what all the fuss was about."

"If I were you I'd get the last train back to Bromley," Kayla said. "You'll probably just make it if you hurry."

"Excuse me, Jamie," I said, getting to my feet. "My friend and I need to have a little chat in private."

I gestured for Kayla to come with me. For a few moments she sat there, perched on the kitchen counter, staring at Jamie as though she was going to ignore me, but at last she hopped down and followed me out of the room.

"What?" she asked once I'd shut the door behind us.

"Exactly what do you think you're doing?"

"We need him hanging around here like we need a damn great hole in the head. He's bad news."

"He needs help."

"Not from you."

"Then who else?" I countered. "If he really is seeing the dead—and if he can see you, then I suspect he is—who else can help him?"

"You can't help him. Don't you see that? *No one* can help him. He'll just have to learn to live with it like you did."

"I had you," I said, and I stared at her until she lowered her eyes. "He hasn't got anyone."

"Then maybe he should call up his girlfriend," she said with a wicked smile.

"Why are you being such a bitch? You know as well as I do that the chances of him connecting with her are practically negligible."

She started paying a lot of attention to the strand of hair she was twirling around her finger.

"He might even end call up something deeply unpleasant—not to mention the matter of old Henri le Dent, which we still haven't dealt with . . . Do you really want to risk him turning up here because Jamie started messing around with the other side?" Her eyes met mine and a frown creased her forehead. "I guess not," I said.

"There's no need to be mean," Kayla said.

"I'm not the one being mean. Jamie has asked for my help and I'm going to do my best to give it to him."

"Well, it's all settled then," Kayla said with a sniff. "But don't come crying to me when it all goes horribly wrong."

"What on earth could go wrong?"

Kayla muttered something under her breath then flounced off into the living room, leaving me to return to the kitchen—and Jamie—alone.

"Is something the matter?" he asked, as I entered the room.

I sat down across the table from him. "Not really, Kayla's just being a pain."

"She doesn't want me here, does she?"

I opened my mouth to lie, then seeing his expression, thought better of it. "I think she's a little surprised you can see her. It's always been just her and me and I think maybe she wants it to stay that way."

His forehead furrowed. "Don't you have any friends? I mean human ones."

I laughed. "Do you, since you began to see ghosts?"

He slumped back in the chair. "No, I guess I don't. I've sort of distanced myself from them—they can't understand what I'm going through." He started fiddling with his half-empty glass. "To be honest, I think most of them think I'm crazy, or I'm having some kind of breakdown."

I gave him a sympathetic smile. "Look, I've been seeing the dead all my life. I was the weird kid who talked to herself—I was always bullied, so I got used to being alone and apart from everyone—except for Kayla, of course."

"So it's just the two of you?"

"Pretty much. I go to the village pub for a drink with the locals now and then. I've got an agent who I see several times a year, and my editor of course."

"No boyfriends?" he asked, then he flushed pink and apologized.

"Actually, I have had a few boyfriends, but after a couple of months they usually end up leaving because I'm too weird."

"That sucks."

"Not really. They were pretty high maintenance emotionally."

"Did they know about Kayla?"

"Do you think they'd believe in her?"

He gave a small laugh. "No. If we'd been having this conversation last year I'd have thought you were bonkers."

He chugged back another mouthful of beer and sat back, concentrating on the last drop as he swirled it around the bottom of the glass. This gave me the opportunity to concentrate on him. When I first saw him standing on my doorstep I'd thought he was probably about twenty, but once he'd taken off his hooded jacket I could see he didn't have the gangliness that comes with adolescence, and judging by his biceps, he had either been working out or doing some kind of manual work. Looking at him now, I would have said he was probably only a year or two younger than me. Fine lines radiated out from his eyes. I wasn't at all sure whether that was from laughter or pain. I doubt he'd had much to laugh about over the past year, though before then I assumed he'd probably been happy.

"What do you do for work?" I asked.

"Not a lot," he glanced up from his glass. "I was training to be a vet, but after . . . you know . . . I couldn't concentrate on anything. I've done a bit of casual work here and there just to keep myself in cash and to pay the rent, but"—he grimaced—"that's part of the reason I need your help: I want to get my life back, or at least some semblance of it."

His eyes met mine, and for a moment, they were all I could see. "You can stay here for a while," I heard myself say, and even as the words came out of my mouth, I thought, *What?* And yet I couldn't stop. It was like my voice was coming from somewhere very far away. "You can't afford to be paying out for a room at the pub."

His eyes stayed locked with mine and then he blinked and I was left feeling a little lightheaded.

A small hint of a smile curled the sides of his mouth. "You're going to let me stay here?"

I opened my mouth to say, *No, no, you can't; I don't know what I was thinking*, instead a murmured "yes" came out, and although I knew inviting a strange man to stay in my home was downright crazy, the hope in his eyes and longing in his voice was so much I couldn't bring myself to disappoint him.

"We're going to help each other," I said, though I still wasn't sure where the words were coming from.

"Me, help you?"

"Can you drive?" I asked. I reached for the bottle and refilled my glass. I was probably going to need it.

"Yes."

"Well, that's one way you can help me right away," I said, at last feeling like I had regained control of myself. "I hate driving, but it's the only way to get anywhere from this damn village other than the daily train or twice-daily bus."

"I can't afford a car," he said.

"No problem. I have a car, I just don't like driving it."

"Thank you," he said, and looked back down into his empty glass, but not before I saw his smile.

"Do you want to go and get your stuff from the pub?" I asked.

"If you're sure you don't mind me staying here? I can afford the pub for a few days," he said, his eyes once again meeting mine.

Another chance for me to back out but I didn't; no: I *couldn't*. "Can you afford to have Batty Bill messing with your head?" I heard myself say.

He blinked. "Who?"

"He's the one I told you about. He was the pub's alcoholic landlord about thirty years ago," I managed to explain, now back in control of my own vocal cords, "I think what makes him so grumpy is that he's haunting a pub, but can never have another drink." I reached for my glass, then stopped: I was already feeling rather odd. "Come on, I'll show you to your room and you can decide what you want to do."

When I took him out into the hall, I saw Kayla sitting on the stairs.

"He's staying then," she said, as she got up and moved out of our way. She had clearly been eavesdropping.

"For a few days," I said.

"Sorry?" Jamie said.

I turned to look at him and I realized he could no longer see Kayla, although she was directly between us.

I glanced at Kayla with a frown. She and I were definitely going to have to have a long talk, and not just about her friend Henri. It was becoming increasingly apparent she had deliberately let Jamie see her earlier in the evening and now she was hiding herself again. Kayla wasn't averse to playing games, but this was one I didn't understand, not in the slightest.

I gave Jamie what I hoped was a bright smile and, ignoring the question, gestured for him to follow me up the stairs. I threw open the door of my spare bedroom and switched on the light.

"It's not massive," I said, "but there should be enough room for you and your stuff."

He walked over to the window and looked out into the night before turning back and surveying the room. "It's great," he said. "Bigger than my room at the pub and probably with a better view; I was overlooking a yard full of empty beer crates there."

"Okay," I said, leading the way back downstairs, "let's go and collect your things."

I grabbed a coat off the hook by the front door and he pulled on his jacket.

"You coming?" I asked Kayla, over my shoulder.

"I'm sure you don't need me around," she said.

I let Jamie by and turned to face her. "Come on, you know Bill's bound to be around."

"I'm sure you and your new best friend will do fine without me," she said with a sniff.

"Suit yourself," I said.

I hesitated for a moment to see if she would follow, but she turned away and I pulled the front door shut. I could do without Kayla in one of her moods.

"Have I caused a problem between you two?" Jamie asked, as I joined him out in the lane.

"Not really. I think this has more to do with something that happened earlier in the day. You turning up when you did just gave her an excuse not to talk to me about it."

"Sorry."

I flashed him a smile. "Don't worry about it, Kayla and I are just the same as any other two girlfriends: we argue sometimes and we get on each other's nerves, but it's never serious."

"It is kind of weird your best friend being a ghost," Jamie said.

"Once you get to know me, you'll find I am kind of weird."

By the time we reached the pub the moon was obscured by black, rolling clouds racing across the sky and it was trying to rain again. Despite being escorted by Jamie, it had been a relief to reach the end of the unlit lane and see the lights of the village come into view, but now it looked like the journey back home was going to be a very dark one. I wasn't looking forward to it one bit, not with Henri around.

Jamie opened the door to the public bar and ushered me through first. An open fireplace split the bar in two and the heat of the fire roaring away inside it instantly chased away the chill that had seeped into my bones during the walk.

"Lucky, darlin', lovely to see you," Rita, the landlady, called from behind the bar.

Roger, her husband, raised his eyes from the pint of beer he was pulling and glanced our way. "You found her then," he said to Jamie.

"The usual?" Rita asked, ignoring her husband.

"Please; Jamie?"

"Lager, thanks."

"You go and get your stuff," I said.

Rita and Roger exchanged a look that wasn't lost on me, but I waited until Jamie disappeared upstairs before explaining.

"He's staying with me," I said, giving them both a hard stare and daring them to pass any comment, mainly because I doubted I could disagree with anything they were likely to say.

Rita, unfortunately, was completely oblivious to the warning. "Darlin', are you sure? I mean, do you know him?"

"He can't afford to stay here," I said.

"Well, he's not getting a refund for tonight," Roger said.

Rita flapped a hand at him to shut up. "Lucky, you can't let a complete stranger sleep in your home."

"Why not?" I asked, immediately defensive. "You do it all the time."

"That's different. Anyway, I have my Roger to protect me."

Roger gave a snort and slammed an overflowing pint of beer on the bar, slopping the contents. A customer opened his mouth to protest then thought better of it, paid and shuffled across the bar to a table as far away from the irritable landlord as he could get.

"What is the matter with you this evening?" Rita asked.

"You know full well what's the matter. This f—" he took a deep breath. "This flaming place, that's what."

I raised an eyebrow at Rita. She gave me a tight smile and reached across to pat Roger's hand. "It's our little problem," she said. I must have looked puzzled as she leaned closer across the bar and whispered, "You know the one."

"Sorry, you've lost me."

"For goodness' sake," Roger said, joining his wife, "you of all people should know what we mean."

It finally clicked. "Batty Bill."

Roger shushed me and glanced around the bar to see who might be listening. "Keep your voice down, will yer?"

"What's happened? I thought you hadn't had any trouble. In fact, I remember you telling me that it was all a load of old nonsense."

Roger's cheeks puffed out and took on a rosy hue, which had nothing to do with the heat from the fireplace. "I know, and I'm sorry," he said. "I still think it's a load of old nonsense, but . . ."

"But?" I asked.

He glanced at Rita.

"Tell her," she said.

Roger beckoned me closer and leaned across the bar. "Last weekend we had a young couple stay a few nights. First night was no problem, but the second night she woke half the damn village screaming the place down."

"I thought she'd never stop," Rita added. "She just went on and on and on."

"What did she say happened?"

Roger's lips twisted into a sneer. "Couldn't get any sense out of the woman, didn't hear anything she was saying through the screeching, other than that she'd woken up and seen some horrible old man peering down at her. They packed up and left right away, didn't even wait until morning. She refused point-blank to go back into the room—she got dressed right here in the bar."

"Is there any way to get rid of him?" Rita asked. "From now on I'm going to be scared half to death that another guest is going to wake me up with their screaming."

"You could try getting an exorcism," I said. "I know there are priests who'll do it, but they have to have permission from their bishop, or sometimes even higher."

"That's all I need, a bunch of damn God-botherers chanting and burning incense around the place," Roger said.

"Beats the alternative," I said.

"Do you know someone who could help?" Rita asked.

I took a sip of my wine. "Not personally, but I'll ask around."

Before I had a chance to think on it any further I was distracted by the sound of hurrying feet on the stairs: feet moving too fast for the narrow wooden steps. The door at the bottom of the stairwell flew open and Jamie burst out, stumbled, righted himself and almost ran across the bar to the exit.

He was followed by a low, insistent voice hissing venomously, "Run, little boy, run as fast as you can, but it won't do you no good; when your time comes, you'll have nowhere to run to. When your time comes, we'll be waiting."

"What about your beer?" Roger called as Jamie tugged open the door and ran outside.

"Oh God, it's not happened again, has it?" Rita asked me. I ignored her as I moved across the room and positioned myself between the stairs and the exit.

Bill was still uttering his poison as he entered the bar. His malicious smile slipped a little upon seeing me, but then his eyes flicked around the room and his smile returned. *No Kayla.*

"Lucky, lucky me," he said, then laughed at his own joke. "I should have known you'd be around somewhere. You attract freaks like flies to a turd."

Bill came a little closer, his piggy eyes glistening with glee. I'd heard he hadn't been a pleasant man when alive. Being dead hadn't improved him any. "I would have thought you'd have known better than to come here without your bodyguard," he said, taking another step toward me. "She deserted you as well?"

I frowned. "As well?"

He grinned, showing custard-colored teeth punctuated with blackened stubs. "Haven't you wondered why she's the only one who doesn't leave? First your mom, then your dad."

"My dad died," I said, before I could stop myself.

Bill's grin turned up a notch. "Poor Lucky. You'd be better off if you joined him. You'd be better off dead."

"And we'd all be better off if you left this place and went to where you belong," I said, trying to take charge of the situation.

Bill laughed again. "Don't you think it's odd she bothers to hang around such a loser like you? Why don't you ask her? Why don't you ask why . . ." His mouth snapped shut and he stumbled backward a few steps. His eyes grew wide and he shrank away.

"You have a big mouth, little man," Kayla said, stepping between Bill and me.

If he had become smaller, Kayla had grown: I could only see her back as she towered over him. But, though I knew it was Kayla, somehow it wasn't. She was taller, wider; her voice was deeper, darker.

"I didn't mean no harm—"

"Yes, you did, you horrible little insect," Kayla said. "Now leave this place and never come back."

"No," he whimpered, "please don't make me leave, this is all I have." He dropped to his knees, his hands clenched together as if in prayer. "Please, I beg you."

"You should have thought of that before," she said, and I could feel the fine hairs on my arms and at the back of my neck bristle. Never before had I ever felt an ounce of fear toward my friend, but for a brief moment she could have been a malevolent stranger. "Be gone from this place and never return."

"No," he said, "please, no."

And he began to fade at the edges—no, not fade: it was as if he were draining away like water down a plughole, or sand slipping through fingers, or autumn leaves swirling away on a breath of wind. Before I could make up my mind on exactly what was happening to him, all that was left of Bill was a small, shimmering ball.

And then he was gone.

Kayla stood there for a moment, staring down at where he had been, and then with a toss of her head she swung around to face me, and suddenly she was the same old Kayla. The confusion must have shown on my face as her smile was grim.

"He won't be back," was all she said as she walked past me and to the door.

I turned and watched her leave before returning to the bar. Rita was clinging to Roger's arm as if it was a lifeline.

"What happened?" she asked. "Something happened, I know something happened."

"Your unwanted guest won't be back," I said, and as I said it, I was pretty sure it was true. Despite myself, I almost felt a little sorry for the unfortunate Bill. I had no idea where he had gone to, but I didn't think it was anywhere good.

"You sure?" Roger asked, and I nodded.

All at once I felt very, very tired. It had been a long day and I was physically and emotionally exhausted. I knocked back my glass of wine, though it could have been water for all the kick it had, and took out my purse to pay.

Roger waved the offered bill aside. "On the house," he said.

When I left the bar Jamie and Kayla were waiting outside. Jamie was leaning against the parking lot wall and Kayla was sitting on one of the picnic tables outside the pub, swinging her legs like a little child. They were ignoring each other, although I wasn't sure whether that was just because Jamie couldn't see my friend or not.

"Is he really gone for good?" I asked Kayla.

She shrugged, not meeting my eyes. Jamie glanced over to where she was sitting and frowned. Then an unreadable expression passed across his face and almost immediately was gone.

"You saw him?" he asked.

"Yes," I said, when Kayla didn't answer. "He was his usual nasty little self, but apparently he won't be anymore." Jamie dragged his eyes away from my uncommunicative friend. "She," I said, indicating Kayla with a head movement, "sent him away, and by all accounts he won't be coming back."

"She can do that?" he asked.

"Unchartered territory as far as I'm concerned; she says so."

"He won't be back," Kayla said, as she hopped down from the table and started walking toward home. "You coming?" she called, glancing back.

Jamie picked up his knapsack and heaved it over his shoulder. "You still sure it's all right for me to stay?" His eyes met mine.

I could have said no, I could have said that now Bill was gone there was no need, that we could meet up tomorrow, but I didn't. I was too damn tired and my head felt like it was full of cotton balls. "Bill may be no more, but I suspect you'll sleep easier at mine. I don't get any unwelcome guests—Kayla sees to that." And for the first time it occurred to me that this was probably true. Not once had I ever had a problem with spirits in a place where I was living, other than at the school and, in retrospect, that hadn't actually been my problem. I had just ended up in the wrong place at the wrong time.

Four

I was relieved to be safely back inside my cottage. The narrow lane leading home had felt almost menacing, and when I'd reached my front door step, I could have sworn I caught a whiff of Parma violets again. I suspected it was due to my overactive imagination. My encounters with Henri and Bill had left me more shaken than I would have believed, and it wasn't helping that my best friend was somehow at the center of it all.

While Jamie stowed his stuff I made a cup of tea. I wanted a few minutes alone with Kayla so I could start trying to make sense of what was going on, but as soon as Jamie started up the stairs she disappeared and didn't return until he did. Knowing that she was avoiding me wasn't lowering my anxiety levels.

"Tea?" I asked him.

"Thanks," Jamie said, joining me at the kitchen table.

"There's a beer in the fridge if you'd prefer?" I offered.

"I'm not much of a drinker. I tried for a while hoping that if I was drunk it wouldn't matter what I saw, but it didn't help."

"It's easier for them to mess with your head if you're not in control," I said. "I imagine drugs would make it even worse."

He gave me a sideways glance. "They do," he said. "Much worse."

Now the door to the other side had been opened to him I doubted anything would close it again, so all he could do was learn to live with it. If not . . . well, I didn't really want to think about the other option.

"So, when did you first realize you could see ghosts?" Jamie asked.

I put down my cup and relaxed back into my chair. "I don't really know. Probably from the moment I was born."

"How about Kayla?"

I hesitated, trying to think back to when I was a child. "I'm not sure; I certainly can't remember a time when she wasn't with me."

"Did you ever consider she might be your twin or something?" he asked

"Yes, but Dad assured me that wasn't the case."

"What about your mother?"

I sighed. After all these years it still hurt me to think about her. "She left when I was very young. I think I scared her. Dad said that wasn't true, but . . . I don't know."

He gave me a sympathetic smile. "That must have been rough?"

"My dad loved me enough for two—and I had Kayla. Of course having an invisible best friend brought its own problems. I was bullied until I realized Kayla was best kept a secret, so I learned not to look at her if other people were around when she was talking to me."

"How did your father cope?" Jamie asked. "It must have been difficult for him?"

"It was. We went to a succession of child psychiatrists before he decided they were doing me no good at all. Once he knew it was more than me having an overactive imagination, he started taking me to psychics. Unfortunately, most of them were frauds and I suppose that's why I despise them so much: I've seen firsthand how they prey on the vulnerable, on people who are desperate for answers."

"Did he ever see her?"

"Who, Kayla?" I shook my head. "No, until today you're the only person who has. The only *living* person, I mean."

"I can't see her all the time, though." He looked to my left, then my right. "Is she here now?"

Kayla hopped down from the kitchen counter where she was perched and sat on the chair between us, and Jamie gave a little start.

"Oh," he said. "There you are."

"Yes, here I am," she said, a slight edge to her voice. Jamie looked away, slumping down in the chair.

I glared at Kayla and mouthed, "Be nice!" She wrinkled her nose, so I gave her what I hoped was a killer glare; it must have worked as she immediately plastered a smile on her face.

"So, Jamie," she said, "you were training to be a vet?"

Seeing her smile, his shoulders relaxed a bit and he sat up in the chair. "I was," he started, "but . . ."

"Maybe if you went back to college it would take your mind off things?" I said.

"How could it? Even if I wasn't seeing—you know—I would be thinking of Sara everywhere I went."

"You met her there?" I asked, and when he gave me another lopsided smile, I suggested, "Perhaps you could transfer to a different college?"

"Maybe—I did consider it for a while, but . . ."

His voice tailed off again and I could tell his heart wasn't in it—and who could blame him? It was bad enough he'd been blown up and lost his girlfriend, that would be enough to derail anyone; but seeing things no one should have to see on top of that?

"Well, haven't you still got a while before you have to go back?" I said. "Perhaps you could ask if they would extend your leave of absence to the beginning of a new academic year?"

"I suppose," he said, then added, "If you don't mind, I think I'll go to bed."

I gave him a smile. "Of course, it's fine. I'll see you tomorrow."

He said goodnight and was gone. I got up and started cleaning up, waiting until I heard the bathroom door close before forestalling Kayla by saying, "I've got to do something to help."

"I don't see how you can help," she muttered.

"Well, no one else can."

"You think he's for real?"

I turned to face her. "Don't you?"

An earnest look came over her face. "There's something not quite right with him."

I regarded her for a moment. "I'll tell you what isn't 'quite right,'" I said, "a demon asking after you and a nasty little spirit casting aspersions: what's that all about?"

"I don't know what you mean," she said, and started toward the door.

I crossed the room and stood in her way. "Oh no you don't, Kayla. We really need to talk about this."

"Not now."

"Yes, now."

She stepped around me.

"Kayla?"

"Lucky, just for once, let it be," she said. I hadn't heard that tone in her voice before and it pulled me up short.

"Kayla, we need to talk about this because I'm willing to bet that we haven't heard the last of Henri Toothy Pegs."

"Don't worry about him," she said.

"All very well for you to say—he wasn't drooling all over your face. Anyway, wasn't it you who said that if he threatened me I should be worried?"

She raised her eyes to meet mine. "I won't let anyone hurt you," she said. "I promise." Then she turned and disappeared through the door, leaving me staring at empty space.

I woke up to raised voices. "What the f—?" I mumbled, rolling over to look at the clock. Two-thirty in the morning. I sat up and swiveled my legs around, searching for my slippers with my toes while the voices kept rumbling on. I grabbed my bathrobe from the end of the bed and shuffled out into the hallway.

"Like hell I will," I heard a male voice say from downstairs.

"Wonderful," I muttered to myself. My guest had been in residence only a few hours and I was already losing sleep over him.

"What business is it of yours anyway?" I heard Kayla say.

Great, so Kayla was involved. I was tempted to stomp down the stairs—but then I might never know what was going on. Instead, I padded down as quietly as I could, avoiding the squeaky step third from bottom, and crept along the passageway toward the kitchen.

"I'm making it my business," I heard Jamie reply. "And did you really have to extinguish the spook at the pub into nothingness like that? That was cruel, even for you."

"If you had dealt with him I wouldn't have needed to. Anyway, don't try and change the subject; what's this 'now you see me, now you don't' act all about? Are you trying to alienate me from her?"

"We can all play games, Kayla."

"I'm not playing games! She was visited by a court assassin this afternoon."

"Why do you think I'm here?"

"You'd protect her?"

"Better than you can."

Protect me? Court assassin? What the hell was going on?

I pressed my ear against the door and heard Kayla sigh. "All right, but the sooner you're gone the better."

"I'm not going anywhere."

"We'll see," she said, and the door jerked open so suddenly I almost fell flat on my face.

"Lucky?" Kayla said, giving Jamie an anxious look.

"All right, what's going on?" I asked. I crossed my arms and willed my cheeks not to flush scarlet.

"Nothing—nothing really," Kayla started.

I glanced at Jamie and did a double-take: gone was the frightened young adult and in his place stood a confident, fully grown man.

I looked him up and down. "What—?" I started to say as his eyes met mine and the strange fuzziness came back over my thoughts.

"Hi Lucky, are you all right?" he asked. "You look pale."

"I . . . I . . ." *I what?*

"You should go back to bed. You're dreaming: weird dreams, strange dreams."

Cotton-ball weariness filled my head and my eyes began to droop.

"Here, let me help you," he said.

★ ★ ★

Considering the day I'd had, I hadn't thought sleep would come easily, but I must have dropped off as soon as my head hit the pillow because I didn't wake until it was almost light. I had dreamed though, I could remember it vividly. I must be more worried about this whole situation than I thought to dream in such detail. I lay there for a moment, trying to push the fog of sleep away. When I sat up I found Kayla staring out through my bedroom window.

"Hey," I said with a yawn.

She glanced at me over her shoulder and gave a small, crooked smile. "You slept well," she said, "which is more than can be said for your guest."

"Oh?"

"He spent most of the night pacing and finally fell asleep with the dawn chorus."

"Did you speak to him?"

"Nope. I don't need his emotional garbage—and neither do you."

"Change the record," I said. "I told him I'd try to help and I will."

She crossed the room and sat down on the bed next to me. "Lucky," she said, then hesitated. It was unusual for Kayla to be unsure of herself, and added to what had happened the previous day I immediately began to feel edgy.

"Kayla, what's wrong?"

"Sometimes you are far too trusting," she said. The room was still filled with the gray of early morning so I couldn't see her expression, but there was sadness in her voice, tinged with another emotion I couldn't quite place.

"What do you mean?" I asked.

"This business at the school, Philip and now Jamie, don't you think it's all a bit . . . odd?" She kept her eyes lowered as she twisted a strand of hair around her finger.

"At the risk of repeating myself, what I do find 'odd' is how, all of a sudden, the twin girls at the school kick off after fifteen years of nothing, Bill draws attention to himself by giving one of the guests at the pub the heebie-jeebies, I suddenly have a demon at my heels, and in each case, I receive messages either for or about you. So what's that all about?"

She stood up and faced me. "I just don't think it's a good time for Jamie to be here," she told me, ignoring everything I'd said. "Then of course there's Philip Conrad. Okay, it could all be coincidence, but I wish I could be sure."

"Coincidence? Sure of *what*? Kayla, you're talking in riddles. And what on earth has Philip got to do with anything?"

"Exactly," she said, and if I could have taken her by the shoulders and shaken her I would have.

"Kayla, will you just *tell* me?"

"No need to get your panties in a twist. Let me think about it, okay? Once you've had dinner with Philip tonight and found out what he's all about, then we can talk."

"Why not now?"

"Too soon."

"Too soon for what?" I asked in exasperation.

"I need to think," she repeated, and with that she flounced out of the room. I was very tempted to go straight after her, but as I was wearing next to nothing and there was a strange man in the guest room I thought better of it.

I contemplated taking a run before breakfast, but in the end decided against it: it was Jamie's first morning in his new—albeit temporary—home and I wasn't sure what Kayla might say to him if I wasn't there to mediate.

When I got downstairs Kayla was nowhere to be seen and as she'd said Jamie hadn't slept well, I decided not to wake him and ate breakfast alone. I was just pouring more coffee when he appeared in the doorway. His eyes were puffy and red-rimmed and his complexion was dull and pallid. I didn't even bother to ask, just handed him my mug of coffee. His need was greater than mine and I drank too much caffeine anyway.

He slumped down on a kitchen chair, clutching the mug.

"Bad night?"

"A bit."

"Want something to eat?"

He shook his head, then, as if suddenly remembering his manners, mumbled, "No thanks."

I sat down opposite him. After a few minutes the color began to return to his cheeks and I could see he was beginning to focus. By the time he'd finished his drink he was looking a lot better and much more awake.

"Mind if I take a shower?" he asked.

"Be my guest."

"Thanks," he said as he stumbled to his feet. He shambled back upstairs, leaving me to consider how I was going to spend the day. My diary was empty and the only thing I really had to do was pick up some dry-cleaning—and if necessary, I could do that the following day.

The problem was: now Jamie was here I didn't know what to do with him. The best I could think of was to try to rebuild his confidence so he wouldn't be afraid all the time. His meeting with the vitriolic Bill hadn't been the best place to start. There was also the matter of Henri le Dent, who had left me in no doubt he'd be back at some stage. He'd scared the shit out of me and I was used to *weird*; a confrontation between him and Jamie just didn't bear thinking about.

You have something we want, he'd said.

I shivered. I could almost feel his breath on my face, the touch of his fingers as he stroked and sniffed at my hair. Although my dreams had been strange I was surprised they hadn't been nightmares—actually, I was surprised I'd slept at all. The scent of him was everywhere, but I knew it was all in my head.

At least, that's what I told myself.

Then there was Philip Conrad. Now I thought about it, I realized Lydia Mitchell hadn't explained who he was, or how he was involved. Kayla had said he was troubled, but in retrospect I thought it was far more likely my first impression of him was right: that it was he who was trouble.

And now there was Jamie. Men were like buses in my life: not one for months, and then three (if you could count a demon) came along at once: Henri: evil and terrifying; Philip: powerful, but with a slight air of vulnerability, and Jamie: scared and helpless. They couldn't be more different.

"Penny for them," Kayla said, dropping down onto the chair next to me.

"I was thinking about your comments on coincidence," I said.

Kayla gave me a smug smile.

"I was also thinking about what Henri and Bill had to say about you."

That knocked the smile off her face. "I told you, we'll talk about it later."

"I want to talk about it now."

"Well, I don't," she said.

"Henri said, 'We want Kayla back.' So who's 'we'?"

"What are you going to do with Jamie today?"

"Don't change the subject."

"He's actually quite good-looking in a scruffy, down-and-out sort of way."

"Really?" I said with a sigh. When Kayla was in one of these moods she would just disappear if I tried to push the point, but she was making me way beyond cranky.

"And that Philip Conrad is decidedly yummy."

"Too slick for my liking."

"Wealthy."

"Looks can be deceptive."

"Fancy car, expensive suit."

"Both can be rented," I said.

"Buffed skin and polished nails. Expensive aftershave."

"A vain man, that's all I need."

"A rich man is what you need."

"No, I don't. Men just complicate things."

"Then why did you say you'd go to dinner with him?"

"Business."

"I didn't hear him mention payment."

"If all he wants is advice, dinner will suffice."

"What if he wants more?" Kayla asked.

"He'll be out of luck."

"It'll do you good to have a little fun."

"That sort of fun I can do without. Especially with someone like him."

"We'll see," she said with a smirk.

"Kayla, if you're right about him and he really is troubled, then he'll have a whole lot of emotional baggage I can do without. I've got enough of my own, thank you very much."

"So why is Jamie here?" she countered.

I sighed. I could hardly tell her I wasn't at all sure why he was here either. "I told you, he doesn't have anyone else."

A sudden *tap, tap, tap* on the kitchen door made my heart skip a beat and my head jerk up in surprise.

Kayla glanced at me. "Jumpy," she commented.

"Can I come in?" Jamie's muffled voice asked from the hallway.

"Of course," I said.

The door opened and he hesitated just outside. "I'm not interrupting anything?" he asked, and glanced around the kitchen. "Is she here?"

"I wasn't talking to myself," I said.

Kayla glared in his direction and Jamie's eyes widened a little before he gave her a tentative smile.

"I don't think I'll ever get used to her doing that," he said to me.

"Why does everyone talk about me as though I'm not here?" she asked.

"If by 'everyone' you mean Jamie, it's because half the time he doesn't know if you *are* here." I gestured for him to take a seat. "Feel like some breakfast now?"

"No, thanks. A cup of tea would be good though."

My nerves were so frazzled a coffee was probably not a good idea, so I made myself a cup of tea to keep him company. I dug out a box of cookies from the cupboard, too. Fortunately they were still in their cellophane and only out of date by a couple of months but Jamie wasn't interested.

"If you're interested in a drive we could go shopping to get some food in," I suggested. "You'll need something for tonight as I'm going out."

"On a date?" he asked.

"No," I said, with a wave of the hand. "Business."

"That's what you say," Kayla mumbled.

I gave her a look. She could be such a pain at times. "Kayla, you know very well it's business."

"Does he, though?" she asked.

I ignored her and turned back to Jamie. "I met him yesterday afternoon." I chose my wording carefully. "I think he has some *issues* that he wants to talk to me about. He suggested we have dinner."

"Issues as in ghosts?" Jamie asked.

I decided to be a little economical with the truth. He was having quite enough trouble coping without throwing demons into the mix, at least at this stage. "I think so. To be honest, I know very little about him."

Jamie turned his attention back to his drink but not before I saw a strange expression pass across his face . . . again.

"What?" I asked, but he continued staring into his cup. "Jamie?"

His eyes jerked up to mine. "Sorry?"

His face was so completely guileless I thought I must have imagined the previous expression. "Never mind," I said. "Let's go shopping."

I *really* don't like driving; when I told Jamie that it wasn't a lie. Every trip for me is a white-knuckle ride: after a long journey my fingers are tight claws and my shoulders and neck ache with tension. Really I should be living in a big city where public transport isn't a problem, but then, cities mean other issues, like the number of lost souls wandering the streets, many of whom haven't even realized they've died and should have passed over.

Now Batty Bill was gone the village had only one spirit in residence: an old lady, fortunately of a much nicer disposition. She doesn't know she's dead and carries on just the way she did before she passed away. She lived alone and was quite old, very deaf and terribly short-sighted, so she doesn't realize people can't see or hear her. I always give her a cheery wave and if she sees me she waves back. Kayla usually ignores her, but then, that's Kayla. She can be a complete bitch at times.

My blue Ford Fiesta is a few years old but hardly has any miles on it thanks to my totally incomprehensible aversion to driving. Jamie fortunately didn't share my hang-up. In fact, once behind the wheel he was the happiest I had seen him since we had met. He certainly put the old girl through her paces; he had her racing through the country lanes at speeds I'd be incapable of reaching while driving, at least not without my knuckles shattering. I might've been a rotten driver, but I was a great passenger, so I just leaned back and enjoyed the ride.

We went to one of those out-of-town shopping malls where you can buy almost anything, from groceries to a three-piece suite to a garden shed. I always prefer the local corner shop, but our village store is rather limited when it comes to stock: if you want bread, milk, eggs or basic mild Cheddar cheese you'll be fine, but if you have a sudden interest in an Oriental meal for two or a nice piece of Brie, you'll be right out of luck.

Jamie very gallantly pushed the cart while I scanned the shelves and generally tried to discourage him from his terrible choice of foods. Kayla followed along behind us, completely uninterested in the whole process.

Occasionally we'd pass a child in a stroller, or a baby seated in a cart, and Kayla cheered herself up by making them burst into tears or start screaming the place down. I've never actually caught her at it, so I don't know exactly what it is she does, but for all her hurt denials, I've always known it's her causing all the tears and tantrums.

This time I just ignored her and hoped Jamie didn't realize the trail of whimpering children was something to do with my best friend.

There wasn't much of a line at the checkout, which was a relief: Kayla hates hanging around waiting to be served and she's quite capable of causing mayhem among the shoppers. I shuddered, remembering the time the police had to be called after a fight broke out when a young woman accused an old boy in the line behind her of patting her bottom. She'd started screaming obscenities, then her boyfriend, a tattooed skinhead with a stud through his bottom lip, had joined in, pushing the bewildered—and entirely innocent—pensioner in the chest, then going to thump him. In the end I'd managed to calm everyone down by somehow convincing them it was the old guy's basket that had knocked the woman's backside. I'd impressed myself with my quick thinking—I might have had to lie through my teeth but at least I saved some hapless old guy from being beaten up or arrested. Kayla, of course, thought the whole thing was hilarious.

This time, to my huge relief, she behaved herself, although I did have a minor heart attack when she started eyeing up a rather stuck-up woman being served at the opposite till. Fortunately, our last item was being scanned by the time Kayla had noticed her and I shoved my card into the little machine and tapped in my number as fast as I could manage, praying that just for once, there wouldn't be any hold-ups in the processing.

Jamie, blissfully unaware of the potential calamity that had been narrowly avoided, strolled out of the supermarket pushing the cart while I bustled ahead, trying to put as much distance between me and the store as possible. I was really hoping Kayla was right behind me.

"Where to next?" Jamie asked, as he turned the key in the ignition and the engine roared into life.

"Yes, where to next?" Kayla asked, with a smirk that made my heart sink. She'd been up to something, I was sure of it. All I could do was pray that I wouldn't be reading about a riot in Sainsbury's in a few days' time.

"I think home," I said, "unless there's anywhere you want to go?"

Jamie put the car into reverse and checked over his shoulder. "No thanks, I'm good."

I heaved a sigh of relief, but it was short-lived.

"I was surprised at the bill," Jamie commented as he pulled out of the parking lot and onto the highway. "I'd have thought it'd come to a lot more."

"I didn't notice," I said, digging in my handbag for the receipt and trying to ignore the sinking feeling in the pit of my stomach.

Kayla peered over my shoulder from the backseat. "Looking for something?" she asked.

"My purse," I said through gritted teeth. "The till receipt. What did you do?"

"Me?" She flopped back in her seat, smiling.

The receipt was wrapped around my credit card. I took a deep breath and unfolded it.

"Oh, Kayla," I sighed. I had apparently bought four gallons of milk and a bag of potatoes, making the total considerably less than it should have been. I glared at her, but she just smirked back, knowing I could hardly say anything in front of Jamie. I was angry, but this time I had to let it go. At least it was a better than an all-out super-market riot.

Five

I took a lot of care dressing for my evening out, though I didn't know where Philip intended to take me. I chose my favorite black strappy dress—I loved the chiffon skirt that fell to just below the knee—and slipped a silvery-gray cardigan over the top, then added a pair of black round-toe courts and glittering silver earrings. I wore my shoulder-length chestnut hair loose.

"Are you coming?" I asked Kayla.

"It really isn't a date?"

"No," I said with a smile, "and you might be able to help."

She bounced up from the edge of my bed where she had been sitting as I got dressed. "Then I'd better get ready," she said.

"Kayla, only I can see you."

"Even a—" She faltered for a moment, then she lifted her chin high and gave a defiant toss of her head. "Even a spirit likes to look good when they're out on the town. Well, I do, at least."

She twirled around in a blur of blues, blacks, purples and greens and when she stopped she was wearing a fitted emerald-green dress that ended midthigh. Her dark blond curls were piled loosely upon her head and she was wearing a necklace of gold and deep red stones of some sort. She was breathtaking, and I was suddenly very glad that Philip wouldn't be able to see her.

My doorbell rang at eight o'clock on the dot. Philip was punctual, at least; I liked that in a man. There's nothing worse than being all dressed up and fragrant, then having to wander around aimlessly for twenty minutes because your date's running late.

When I opened the door he was standing with his back to me, looking down the path toward the gate. He turned toward me with a smile.

"Hello," he said, and handed me a huge bouquet of peach roses.

I said, "Thank you, they're beautiful," but I felt distinctly awkward: I didn't even know the man and he was giving me flowers. Now I would have to invite him into my home while I put them in water because I was too polite to leave him standing on the doorstep.

I forced a welcoming smile onto my face and showed him into the sitting room. "I'll just find something to put these in," I muttered, and hurried through to the kitchen to find a vase. The roses were lovely—they *were* lovely, but . . . Their scent filled the air and the cellophane crackled beneath my fingertips. These were not flowers picked up from a nearby garage or supermarket; everything about them said *expensive*. I shivered. Philip Conrad was too slick by far and although I had no reason to think so—*yet*—I couldn't help but feel like I was being played.

I couldn't remember where I'd put the damn vase, so I stuck the flowers in the sink.

"A bit over the top," Kayla said, then pushed her face into the blooms. "They smell nice, though."

"Hmm," I murmured. I didn't want him to hear me and think I was talking to myself.

"What do you think he's up to?"

"I don't know," I whispered. "Maybe this isn't such a good idea."

"Maybe what isn't such a good idea?" Philip said from behind me and I whirled around to find him leaning casually against the doorframe. He had an amused smile on his lips and once again I had the overwhelming impression that he knew things about me he shouldn't.

"Putting the roses in the sink," I lied. "I didn't want to keep you waiting while I looked for a big enough vase." I realized I was on the verge of babbling so I shut up before I made a total idiot of myself.

"We have time," he said. "The table is booked for nine."

"There's a vase in the top cupboard," Kayla said, leaning against the fridge.

She might have been speaking to me, but her eyes were fixed on Philip and the light must've been playing tricks on me because her eyes looked almost black and her expression was very strange. I couldn't ask if there was something wrong so I found the vase and attended to the roses.

"That's better," he said.

"They're lovely, thank you," I said.

"My pleasure." And once again, there was something in his voice that hinted at hidden meanings to whatever he said.

"Shall we go?" I asked. Suddenly I was eager to get him out of the cottage.

"We have plenty of time," he said. "Why don't you show me around?"

I laughed, though even to me it sounded off-key and nervous. "There's not much to see. This is more or less it downstairs, and it's just two bedrooms, my office and the bathroom up top."

"You have an office?"

"Converted bedroom—it's tiny, just about room for my desk, a chair and a filing cabinet."

"I'd love to see it."

I stopped and stared at him. "What is it you want, Mr. Conrad?" I was trying not to sound rude, but however nicely he was asking, he was still trying to invade my personal space.

His smile slipped a fraction. "Philip," he said. "Please, call me Philip."

"Okay, Philip—let's cut to the chase. You've invited me to dinner, brought me roses and you certainly appear to know a lot about me, but I don't know one thing about you. So I'm going to ask again: what do you want from me?"

He was still smiling, but the expression was tight, almost as though he was wearing a mask. "Let's go to dinner," he said.

I was about to tell him I'd changed my mind, but Kayla quickly moved between him and me and put a finger to her lips. "I don't know about you, but I'd be interested to hear what he has to say."

I hesitated; she was right: he had piqued my curiosity. I took a deep breath and followed him out into the hall. When he turned toward me I could see his tight smile had relaxed into a more natural expression—but why wouldn't it? I was doing what he wanted, after all.

He opened the front door and gestured for me to go first. I snagged my handbag off the hall table, checked I had my front door key and walked past him out into the night. He closed the door behind us and there was a soft *click* as it locked. Then, putting a hand beneath my elbow, he guided me along the path. I had another moment of unease. It felt like I was being escorted off the premises.

Kayla had skipped around us and was standing by the gate. "Nice wheels," she said.

Another shiny limousine waited in the lane, this one in metallic dark gray. As Philip opened the gate the driver—no, not a driver, a *chauffeur*—hopped out of the car and hurried around to open the door for me. Kayla clambered in first while Philip walked around to get in the other side.

"Where are we going?" I asked, as the chauffeur started the engine and pulled away.

"The Riverview Hotel," Philip replied, his teeth a flash of white in the darkened interior. I shivered at the sudden reminder of the dreadful Henri.

"Oh, won't that be fun," Kayla said. "It's only probably the most haunted damn place for miles."

"At least they're harmless," I said, then cringed. I hadn't meant to speak out loud.

"Excuse me?" Philip asked.

"Sorry, just speaking to myself."

Another flash of teeth. "Really?" he said, and again there was that tone to his voice.

I let it ride. At some point during the evening all would become clear, and if not, well, it was his choice if he wanted to waste a lot of time and money. As well as being one of the most haunted venues in the area, The Riverview was also the most expensive, patronized by celebrities and politicians who liked to hide away there for dirty weekends.

Staff, mostly of the living variety, hurried to meet us as soon as we walked into the building, greeting Philip with deferential familiarity. To my immense satisfaction the maître d' also welcomed me by name.

Philip's smile faltered a fraction. "You've been here before?"

"It's a popular place."

Kayla giggled, and I must admit I found it hard not to laugh myself: Philip looked like a little boy who's just found the terrific surprise he'd been planning was neither as terrific, nor as surprising as he'd expected.

But Philip's smile soon returned as we were seated next to the long window that ran the whole length of the restaurant and provided an unimpeded panoramic view of the river as it swooped around the hotel before widening and flowing into the sea. It was spectacular during the day, but looking out across the water at night was magical: reflections of the lanterns set along the banks glittered like fairy lights and shone across the rippling surface. I could have stared out at the scene all evening.

"It's beautiful," I said.

"My favorite place to eat."

"You come here a lot?"

"Whenever I can," he said. "I've never seen you here, though, and I'm sure I would have noticed."

"I usually come here for lunch with my agent and publisher. All business, no pleasure."

"A shame. This view was meant to be enjoyed."

The wistful edge in his voice made me look at him. He was staring out into the night, his expression sad. Then it was as though he gave himself a mental shake, his smile returned and I became the focus of his attention once again.

After asking if there was anything I couldn't or wouldn't eat he ordered for both of us, and while we waited for the first course, we sipped a delicious Puligney-Montrachet and chatted easily. But it wasn't long before my earlier disquiet returned: he was trying just a bit too hard to make me comfortable and his smile had an odd, fixed quality. Kayla didn't appear to share my concerns and, despite her telling me she wanted to hear what he had to say, drifted off somewhere, leaving Philip and me alone together. I hoped she would behave herself; I had enough to worry about.

He still hadn't mentioned the school or the demon by the time we were served coffee, and he'd swerved around all my attempts to lead the conversation in that direction. But once we'd finished eating, he became strangely uncommunicative, and I found myself getting a little annoyed. After all, hadn't the purpose of our dinner been to discuss the demon issue?

"So, what have you got to do with St. Agatha's?" I asked, trying to end the uncomfortable silence and—hopefully—get to the point.

He took a sip of his coffee and leaned back in his chair, then studied my face for such a long time I could feel my cheeks begin to burn.

"My wife was an old girl," he said at last. "When we enrolled our daughter I wanted to be involved, so I became a governor."

"You have a daughter?" I asked, although I had no idea why I should be surprised.

He didn't reply, just looked at me with the same sad expression I had noticed earlier. Then his eyes swung away from me and he lifted a hand to catch the attention of a waiter. Within moments the bill was paid and we were leaving, so quickly I wasn't quite sure what had happened.

As he hurried me out of the hotel, I glanced around, trying to catch a glimpse of Kayla. Where on earth was she? I wasn't worried she'd be left behind—she'd catch us up when she was ready—but I was beginning to get concerned about being alone with Philip Conrad.

The car was waiting out front and the chauffeur was opening the door for me before we had even reached the bottom step. I had another quick look over my shoulder to see if Kayla had reappeared, but it looked as if I would be making this journey without her.

"I thought you wanted to talk?" I said, as soon as Philip had settled in his seat.

"I thought we had."

"Mr. Conrad"—he gave me a look—"*Philip*, you were insistent I have dinner with you to discuss what happened at the school."

"I thought I could talk to you over dinner, but I couldn't." His voice quavered slightly. "Not there."

"Okay, so how about now?"

He gave a short laugh that had nothing to do with being amused. "There are some things better not discussed in the dark."

There I had to agree with him, but I was beginning to think I needed to know what he wanted and how he fitted in to the events of the last few days. I sighed inwardly; I was probably going to regret this. "How about you come in for a coffee or nightcap?"

He smiled, then he leaned forward and pressed a button; the tinted screen between us and the chauffeur slid down with barely a sound.

"We'll be going straight back to Miss de Salle's cottage."

"Yes, Mr. Conrad," the chauffeur replied, his eyes not leaving the road, then, "What the f—?"

He slammed on the brakes but as tires screamed on pavement, the car carried on moving as if in slow motion. I looked past the chauffeur at the road ahead. The unlit country road was pitch black, but Henri le Dent was clearly illuminated in the stark white beams of the headlights. He stood there, legs apart, right hand resting on his cane, left hand on hip, a very wide and arrogant grin showing off almost every single one of those horribly pointed teeth.

The chauffeur leaned back in the seat, his foot no doubt pressing the brake pedal into the floor, but we still plowed on until Henri disappeared under the front of the car and the whole vehicle juddered as if it had driven over a speed hump. At last the car slithered to a halt and for a moment there was silence.

"Davis, what happened?" Philip asked.

The chauffeur began to struggle with his seatbelt. "There was a man, sir—he appeared from nowhere, right in the middle of the road—" He flung the door open and jumped out.

"Stay here," Philip ordered.

I reached out to stop him, but I heard Kayla say, "It's all right." And there she was, sitting by my side. "But you stay inside the car." Once I'd promised I was going to stay put, Kayla disappeared again.

A few minutes passed. Inside the car it felt like I was cocooned from the outside world. I couldn't hear what was going on, or see much through the tinted side windows, and it wasn't until Philip and his chauffeur appeared at the front of the car to examine the hood and front bumper that I knew for certain they were still there. Henri could have carried them away to some terrible demon place for all I knew.

I saw Philip put his hand on the chauffeur's shoulder and the man nodded his head a couple of times as if to say he was all right, though his face was milk-white in the harsh brightness of the headlights.

Kayla appeared beside me. "What happened?" she said.

"Henri happened."

"The chauffeur's terribly shaken up," she said, sounding very matter-of-fact. "He thought he'd killed someone."

"I did too: I felt the car drive over him."

"You felt the car drive over a hole in the road."

"Not Henri?"

"Of course not, silly! You can't run over a demon. He was just playing with you."

"I'm glad you think it's funny."

She smiled a dark smile. "Oh no," she said. "I don't think it's funny at all."

The back door swung open and Philip leaned in. "It's okay, just a pothole."

"Is your driver all right?" I asked.

"A bit shaken, that's all. He thought he saw someone standing in the middle of the road."

Kayla looked at me and put her finger to her lips. "Was there?" I asked.

He stood there, once again studying my face. I stared back.

"No, apparently not," he said at last. He lingered a few seconds more, looking at me, and then stepped back and shut the door. I saw him join the chauffeur at the front of the car. The poor guy was puffing on a cigarette as if his life depended on it.

"I'd just invited Philip back home for a nightcap," I said to Kayla. "Is there any reason Henri le Dent wouldn't want that to happen?"

She considered the question, her forefinger tapping her bottom lip. "No, I suspect this is about you."

"No, Kayla, this has *your* name written all over it."

She didn't deny it, but she still avoided the question hanging in the air. "Anyway, I doubt Philip will be coming back to the cottage now; his man's a bag of nerves."

"Probably just as well," I said, "because you and I still need to talk. I don't imagine Henri turning up again so soon is a good sign, do you?" Again there was no denial.

The back passenger door opened and Philip climbed in. A moment later the chauffeur slid back into the front seat.

"Do you want to take a rain check on the nightcap?" I asked.

"No, I need to talk to you."

"What about—?" I struggled to remember the man's name.

"I've arranged for a car to be waiting at your cottage with a replacement chauffeur, and someone will ferry Davis home for the night."

"Oh." I couldn't think what else to say, though I did begin to wonder just how many drivers and cars he had at his beck and call—and what he did for a living, to amass such wealth.

Sure enough, as I climbed from the car outside my cottage another limo pulled up behind us and I wondered how it had got here so fast. I left Philip outside with his entourage while I went in to turn on the kettle and put the door on the latch, telling him he could come in when he was ready. I could hear Jamie moving about upstairs and wondered what he'd been up to all evening.

Kayla followed me inside and plunked herself down on the kitchen table while I puttered around the kitchen.

"Philip must live locally," I said.

"Really?"

"His other car was right behind us."

"His other car followed us back from the restaurant," Kayla said, "I hitched a ride until the *accident*."

"What?" I said and she gave me a smug look.

"He has two bodyguards."

"Bodyguards? Who the hell is he to have bodyguards?"

She sniffed. "I can't say who he is, but I can tell you what he is: one very scared man."

"This is getting weird."

"Did he tell you anything interesting over dinner?"

"If you had stayed around you would know."

"I got bored with all the small talk."

I shooed her out of my way so I could put milk and sugar on the table. She hopped up on the kitchen counter. "Anyway, it was beginning to feel like a date so I didn't want to cramp your style."

"He's married with a daughter," I said.

"Really? Are you sure?"

"That's what he told me."

"Men are such liars."

"Why would he lie about that?" I said.

"Who knows? I'm just making an observation."

"Anyway, what experience have you had with men?"

"Same as you." She gave me another smug smile. "Remember, I've been there for almost every tragic moment."

I was about to come back at her with a sharp retort when I heard the front door open and close, then footsteps in the hall.

"Sorry about that," Philip said from the doorway. "I was just making sure Davis was okay. He really was shaken up."

"I'm not surprised if he thought he hit someone." I fiddled with the milk jug so I didn't have to look him in the eye.

"I don't know—it was really odd. He described the guy in detail—in fact, he could have been describing your demon—didn't you say he was dressed like an eighteenth-century gentleman?"

"Whoops," Kayla said, with far more cheer than was strictly necessary.

"Shall we go into the living room? It's more comfortable," I said.

An amused expression crossed Philip's face; Henri wasn't the only one playing games. Without waiting for a reply I plunked the two mugs on a tray and marched through to the other room. My cheeks felt hot; I needed to regain some measure of composure. It didn't help that I could hear Kayla laughing as she followed me into the sitting room.

I sat down on the couch and immediately realized my mistake when Philip chose to sit down next to me.

Kayla settled herself down in the armchair. "Told you it was turning into a date," she said. "Do you want me to leave?"

I risked giving her a glare, then shifted slightly so I was facing him, but as far away from Philip as the couch would allow.

"Milk? Sugar?"

"Thank you," he said, but ignored both.

I sipped my coffee and studied him. He had unbuttoned his jacket and was leaning back, surveying the room. I doubt he missed much. He had an agenda, I was sure of it, but he obviously wasn't in any hurry to share it with me, and I couldn't work out what it was. Maybe he was a long game man.

"So," I said, when it became quite clear we would be sitting here all night if I waited for him, "what is it you want from me?"

His attention drifted back to me. "Demons," he said, after a moment's hesitation. "I want to know about demons."

I glanced at Kayla. She had such a lack of expression her face could have been sculpted out of marble, but the dark glitter of her eyes told another story. They held an emotion I didn't understand, though if I had to put a name to it, I would have said it was anger: burning anger. I was puzzled, but I didn't have time to dwell on it; Philip was watching me closely and waiting for some kind of answer. I had a feeling I was about to disappoint him.

"What I know about demons I could write on a postage stamp." That wasn't, strictly speaking, true, but I needed to know his true intentions before I started giving out potentially dangerous knowledge: you never messed with the other side unless you really knew what you were doing, and you *certainly* didn't mess with demons. Henri le Dent was a case in point.

"I've been led to believe you're an expert—or you know someone who is at the very least."

I heard Kayla gasp from across the small room, though I resisted the temptation to look her way. "Who told you that?"

"It doesn't matter."

"I think it does."

His smile had disappeared, along with his aloof self-assurance. An emotion somewhere close to desperation clouded his features. The color had leached from his face.

"Please, Lucky—Miss de Salle—I need your help."

He looked like his emotions were laid bare, and Kayla was right: he was a troubled man. I turned my head away as if I was considering what he had said, but I was actually risking another look at Kayla.

"We already have one demon knocking at our door. I'm not sure we need any more," she said, not taking her eyes off him.

I really needed to talk to Kayla alone. I don't believe in coincidences, and certainly not like this. I'd had no dealings with demons before, at least not that I knew of, and now Henri le Dent was on the scene and Philip Conrad seemed to think I was an authority. What the hell was going on?

"Mr. Conrad—Philip—I am *not* an expert on demons. I'm not sure I know anyone who is. Most of what's been written about the other side is plain hogwash, and I would imagine the same can be said for demons; the truth is, we just don't know anything, not for sure. There are theories about how to call them up, and what to do to protect oneself if a demon should appear, but I wouldn't like to risk it as I couldn't be sure they're actually correct."

"I was told you had access to this knowledge."

"By whom?"

"I . . . I'd rather not say."

"I'd rather you did." I crossed my arms, leaned back in my seat and waited, staring him out.

This time he looked away first. He spent a long time studying his fingers before he finally raised his eyes back to mine.

"Do you know what a bokor is?" he asked, and I don't know who was more shocked, me or Kayla.

"Yes," I said, wondering where this was leading—nowhere good, that was for sure. "I suppose you would describe a bokor as a voodoo priest or sorcerer."

"This man is dangerous," Kayla said, referring to Philip.

We were agreed on that.

"What's this all about?" I asked again, and this time I wasn't prepared to let it go.

"For months I've been visiting psychics, clergymen, witch doctors—if they claim to have power, or anyone else who might possibly know about demons. Eventually I was introduced to a man in South London who knew a man, who knew another man who could arrange a meeting for me with a bokor."

"Philip, why would you even want to meet such a man? And more importantly, from my point of view, what's it got to do with me?"

He looked me directly in the eyes. People say the expression "eyes full of pain" is pure fiction, that no one's eyes cannot convey such an expression. Whoever said that was dead wrong. What I saw in his eyes made me shudder.

"A demon murdered my wife, Miss de Salle. It murdered my wife and then stole my daughter and I will do anything—absolutely *anything*—to get her back."

"Hell's bells and buckets of blood," Kayla murmured under her breath. "Why did I not see *that* coming?"

Why would you? I thought, but couldn't ask her so, I asked Philip if he wanted a drink of something stronger. I knew I did. "Although I'm afraid it's just wine or beer."

"You've got that bottle of cognac," Kayla reminded me.

"Oh, and I do have some cognac."

"That would be great."

I thought Kayla would follow me into the kitchen so we could have a quick talk, but she remained behind, her eyes fixed on Philip, and when I returned with the drinks, they were both where I had left them: Philip slumped forward on the couch, his elbows resting on his thighs, hands clenched together, forehead resting on knuckles; Kayla watching him, her face a mask. I had no idea what was going on in her head, and—not for the first time in less than forty-eight hours—I began to wonder whether I really knew my best friend at all.

I put a glass of cognac on the coffee table in front of Philip and he straightened up and gave me a small smile of thanks.

I put my own glass down by the armchair, hoping that Kayla would get the message. Her dark eyes met mine and for a moment I thought she was going to ignore me, then she stood with a sniff and moved to sit on the arm of the chair. I sank down beside her and reached for my drink. Philip was studying the contents of his glass, swirling the amber liquid around as he stared into its depths.

I took a sip. It was velvet on my tongue, with a kick as it hit the back of the throat. A gradual warming sensation followed, filling my chest then the pit of my stomach. Philip was still pondering on his glass and hadn't drunk a drop.

"The bokor sent me to you," he said at last.

I was genuinely puzzled. I had never had any dealings with these so-called black magicians or voodoo priests or whoever they were. I had quite enough on my plate with fraudsters pretending to be psychic without antagonizing some seriously scary people.

"He mentioned me by name?"

"Well, sort of," he said, swirling the cognac, then breathing in the fumes.

"Go on."

"I met him at this house in a rundown part of London, somewhere near the river. I was taken there by the contact, and to be honest, I doubt I could ever find the place again. It was dark, it was raining and it was very late." He finally took a sip, although I doubt he even tasted it. "It wasn't an experience I'd recommend, nor is it one I'd be prepared to repeat." He swirled the glass again, then downed it.

"I'd get the bottle if I were you," Kayla said, reading Philip's mood the same way I was. I went and got the bottle and poured him another.

"The bokor spoke to me in something like a French patois. I couldn't understand a word, but the man who took me to him translated . . ."

He stopped talking again, and at last I asked, "What did he say?"

"He told me to forget my daughter. He told me she'd gone some-where I could never reach her." He raised his eyes to mine. "He told me all this, without me having said a *word*—I hadn't even told him why I'd come to him."

"Philip, he probably had his people research you. It wouldn't be difficult to do. I guess if I Googled you I'd find some mention about your wife's death and how your daughter had gone missing."

"I know you're right and I told myself the same thing, but if you'd been there, if you'd seen him . . ." He shuddered. "He was very convincing."

"They always are."

He sighed. "I said to him, 'So you won't help me?' then he and the other guy jabbered away to each other until the bokor did some mumbo-jumbo with some bones, stones and bits of twig. He started muttering to himself while the other man went off and returned with a large bowl and a hen."

"I don't suppose I have to guess what happened to the chicken?" I said. I don't know if it was the brandy or not, but I was feeling slightly nauseous.

"It wasn't pretty, and I'd had enough, so I got up to leave. Then something weird happened: the guy—the bokor—started speaking in English, cultured English. His friend, the translator, went all wide-eyed and started crossing himself, again and again."

"So what did he say?"

"He said I should visit my daughter's school and that I'd find help there. He said there was a woman, a lucky woman who would come to the school and that it was she who had the knowledge I sought."

"This isn't looking good," Kayla murmured. "I think it's time you and I had that talk."

I ignored her. "Was that it?"

"No. The bokor went into some kind of fit, then the room filled with people and they all started fussing over him. I was ushered out-side and into the car and driven away. The man who had taken me there more or less threw me out of the car when we got to our original rendezvous—he didn't even ask for the money I owed him for setting up the meet."

"So you contacted the school?"

"I didn't need to. I had a missed message from Lydia Mitchell when I got home. The woman doesn't particularly like me, but I think she thought I was the only governor she could turn to who wouldn't immediately panic—and probably the only one who would cough up the money needed. The rest of the board is made up of windbags and old farts."

"She's a practical woman."

"Very. Of course, when I met her the following day and she told me about you I couldn't help but wonder: I was told a lucky woman would come to the school and she starts telling me about this ex-pupil called Lucky de Salle."

"That's definitely one coincidence too far," I said, speaking my thoughts aloud.

"Excuse me?"

"Philip, I have to think about this."

"Lucky, I really need your help—and he said you were the one who could help me—"

"I . . ." I started to protest, then stopped. I could hear the desperation in his voice, but I didn't know what to say to the man.

Fortunately, I was saved from having to answer him as the door swung open and Jamie stood framed in the doorway. He was shirtless, and his jeans hung low on his hips, showing a dark silky line of hair running downward from his navel.

"Oh, I'm sorry," he said to me, seeing Philip. "I didn't realize you had company."

"Clearly," Philip said, getting to his feet.

I managed to tear my eyes away from Jamie's bare chest, though it was difficult. "Philip, this is a friend of mine: Jamie. Jamie, this is Philip Conrad."

Both men stood there eyeing each other up and there was an undeniable, almost physical tension spanning the room between them.

Kayla and I exchanged a perplexed glance.

"It's like two tomcats getting territorial," Kayla said. "Let's hope they don't start marking the room."

I almost giggled, and had to disguise it with a small cough. Philip's distraught expression had hardened into one of arrogant disdain, and Jamie too had lost any sense of vulnerability. Kayla's description was perfect: they were eyeing each other as if they were rivals for the same piece of turf.

"I didn't realize you had someone living with you," Philip said.

"Jamie's a guest," I said, and was immediately angry with myself for trying to justify Jamie's presence. It was none of Philip Conrad's damned business.

"I'd better be going," he said as Jamie stepped into the room. If Jamie had actually said, "Off you go then!" he couldn't have made it plainer.

Philip walked out and I followed, frowning at Jamie as I passed him, but he just smiled. Now I remembered why I had stopped bothering with men: I couldn't be doing with the continual games they played, the constant bolstering of their egos and all their other shit; it was far too emotionally draining. I walked Philip to the gate and he stopped when he got to his car.

He stood there looking at the ground, then took a deep breath, as though he was having difficulty finding the right words to say. His eyes rose back to meet mine.

"Will you help me?"

I waited a heartbeat. I didn't know what I could do to help this man.

"Please."

"I'll do what I can." What else could I say? "I'll think on it and give you a call tomorrow."

"Here," he said, pulling a wafer-thin card case from his inside breast pocket. He flicked it open and handed me a card. "I'll speak to you tomorrow."

"Right," I said, as he slid into the car. I watched the limousine until its rear lights disappeared into the night before going back inside. What on earth was going on? I was suddenly involved with two men who both wanted something from me I wasn't sure I was able to give, and it had started to weigh mightily on my shoulders.

When I got back inside Jamie was in the kitchen getting a glass of water and Kayla was perched in her normal spot on the kitchen counter, watching him.

"You'll go blind," I whispered to her, and was surprised by her expression when she looked my way. I had expected a cheeky grin; instead what I got was a weak smile.

"Pardon?" Jamie asked.

I ignored him; I couldn't be bothered to explain. He frowned, glanced around, then his eyes shifted to the counter as Kayla obviously decided to show herself.

"I'm sorry if I interrupted anything," he said.

"You probably turned up in the nick of time," Kayla replied. "We don't need her taking in another stray, particularly one who's demonically challenged."

"Kayla," I said, warning her to shut up.

"If you've got a problem with me being here, why don't you just come out and say so?" Jamie said.

"Thought I just did," she said, giving him a bitchy little smile.

"Okay, I'll go and get my things," he said, slamming the glass down on the worktop and making for the door.

"Stop," I said, putting my hand out in front of him. He was too angry to see and it was only when his chest slammed against my palm that he faltered and stopped.

"I . . . um—" My hand dropped to my side and I hoped the flush to my cheeks wasn't as noticeable as it felt. Fortunately, he wasn't looking at me; his brow was creased and his hands were in tight fists.

"Jamie, I invited you to stay because I wanted you to."

"Are you sure?" he asked, his eyes meeting mine.

"I wouldn't have said so if I wasn't," I said, though actually I had done just that. I was still having trouble working out what had been going on in my head.

"What about him?" he asked, jerking his head toward the front door.

"Yes, what about him?" Kayla asked.

I looked back over my shoulder as if Philip's presence lingered in the room. "I'm not sure about Philip. As I told him, I'll have to think about his problem." I sat down on a kitchen chair.

Jamie leaned back against the fridge. His brow furrowed and he glanced at Kayla and then me. "What did Kayla mean by 'demonically challenged'?"

I closed my eyes and massaged my temples. This I didn't need. "My friend sometimes has a very big mouth."

When my eyes opened Kayla was doing one of her girly pout things, which I'm sure she thinks makes her appear adorable.

"Not nice," she said.

"Nor are you sometimes." I was hoping we had deflected an awkward question, but no.

"Demonically challenged?" Jamie asked again.

"She was trying to be funny," I said, hoping he'd buy it.

"Ha-fucking-ha," Kayla said.

I shot her a glare, which she returned twofold. "If he's staying here you should tell him," she said.

Jamie looked from me to her and then back again. "Tell me what?"

Kayla hopped down from the table. "It's up to you, but should Henri come calling, he might want to leave you a little message of his intentions. I would if I were him and I'm sure you wouldn't want your new lodger getting caught in the crossfire." And with that, she gave me another bitchy smile and vanished, leaving me utterly bewildered.

"What's she talking about?" Jamie asked, dropping down onto the chair opposite me.

"Sometimes she talks in riddles, but I think the gist of it is she believes you could be in danger if you stay here."

He leaned back in the chair and I couldn't stop myself from noticing that his chest and shoulders were a golden tan. He said he'd done some laboring jobs to earn some money, so I guessed he must have spent most of the summer with his shirt off. But if I was going to start thinking straight, I was going to have to tell him to put his shirt on.

I gave myself a mental shake. I had a monumental demon problem and I was letting myself get distracted by the bare chest of a man I hardly knew.

"Lucky?"

"When you arrived yesterday"—*was it really only a day ago?*—"I'd just got back from the school I'd been expelled from as a child. They had a problem they hoped I'd make go away."

"A ghost?"

"Twin ghosts, actually. Unfortunately, it turned out the girls were the least of the school's worries." I explained about the boarders playing with the Ouija board the previous weekend. "But the twins were already there—hell, they were there when I was at the school fifteen years ago, so you wouldn't need a Ouija board to get them to appear. And this is what I meant by it being dangerous to call upon the dead: the boarders called up a demon instead, and apparently once called they can be the devil of a job to get rid of."

"They called up a demon?" Jamie was surprisingly unperturbed. "As in horns and a tail?"

I grimaced. "I wish. This one looks like an eighteenth-century gentleman and has a mouth full of very sharp teeth, which, I get the impression, he would be more than happy to use to take a chunk out of someone."

"He threatened you?" Jamie said, echoing Kayla is such a way that it made me frown. Now I was getting paranoid. "Lucky?"

"Sorry, I was just . . . I'm tired. Yes, he threatened me and then I saw him again tonight on the way home from the restaurant."

"Did anyone else see him?"

"Our driver. The poor man thought he'd run someone over."

"Did your friend see him?"

"Kayla?"

"No, that guy—Philip."

"No—at least he said he didn't." Did he say that? I tried to think. "No, I'm pretty sure he didn't."

"So what does this demon want?"

"I have no idea," I lied.

I didn't want to mention Kayla's involvement until she and I had talked, and although I was tired and cranky, that was going to have to be tonight. If she really thought Jamie could be in danger, I needed to know.

"I'm going to bed," I said. "I'll see you in the morning."

He wasn't really listening, more gazing into space, a slight frown wrinkling his forehead. I obviously wasn't the only one with a lot of thinking to do.

Kayla was in my bedroom, sitting in her usual spot by the window. She was staring out into the darkness and didn't acknowledge me when I entered the room. I turned on my bedside lamp and started to undress.

"So," I said, "what is it with you and this Henri? And I won't take 'I don't want to talk about it' for an answer."

Kayla slowly turned around in the seat until she was facing me.

"He said they want you back—what did he mean by that?" I asked.

I pulled my nightdress on over my head and then sat down at my dressing table and started to brush my hair. I glanced back over my shoulder and did a double-take. My friend's face was a mask of abject misery, mixed with another emotion that gave me goosebumps. "Kayla?" A cold chill at the nape of my neck made me shiver.

My friend was afraid, for the second time in as many days. She hadn't wanted me to go back to the school and had refused point-blank to go in there with me. She had blamed the two girls. It's true, the last time we met they'd scared the hell out of me, but then I'd only been ten. I didn't remember her being afraid back then, in fact, I'm pretty sure she'd found it quite funny.

Then it clicked—she had known there was a demon waiting in there for me.

I got up off my chair and crouched down in front of her. "What's going on Kayla? What's this all about?"

"If I tell you, you may not want me hanging around anymore," she said, in a little-girl whisper.

"Kayla, we have been together since I was . . . I don't know, as long as I can remember. You're my friend—you're an important part of my life and you're part of me."

"You promise you won't hate me?" she said, her dark eyes glistening.

"Kayla, you're my best friend—you always have been and you always will be. There's nothing you can say or do that'll change that. If, for some reason, we've got to take on old Henri Toothy Pegs then so be it, but you are my friend."

She didn't seem so sure. My legs were cramping, so I got up from my crouch and sat down on the bed opposite her. I had been a bit pissed off before, but now I was more than a little concerned. This wasn't my ballsy, capable Kayla, who could make the meanest of spirits run for cover with a few well-chosen words. This was something unfamiliar.

She sighed. "The demon you met today"—she raised fearful eyes to mine—"he and I aren't so different. You've always assumed I was a spirit, but it isn't really true. We appeared to grow up together, but that's not true either."

"Kayla? I don't understand."

"Lucky, I'm more than three thousand years old and I'm a . . . I'm a demon."

I was about to laugh: she could have been introducing herself at an AA meeting. But the merriment drained out of me when I saw how serious her expression had become. As I stared at her she solidified in front of me. I could always see her when others couldn't, but sometimes she looked more solid than others. Now there was no transparency to her at all and she looked as human as . . . me.

"You can't be! You're good and kind—you're my friend—how can you say you're a demon? I could feel the evil oozing out of Henri—you're not like him." I was jabbering and I knew it.

"When you were born," she said, her voice soft and gentle, "you were like a beacon. Even from the moment you first took a breath there was a glow inside you that bloomed up into the skies and down into the Underlands."

My friend leaned forward, her hands clasped together between her knees. "You drew us to you like moths to a flame, and there were some of us who knew that without help, without someone to guide and protect you, you would probably be swamped by every lost soul out there.

"There was a lot of argument. The days were long gone when our kind used to interfere in the human world, but some said those times were returning, that your coming was proof our two worlds were about to collide. While all this arguing was going on, you were already beginning to feel the effects of your power: spirits surrounded you. You were a baby so you didn't understand, but your mother and father were terrified."

"She left us," I said, and it still made me ache inside. "She left us both."

"I know. And it was then I decided I had to be with you. To protect you from the spirit world and those from mine, who might not have your best interests at heart."

"But surely demons can't move between worlds just like that?" I said with a shudder, thinking of the terrible Henri.

"No, of course not. There are some demons who can travel to and fro between our worlds at will, but they are very few. Usually a demon has to be summoned to this world, and then, having crossed over once, they can continue to travel between the two unless the door is closed—and before you ask; no, the closing ritual you performed with the Ouija board was not strong enough—that's usually just for spirits."

"So Henri can come back and forth now whenever he likes?"

"For the moment," she said.

"So, how did you cross over?"

She laughed. "I just had to be patient and wait for some silly girls to play with a Ouija board, or some idiotic psychic to call upon the spirit world. It didn't take long. A group of people playing at being Satanists attempted to make a demon manifest. They got me."

"And you've been with me ever since."

"I came to watch over you."

"So, what happened to the Satanists?"

A strange expression crossed her face. "Not sure, though I doubt they ever held another ceremony."

I knew my friend well enough to know when she was being evasive. But then, did I really know her at all? "Kayla, I don't understand. Why has Henri come looking for you after all this time? Why did you come to me in the first place? Why didn't you ever tell me any of this before?" I had a hundred and one questions buzzing around in my head, but these were the only ones I could immediately put into words.

She had a distant look in her eyes and it suddenly hit me that I might be losing her. "Henri, as he calls himself, hasn't come here just for me. He's told you this because he wants you to distrust me."

"Why?"

She smiled. "I would guess he's trying to 'divide and conquer.' It's what I'd do in his position."

"What possible reason would he have for doing that?"

"Because, my dear girl, he doesn't just want to take me back to the Underlands. He wants to take you too."

I was dumbstruck. I jumped up and strode across the room to my dressing table, then stopped, turned and walked back. Kayla sat watching, not saying a word. Why would she? She'd said quite enough.

"Why on earth would he want to take me back to—back to wherever it is he comes from? What possible reason would he have to do that?"

Kayla looked up at me, her face twisted into a cynical smile. "New blood," she said.

"I don't understand."

"We are immortal, though we can be destroyed, and unfortunately, like any being, the older we get the more difficult it is for us to procreate. To make things worse, there are not many female demons left, so we have had to start slipping into the world of humans to find mates."

I sank down onto my bed. I didn't think my legs would hold me upright for a moment more. "You're saying Henri wants me for *sex*?"

She laughed, a hollow sound that echoed with bitter tears. "If only that were the case. No, Henri's just a minion. You're meant for greater things."

I wrapped my arms around myself. I'd been a little frightened before, but now I was completely terrified.

"Surely he can't just take me?" I said.

"Just as I once did he found the chink in your world's armor: three silly girls playing with something they shouldn't. Now he can move around in this world as he chooses."

"Is there nothing that can stop him?"

"Not much, unless . . ." She paused, her forefinger drifted up to her lips and she began to tap them in an irregular tattoo.

"Unless?"

Her forehead creased in concentration and her eyes focused on some point in the middle of my chest. Suddenly she grinned. "Unless we take the battle to him!"

She might have been happy with that scenario, but my bowels gave an uncomfortable lurch and for a moment I thought I might be about to throw up my very expensive dinner.

"That's an option, is it?" I asked, in a voice a couple of octaves higher than usual.

"Hmm, could be. I'll give it some thought."

"You do that," I said, as I got back on my feet and started to pace the floor.

I was so tired my eyes hurt, but I knew there was no way I was going to get a wink of sleep. I pulled on my bathrobe and made for the door.

"Where are you going?"

"To have a cup of tea."

"It'll keep you awake."

"Like I want to sleep when the bogeyman is very likely to come get me at any moment? I doubt I'll ever fucking sleep again."

Kayla frowned. "I told you I'd protect you, and I will. From now on I'll never leave your side, not unless I am certain it's safe."

"You let me go into that school when you knew he'd be there," I said, and I couldn't help the bitter edge that had crept into my voice.

Her frown deepened and she looked away. "I'd hoped I'd be wrong."

I stared at my friend. She was lying. She said Henri would try the "divide and conquer" approach, but she was doing a pretty good job of that all by herself.

I walked down the stairs and into the kitchen, but if I thought I was going to have time alone to think I was wrong. Jamie was sitting at the kitchen table more or less where I had left him, except he was cradling a glass of milk.

He gave me a wry smile. "Want to talk about it?"

"What?" I said, immediately feeling flustered.

"This is a small cottage with very thin walls."

I turned away from him, my excuse being to put the kettle on, but in reality I was trying to remember what had been said that was heated enough he could have heard it downstairs; if, of course, he really had been in the kitchen all through my conversation with Kayla; he could well have been listening outside the door for all I knew.

"It wasn't about you staying here if that's what you're worried about."

"You made your thoughts on that very clear. Were you arguing about this Henri character?"

I reached up and took a cup and saucer from the cupboard and rattled around in the drawer looking for a teaspoon. I didn't really want to talk about this with Jamie—but then, why not? I thought he'd have gone running for the hills at the mention of a demon, particularly as he was coping so badly with everyday spirits, but no, he was taking it all in his stride.

"What do you know about demons?" I asked.

He gave a derisive snort. "How much do you think? What about you?"

"Apparently not as much as I should," I said, dropping a teabag into a cup. "To be truthful, I didn't really believe they existed. I've read accounts of demonic possession and exorcisms, but in most cases they were either at a time when people didn't know any better or in poor, very religious countries. Nine times out of ten I would have said the so-called possessed had a psychiatric disorder."

I poured boiling water into my cup, added a splash of milk, took out the teabag and slumped down on the chair opposite him.

"What does this one want?" Jamie asked.

"Who says he wants anything?"

Jamie gave me another smile. "If you don't want to talk about it just say so, but if you've seen him twice in as many days it's pretty obvious to me that he's after something."

I took a sip of tea while Jamie waited, watching me. "Kayla seems to think he wants to take her, and me too, for that matter, back to wherever it is he comes from," I said, with a small laugh, trying to make a joke of it.

Jamie obviously didn't see the funny side. The smile slipped from his face and his forehead crinkled into a concerned frown.

"You're not serious?"

I took another sip of my tea. "Kayla seemed to be."

"Aren't you worried?"

I started to shake my head but then stopped. What was the point in pretending? "Of course I am. Who wouldn't be?"

"Did she say why he wants you both?"

I made a small *huh* sound. "Something to do with a declining demon population."

He looked a little baffled for a few moments and then the proverbial lightbulb turned on, and with a blinding flash. "He wants you for—? He wants to—"

I decided to put him out of his misery. "Apparently they need baby demons and there aren't many lady demons to fulfill the demand."

"Really?" For a split-second a puzzled expression flickered across his face.

"That's what Kayla said."

"I don't believe it."

I had been thinking more or less the same thing ever since Kayla had given me the bad news—or at least her version of it. In fact, the longer I thought about it, the more certain I was that there was a great deal she was still keeping from me.

"Why Kayla?" he asked. "I mean, she's a ghost, so what good would she be? You, well, I can sort of understand, but not her."

I didn't want to tell him what she really was, not at this point—I hardly knew him, and I was having a pretty hard time taking it all in myself. My whole relationship with my best friend had been based on lies, and those lies were still continuing.

"Maybe where he comes from spirits become flesh, I don't know," I said.

From his expression I could see he wasn't convinced, but he didn't voice any opinion, for which I was grateful. I didn't want to lie to him more than I had to.

"This Philip guy," Jamie said, "what's he got to do with all this?"

I looked up into piercing blue eyes. "Nothing—well, nothing to do with Henri at least." Jamie didn't need to know about Philip's little problem.

"Yeah, right! You've never seen a demon before—weren't actually convinced they existed—then suddenly you see a demon and on the very same day you meet a man who is 'demonically challenged,' then this guy takes you out to dinner and hey, guess what, your old friend the demon shows up again. *Please!* There must be a connection."

Maybe I wasn't as paranoid as I thought.

"Maybe it has nothing to do with Kayla and more to do with Philip," he added, a pensive expression on his face.

"I wish."

He looked even more concerned. "You're sure?"

I took a deep breath. *In for a penny . . .* "Henri asked me to give Kayla a message. He said they want her back."

"Back?"

I looked away, not wanting him to see how miserable I was. She was my friend and despite everything I still loved her and I was beginning to be afraid I was going to lose her.

I obviously wasn't fooling Jamie one bit. He got up and walked around the table and crouched down beside me. "It'll be okay," he said, resting his hand on my arm and giving it a squeeze.

"I wish I could be so sure."

I tossed and turned for hours, and then overslept until almost nine. Kayla was nowhere to be found and I suspected that once it had got light she'd probably become bored. Then I wondered—did demons sleep? Why wouldn't they? And if they did—if she did—why had I never seen her sleeping? Where had she gone to sleep? Yet more things my *best* friend had been keeping from me. Well, wherever she was now, I just hoped that she wasn't tormenting Jamie.

I took a shower, but I was too wound up for it to be relaxing, and then stomped downstairs. The aroma of toast and freshly made coffee wafted out of the kitchen: Jamie had obviously made himself at home. He glanced over his shoulder and gave me a smile as I walked in. Fortunately he was wearing a shirt, although when he turned around it was hanging loose, giving me another glimpse of tanned, muscular chest.

"Coffee?" he asked.

I gave him a distracted nod as I looked around the kitchen. "Seen Kayla?"

"No, but then she only appears when she wants to. She could have been sitting in here the whole time and I wouldn't know. Does she do that to you?"

"I would have said no, but now I'm not so sure," I said.

He gave me a sympathetic smile, which only made me feel worse. And I really was getting worried. Where on earth was she?

"So what have you got planned for today?" Jamie asked.

"Nothing special. I've got some dry-cleaning to collect and some correspondence to catch up on, but apart from that not a lot."

"I'll go and get your dry-cleaning, if you like."

"Thanks," I said.

"Did you get any sleep?"

"Not much. You?" I said, accepting the mug and the plate of toast he was holding out.

"Yeah, like the dead."

I gave him a look; that wasn't an expression I ever used. His face crinkled into a grin. "Stupid thing to say."

"A bit," I said with a smile.

"Do you ever get used to it? You know, seeing ghosts?"

"I think I'd have trouble getting used to not seeing them now. They've been part of my life for so long."

He sat down at the table across from me and started spreading marmalade on his toast.

"What you've got to remember is that they can't hurt you," I said. "They can try and scare you, they can play with your head, but physically hurt you? No way."

"How about throwing plates at you and stuff like that?"

"Very few can. Some can slide things across a floor or table, but lifting something up and throwing it takes a lot of power and most spirits haven't got it."

"But demons are different?"

I shuddered. The memory of Henri's tight grip, the flicker of his reptilian tongue as it ran down my cheek and the touch of his hand caressing my hair was still fresh in my mind. "Oh yes," I said. "Or, at least, Henri was."

"How about Kayla?" he asked.

The question made me think. "Yes," I said, wondering why I hadn't ever questioned her abilities before. "She can move things, and I have known her to throw things."

"So she's quite a powerful spirit?"

"Hmm," I mumbled into my coffee.

Now I knew what Kayla really was—or at least what she *said* she was—I was beginning to realize there were a lot of things I had accepted about her that didn't fit with the other spirits I'd come across. In my mind I suppose Kayla had always just been Kayla, and I had accepted her at face value. Why wouldn't I? When I was a child I hadn't known any different, and as we grew up I simply hadn't put her in the same category as other spirits.

"I wonder where she is," he said.

"I don't know."

"You're worried about her?"

"A bit." I gave him a half-hearted smile. "Well, a lot, actually."

"Was she upstairs when you went to bed last night?"

"Yes, she was sitting by the window. It's her normal spot."

"Does she go to bed? Or sleep?" he said, asking the same question I had been thinking on earlier. I tried to answer him based on what she always had done—hopefully not giving away too much of my distress at her lies.

"Sometimes she lies down next to me, but usually she just sits looking out of the window," I said.

"Must be boring for her when you're asleep."

"Oh, she reads sometimes," I said. "When I was a kid she would do my homework for me."

"You're kidding?"

I smiled at the memory. "I was always useless at history, so for tests and exams she used to read up on whatever period we were studying and tell me the answers to the questions." Then I remembered she'd said she was more than three thousand years old. Maybe she hadn't had to read up on the history.

Jamie went off to collect my things from the dry cleaners and pick up a newspaper. Kayla still hadn't made an appearance and the dull ache that had started in my chest had progressed to anxiety and full-blown panic was beginning to set in. I had thought I might be losing her, and now I was beginning to believe I really had. She had promised she wouldn't leave my side unless she knew I was safe—so where was she?

I tried to take my mind off her by catching up on my correspondence, but it was nigh on impossible to concentrate. I went downstairs and put the kettle on, then switched it off again—better wait for Jamie. I wandered into the living room, but she wasn't there, then I marched back upstairs and rechecked my bedroom, then Jamie's. I went back into the office, sat down, stared at the blank screen of my laptop, then stood up and went back to my bedroom.

I could smell him as soon as I walked through the door. This time I knew it wasn't my imagination: Henri had left a calling card, a frothy, white lace hanky lay on my pillow, redolent with the scent of Parma violets. I stared at it from across the room. My heart tried to pound its way out of my chest, then I started to get really angry. Henri was trying to scare the crap out of me, and he was succeeding quite nicely actually, but invading my home—that was *intolerable*.

Then a noise downstairs made me jump. Could it be Henri? I glanced at my bedside clock: not quite midday, so too early for Jamie to be back. Maybe Kayla had finally returned. I took a deep breath and crept down the stairs. I tried the kitchen first, but it was as I had left it. I didn't want to run into Henri empty-handed, so I grabbed the frying pan off the stove, crept across to the living room, threw open the door—

—and froze. I had visitors, and suddenly Henri was the least of my worries.

Six

Two men were perched on the edge of my couch, their hats resting on their knees gripped with both hands. Upon seeing me in the doorway they stood.

Of course, when I say "men," what I mean is, they were *male*—that much was obvious—but while Henri le Dent looked every inch the English gentlemen—except for those vicious teeth, of course—these two were from a place far closer to Hell than I would ever want to be.

I would have turned to run but my legs had stopped working and I had to grab hold of the doorframe to steady myself.

"Mistress, we mean you no harm," the smaller of the two creatures said quickly.

He was only about four feet tall with a head as bald as a baby's and at least two sizes too large for his body. His face was pink and plump and his cheeks and chin had a softness to them that made me think of marshmallows. Impossibly large dark blue eyes bordered with long black lashes filled his face, while his lips were tiny: a deep red cupid's bow. His midtan knickerbockers—*knickerbockers!*—came straight out of a Victorian costume drama; he wore them with a tightly fitting short jacket, long brown socks and leather shoes.

If it had just been him standing there in my living room, hat in hand, I might have believed him as he wasn't scary at all, just . . . well, *odd*. But his partner was another thing altogether. He was close to seven feet tall and had to stoop to stand in my low-ceilinged room. His skin was a luminous emerald color, offset by the ivory tusks sprouting from the center of his forehead and the top of his snout and the large ivory fangs protruding between thick rubber-band lips. Smoke puffed from cavernous flared nostrils. In fact, his eyes were the only things small in his face: they were mostly hidden within his wrinkled hide.

He too wore a Victorian suit, but his mighty frame strained against the material and the collar of his white shirt looked like it was choking him.

"Truly, mistress, we mean you no harm," the short one repeated.

"Who are you?" I managed to ask.

The short one smiled and I had to stop myself from flinching; Henri le Dent wasn't the only demon around here sporting a fine set of dentures.

"I am Mr. Kerfuffle," he said, with a courtly bow, "and this is Mr. Shenanigans."

The huge creature also gave a bow, which made his suit creak alarmingly.

"And to what do I owe this pleasure?" I asked, checking out my exit route; I'd be making a bolt for it the moment I thought my rubbery legs would hold me. The frying pan would be of no use at all.

"We are here to protect you," said Mr. Kerfuffle.

"From what?"

He smiled again—if that was meant to be reassuring, I had news for him. "We have been sent to watch over you until such time an agreement has been made."

"'Agreement'?"

"Negotiations have already begun to ensure your safety upon your return to our world."

"'Return'?" I knew I sounded like a moron, just repeating words, but nothing he'd said made any sense yet.

"I've never been to your world, so how can I return?" I was jabbering now, but under the circumstances I think I could be forgiven. "I think you must have me confused with someone else." Now I sounded like I was in control . . .

"No, no," said Mr. Kerfuffle. "You are Lucky de Salle are you not?"

I hesitated a moment before replying. "Yes . . . but I . . ."

He and his large friend exchanged a look. "It is definitely your person that requires our protection until negotiations are complete."

They sat down in unison.

"Who sent you?" I asked.

"The Lady Kayla," the little man said, and his horned friend nodded in agreement.

"Kayla? Where is she? Have you seen her?" I stepped fully into the room, my concern for my friend outweighing any fear I might have had for myself.

"She has returned to our world and it is she who is negotiating for your safety," Mr. Kerfuffle said.

I sank down into the armchair. Kayla had left me. Tears started welling up and I could do nothing to stop them. She had promised to stay by my side but had instead returned to wherever it was she had come from. I knew why she had gone home—she was trying to protect me—but the fact she hadn't even told me her plans somehow made it worse.

"There, there," the little man said, leaning forward and offering me a huge white handkerchief. "There's no need to upset yourself. You'll see her again shortly."

I took the proffered hanky and dabbed at my eyes. When I looked up, Mr. Shenanigans was eyeing me with a strange expression.

"What is it that leaks from her eyes?" he asked, in a low, ponderous voice. "Is it venom?"

"No, no," his friend replied, "it's a human expression of emotion. Sometimes it means they are happy, but usually it means they are sad."

"Does it hurt?" Mr. Shenanigans asked me.

I glanced at Mr. Kerfuffle and then back to Mr. Shenanigans.

The little man patted his friend's arm. "It's his first time in the Overlands," he explained. "The ways of humankind are new to him."

"No, the tears don't hurt," I replied.

"Good," he said. "I wouldn't wish you to be in pain."

"Don't let us disturb you," the little man said. "Just carry on as if we weren't here."

"I have a friend staying at the moment," I said. "Will he be able to see you?"

The two creatures exchanged a glance, both frowning. "Who is this friend?"

"His name is Jamie and I don't want you frightening him."

"Is he your friend?" Mr. Shenanigans asked.

"He's a friend."

"What my young colleague was politely trying to ask is whether your gentleman friend shares your bed?" Mr. Kerfuffle said.

"It's none of his damn business," I said.

Both men shifted forward in their seats and Mr. Kerfuffle's smile darkened into a malevolent scowl.

"He's a friend—j-just a friend," I stuttered. "In fact, we hardly know each other at all."

Both creatures relaxed back onto the couch and the little man's features slipped back into a gentle smile so swiftly that I could almost believe I had imagined his former expression. Almost, but not quite.

"It might be better if your friend were to leave."

"He can't," I said, feeling my hackles rising. "He has nowhere else to go."

The two creatures exchanged another look and then they both returned their attention to me. It was almost as if they had just had a conversation only they could hear.

"If your friend stays out of our way, we will stay out of his," Mr. Shenanigans announced.

"I don't need your protection," I said.

He chuckled, and Mr. Kerfuffle said, "You most certainly do. You wouldn't see another sunrise in this world if we should leave—in fact, whether you will last another day here, with or without our protection, is very much in the balance right now."

"Why should that be? I don't know anyone in your world."

"But it's your misfortune that they know of you."

"How? I only—"

I was interrupted by the sound of the front door opening and then slamming shut. I glanced over my shoulder at the closed door and then back at the two creatures. "You both stay here," I said, getting up.

They both nodded and, as I guessed it was the best I would get from them, I hurried from the living room and into the hall, shutting the door behind me. I leaned back against it for a moment and took several deep breaths. God alone knew what Jamie would make of two demons sitting on my sofa. Bill had practically scared the shit out of him and he was just a lowly spook, albeit a spiteful one.

I found Jamie in the kitchen. He had hung my dry-cleaning on the hook on the back of the door and had dropped the newspaper on the kitchen table. The aroma of freshly baked bread filled the small room. Freshly baked bread is a weakness of mine, but at that particular moment I was too nervous to even peek into the bag.

He looked up from unpacking groceries and smiled. "I got us some lunch while I was out—just bread, ham, cheese and olives; I hope that's okay?"

"Sounds yummy," I said, forcing the panic back down.

"Has Kayla shown up?"

"Jamie . . ." I began.

"What's up?" he asked.

"We might have a small problem."

"Such as?"

"Where to begin?" I said, almost to myself. I had no idea how I was going to explain any of this when I didn't even understand what was going on myself.

"What's the matter?"

I took a deep breath. "Jamie, there are two demons sitting in my living room who say they're here for my protection."

Jamie stared at me for a long moment and then began to laugh. "Very good," he said. "You nearly had me going then."

"I'm not joking."

He flapped a hand at me, still laughing, and moved across the kitchen to fill the kettle. "Have you been in the cooking sherry or something?"

Well, I had tried to tell him. I dropped into a chair and slumped there, resting my elbows on the kitchen table and my head in my hands. My energy levels had drained to zero and I was exhausted.

Jamie placed a mug of coffee by my elbow and slouched down in the chair across the table from me. "She'll be back. Don't worry."

I picked up the mug and wrapped by hands around it, savoring the comforting smell, but it didn't make me feel any better. "I'm not sure she will. She's gone back to wherever she came from—to negotiate for my safety, or at least that's what they told me."

"Who told you?"

"The two demons," I said.

He pushed his chair back from the table with a scrape of wood against tiles. "You, Lucky de Salle, are losing the plot," he said as he got to his feet. "There are no demons in your living room."

"Suit yourself."

He stared at me for a few seconds, then stalked out of the kitchen.

I sighed. "I wouldn't if I were"—I heard the living room door open—"you." The door closed and it all went quiet. There were no shouts of alarm, no yells, no pounding of feet as Jamie raced from the house screaming—nothing.

A minute passed, and then two. I got to my feet. They'd done something to him; they must have. I walked slowly to the kitchen door and poked my head out into the hallway. Silence. I padded across the carpet to the living room and reached out to turn the doorknob, then hesitated. What if Mr. Shenanigans had eaten him? Or Mr. Kerfuffle? He might be small, but his teeth looked every bit as vicious as those of Henri le Dent. I took the doorknob in my hand, breathed in deeply, and turned it.

I let the door swing open and stood waiting in the hallway, too scared to take that first step into the room and look. But I couldn't just stand there, so I forced myself to move, first one step then another. I peeped inside.

The two demons were exactly where I'd left them, but Jamie was nowhere to be seen.

"What have you done with him?"

"Done?" Mr. Kerfuffle said, frowning. "We have done nothing."

"Where's Jamie?"

The demons exchanged another of their long glances, then Mr. Kerfuffle gestured toward the window. "He went outside."

I crossed the room with a frown. What was Jamie doing out in the front garden? Had he made a run for it? Why hadn't I heard him go? I'm not sure what I expected to see through the window as I pulled back the curtain, but it certainly wasn't the scene being played out on my narrow strip of lawn. Kayla had her back to me, but somehow she had become taller, just as she had in the bar when she faced down Batty Bill. I knew I hadn't imagined it.

"Why are you still here?" she said in a deep voice, just loud enough for me to hear. "You are no longer needed. She has my protection now."

Jamie stared at her, and there was no trace of the frightened young man I had befriended; he stood his ground and met her eye to eye. "I might ask the same of you," he said.

They began to move, circling like barroom brawlers getting the measure of each other. Jamie sidestepped toward the house so he and Kayla were face-to-face across the path, and for the first time I saw my best friend as what she no doubt really was.

I gasped and Kyla turned toward me, myriad emotions crossing her face: anger, fear, sorrow, then a strange expression I would almost have called relief.

I stared at her and she returned my stare. She was still Kayla, but a terrifying version of her. From five foot five she had grown to over six feet tall. Her dark blond hair was now a mass of blood-red and venom-green curls interspersed with long writhing serpents. Her normal sapphire-blue eyes had become bottomless pits of black, and her rosy skin was now an opalescent white, shimmering with green and blue tones. She was undeniably beautiful, but it was a terrible beauty.

"Seen enough?" she asked through the glass.

I nodded, quite incapable of coherent speech—and besides, I had no idea what to say. I hadn't really believed her when she told me she was a demon, not in my heart.

Now I knew she hadn't lied.

She stared at me for a moment more and then shimmered and shrank back to the Kayla I knew and loved. She cast an angry look at Jamie, then stalked through the front door and into the house.

As she entered the living room, Mr. Kerfuffle and Mr. Shenanigans jumped to their feet and dropped down to one knee, their heads bowed. For a crazy moment I had the overwhelming urge to copy them, but instead I clung to the back of a chair to stop my legs from giving way beneath me.

Kayla stopped in the middle of the room, her eyes searching mine. I don't know what she saw, but her lips curled into a sad smile. She walked over to me and reached out a hand to touch my face, and I couldn't help but flinch away from her.

Her lips compressed into a thin line. "Lucky, I would never hurt you."

"You already have," I whispered.

"You don't have time for this," Jamie said from behind her.

She twisted her head to glare at him again, but when he just shrugged she returned her attention to me. "Lucky, listen to me: these two . . . gentlemen"—she pointed at the two kneeling demons—"are here for your protection. Do as they say and you won't get hurt." I must have looked uncertain, because she added, "I mean it!"

"Kayla, what's going on? They told me you were negotiating for my safe return to your world."

Her forehead creased into a frown and she shot a look that would wither roses at the two demons. They must have sensed her displeasure as they both raised their eyes and Mr. Kerfuffle clasped his hat to his chest and gave her a tentative, lopsided smile.

"My lady, I had to tell her something—she was afraid and about to run."

She tapped her bottom lip with her forefinger. "All right," and both demons visibly relaxed, "but it was a bad choice of words." She said to me, "I don't have time to give the reasons for my actions now, but as soon as I know you're no longer at risk I'll return and explain all. Will you trust me?"

"Yes," I whispered. What choice did I have?

She stared at my face for a long moment. "Trust no one that you have met in the last few days, particularly not Philip Conrad."

"What has he got to do with anything?"

"I'm not sure he has," she said, "but I'd rather you were safe than sorry."

I looked at Jamie, who was now leaning against the doorframe. Something about him had changed. He'd completely lost that "young, frightened and vulnerable" vibe.

"Are you including Jamie in that instruction?" I asked.

She narrowed her eyes and set her lips in a grim line. "The jury's out on him," she said. "I don't think he means you harm, but"—she glanced back over her shoulder at him—"if he should hurt one hair on your head . . ."

Jamie stared her down as if to say *you and whose army?*

"No, he won't hurt you," she admitted. Then she leaned in close until her lips were almost brushing my ear and whispered, "But don't let him trick his way into your bed."

"Kayla!" I said, embarrassed, though I knew he couldn't have heard. "I would have thought you knew me better than that."

Her face lit up in a grin and for a moment she was my old friend again. "Only joking."

I glanced at the two kneeling demons. "They gave me the impression they wouldn't be very happy if he was more than a friend," I whispered back.

"They're here to keep you safe and that includes protecting you from men like him and Philip," she said. "Just be patient and I'll be back really soon." She looked at the two demons again. "You make sure that nothing happens to her while I'm gone, you understand?"

"Yes, Lady," they chorused, both bobbing their heads.

Jamie straightened up as she focused her attention on him. "If you're not going to leave, at least take care of her," she said.

"Why wouldn't I? That's why I'm here."

She looked from him to me, and back again. "Just make sure you do."

She walked back to me, and pulling me into a tight embrace, she whispered, "Be very careful. Remember, I love you so very much."

And then she was gone, just like that.

I looked around the room. One moment she had been holding me and murmuring into my hair, then, without even a *poof*, she had vanished. If Jamie was impressed he didn't show it. He was leaning back against the doorframe, watching the two demons get up off their knees. I could have sworn I saw an amused twinkle in his eye.

"You two stay here," I said to them, and then walked to the door, took Jamie by the arm and pulled him outside with me. I shut the door behind us.

"What was going on between you and Kayla?" I asked, once we were in the kitchen.

"She was telling me to leave."

I frowned, trying to remember what I had heard. It had sounded a bit like she was, but not quite. "It was more than that—and anyway, when did you get so brave? A few spooks have you quivering like a jelly, yet being in the company of demons leaves you completely unmoved? Come on, Jamie, what's going on? Who are you? You're certainly not some traumatized veterinary student."

"It has to be said I haven't been completely honest with you."

"Well then, it's time to 'fess up. What the hell is going on—and what have you got to do with all this?"

He started to unbutton his shirt. "Prepared to be amazed," he said.

I was completely confused. "What are you doing?"

He shrugged off his shirt and turned away from me, then glanced back at me over his shoulder. I stared at him for a moment, not understanding, and then suddenly, in a flurry of feathers, it all became abundantly clear.

"Oh shit," I said, as the room lurched and I grabbed for a chair.

Seven

Jamie tried to explain, but I wasn't having any of it. He had lied to me, Kayla had lied to me and Mr. Kerfuffle and Mr. Shenanigans were probably lying to me too.

Jamie offered to make lunch and I almost told him what he could do with it, but even though I was furious, swearing at an angel seemed plain wrong. Instead I told him I was going for a nap. I had intended to think about what was going on, but in no time at all I had dozed off.

I woke up feeling the better for my nap—until I opened my eyes and Mr. Shenanigans's face filled the whole of my vision.

"Christ," I mumbled, pushing myself up the bed until I was huddled against the headboard and as far away from the huge demon as I could get.

"Hush, hush, Mistress Lucky, I will not harm you."

"Just scare the shit out of me, why don't you?" I grumbled.

He backed away and sank down onto Kayla's chair by the window. *Kayla*. This was all getting too weird. I was beginning to think I might be going mad: my best friend really was a demon, just as she'd said, but I had thought there were no such things as demons, but when I looked across the room there was still a very large one sitting opposite me.

It was dark outside and the only light in the room was the yellow glow from my bedside lamp. My stomach gave a little growl. It was dark, but last time I checked the time it hadn't been quite midday. The alarm clock on my bedside table said it was almost seven o'clock. My stomach growled again: I needed to eat, and I realized I also needed to pee. I swung my legs out from beneath the blanket and sat on the edge of the bed, then clambered to my feet.

"Mistress, can I help?"

I shuffled into my slippers. "No, I'm going to the bathroom."

I hurried out of my bedroom and across the landing and felt mightily relieved as I closed the bathroom door and slid the bolt home. I had half expected my demon minder to try and come with me.

I studiously avoided looking in the mirror as I washed my hands and face. I was scared at what I might see. Would I have changed, like my friend? Would it be like looking into the face of a stranger? Then I forced myself look, but it was just me.

I wandered downstairs, the aroma of roasting chicken wafting up to greet me. Jamie was at the sink with his back to me—thankfully, he was wearing his shirt, but it didn't erase the memory of what I had seen. In fact, I wondered how he could wear a shirt at all. It fitted flat across his shoulders: no bumps, no lumps, nothing, but he had shown me his huge, glossy white feathered wings that Pegasus and the Archangel Gabriel would both have been proud of.

He must have felt me watching him as he glanced over his shoulder and smiled. "Sit down," he said, pulling out a chair. "Dinner's almost ready."

He poured a glass of wine and handed it to me, then busied himself with the vegetables. How could he go on acting as though nothing had happened? There he was peeling spuds while I felt like I was in some sort of alternative universe.

I took a tiny sip of the wine; I hadn't eaten all day and I didn't want the wine going straight to my head. Under the circumstances I wanted to have my wits about me. Although I *had* been asleep for several hours and nothing alarming had happened—if any of them had wanted to do anything, they would have done it while I was out for the count, surely?

The kitchen door swung open and Mr. Kerfuffle appeared in the doorway with Mr. Shenanigans hovering behind him.

"What do you want?" Jamie asked. His tone was far from friendly.

"We have been charged with the protection of Mistress Lucky and we intend to fulfill that obligation to the best of our ability," said Mr. Kerfuffle.

"She's safe with me."

"So you say."

"I, at least, have no allegiance to the Lord Baltheza. If he were to order Lucky's assassination, would you defy him?"

Mr. Kerfuffle shuffled his feet and looked away, but his huge friend puffed out his chest. I guessed he would have pulled himself up to his full height had the kitchen ceiling allowed. "I have sworn to protect Mistress Lucky with my life and I will defend her to my last breath, even if it means offending Lord Baltheza himself," he said in his slow, deep voice.

"Your little friend doesn't seem so sure."

Mr. Kerfuffle raised his eyes to meet Jamie's. "I have also sworn to protect the lady, and I shall."

"Even if that means being thrown into the Chambers of Rectification?" asked Jamie.

The little demon shuddered. "Yes, even if I had to suffer that."

Jamie looked at him. "Hmm, we'll see."

Chambers of Rectification? And who the hell was Lord Baltheza? I went to interrupt but Mr. Kerfuffle beat me to it. His strange, puffy cheeks flushed with anger and he stood, glaring up at Jamie. "I don't know why you're even here," he said. "What's your interest in this matter?"

"Everything that interests Lord Baltheza interests me," Jamie said, "especially anything that causes such major rifts in his household and overspills into the Overlands."

"I don't trust you."

"Nor I you."

Mr. Kerfuffle snorted. "I'll be watching you," he said.

"And I you."

Then he turned to me and bowed. "We'll leave you to eat."

"Won't you join us?" I asked. I wasn't really sure whether I wanted them to or not. The very sight of them freaked me out, but I wouldn't get any answers if I didn't get the chance to question them.

Both demons gave low chuckles. "We have already eaten." Mr. Shenanigans also gave a little bow before backing out of the door.

"Who exactly are they?" I asked once the door had closed behind them. Not sure whether I was relieved or not that they'd gone.

Jamie glanced up from gravy he was stirring. "Kerfuffle and Shenanigans?" He paused to taste the gravy, screwed up his nose and added some more pepper. "I suppose in this world you would call them fixers," he said.

"Fixers?"

"They do the things that are a little bit shady or a little bit risky when powerful people want something done, but don't want to get their own hands dirty."

"So what's in it for them?"

"It's doubtful they get paid much for their trouble, but it's sometimes safer to help members of the upper classes than not. Kayla's more generous than most, so they'll probably be looked after when they return home, as long as they don't mess up."

"What happens if they do?"

"What, mess up? They won't."

"You sound pretty sure."

"They're very capable."

"So you do know them, then."

"By reputation," he said, as he began dishing up the meal. By the time he placed the plate in front of me my stomach was growling in a most unladylike fashion. If he heard, he didn't remark upon it, although his lips were curled into a smile.

"This is lovely," I said, as I tucked into the chicken. "You needn't have gone to so much trouble." Then I wondered why on earth I was being so damn polite. Jamie had lied to me, manipulated me even. Then he looked across at me, his eyes meeting mine, and the anger that had been building up inside me drained away, leaving me slightly lightheaded.

"It was the least I could do," he said and looked like he was trying not to laugh.

I was finding it hard to concentrate, but I needed some answers and I hated this feeling of not being in control. "You eat, Kerfuffle and Shenanigans eat; why does Kayla never eat?" Then I thought, *What an inane question*. I had demons wandering around my house and I was asking about Kayla's eating habits.

Jamie laughed out loud. "Of course she eats—she just made sure you never saw her. Would you have believed she was a spirit if she was forever stuffing her face with Big Macs?"

"Okay, but why is it I'm the only one who can see her? Shouldn't she be solid, like you?"

He obviously thought this equally funny, as he laughed some more. "In your world we can be as solid as you or any other person, but we aren't *of* this world, so we're not bound by its rules."

"So it's normal for demons to visit our world?" I asked in alarm.

"No, it's not really allowed. Though there are some demons who cross over into your world just to cause mischief, even though it's against the rules. Then there are others who do mean to cause harm." A small frown creased his forehead. "They're the ones I have to worry about."

"Why?"

He thought about it for moment. "Just think of me as a sort of border control officer."

I placed my knife and fork down on my plate and looked at him across the table. "Is your name really Jamie?"

"James, actually, but I quite like Jamie."

"But the story about you and Sara, at the station, that's not true . . ."

"It's true all right; it's just not *my* story."

"So the real Jamie is . . . ?"

Jamie put down his own cutlery and gave me a gentle smile. "He didn't make it. He's with his Sara."

It was so sad—poor Jamie Banks . . . Then it occurred to me I was mourning someone I had never met and never would. I really was losing the plot.

"Might I make a suggestion?" Jamie said. "You need to toughen up. If you're granted safe passage to the Underlands you're going to see and hear things more terrifying and more wonderful than you could ever have believed—if you show fear or sadness, these emotions can be used against you, and you must believe me when I tell you that there are those who will be eagerly awaiting such emotions."

"Everyone keeps talking about me getting 'safe passage' to somewhere or other, but no one appears to have considered the possibility that I may not want to go. In fact, let me make it quite clear: I'll pass. I don't want to go to your world—this one's bad enough and yours sounds a whole lot worse."

Jamie gave me another of his smiles, though this time it was more like the look a patient father gives to his child while carefully explaining what's good for her. "I'm afraid you have little choice. If Kayla is to return, you must go with her."

"Why?" I was getting more and more frustrated with all this "you will" and "you won't" nonsense.

"You'll have to ask Kayla."

"Wonderful," I said, picking up my fork and jabbing it into a roast potato. "I'm threatened by a demon, my best friend is a demon, I'm being protected by demons and now I'm expected to go and live with demons, and all for reasons no one damn well cares to explain."

I shoved the potato into my mouth and started chewing. I could feel my face setting into a stubborn frown, the sort that gives one permanent lines, but couldn't help it. I *hated* being told what to do at the best of times, especially when it was something I didn't want to.

"Lucky," Jamie said, "if it's any consolation I will be with you every step of the way."

"Why did you lie to me? Why did you make me feel sorry for you?"

"Because I needed to get close to you so I could protect you. I knew you had a kind heart, and wouldn't turn away someone who needed your help."

"How? How have you even heard of me?"

Jamie began to laugh. "You have no idea," he said.

"No, that's the whole point! I have no idea—about you, about anything!" If I'd been fed up before, now I was seriously grumpy. "I've fallen down a rabbit hole and everyone is too damn busy being mysterious to tell me anything!"

I might be living a strange life, but as it had never been any different, I was used to being the weird kid, the strange teenager, the odd woman. But now it was getting seriously bizarre and I didn't like it. My kind of strange I could do, but this—no way.

I picked up my cutlery and carried on eating in silence. I could have hit Jamie—but then I guess I really would end up going to Hell. I could see that thumping an angel would probably be frowned upon.

By the time I had finished my dinner and a second glass of wine I was feeling slightly less panicked and slightly more logical: refusing to talk to the one person who could tell me what on earth was going on was definitely counterproductive.

"So, Jamie, do you live in the Underworld?"

"The Underlands, we call them, and yes, I do."

"Angels live in the same place as demons?" The idea sounded preposterous.

"I'm not an angel."

"You certainly look like one."

"Demons, angels—they're just names given to us by humans."

I thought about that for a moment. "So what do you call yourselves then?"

"Daemon—that's spelled a-e—but demons, angels, whatever, they're as good as any names."

"That's it?"

"Pretty much. But you shouldn't be worried about what *we* are."

I gave him a puzzled look and he stared back; his expression was still patient, but as though he was waiting for something.

"You're talking in riddles." My grumpy mood was fast returning.

"Think about it: what did Kayla tell you?"

"She said they wanted her back, and me too, because there was a dearth of lady demons and they needed to procreate."

He looked pensive for a moment. "Hmm. I think she was being a tad selective with the truth—but that aside, if it is the case, then why would they want you?"

"I don't know—maybe for the same reason they kidnapped Philip Conrad's daughter? I guess if there are no female demons, then female humans will have to do."

"Is that what Philip Conrad told you? Demons kidnapped his daughter?"

"Murdered his wife and stole his daughter," I corrected him.

"Interesting," Jamie said, though I could see he was taken aback. Then his eyes refocused on me. "Putting all that to one side for a moment, I will reask the question: why do you think they would want *you* in the Underlands?"

"By all accounts, not everyone down there does, if Kayla, you and Tweedledum and Tweedledee all think I need protecting. Henri le Dent certainly seemed much more interested in gnawing on my neck than taking me anywhere."

Jamie grunted. "He's like them"—he gestured toward the living room—"a minion doing his master's bidding."

"Is this Lord Baltheza Henri's master?"

"Yes and no."

I massaged the bridge of my nose between thumb and forefinger. This was worse than pulling teeth.

Jamie finally took pity on my frustration and he added, "Lord Baltheza rules the Underlands, but there are other lords beneath him, all juggling for power, all plotting and planning."

"So, not that different from our world's governments."

"No," Jamie said, "not that different at all."

"So, who *is* Henri's master, why does he want Kayla home, and, more importantly, why does he mean me harm?"

"Henri's master is Lord Daltas and his intention is to use Kayla's fear for you to manipulate her into doing what he wants."

"And what he wants is for her to return to your world?"

Jamie nodded.

"But why?"

"He wants her as his consort."

I raised my eyebrows. "'Consort'? As in wife?"

"If she gives him an heir, most certainly, but politically I think he will probably take her as his wife anyway."

"Politically?" This was really blowing my mind. "Why 'politically'? For goodness sake, Jamie, just tell me why he wants Kayla—and possibly me—to return to your world."

"Your friend is of royal blood, so if Lord Daltas takes her as his wife, he will be several steps closer to the throne."

"Okay—and he thinks if he threatens me Kayla will do what he wants?"

Jamie grinned. "Exactly. But he's underestimated her. She has begged her father to intervene."

"And has he?"

"You have two demons guarding you, do you not?"

"For the moment."

"Her father wants her to return to him and I think he will grant her anything. He's also more than a little interested in meeting you. All the negotiation is for show, although one can never really tell with Lord Baltheza. In this particular instance, however, I think I can safely say he will do anything to get his daughter to return to the Underlands."

"Kayla is his daughter?"

Jamie nodded, but his smile had slipped a little. "Your friend will probably become one of the most powerful women in our world, should she return permanently."

"If she agrees to return, why should I go with her?"

"It may well be part of the deal to keep you safe, though I'd fear just as much for your safety in our world as in your own."

"But I'm a human—I can't live in your world."

He started to say, "Lucky, you are just as—" but the phone rang, interrupting him, and he slumped back in his chair with a resigned sigh.

I hesitated—I'd finally got Jamie talking and I really wanted to know what he'd been about to tell me—but the ringing of the phone was insistent.

"One moment," I said, raising my forefinger to halt him, then crossing the room to pick up the phone. "Hello?"

"Lucky," a familiar voice said, "it's Philip. You said you would call me today."

I screwed my eyes shut. *Damn.* "Sorry, things got a little manic here today."

"Can I come over?"

"It's probably best you don't," I said, thinking fast. "I'm not feeling too well."

"I'm sorry to hear that."

"Can we leave it until tomorrow?"

"I'd like to meet with you."

I raised my eyes to the heavens. Philip was a complication I could well do without right now. I could understand his persistence—but was he telling the truth? Jamie had certainly been puzzled by his story.

"Okay, where and when?" I said at last.

"How about lunch at my golf club?"

"Okay," I said. I really hoped he wasn't trying to impress me, because he'd be wasting a lot of time and energy, not to mention money. "Which golf club?"

"I'll send a car to collect you."

"No need, I have a driver."

"You do?" He sounded taken aback, which pleased me.

"Jamie will bring me, and before you say a word, I'll be paying for our lunch, and it'll include Jamie."

"I need to speak to you in private—"

"The restaurant of a golf club is hardly private," I replied, "and anyhow, that's the deal. Jamie has taken on the role of my assistant and bodyguard for the foreseeable future."

"Bodyguard? Why would you need a bodyguard?"

"I don't know, Philip, but it seems like ever since the afternoon we met there's been a demon waiting in the wings, so I think I have a right to be cautious."

He was silent for so long I might have thought we'd lost the connection, except I could still hear the gentle hum of traffic in the background.

"All right," he said, though he didn't sound happy. "The Longley, tomorrow at twelve-thirty."

"I'll see you then."

He grunted and was gone. It was interesting that he hadn't tried to tell me he wasn't responsible for demons stalking me—he hadn't even argued or acted insulted, which would have been a more normal response.

"You don't trust him?" Jamie asked.

"No. Kayla said she didn't, and I get the impression you don't either, though you've not said as much. And I'm not sure I trust anyone at the moment, to be honest. No one seems to be who they say they are, and you're a case in point."

He had the good grace to dip his head in acknowledgment, but he still wasn't in the least embarrassed. He was so different from the original Jamie who had arrived on my doorstep he could be another person entirely. But I guess he was.

He even *looked* different. Before, he'd been a scared and vulnerable boy, but the man sitting across the table was none of these things. He was calm, confident, maybe even a little arrogant.

A thought occurred to me. "Jamie, apart from the wings, is this how you really look? Or are you like Kayla?"

"This is it," he said. "The wings are my only surprise."

"They were enough."

"There are others of us who are winged, but they're from Lord Baltheza's Court and more like Kayla or our friends in the other room."

"So whose court are you from? Not this Daltas character?"

"Oh no, Daltas and I don't get along. No, my kind serve no one. We're neutrals; we maintain the balance between the kingdoms."

"So there are other angels?"

"We call ourselves Guardians."

"This is all very confusing," I said and it was true that my head was beginning to ache and I was already regretting the second glass of wine.

"Once you reach the Underlands you'll soon get used to it."

"Jamie, I don't *want* to reach the Underlands. I want to stay right here in my world."

He gave me a sympathetic smile. "I know you do, but I don't think that will be possible now."

"Why?"

"Kayla has to return to the Underlands. If you choose to stay here you might never see her again—have you thought of that?"

I had thought of it, and I had promptly pushed the thought from my mind, but Jamie saying it out loud made my chest ache. It was like I was being held down by lead weights, and I was finding it hard to breathe, let alone speak. I couldn't bear to think of what life might be like without Kayla by my side. She had always been there—she was the sister I'd never had. She was my best friend, my confidante: she was the one who always told me the truth, whether I would like what she was saying or not. Mind you, she'd not been doing a lot of that lately.

My anguish wasn't lost on Jamie, but I suspected that had been his purpose. "You were sent to convince me to go with Kayla when the time came, weren't you?" I said.

"Lucky, she'll still be your friend. She's spent more than twenty years in your world—so isn't it fair that you spend some time in hers?"

"I have a life here. I can't just disappear."

"People disappear all the time."

"I'll be missed."

"By whom?"

I opened my mouth to speak and then shut it again. I frowned. He was right: who exactly would miss me? I had no real friends, just acquaintances I hardly met from one year to the next. The villagers only saw me now and then, and I was often away for long stretches, so I doubted they would notice my absence much. My agent might miss me for a few weeks when I hadn't returned his calls, but then he would move on to the next client and forget me. Jamie was right; no one would miss me at all.

"You might even find you grow to love our world," Jamie said, his voice soft. "It is an incredible place."

"All the demons I've seen so far are scary," I said.

"You find me scary?"

"You're not a demon."

"I told you, demon is but a human name for creatures they do not understand. There are others like me; others barely different from humankind."

"Like Henri?"

Jamie's smile disappeared and he gave a snort. "No, not like Henri; he's an assassin. If he calls on you again you get out fast. Let me or the other two deal with him."

"You're not actually selling your world to me . . ."

"Did you not think Kayla beautiful?" he asked.

"Yes, I guess I did, but in a terrifying way."

"Only because you've never seen anyone like her before. If you come to my world, you'll soon get used to it."

"I don't think so."

"Did you never dream of a world full of dragons and trolls and goblins as a child? Did you not dream of fairies with gossamer wings?"

"Yes," I whispered, and in my head I could almost see them.

"Centaurs and fauns? Giants and dwarves?"

I remembered lying in my bed, staring at the ceiling, while Kayla told me stories of such creatures: beautiful stories that always had a happy ending.

"Given the chance, wouldn't you want to see such things?"

I started to nod, then with a jerk I came back to reality. I glared at Jamie across the table. "You were trying to hypnotize me."

"Why would I do that?" he asked.

I eyed him suspiciously. "I don't know," I said. *Was that how he got me to invite him to stay in the first place?*

But before I could wonder more about that, he went on, "I was just trying to tell you about my world."

"Kayla used to tell me stories when I was a child, but I thought they were just that—stories."

"It is a strange but wonderful place—a place where all your dreams can come true."

"Or they can be broken."

He smiled, and this time it was a sad smile, one that made me want to reach across the table and take his hand . . . and it wasn't until my fingers brushed his skin I realized that's what I had done. I went to pull away, but he enclosed my fingers in his.

"Let me take you there," he said, "only for a few hours, if you wish—just to see what it's like."

"I wouldn't have to stay if I didn't want to?"

"No," he said, squeezing my fingers again.

"I'm afraid."

"No need to be; I'll protect you from harm."

"Can I think about it?"

"Don't take too long. It would be better you come with me willingly than go with someone else against your will."

"I have to meet Philip tomorrow. I need to know what he has to do with all this, if anything."

Jamie's eyes dropped to our hands and his thumb caressed mine. "I too am interested in what Mr. Conrad has to say," he said. "If his daughter truly has been stolen by some creature from my world, this would be a disturbing turn of events."

"If I went with you to your world, could you help me find her and bring her back?"

He sat and thought for a moment. "I'll make inquiries, but I can't promise anything."

"But you will try to help me find her?"

"You have my oath." He said the words with such gravity that I was pretty sure they meant something: that if he gave his oath, he kept it. Maybe I was being a fool, but I couldn't believe Jamie was one of the bad guys.

Eight

The following morning I woke to birdsong and a swathe of sunlight shining under my curtains and across the floor. My eyes automatically went to Kayla's chair, but of course she wasn't there. I had slept late; if I was to meet Philip at twelve-thirty I was going to have to get a move on.

I was feeling strangely nervous—and as I had two handsome men to impress I was probably going to take twice as long to get ready, more than likely changing outfits at least three times before I was happy. Usually I had Kayla to help me decide—and as soon as I remembered that, it didn't matter anymore.

After showering, I padded downstairs in my slippers and bathrobe to grab a mug of coffee. Jamie was leaning against the kitchen counter scoffing toast.

"Want some?" he offered.

"No thanks, I'm saving myself for lunch."

He snorted. "I'd fill yourself up now. It'll probably be nouvelle cuisine, not enough to feed a water nymph."

I paused a moment. "Water nymph?"

"Tiny, perfectly formed, and can quite literally eat a horse."

"Oh," I said, and hoped he was joking, though somehow I thought not. "Comments like that are hardly going to help persuade me to visit the Underworld."

"Underlands."

"Underlands," I said, rolling my eyes.

He gave me a happy smile. "What are you going to wear for your date?"

"It's not a date. If it were, I'd hardly be likely to have you tagging along."

"I think you should wear the green silk dress."

"Bit over the top for lunch, don't you think?" I replied, and then something occurred to me. "How do you know what's in my wardrobe?"

"I don't, but I collected it from the dry cleaner's, if you remember."

"Oh," I said with a frown, not quite believing him.

"The Longley seems a bit . . . upscale," he said.

"You mean pretentious."

He grinned.

"So what are you going to wear, then?" I asked.

He just shrugged and picked up another piece of toast. For an angel he had a remarkably healthy appetite.

At a quarter to twelve I was ready. I had to admit the dress Jamie wanted me to wear looked good on me, but it really was too much for lunch, even for somewhere like The Longley. I chose instead a collarless silk blouse of emerald green that fell in a "V" at the front and showed just enough flesh for it to feel both sexy and businesslike. Then I added a black pencil skirt (the handy slit at the back meant I could walk with a confident stride) and black, slightly pointed stilettos. I looked pretty damn hot even if I did say so myself.

I grabbed my jacket and carefully negotiated the stairs down to the living room, where I hoped Jamie would be waiting. He was nowhere to be seen, but my two demon bodyguards were there. Mr. Shenanigans was sitting on the couch; as soon as he saw me he struggled to his feet. He might have been a demon, but he was very polite.

Mr. Kerfuffle had been peering through the window, but when he glanced around at me his forehead wrinkled into a displeased frown as he looked me up and down. "You are going somewhere?"

"Out to lunch," I said, "and before you ask, Jamie will be escorting me so I'll be quite safe."

The two demons exchanged a look and Mr. Shenanigans cleared his throat. "We'd rather we were in attendance."

"I'm sure you would, but don't you think you might cause a bit of a stir?" I said. And before I could stop myself, I added: "I mean, look at you."

Mr. Kerfuffle's strange chubby face creased into a solemn frown. "If necessary we can make ourselves fit in."

"Really?"

Both demons nodded and he added, "Mistress Kayla did tell you to do as we instructed."

That was true—and for some reason Kayla had been more comfortable with their presence than Jamie's. I sighed. "Okay, you can come with us—*if* you can pass as human and *if* you keep a low profile."

Mr. Kerfuffle gave me a happy smile and the air around him shimmered and shook outward, almost like ripples in a pond. In a moment he had transformed into a rosy-cheeked, elderly gentleman, although he was still wearing his strange old-fashioned suit. Mr. Shenanigans did the same and while he was still well over six feet tall and broad of chest and shoulder, he now looked every bit the Mafia bodyguard in his black suit and tie with white shirt and dark sunglasses. His black hair was slicked back and he had even remembered to add an olive tan to his skin. His tusks were nowhere to be seen; instead, he flashed white tombstone teeth.

"Wow," I said. "Just look at you two."

"Suit," Mr. Shenanigans said to his partner, gesturing at his own attire. "This is what they wear these days."

Mr. Kerfuffle looked down at himself and then, with another shimmer his suit changed into a replica of his larger friend's. Thankfully, he went without the sunglasses.

"Okay," I said. "Just Jamie to go."

"I'm ready," a voice said from the hall behind me.

"I hope you've dressed up," I said as I turned, "because this place really is quite . . ."

I stuttered into silence.

He had said the wings were the only surprise, so I wasn't sure if I was seeing the real Jamie or not, but he looked a little taller, his hair was a little blonder and his eyes were a whole lot bluer. He was dressed in a suit that was just slightly lighter than black, with a deep gray trim; his intensely blue tie against his crisp white shirt really set off his eyes. The expression "drop-dead gorgeous" could have been made for him.

"You certainly scrub up well," I said, once my power of speech had returned.

"So do you," he said. His eyes sparkled as he looked at me, then they shifted to the demons and his smile became grim. "They're not coming with us?"

"I'm afraid they are," I said.

"You're going to have to get a bigger car," he grumbled, as he picked up my car keys from the hall table.

"It *is* going to be a tight squeeze," I admitted.

"Don't you worry about us," Mr. Kerfuffle said.

"We won't," Jamie said.

"Children, children," I said, following Jamie out of the cottage, "play nicely."

It was a bit of a struggle for Mr. Shenanigans to get into the back of the car and I'm pretty sure he resorted to a bit of demon jiggery-pokery in the end, but after a few minutes the two demons were ensconced in the backseat. I had moved mine as far forward as I could, but poor Mr. Shenanigans still looked as if he had been folded in half. His knees were up near his chin and his head and shoulders were hunched forward.

"It's not too far," I assured him.

"I'm all right," he managed to mumble, but I did wonder what would happen if he should sneeze or cough—and whether my poor little car would be split open like a blown can of baked beans.

Fortunately, neither occurred before we reached the golf club, and although I really didn't like sharing the back seat with Mr. Kerfuffle, I thought maybe on the return journey the larger demon should sit up front.

Jamie swung the car into a free parking space, and when I climbed out and looked around it became apparent that my little Fiesta was completely out of place. The cars on either side of us—a Mercedes and a Jaguar—were probably worth more than the total of all my worldly possessions put together—including the cottage.

"It looks like your date's already here," Jamie said, gesturing with his head to a Mercedes parked close to the main entrance and it did look like one of the limousines Philip had sent for me previously.

"Date?" Mr. Kerfuffle said.

I gave Jamie my "shut up, why don't you" look, but he just grinned.

"Don't get your panties in a knot," I said. "It's a business meeting, sort of."

"Sort of?"

"It's important I meet with this guy."

"Why?" he asked.

Before I could reply, Jamie interrupted. "Because if what this *gentleman* says is true, someone from the Underlands is not playing by the rules"—the two demons exchanged a glance—"and I don't have to tell you what that means."

"You said 'if he's telling the truth'?" Mr. Kerfuffle said.

"If he isn't, I want to know whose game he's playing, but at a guess I would say it has Daltas written all over it."

Mr. Kerfuffle managed to look even unhappier, if that was possible.

Jamie placed a hand at the small of my back and escorted me up the steps into the club, leaving the two demons trailing along behind. I wasn't quite sure how I was going to explain their presence to Philip. I'd told him Jamie was acting as my bodyguard, but I hadn't envisaged turning up for lunch with an entourage. I just hoped Philip wasn't easily intimidated.

I needn't have worried: when we walked into the restaurant the maître d' immediately guided us to a table in the corner, where Philip was sitting studying a menu. Standing behind him were two men in dark suits, both tall, with the hard, chiseled look of ex-military personnel. Kayla had told me he had bodyguards and it appeared she was right.

Their hands hung loosely at their sides, though they were obviously alert and constantly scanning the room. When they saw us their eyes narrowed and the slightly taller of the two men leaned forward and whispered something into Philip's ear.

Philip looked up, and though the smile on his face faltered slightly when he saw us he recovered almost immediately and stood to greet me.

"Lucky," he said, as he moved around the table. He took my hand and to my surprise, kissed me on both cheeks then led me to the table. "You mentioned bodyguards but I didn't expect you to be taking it so seriously."

"Nor I you," I said, cocking my eyebrow at his two men.

He smiled and pulled a chair out for me. The table was set for three and Jamie made himself comfortable in the third seat.

"James," Philip said in greeting.

"Philip," Jamie replied.

I sighed inwardly. I should have known this would be a mistake. If I'd had any sense at all I would have left Jamie at home and just brought the demons—if I'd realized Philip would be similarly protected it would have been a no-brainer. Instead, I had his bodyguards eyeing up my bodyguards and vice versa while Philip and Jamie were doing that testosterone-fueled man-thing that guys do whenever two or more are alone with one woman. And Jamie was an *angel*, for Heaven's sake!

A waiter appeared by my side. "Would Madam like something to drink?"

I had promised myself I'd be good and stick to Perrier, but my resolve faltered and then dissolved. "White wine, please."

Philip consulted the wine menu and ordered a bottle of something called Picpoul de Pinet.

"I think they serve beer here," he said to Jamie.

"The Picpoul will be fine," he replied with a charming smile, "although I'd have chosen the 2013."

I kicked him under the table and he grinned at me.

"Let's get down to business," I said, taking a notebook out of my bag.

"I think we should eat first," Philip started, "then we can go somewhere private to talk."

I gave him a long, hard look. *Why was he always doing this?* But before I had a chance to speak, I felt rather than heard the two demons step a little closer to my chair, and Mr. Kerfuffle said, "We are charged with Mistress Lucky's protection. Where she goes, we go too."

Philip's two goons closed in behind him and there was no doubt in my mind that they were just aching to take a pop at Mr. Shenanigans. I could see that they were thinking Mr. Kerfuffle was just some little old guy who should have been put out to pasture. If they'd had any idea *what* my two protectors really were . . .

I looked up at his two men and then back to Philip. "I suggest you tell your two . . . companions to back off," I said, and when he gave me a supercilious smile, "Philip, I'm serious."

"Come now, no one's in danger here."

"Tell that to your two boys."

"They're just doing their job."

"Why are they here?"

"You're not the only one who feels threatened."

"I don't feel threatened," I said, lying through my teeth. The memory of Henri's teeth flashed into my mind.

"Then why all of this?" he said, gesturing at my bodyguards.

"I might not feel threatened, but they seem to think I'm in danger, so for the foreseeable future I have around-the-clock bodyguards."

"Haven't you considered that if you have a demon after you these three bozos won't be of any use at all?" Philip said.

"Have you?"

"At least mine are military trained."

"Philip, for Heaven's sake! I haven't come here to argue about who has the better bodyguards."

"If she had, I know who I'd put my money on," Jamie muttered.

I tried to kick him again, but he'd obviously learned his lesson and moved his ankles out of reach.

"Who exactly are you?" Philip asked Jamie.

"Enough," I said. "I didn't come here to play stupid games. In fact, let's cut to the chase, shall we? I seem to have lost my appetite."

Jamie completely ignored me. "I'm Lucky's friend and I'm here to look after her interests."

I glared at Jamie.

"Really?" Philip replied. "My understanding is that you turned up on her doorstep unannounced just a couple of days ago. I'd say you could very easily be her enemy."

"As could you," Jamie said, his frown mirroring my own: how on earth did Philip know that? Had he been checking up on me?

Philip's bodyguards shifted their positions slightly: one had his eyes glued on Jamie while the other was glaring at the two demons behind me. The tension around the table was palpable.

Mr. Shenanigans rested a hand on the back of my chair and Kerfuffle moved in close beside me. The taller of Philip's bodyguards moved his hand so his fingertips were just inside his jacket. This was all going too far—and it was also vaguely ridiculous. We were meant to be having lunch, for goodness' sake.

"I can't be doing with all this macho shit," I said, throwing my napkin down on the table. "Lose the bodyguards."

"I can't do that."

I kept eye contact. "Well, get them to back off. Your pal there looks too trigger-happy by far."

"And your guys don't?"

"My guys don't carry guns," I said, although I had no idea whether they did or not—I just assumed demons didn't need anything as déclassé as loaded weapons.

"How about him?" Philip said, indicating Jamie.

Jamie stood and slowly pulled open his jacket. Nothing. "I've shown you mine, now you show me yours."

Philip smiled, but his lips were twisted as though he was sucking on something very bitter. He pulled open his jacket. Unlike Jamie he *was* carrying a weapon, and in a very professional-looking holster.

"Fantastic," I said. "You invite me to lunch and come armed to the teeth." I would have said more, but the waiter arrived with the wine and we had to go through all the pouring and tasting thing, which to my mind is a complete waste of time unless you're buying a twenty-year-old red that costs more than the rest of the meal put together.

Of course, then another waiter appeared and hovered, wanting to take our order. Any interest I'd had in eating had long since vanished. "I'll have the smoked salmon to start and then the filet steak cooked blue," I said closing the menu.

As soon as the waiters left us in peace I resumed the conversation. "Why the hardware, Philip? What's happened since the other evening that's scared you so much?"

He took a sip of his wine. "I really don't want to talk about this in front of *him*," he said, glaring at Jamie.

"You knew he was coming."

"I thought he was just a . . ." His expression grew puzzled and he trailed off. "He seemed very different the other night."

It was my turn to be puzzled. "What do you mean?"

"He didn't look so . . . I thought he was just some . . . I don't know. He seems different somehow."

He was right, of course: the real Jamie was very different from the young man I'd first met, but I couldn't possibly explain it to Philip—and actually, I didn't *want* to explain it to him. He had his guns and I had my demons, so we were both keeping secrets.

We fell into an uncomfortable silence. As we sipped on our wine we studied each other surreptitiously. Jamie was the only one who appeared to be completely at ease. He relaxed back into his chair and watched both of us with a small smile playing on his lips. For some reason, he was finding it all terribly amusing.

The starter arrived and we ate in silence, but when they cleared away the plates I couldn't bear the strained atmosphere any longer. I decided to change tack, as my demands for information were being ignored. "So, Philip, what do you actually do for a living?"

"I buy and sell businesses," he said.

"Oh, that sounds—"

"Boring?" he finished for me with a wry smile; his first for quite some time.

"Well, now you mention it."

He laughed. "Not as interesting as exposing fake psychics," he said.

"That sort of happened by accident."

"I read your first book. It was very interesting."

"Yet you still went to see a bokor?"

"I was desperate."

"And he does sound like he may have been the real deal—either that or he was incredibly lucky."

"He was scary, that was for sure."

"I guess you didn't take your entourage with you to that meeting?"

He patted his lips with his napkin. "It was a risk I had to take."

"I'm not sure I'd want to. I've always steered clear of so-called black magicians and the like. Ghosts I can handle, but witchcraft—no way."

"How about demons?" Philip asked.

"Until recently, I hadn't had the pleasure. Now things have changed—and coincidentally, they changed at exactly the same time as I met you. So what's going on?"

"I haven't the slightest idea," Philip replied.

"Really?" Jamie asked. "It seems to me you know exactly what you're doing."

Philip gave him a long, cold look. "What the fuck do you know about anything?"

Jamie returned his stare, and this time there was no humor in it. "More than you can possibly imagine."

Lines grooved into Philip's face, ugly lines that looked like they would scar his skin forever if he kept the expression for long. "Yeah, right. So what and who have you ever lost?"

Jamie's expression was a chiseled mask; his blue eyes darkened by two shades—a trick of the light, or just his real self breaking through?

"We all lose people and things important to us, Mr. Conrad. It's just how and why we lose them that matters, and then how we deal with that loss. Some lie to themselves to ease the pain. Some just lie. I have this feeling you fall into the latter category."

"And I care what you think because?"

Jamie picked up his wine glass and twisted the stem between his fingers, a smile curling his lips.

"I don't think we can really have any sort of serious conversation with him present." Philip said with a contemptuous sniff in Jamie's direction.

"For fuck's sake, Philip," I hissed leaning across the table and trying not to make a scene even though I felt like screaming at him, "if you want me to help you, I have to know how you got yourself into this mess. But, if you won't talk to me I might as well go home right now."

"Please, don't go," he said reaching across the table and grabbing my hand.

I looked him in the eyes and then pointedly at his hand holding mine. He let go and sank back in his seat.

"Fine. Then let's just eat," I snapped.

As if on cue two waiters arrived and began serving the main course. To my mind we were halfway to having yet another wasted meeting, but this time I was determined to find out what was going on, though I wasn't yet sure how I would manage to do that. Jamie had hinted that Philip was either lying or not telling the whole truth, and if the last few days had taught me anything at all, it was not to take the things people said for granted. I certainly wasn't about to take Philip Conrad at face value.

As for Jamie—was there any reason I should really trust him either? Kayla had clearly not been very pleased to see him when she realized who he was.

I accepted another glass of wine; my head was spinning anyway.

"When we've finished eating, why don't we take a walk around the grounds? They have a very nice walled garden around the back," Philip said.

"Okay," I said, guessing it was his way of putting a few yards at least between me and the others so we could talk with a little bit of privacy.

I decided against a sweet and opted for a coffee: wine and stiletto heels were not a good combination for me at the best of times, and if I was going to have to walk as well as think, a shot or two of caffeine was probably a necessity. A visit to the bathroom was also called for.

I excused myself, and Mr. Shenanigans promptly followed me and took up his post outside the door to the ladies' room. Even in human form he looked quite threatening, so it was no great surprise to me that no one else ventured inside while I was using the facilities.

I took my time freshening my makeup. It was quite a relief to get away from the testosterone-fueled atmosphere engulfing the table—turned out even demons and angels were full of it.

I knew I couldn't prolong my visit without Mr. Shenanigans coming to look for me—in fact, I was surprised he'd not already checked to make sure I hadn't been taken captive by the wicked Lord Daltas, or had a visitation from Henri le Dent. This thought alone spurred me into leaving the privacy of the bathroom: I didn't want to chance another meeting with him anytime soon, not unless I was in the company of Jamie and my demon guards.

It was clear to me, even from across the room, that all was not well. Philip was standing, his chair pushed back and his face flushed, flanked by his bodyguards. Jamie was still seated, but he was leaning forward slightly with the palms of both hands flat against the table. Mr. Kerfuffle was by his side, and when he saw me, he bent toward Jamie and murmured something. For a second Jamie didn't move, just continued to stare at Philip, then he slowly relaxed back against the chair.

"Did I miss something?" I asked, as I joined them.

"Let's walk," Philip said.

"Let's," Jamie said, standing.

It looked to me as though Philip was working hard to suppress his anger: his lips were pressed together so tightly they had all but disappeared. But he said nothing as he ushered me out of the restaurant and into the entrance foyer. A waiter helped me with my jacket, which had magically materialized from the cloakroom, and as Philip shrugged on a full-length cashmere coat it crossed my mind that he looked more and more like a mobster every time I saw him.

"I said I would pay for our lunch," I reminded him as he led me outside.

"I wouldn't hear of it," he said.

When I glanced over my shoulder, Philip's bodyguards were right behind us, sandwiched between Mr. Kerfuffle and Mr. Shenanigans. Neither of the men looked comfortable, but the demons were both smiling happily. Jamie was nowhere to be seen, but I guessed even angels needed to use the bathroom occasionally.

Although it was late autumn, the gardens surrounding the golf course were still very impressive. I didn't like to think how much it must cost to join the Longley; the luxurious club interior, the Michelin-starred restaurant, and the lush, well-tended grounds all suggested a very expensive membership fee. Once again it looked as if Philip was trying to impress me.

"So, do you get to play here very often?"

"Too busy most of the time."

"But you keep up the membership?"

He gave a tight smile. "The waiting list is so long they had to close it. If I were to give up my membership now I'd never get back in."

Except for the clicking of my heels on the paving stones, we walked in silence. It crossed my mind that anyone watching from the clubhouse would think us a strange group: a man and woman strolling through the grounds with four men trailing behind them, and three of those built like heavyweight wrestlers.

"Well," I said, when the brooding silence got too much, "are you going to tell me what this is all about, or are we going to arrange yet another dinner or lunch date and discuss nothing?"

Philip glanced over his shoulder, probably to see whether the four men were within listening distance. When he was satisfied that they were a few yards away he started, "When I told you my wife was murdered by a demon and my daughter stolen, I wasn't lying to you, but what I didn't tell you was it was all my own stupid fault."

I glanced up at him. His face had a pinched, weary look to it.

"You know that old saying, 'if something's too good to be true it usually is'?"

I nodded, but didn't say anything; I didn't want to interrupt him in case he stopped talking.

"When I think back on it I can't believe how stupid I was," he said keeping his voice low. "I can't believe I let myself get sucked into something so insane."

He paused, but I still held my tongue. I had no idea where this was going, but he'd get there in the end.

"Business was great and I'd just closed a deal, one that was worth millions. I had a wife I adored and a beautiful daughter who had just started at one of the best schools in the country. I didn't need anything else; I had it all." He paused, his lips twisting into a bitter smile. "Laura and I had been invited to a party by a casual acquaintance who worked in the City—Laura didn't want to go because she knew it would be all business talk and networking. I very nearly didn't go either; after all, I have enough contacts, I know enough 'people'"—he made quotation marks with his fingers—"but I just couldn't help myself: what if I missed out on meeting that one special person who could make me the next million? If only I'd known then . . ."

He hung his head, stuffed his hands deep into his pockets and carried on walking, his shoulders hunched. After a moment he went on, "The party was in full swing when I arrived, but it was the same old faces, same old patter. I got myself a drink and mingled a bit and by eleven decided I'd had enough and it was time to call it a night."

The path we were following divided into two and Philip signaled that we should follow the left-hand path. I hoped it would lead back around toward the clubhouse, as it would be getting dark before too long. The afternoon sun was already a pale globe dropping down out of the sky and the air was getting that damp, autumn chill to it that comes just before dusk.

Philip continued, "I got as far as the foyer and was waiting to collect my jacket when a young guy joined me at the desk. The coat-check girl was having a problem finding someone's coat, and while we were waiting we started to chat. I'd never seen the man before—I would have remembered him if I had. He was tall and slim and looked a bit like a young Barrack Obama. He even had a slight American accent."

We had reached a wrought-iron gate, through which I caught a glimpse of what looked to be a walled garden. "Shall we?" he said, gesturing to the gate.

"Why not?"

The gate opened with a reluctant squeal of aged metal against metal. One of his men stepped forward and pulled the gate shut behind us, blocking the others from entering and leaving Philip and me alone. I doubted this would sit happily with my demon friends, but I'd let them deal with it.

We walked along a path leading into the center of the garden, where a sun-bleached wooden bench overlooked a small rectangular pond. He gestured for me to sit, and then sat down beside me. It was unnaturally quiet within the confined area: no breeze, no rustling of autumn leaves, and the fountain sculpted into the shape of two cherubs wrestling a dragon had been turned off for the winter. The surface of the water was a still expanse reflecting the gray sky.

"He said his name was Joseph," Philip continued, jerking me back into the story, "and that he was visiting Britain on business. He said he was meeting with a man who could make him a leading player in, not only Britain, but in the world—it was he who introduced me to the bokor."

I frowned. "But you said . . ." *What had he said?*

"I'm sorry, Lucky, you seem like a very nice young woman, but you're far too trusting."

I opened my mouth to ask him what he was talking about, but I was distracted by something in the pond. The surface had been changing from gray to black in the fading light, but now it had started to glow red. I glanced up at the sky, but there was no answer there. The water rippled and began to heave and bubble as though boiling. Curious, I stood up and took a step toward it.

"Philip, can you see that?" I asked, although he'd have to be blind if he couldn't. "What's happening?"

I heard shouts from outside the gates: shouts, and then screams, and I tried to turn away from the pond—I knew something was very wrong, but my feet didn't want to move. Then the whole surface of the pond erupted upward in a bloody red tower, then shrank in on itself as it gradually molded into a distinct shape, first a head, then shoulders, arms, waist appeared, and finally legs. The creature towered above me as it took shape, and finally I managed to open my mouth and scream, "*JAMIE!*"

Even as I screamed, I had no doubt in my mind what this creature was, for he was truly the stuff of nightmares. He could have been carved out of ebony, his skin was so black. The only color about him was in the rivulets of scarlet running down his body and the glowing coals that were his eyes. Two small horns grew out of his forehead, one on either side, just below his hairline. When he smiled, he showed another glimpse of color: ivory teeth and, for a moment, a pointed tongue of dark pink.

His muscular chest shimmered as if made of polished stone; his upper body could have been that of a Greek god—but this was no deity, or at least not a holy one, for below the hips his body was scaled like a lizard. He was naked, and obviously *very* pleased to see me—I could see that from the monstrous object between his legs. What he intended to do with that thing scared me beyond measure, and I started to shake.

He laughed and reached out a hand toward me, and I finally managed to stagger backward. I couldn't bear the thought of his long, slender and strangely disproportionate fingers touching me.

I shrieked for help again, and then there was a noise above me like the beating of wings through still air and the demon's head snapped back as he looked upward. I felt something drop down behind me and I was suddenly surrounded by a warm shield of feathers.

"She is mine, Guardian," the demon cried. "Do not interfere in this matter."

"This woman is under the protection of Lord Baltheza, and until I hear otherwise from his lips, she will remain in my charge."

"I have been summoned to the Overlands; I cannot return empty-handed."

"Then you must look elsewhere," Jamie said, "for he who called upon you should take her place, as is the law."

The creature took one step out of the pond and as he loomed over us Jamie's wings closed tighter around me and he pulled me back against his chest. From behind us there was a screech of tearing metal and the heavy pounding of feet upon paving slabs.

"About time you two turned up," Jamie said, and I stood on tiptoe and peered over the wings just in time to see Mr. Shenanigans appear between the demon and us, his smaller friend by his side. The creature from the pond backed away.

"Return to where you belong," Mr. Kerfuffle ordered.

"I demand my right to return to the Underlands with a soul," the pond demon said, his lips curling downward into a very un-demon-like pout.

"Then take he who called you," Jamie repeated.

The pond demon straightened. "Step aside," he said.

Jamie did as he was asked, still holding me close within his winged embrace, and my demon bodyguards followed suit, positioning themselves so they were still between the pond demon and us.

"You," the pond demon said, raising a hand and pointing past us, "you will come with me."

"You may not want to see this," Jamie whispered to me.

"What?" I said, again peering over his feathers at where the demon was focusing his attention.

Philip was backing away from the demon's pointing finger, then his calves hit the bench and he fell, sprawling back onto the seat. The demon moved forward, then reached out and grabbed Philip by the throat.

"Jamie, shouldn't we do something?" I asked, although part of me was thinking, *Serves the backstabbing little shit right*.

"There is nothing that can be done, mistress," said Mr. Shenanigans, "for once a demon is summoned to this world with the promise of a soul he won't return without one."

"Stop," Jamie called. "Did this man command you to come take this woman?"

The pond demon hesitated, then leaned forward and sniffed the air surrounding Philip. "He is a servant of the one who called upon me."

"Then go and find his master."

His black lips curled into a bow-shaped grin. "No need: he bears the mark of he who called me forth and therefore I have every right to his body and soul—"

"No, please, I beg of you," Philip cried, almost sobbing in fear, "I have no mark—I have *no mark*!"

"Can he do that?" I asked Jamie. "Just carry him off?"

"If Philip truly does bear the mark of whoever is manipulating him, Argon is well within his rights to take him."

So the pond demon had a name. I couldn't stop shivering. I really wouldn't want to be in Philip's shoes, though if it'd been up to him it would have been me hanging in the demon's grasp.

"Lord Argon," Jamie said, "why waste your time on the monkey when you can have the organ-grinder?"

The demon laughed, a deep roar from the pit of his stomach. "Nice try, Guardian, but why settle for one when I can have both? If I bide my time, I will take both master and servant, for I have all eternity, or at least as long as these puny humans live."

"He is not worth your bother," Jamie said. "Just look at him snivel."

The pond demon smirked. "But that is the way I like them: pleading for their pathetic lives, cringing like whipped pups." Argon let go of Philip's throat and set him down, but it was only momentary; with his other hand he picked Philip up by the collar of his coat and held him up so they were eye to eye.

Philip looked like he had given up. He just hung there, his face pallid, his eyes closed, his chest heaving.

"What will he do to him?" I whispered to Jamie.

"You really don't want to know."

Awful images filled my head of what might be awaiting him in the Underlands—what could have been awaiting *me*. But, although he had betrayed me, I couldn't just stand by and watch this happen—maybe he thought giving me up to some lord or other from the Under-fucking-lands would get him back his daughter. I struggled to break free of Jamie's grasp.

"What on earth do you think you're doing?" Jamie asked.

"Let me go! I have to at least try and reason with your Lord Argon."

"Are you mad?"

"I will be if you don't let me go this instant," I said, and I stamped down on his foot with all the strength I could muster.

"Humph," he mumbled, but he still held me tight.

"Next time it'll be with the heel if you don't let me go."

"All right, all right," he said, and slowly unfurled his wings.

I took one step toward the pond demon, but before I could take another, Mr. Shenanigans had scooped me up into his arms and was striding away with me toward the gate.

I fought him, pummeling his broad chest, thumping his arms and shoulders with my fists, trying to make him drop me, but it was no good; I could have been an insect for all the attention he paid me. By the time he stopped, just beyond the gate, I managed to pull myself up to look over his shoulder. Lord Argon was sinking back down into the pool with Philip dangling from his fist.

Philip looked as though he might be dead already. From the grim expressions on my bodyguards' faces, I rather hoped he was. I had a feeling "a fate worse than death" was the appropriate term for what awaited Philip Conrad.

Finally, all that was left of them was a ring of slowly diminishing ripples. Mr. Shenanigans lowered me to the ground and we all stood there, staring, until the pond's surface returned to a mirrored reflection of the darkening sky.

Jamie gave a little shrug, and with a ruffle of feathers, his wings vanished and he was once again a man in a sharp suit.

"Are you all right?" he said, turning to me.

I nodded, but I was numb inside. I wrapped my arms around myself; I felt icy cold and I was pretty sure that wasn't anything to do with the temperature.

Jamie's brow creased with concern and he strode over to me, placed warm hands against my cheeks and glanced up at Mr. Shenanigans, who stood behind me with a hand resting on my shoulder.

"She's in shock," he said.

"No," I said, "I'm just—" I closed my eyes and my legs gave way beneath me.

Someone caught me and I felt myself being lifted.

"Take her back to the car," I heard Mr. Kerfuffle say. "We'll clear up here."

"Clear up?" I heard myself say, but my voice sounded like it was coming from such a long way away. "What does he mean by 'clear up'?"

"Hush now," Jamie murmured against my hair. "I'm taking you home to bed."

"Is that a promise?" I heard myself say, with a giggle. And then it occurred to me I had just propositioned an angel. I giggled again. "Will I go to Hell?" I asked, and then everything faded to gray and then black.

Nine

I awoke to the sound of muffled voices. I stretched and yawned and stretched some more. I was all warm and cozy and my head felt pleasantly fuzzy, like it does when you've slept really long and well. I pushed myself up the bed until I was sitting, and realized that I was wearing only my underwear.

I paused to think about that for a while. Someone had undressed me, which was embarrassing enough—but had I been naked, I would have been mortified.

Then the events of the previous day started to come back and I slumped against my pillow. Philip had betrayed me, and had paid a terrible—if not undeserved—price. Kayla had deserted me, and my new best friends were two demons and an angel.

My eyes flew open. Oh my God! I had more or less asked Jamie to sleep with me—what had I been thinking? Was it he who had undressed me? Just as well I hadn't woken up naked! Damn it; I wouldn't have known what to think.

I could still hear the hum of voices from downstairs, so I scrambled out of bed, pulled on a robe and scampered along the corridor to the bathroom. I would feel better after a shower, or at least that's what I told myself.

The shower is the place where I recharge my batteries. When the whole world has turned to shit, I close my eyes, empty my mind and just let the water wash away all the bad stuff. I shrugged off the robe, discarded bra and underwear and turned the shower onto full power, then leaned forward under the jets, both hands flat against the tiled wall with my head and shoulders directly under the shower head. I closed my eyes and relaxed, letting the water pound over me.

In my mind I envisaged a black stone wall to shut everything else out, but as soon as that was in place and I let my thoughts wander, the image of Philip hanging from the demon's grasp flashed into my head. I screwed my eyes tight, rebuilding my wall, but as soon as I tried to relax there was Philip with the demon, slowly sinking down into the pond.

As it was becoming increasingly apparent that my shower wasn't going to work its usual relaxing magic, I soaped up, rinsed, washed my hair and rubbed myself down as quickly as I could. I was beginning to think that maybe time was running out. Perhaps I should take up Jamie's offer of visiting his world while I still had some choice. If it came down to it, I would rather go there of my own accord than be taken against my will hanging from some monster's talons.

I went back to my room and dressed in black jeans and a black T-shirt, trying not to look at the seat by the window where Kayla usually sat. I missed her so much it physically hurt. My chest ached and there was a hard ball of something in my solar plexus that made me feel nauseous every time I thought of her—and of how I might never see her again.

I felt like throwing myself down on the bed and weeping, but that would have been weak and self-indulgent. I needed to speak to Jamie and my two bodyguards—I didn't think any of them had foreseen what was going to occur at the golf club, and I wondered if the events meant something had changed.

I took a few minutes to put on a bit of makeup—nothing too obvious, just a smear of lip gloss, a coat of mascara and a smudge of color across my cheeks to brighten up my very pale skin.

I was ready. With back straight, head high and chest out I marched out of my room and down the stairs. I hesitated on the bottom step, listening to the voices coming from the kitchen, then changed my approach. Maybe better to check out the lie of the land first. I padded along the hall and leaned against the doorframe, my ear almost resting against the door.

"Can we get on with this?" I heard Jamie say.

"If you can do any better, be my guest," Mr. Kerfuffle said.

"I think maybe this would be a more appropriate receptacle," Mr. Shenanigans suggested.

"It shouldn't matter," the other demon said.

"Well, it obviously does," Jamie said. "Let's try it."

There was the sound of the tap running and slopping water, then a thud as something heavy was probably being placed upon the table.

"This is more like it," Jamie said.

Then something weird happened: the air around me grew heavy, pressing down on my skin, and then it began to vibrate and hum. Pressure in my ears grew and grew until I thought they were going to pop—and then, just as suddenly as it started, it was gone.

"My lady," I heard Mr. Kerfuffle say, "there has been a happening of which I thought you should be made aware."

"Is Lucky all right?" I heard Kayla say.

Kayla? Kayla was back? I pushed the door open and walked in.

Mr. Kerfuffle was standing on a kitchen chair and peering down into my best crystal fruit bowl, which was sitting in the center of the table. Jamie was standing to one side of him, also looking down. Mr. Shenanigans, standing behind them, saw me and hurried around the table to place himself between the others and me.

"I thought I heard Kayla's voice," I said.

"You should leave us," Mr. Shenanigans said, opening his arms wide as if to usher me out of the room.

I could feel my lips curl into a stubborn pout. "I thought I heard Kayla. Was she here?"

I looked from one face to another. Mr. Shenanigans glanced over his shoulder at Mr. Kerfuffle, who hesitated when he saw my expression.

"What harm can it do?" Jamie said to him.

With a sigh Mr. Kerfuffle looked down into the bowl. "My lady, your . . ." He hesitated, glancing up at me briefly, then amended whatever he was going to say to, "Mistress Lucky is here."

There was a heartbeat of silence then, "Bring her to me."

He looked back up and beckoned for me to join him. Mr. Shenanigans stepped to one side to let me pass, though he obviously wasn't happy.

Jamie moved back from the table and gestured for me to stand between him and the little demon. "Look down into the bowl," he said, and when I gave him a quizzical look he smiled and added, "It's okay. Just look into the water."

I looked down—I don't know quite what I was expecting but it certainly wasn't Kayla staring right back up at me in her full demonic glory: beautiful, and at the same time terrifying. She was sitting on a bed, her legs curled up beneath her.

"Lucky, are you all right?" she asked.

"Yes," I said, then, "no, not really."

I felt Jamie put his arm around my shoulders. Mr. Kerfuffle cast me a worried glance and then turned to Kayla. "My lady, the mortal—" He frowned.

"—Philip Conrad—" Jamie obligingly provided the name.

"Ah yes," said the demon, "the mortal Philip Conrad has been abducted by Lord Argon."

Kayla's eyes widened, then her lips curled into a very tight smile. "Tell me."

He explained what had happened at the golf club, pausing now and again for Jamie to add to the story.

By the time they had finished, Kayla's expression was grim. "Someone's playing games," she said.

Mr. Kerfuffle blew out through pursed lips. "Someone is attempting to use a human conduit to disguise their interference."

"I want that human," she said.

"Without the servant, we have no way to find the master," Jamie said. "I think that's why Conrad was taken—once we knew him for what he was, he had outlived his usefulness and had become a liability."

"He told me a demon had taken his daughter; maybe he was trying to get her back," I said, although why I was trying to stick up for the man who had betrayed me so appallingly, I wasn't at all sure.

Kayla's face softened into a smile. "Lucky, you are far too trusting."

"That's what Philip said, but it's not true," I argued. "It's being so untrusting that earns me a living."

She gave a dismissive wave of the hand. "Altogether different. You trusted Philip and it nearly got you into very serious trouble."

"I trusted Jamie and he saved me," I pointed out, though actually I wasn't sure I trusted him much at all. I had already been taken in by his convincing lies. I had also trusted Kayla, though that was something else I didn't want to get into right then.

Her eyes narrowed and she glared past me at Jamie. "I'm not sure what your game is."

I felt him stiffen, then take a deep breath. "I'm not interested in playing games, Lady Kayla. I am interested in keeping Lucky safe from those who would do her harm, and I'm not overly sure I can exclude you from that list."

"Watch it, Guardian," she said, her eyes glinting with barely disguised anger. "I would never hurt Lucky and you know it."

"There are many ways of causing pain," Jamie said, squeezing my shoulder, "and I think you will find Lucky is suffering such as we speak."

She tapped a long pointed fingernail against her lips then gave a weary sigh. "You are, of course, correct." She returned her attention to me. "I want you with me, of course I do, but it's still not safe here."

"Why don't you come back then? I'm not sure I want to go to your world, and I certainly don't want to live there."

"Lucky, you may not have a choice in the matter," she said. "I'm hoping it won't be so, but if I can't get the promise of your safety in our world, I'll never get one for it in your own. At least here, with me, you'll have me to protect you."

"And me," added Mr. Shenanigans.

"Yes," Mr. Kerfuffle said, echoing his friend.

"And I," said Jamie.

"A decision will be made very soon," Kayla said, "and as soon as it is, I'll return for you."

I didn't really understand any of this—and more to the point, I didn't *want* to. My world had been turned upside down and for some reason I didn't appear to have any say in my future. I walked away from the table. I didn't want to see Kayla while she was like that because it was like looking at a stranger.

I paused at the door. "I'll leave you to it," I said, and the despondency and heart-numbing sadness that I was feeling must have shown in my voice as Jamie gave me a sympathetic smile.

"I won't be long," he said.

So I left them to their whispering and plotting and whatever else they were doing and plodded back up the stairs to my bedroom. It was usually my favorite room in the cottage, but not today. Seeing the empty chair by the window made me more depressed than I could have possibly imagined. I flopped back on the bed and stared at the ceiling, not seeing a thing.

I could still hear murmuring downstairs and I wished they'd shut up. I didn't want to hear them, I wanted to be alone—although a little voice in my head persisted in saying, *No you don't*, and it was right, I didn't. I was alone all of the time: I'd lost my mom, I'd lost my dad, and now I'd lost the only other person in the whole wide world I cared about, and without her I didn't know how I was going to carry on.

What made it worse was not that I'd lost Kayla, as in she had gone away—after all, she'd just said she would be coming back for me—it was that I had lost *my* Kayla. She wasn't the person I'd always thought she was. Our whole relationship had been a lie.

So I mourned the friend I thought I'd had.

The murmuring downstairs went on and on—I'd never heard them all talk so much. On reflection, it was probably Kayla—she could always talk for hours. I must have nodded off because a sudden *tap, tap, tap* on my door made me sit up with a jerk.

"Can I come in?" Jamie asked.

I sat up, swung my legs over the side of the bed and rubbed a hand across my face, then quickly ran my fingers through my hair.

"All right," I said grudgingly.

The door opened and he stood there, one hand resting against the frame. "You all right?"

"What do you think?"

"For what it's worth, she really does love you," Jamie said.

"Yeah, right," I said, "she loves me so much she lies to me." I was a little ashamed by the bitterness in my tone.

"When you were a child you wouldn't have understood, and by the time you'd grown into a young woman it was too late," he said. "I think she deluded herself into believing the day would never come when she would have to return to our world."

"But why now?"

"May I—?" Jamie gestured toward Kayla's empty seat.

Well, Kayla wouldn't be sitting there any time soon—then I gave myself a mental shake. Feeling sorry for myself was not just childish and unproductive; it was a waste of emotional energy.

He sat down and leaned forward, forearms on knees, hands laced together. "In some ways my world is no different from yours," he started. "Some humans crave riches and power, some demons are just as shallow."

"Kayla isn't like that," I said. I might not know my friend as well as I thought I did, but I was sure of one thing: she had no interest in either of those things.

"You're right, she isn't. She could have stayed in our world and been the princess she is, but instead she chose to be with you."

"Why would she do that? Why come to me: a little girl she didn't even know?"

Jamie's eyes met mine and there was something in them, some emotion that I didn't understand.

All the same, I shivered. "Jamie, what is it?" And when he looked away, "Jamie, you're scaring me."

"I'm sorry, it isn't my intention."

"For goodness' sake, just tell me what this is all about, why don't you?"

"If you let me take you to my world, Kayla will explain it to you herself."

"She said she was coming back here for me."

Jamie gave a snort. "Wishful thinking on her part. Her father will never allow it. She's his daughter and he's only just managed to get her back to the Underlands; he's certainly not about to let her leave anytime soon."

"So why did she tell me she'd be coming back for me?"

"Because it's what she wants to believe." Jamie got up from the chair and crouched down in front of me. He took my hand. "All I can tell you is this: there is a struggle for power going on in my world. Several of the lower lords are vying to be next in line for Lord Baltheza's throne, and if his daughter were to choose one of them as her consort, it would put them in a strong position."

"This Lord Daltas, for example?"

"He is one of the main contenders. He wants Kayla's hand, but unfortunately for him, she doesn't take kindly to be threatened. Drawing you into this was the worst possible thing he could've done. She'll never forgive him for it."

"So he wanted her back to marry her, and her father—?"

"Just wanted her back."

"So he loves her?"

"Not so you'd notice. But while she's at his court he can keep an eye on her. He has no intention of giving up his throne for anyone, but if he did, he'd want it to go to an heir of his choosing."

"Kayla?"

Jamie gave a wry smile. "I'm afraid that in my world, although females are treasured, they cannot rule alone, only as a consort."

"So whomever Kayla marries will be heir."

"Whoever marries a daughter of Baltheza will be a *possible* heir, but it will still be up to him to choose which husband will be his successor."

I frowned. As usual Jamie was talking in riddles. "Are you saying that Baltheza has more than one daughter?"

"It would appear so."

"But no sons?"

"No," he agreed.

"So, his other daughters—is Lord Daltas going to try to convince one of them to marry him?"

Jamie stood up and peered out of the window into the dark before turning back to me. "Lucky, Daltas is a high-ranking demon lord. He doesn't do *convincing*, or *courting*, or *wooing*. If the person he has chosen will not become his consort willingly, he will take her by force."

"As in 'marry' or 'rape'?" I asked in alarm.

Jamie just looked at me.

"Oh God," I said, trembling, "is Kayla safe?"

When he gave a snort of laughter I looked at him angrily. "Jamie, it's not funny," I scolded.

"Lucky, you know Kayla. It would take the bravest of the lords of the Underlands to try to force her to do anything. I think she has already proved that. No, it's not Kayla who's in danger—it never has been."

He sat back down in Kayla's chair and leaned back, still looking at me with the same unfathomable expression that had made me so uneasy earlier.

"What do you mean?" Then something dawned on me and I stared incredulously at him. "No." He stared back in silence. "No—you can't be serious, it can't be true!" I shivered as a whole platoon of Royal Marine Commandos marched over my grave. "You think I'm Lord Baltheza's *daughter*?"

This time Jamie's expression said it all.

"But that would make me Kayla's sister," I said. "How could I be? I'm not a demon."

He continued to look at me, but I kept protesting, "It can't be true—I *knew* my father; it was my mother who disappeared when I was too young to remember her."

"He was your father in name only," Jamie said, "but he never knew."

I shook my head emphatically. "It cannot be. He *was* my father."

"He thought he was, and he loved you as his own."

"But my mother . . . How? Why—? She must have known—"

"Only Lord Baltheza can tell you that. It's only recently he has even admitted to having another daughter."

"So why did Kayla come to me?"

"Because when you were born your aura shone so brightly that we were drawn to you. Whether Lord Baltheza told Kayla who you were, or whether she guessed—again, I don't know—but she came to earth to protect you . . . or possibly . . ."

He looked like he was about to say something else, but then he stopped and said, "The important thing is, Kayla decided to stay with you and now she loves you like the sister you are."

"'Or possibly' what, Jamie?"

He looked uncomfortable. "Kayla, as the only daughter of Lord Baltheza, would become queen even if only as consort. Another daughter would mean there is a chance she wouldn't. In both our worlds, people have died for less."

My head was spinning. "So when Kayla said there was a shortage of female demons and they were looking for humans to procreate with, she was lying?"

"As I said before, she was being a little selective with the truth," Jamie said, with another of his wry smiles. "What she meant was there was a shortage of *royal* females."

"Great," I said, "so what this boils down to is that I could be a daemon's route to the throne?"

"More or less—but Lord Baltheza would still have to name the demon his heir. He doesn't like Lord Daltas—then again, he doesn't like any of the other lords either. So I guess whomever takes you and Kayla as consorts will have an equal chance—"

I interrupted him, wailing, "But I don't want to marry a demon." The image of Lord Argon's naked body did nothing to help my rising panic.

"It may not come to that, not if Kayla chooses a mate to her father's liking."

"It sounds as though that might be difficult if he doesn't like any of the possible candidates."

"She doesn't have to marry a lord, just someone of sufficient standing to satisfy her father."

"Is there such a person?"

"Probably not—and anyway, Baltheza is not ready to give up his position—why would he? He could rule for millennia yet."

"Then why is this all suddenly so important?" My head was spinning as I tried to come to terms with what I was hearing.

"There are those who would rather he didn't rule forever."

I frowned at him. "Are you saying he could be deposed or . . . *assassinated?*"

"Lord Baltheza is not the most popular of rulers," Jamie admitted, "and his behavior has become increasingly erratic of late . . . erratic—and sadistic."

"Wonderful. So not only am I possibly the daughter of the demon king, but he's also a psychopath."

"I didn't say that."

I didn't bother to argue. "Is there anywhere I can go where I'll be safe? Like for sanctuary—a church, for example, or a convent? Could I join a convent?"

Jamie sniggered, and then he began to laugh. I had no idea what I had said that was so highly entertaining, but it took him several attempts to suppress his mirth.

"I'm sorry," he said, and despite his apology, he started laughing again.

"Ha-fucking-ha," I said, now seriously pissed off. "What's so flaming hilarious?"

"You," he gave a snort. "You in a convent—you wouldn't last five minutes!"

"Would I be safe, though?"

"Why would you be?"

"Well—holy ground?"

"I hate to break this to you, but just because man builds a temple and calls it a place of worship, that doesn't make it holy, at least not to us."

"So basically, I'm stuffed?"

"I keep telling you: I'll protect you and Shenanigans certainly wouldn't let you come to any harm. I'm not entirely sure about Kerfuffle—if Baltheza called for your death I can't be completely certain he would risk Baltheza's wrath over Kayla's—but for the moment he's solid."

"Why would Baltheza want me dead?" I asked in alarm.

"I doubt he does, but Kayla is demanding he keep you safe and despite everything, he does want her back at court. Her antics certainly used to keep him entertained."

"If I agree to go to your world, you say you'll protect me?"

"I give you my oath."

"I don't understand why you should care."

"Let's just say it's in my job description," he said, with a smile.

"Is it part of your job description to talk in riddles all the time?" I asked.

He got down on one knee and took my hand in his hand, then looking me straight in the eyes, he raised it to his lips and kissed my knuckles.

"I swear my allegiance to you and I am yours for as long as you need me," he said. It was almost as if he were performing some ritual I didn't understand. "And now, my lady, are you ready to visit your true home?"

"I'm afraid," I whispered.

He took my other hand in his and drew me to my feet. "Don't be," he said.

He waited while I put on a pair of boots and then led me out of the bedroom and across the landing to the bathroom. He opened the door and the room beyond had vanished. All that remained was pitch-black nothingness.

I stopped in the hallway. "Jamie?"

He reached out to me and after a moment's hesitation I took his hand. He smiled a hundred-watt smile, which made my knees go a little bit weak, and then with a flurry of feathers his wings unfurled and he wrapped his arms around me.

"Ready?" he asked, looking down at me, but I couldn't speak because I was so scared. "It'll be all right," he said, and his grip tightened around me.

He stepped into the room and suddenly the cottage was gone and we were in total darkness. Wind was whistling past my ears and I felt like I was falling, but Jamie was holding me so tight I could feel the steady beat of his heart against my chest, and his obvious lack of fear helped calm me a little. His wings wrapped around me and I wondered why he wasn't trying to fly.

"Almost there," he said, shouting so I could hear him over the wind, and then his wings did unfurl and we shot upward for a second or so before leveling out and then gliding down until our feet touched the ground.

"All right?" he asked, relaxing his grip on me a little and looking down at my face.

I gave him what was probably a shaky smile, not trusting myself to talk, and he released me, although he did keep one arm draped across my shoulders. I looked around, curious and wanting to get my first glimpse of this strange, new world.

It was dark, but not as in pitch-black, under-the-ground, deep-in-the-depths-of-the-earth dark; it was dark like night, and when I looked upward I could see two red orbs above us, one slightly overlapping the other, and dark clouds speeding across the sky.

"They are our moons," he said, following my gaze.

"You have two moons?"

"And two suns."

"Are we under the earth?"

"Not so much," he said with a chuckle.

"More riddles."

"No, just a fact: though we call it the Underlands, our world doesn't exist beneath your world, but rather in tandem with it. Come, I'll take you to Lord Baltheza's court."

He went to step away, but I hung back. I felt a bit like I was going mad, or dreaming, or having some crazy nightmare.

He dropped his arm from my shoulders and faced me, and gazing into my eyes, he promised, "It will be all right you know."

"Kayla said she was bargaining for my safety—" I couldn't stop my voice from wobbling. "What if she hasn't managed to get it yet?"

"She has."

"When I spoke to her earlier she said I still wasn't safe."

"Word came after you left us."

"Call me suspicious, Jamie, but how do I know I can trust you?" I frowned as it dawned on me that we had left the two demons Kayla had entrusted with my safety behind in my world. If Jamie was the enemy, I had just walked straight into his trap. I stepped back from him.

It was as if he knew exactly what I was thinking. "Do you really think Kerfuffle and Shenanigans would let me take you anywhere without their knowledge?"

"We were upstairs—they were downstairs; they might not even realize I've gone yet."

"When a doorway between our worlds is opened, we can always feel it."

I still wasn't convinced. "Can only your kind feel it? Because I didn't feel a thing," I said, crossing my arms and staring up at him.

"When we used the bowl of water in the kitchen to call upon Kayla, did you not notice anything?"

I started to shake my head and then I remembered the strange sensation of the air vibrating and the pressure building in my ears. "Yes, I think I did—like my ears needing to pop . . ."

"They would have felt something similar—anyway, they'll be joining us shortly. When we go to court you'll have a full complement of guard, as befits visiting royalty."

"Royalty?"

"Haven't you listened to a single thing I've said?"

"I . . . It's just too much to take in."

He put his arm back around my shoulders and began to usher me along a narrow path. As my eyes adjusted to the darkness I began to make out some of my surroundings. We could have been in a park or a meadow, I wasn't sure which. We were flanked by grass on either side, and when I picked a stem and brought it closer I thought it might be rust-red.

"Where are we?" I asked.

"In the grounds surrounding Lord Baltheza's court. This path leads to the royal fortress."

"We're going to his court now?"

"Not yet; we have to meet Kerfuffle and Shenanigans, then find you a steed fit for a Princess of the Blood."

"A steed? As in a horse?"

Jamie chuckled. "You'll see."

What I could see was that I was going to get serious frown lines before too long. With a conscious effort I rearranged my face into what I hoped wasn't too stupid an expression and walked along beside the man I really hoped with all my heart was my friend.

The path stretched on and on into the distance. Had we been back at home we would have already walked to the village and back several times, but I resisted the urge to ask how long it would be before we reached our destination. Here on this path, flanked by lawns as far as the eye could see, I felt safe. If danger approached out here, I'd see it coming. In a court, surrounded by demons, it'd be another thing altogether.

Suddenly a thought occurred to me. "Why aren't we flying?" I asked.

"Normally I would," he said.

"Oh," I said, realizing, "I'm too heavy to carry."

He gave my shoulder a squeeze. "Not at all, but there are things that fly the skies at night from which I couldn't protect you if you were in my arms. On the ground it's another matter."

I glanced up at the sky, any feeling of safety I might have been harboring gone. I couldn't stop myself from shivering, but he hugged me. "Don't worry, you're quite safe with me."

I hoped he was right, though I badly wished I was back at home and tucked up in my own bed.

The path led us over a hill, and as we walked the landscape in front of us changed. I could see a long line of trees, standing tall and straight like a wall in front of us. The smell of something like pine but not quite the same scented the air. When we reached the trees we found a road wide enough for two cars to pass each other.

"Do you have cars here?"

Jamie laughed. "There are very few mechanical devices in our world."

"Why?"

"We have no oil and no coal—and so no pollution; a conscious decision has been made to keep it that way."

"No electricity?" I asked, wondering how on earth they had existed living in the Dark Ages for so long.

"Have any of the progressions in technology really made mankind happy? As soon as any advance is made, someone somewhere finds a way of making it into a weapon. This may be a violent world at times, but at least we only kill each other in the singular. There are no weapons of mass destruction here."

I supposed it did make a sort of sense, and who was I to argue? I had only just arrived. Then I had a thought. "So how do you know how to drive?"

He grinned. "It's one of the perks of being a Guardian. I have to fit in when I'm in your world, and I love driving."

Good for him. Maybe this was something I would like about his world—no cars.

His cheerful expression faded. "I learned to drive in the 1920s—it was a bad era for interference between the realms. At that time there were a lot of men in your world who were intent on calling upon those from mine." We started along the road.

I didn't like the sound of that, but I was beginning to flag and was too tired to respond. I'd have to ask about that some other time.

"It's not far now," Jamie assured me.

It was darker walking down the avenue of trees, and I could see very little except the very long and very straight road. The landscape had a slightly orange hue to it and I guessed it had something to do with the color of the two moons glowing down upon the rust-red grass.

Then the road ahead began to widen and the trees opened on either side into an arc, revealing dark stone walls and a building straight out of a children's fairy tale—or nightmare, depending on which books you read. Tall circular turrets rose upward and a drawbridge over a moat led to high walls and battlements that dominated the skyline. I could even see a portcullis at the entrance. It looked like a proper medieval fortress, though this was no English Heritage ruin. Within its walls I could see a castle, with light glowing through its many windows.

"Is this it?"

Jamie nodded, his expression grim. "This is Kayla's home: the court of Lord Baltheza."

"You don't seem very happy we've arrived."

Jamie glanced at me. "I'll be a lot happier when we find Kerfuffle and Shenanigans—and your steed."

I didn't disagree: the demons I had found so disconcerting and threatening when they'd first appeared in my sitting room had proven to be very important to my wellbeing.

Jamie took me by the hand and led me off the road and through the trees. The ground was soft beneath my feet, though it didn't feel quite like grass; it was springy, even spongy—maybe composted leaves, or needles that had rotted where they fell. I could no longer smell the trees' fragrance; it had been overwhelmed by a pungent aroma that filled my nostrils, making me want to sneeze.

"Aren't we going to the castle?"

"Yes, but not through the front door. I would rather your arrival was a surprise to all concerned—particularly if you decide to leave. It won't be so easy to return you to the Overlands once Baltheza knows you're here."

"But I will be able to leave?" I asked in alarm. "I will be able to go home?"

"This is your home," Jamie said, taking me by both shoulders and looking down at me. "This is your *real* home."

"You lied to me, didn't you?" I said, crossing my arms and glaring at him. "You told me you would bring me here just for a visit, but you never intended to take me back."

His eyes dropped and he stood there, head bowed, as if struggling to come to a decision. Eventually he raised his head again and looked me in the eyes. "Lucky, if I think you're in real danger, or if this place makes you so miserable you can't thrive, I'll do everything in my power to take you back to the Overlands."

"You promise?" I asked, though it didn't really detract from the fact he had lied to me, *again*.

"I promise," he said, his fingers giving my shoulders one last squeeze. Then he let me go and took hold of my hand. "Come, now we must fly."

It turned out that he meant that quite literally, and the prospect chased away my apprehension, at least temporarily. He pulled me into his arms and with one beat of his powerful wings we were up in the air and gliding over the fortress walls. The sensation was wonderful—not only was I being held in the tight embrace of an extremely handsome angel, I was flying through the night sky with the wind blowing through my hair.

Sadly, the flight was over far too soon, and we dipped lower and came to rest just inside the fortress walls. Jamie held me for a little longer than perhaps he had to, but when he released me I wished he would take me in his arms again. Despite my reservations, despite his lies, I still felt safe with him.

"This way," he whispered, taking hold of my hand again and leading me around to what I imagined was the back of the castle.

Patches of flickering light from the upper windows marked the ground with pale golden rectangles, though there was little else to illuminate our way. If anything, it was even darker within the walls. I could smell wood smoke, and something meaty roasting, and my taste buds began to tingle. That made me remember our meal at the golf club—how long ago had that been? And how long since Philip had been taken? I couldn't help but wonder what had become of him.

I didn't have time to ponder on Philip's fate for long, though, for my worry was overridden by concern for my own wellbeing when a huge figure stepped out of the shadows in front of us. Jamie stopped and I clung on tight to his arm.

"Guardian," a voice whispered, "over here."

"Shenanigans?" I felt Jamie relax beneath my hand and I managed to breathe again.

"Follow me." He led us through a gate and into a yard lit by burning torches at the far end. Mr. Kerfuffle was waiting for us by a large wooden door of a huge barnlike structure.

"This way," he said, gesturing for us to follow him into the barn.

There were more torches inside and I saw immediately it wasn't a barn really, more a stable block, with a large indoor training area to one side.

"Is he here?" Jamie asked.

Mr. Kerfuffle looked very pleased with himself. "Over there," he said, pointing to a stall at the far end.

The other stalls we passed were empty, although they all had fresh straw on the ground. Even here, in this strange place, the straw smelled the same as at home and that was somehow comforting. What I did find rather odd was the size of each stall. They were high-roofed and very wide; in fact, they were each large enough to house half a dozen horses; I doubted a giraffe would have had to lower its head much to stand upright.

I knew very little about horses, but I did think they usually had separate stalls. Maybe it was different here.

"Look," I said, "I know you said I needed a steed, but to tell the truth, I can't ride. I've never even sat on a beach-ride pony, let alone a full-grown horse."

Mr. Kerfuffle and Mr. Shenanigans exchanged an amused glance and the smaller demon began to giggle, which was a strangely disconcerting and rather scary sound.

"Jamie, I mean it: I can't ride and I don't really want to."

Jamie indicated the last stall.

We stopped outside and I looked in.

"This is Pyrites," he said.

For a moment I was speechless. I closed my eyes and opened them again to make sure I wasn't seeing things. Then I did it again.

"You are joking?" I eventually managed to say.

"You need a steed to get you around."

"Jamie, it's a *dragon*."

"He'll get you out of harm's way if, for some reason, I'm unable to take you to safety."

"Like if he's dead," added Mr. Kerfuffle helpfully.

"No," Jamie said, with a glare in the demon's direction, "just if I'm better served delaying the enemy."

I looked at the creature with trepidation. Even though the dragon was lying flat on his stomach with his head between his outstretched claws, he still towered above me. If he opened his jaws he could swallow me in one gulp, which wasn't exactly comforting. All I could do was hope that Jamie and the demons knew best.

Pyrites was, I suppose, a handsome dragon. His scales were a shimmering combination of reds, oranges and yellows, with the occasional fleck of gold. His eyes were an amazing emerald-amethyst-sapphire kaleidoscope glow, and that alone made it hard to imagine he could be dangerous.

Jamie led me closer. "Hold out your hand to him."

I swallowed hard and tentatively lifted my right hand toward his enormous snout.

"I'd make it your left hand," Jamie added, "just in case."

I snatched my hand back in alarm and the demons both sniggered.

"Only joking," Jamie said.

"Not funny," I said, but my three protectors obviously thought it was hilarious.

I ignored their laughter as best as I could and slowly held out my hand toward the creature. He raised his head from between his claws and stretched forward until his snout was just above me, then sniffed. With a tilt of the head that was almost dainty for a creature so huge, he shifted so his nose was just in front of my hand.

"What do I do now?" I whispered.

"Pet him," Jamie replied. "Stroke his nose."

I took a deep breath and then with my heart in mouth I ran my fingers across his snout. His head pushed up against my hand as if wanting more, so I traced my fingers across his scales again and a small puff of smoke erupted from his nose.

"He likes you," Mr. Shenanigans said.

"He does? How can you tell?"

"Oh yes," said the demon. "If he didn't, it wouldn't have been smoke."

I laughed. "Yeah, right."

"Too right," Jamie said, and this time no one laughed. I swallowed hard. I was beginning to think if I survived forty-eight hours in this place I'd be lucky.

Pyrites pushed at my hand again and I rubbed his nose a little harder and his head flopped back to the ground so his eyes were level with mine. This time when I stroked him, his eyes rolled back in his head and his eyelids fluttered.

"I think he's in love," said Jamie as another small puff of smoke plumed out of the dragon's nostrils and he gave a soft sigh. "Looks like you've made another conquest."

I managed to drag my eyes away from Pyrites—who had begun to make a strange purring sound deep in the back of his throat—and glance at Jamie, who gave a small jerk of the head toward Mr. Shenanigans and with a start, I realized he was right: the big demon had been following me around like a faithful guard dog asking for nothing other than to be noticed. I shivered as though someone had walked over my grave. It made me uncomfortable to be adored so, but on the practical side, I knew in my heart Mr. Shenanigans at least would never betray me.

Pyrites pushed against my hand, demanding more attention, and I stroked him with the palm of my hand as I would a cat. His scales were warm to the touch and felt a little like varnished wood, or maybe a tightly closed pinecone. He lifted his head to one side, his eyes half closed.

"Scratch under his chin," Jamie said.

I did as I was told, and found his scales there were smaller and softer, and lighter in color: a pale lemon with streaks of gold. He was clearly more sensitive there, as his flanks shivered as I scratched and tickled him.

"He's beautiful," I said.

"I'm glad you like him, because he's now yours forever."

I glanced back at Jamie. "Forever?"

"The underside of a drakon's chin is his most vulnerable spot. By offering it to you it means he's trusting you with his life."

"But he doesn't know me. I could be horrible."

Jamie pointed at Pyrites. "A drakon knows his master or mistress from the first moment they touch. If you hadn't been right for him he would have shrunk away and showed his displeasure."

"Which can be a very nasty business indeed," Mr. Kerfuffle added. "Do you remember Lord Raynard's youngest?" he asked the others.

"What happened to him?" I asked, still scratching Pyrites's chin. It was actually quite soothing. "Or do I not want to know?"

"The drakon roasted him to medium-rare, then ate him," Mr. Shenanigans said.

"Mind you, he was a little shit. It would have been the same story whatever the drakon," Mr. Kerfuffle added.

"So if Pyrites hadn't liked me he would have had me for dinner."

"That was an extreme case. Young Pyrites here would probably just have singed you a bit."

"You were never at any risk," Mr. Shenanigans said. "We knew he would like you."

"How?" I asked.

He frowned as though puzzled. "Because we do," he said.

Once again, I was left speechless. Whereas Jamie spoke in riddles, Mr. Shenanigans simply told it how it was: so not only was the demon loyal, he would tell me the truth, which would be very useful if I had to stay in this world for any length of time.

"Right," Jamie said, "we need to find one more to form your guard and then we'll be ready to enter court."

"Another?" I asked.

"You need at least five. With Pyrites we are but four," Mr. Shenanigans pointed out.

"Pyrites counts as a guard?"

"Oh yes," both demons said together.

"Pyrites will defend you to the death," Mr. Shenanigans said, "as will I."

"Come on," Jamie said, "we need to get moving." Pyrites scrambled to his feet and padded forward until he stood by my side. Jamie grinned at me. "Now you even look like a princess," he said.

The others nodded their heads in agreement. "Only those of the Blood are served by a drakon," Mr. Kerfuffle said.

If he thought I would find this comforting, he was mistaken. I didn't want to be "of the blood"; I wanted to go home. But before I knew it we were moving again.

Mr. Kerfuffle handed me a long length of dark gray material. "A cloak, to hide your clothing," he explained. "Your garb will immediately give you away as one from the Overlands."

"What about you?" I asked, but even before the words had fully left my mouth, the air shimmered again and black Mafia-style suits disappeared, to be replaced by shirts, jerkins and breeches.

I turned to Jamie, who was now bare-chested, his wings in full view, wearing pale breeches tucked into tan knee-high boots of soft leather.

"We'll get you something more suitable to wear when we get to court," Jamie said.

I wrapped the cloak around me and Jamie lifted the hood up so it covered my head and hung down over my brow to keep my face in shadow.

We left the barn through a back entrance, close to the stall where Pyrites had been. Mr. Shenanigans led the way, with Mr. Kerfuffle trotting along beside him in an effort to keep up. I knew how he felt.

"Boys," I called, keeping my voice as low as I could, "can we slow down a bit?"

Mr. Shenanigans immediately slowed and looked around at me, his expression apologetic. "Sorry, mistress," he said, and then continued at what must have been a crawl for him, though to me it was still a fast walk. At least Mr. Kerfuffle's little legs were no longer pumping as hard, although the pace didn't appear to worry him the same way it did me. Jamie stayed by my side, as did Pyrites, and every now and then the dragon would rub his snout against my shoulder as if to let me know he was there. The first time he nearly knocked me out but he learned from his mistake and after that he was a lot gentler.

We crossed a small unlit courtyard. The demons went on ahead, just dark shadows in the gloom and the only sound was the clicking of Pyrites's claws on the stone slabs beneath our feet, echoing between the walls.

"Where are we going?" I asked.

"There's a small town within the fortress walls, and where there's a town, there's always an inn. It's there we're most likely to find your fifth guard."

"Why five? Why not four? Or six?"

"A child of a minor lord would have one or two; his father two or three. Lord Daltas has seven, I believe, and Lord Baltheza thirteen. Five is the correct number for your station: it's an acknowledgment that you're royalty, but it isn't pretentious. Once you're welcomed into court I imagine Kayla will see you have more."

"My having bodyguards is all to do with court protocol?"

"Trust me, Lucky, you having bodyguards has nothing to do with protocol—the *number*, maybe, but you need them."

"So Kayla has bodyguards, too?"

"Kayla can largely look after herself, but yes she has. Though I think she has chosen her guards more for their looks rather than for any professional ability."

I wasn't quite sure what he meant, but I didn't have time to inquire because he was ushering me through the gate. To my surprise, the gate closed with Jamie on the wrong side. I was about to protest when I heard the sound of bolts being shoved home, then after a moment or so there was a rustle of feathers and Jamie dropped down beside me. No sooner had his feet hit the ground than we were off again.

Now we were hurrying through dark, narrow alleyways. Shards of golden lamplight cut through gaps between curtained windows or under doorways, staining the path ahead. Occasionally there were burning torches held in brackets next to doors, and the flickering light allowed brief glimpses of my surroundings. I caught sniffs of roasting meat or boiling vegetables, and sometimes more unpleasant odors permeated the air: rotting fish and garbage mixed with other smells I really didn't want to contemplate too deeply.

Often we heard voices from behind the closed doors; some loud and raucous, others low and menacing. In one particular lane Jamie threw his arm across my shoulders and hurried me along so fast I was almost running, but I didn't complain. The place had smelled bad, and the unpleasant crawling sensation on my arms and the back of my neck warned me something unwholesome was loitering in the shadows.

We turned a corner and found ourselves in a courtyard where candlelight blazed from windows. There was music playing and voices shouting and laughing; there was even drunken singing. We had found the inn.

Smoke curled from the chimney and I could smell burning wood and something cooking. A door flew open and bright orange light spilled out across the cobblestones. A demon lurched out, swaying slightly as he staggered around the side, one hand on the wall, presumably to keep him upright.

"When we get inside keep your head down; you look far too human to go unnoticed."

"That's because I am human."

All three gave me looks that suggested differently.

"Pyrites," Jamie said, "wait here and keep watch."

The dragon bowed his head and then sat back on his haunches.

"Good boy," I said, and was rewarded with a small puff of smoke and a low rumble in the back of his throat. "Is that good?" I asked.

Jamie smiled. "You'd soon know if he wasn't happy."

I wasn't at all sure I wanted to find out what Jamie meant—several unwanted images of roasted flesh and the unfortunate Lord Raynard's offspring sprung into my head.

Jamie took me by my elbow and guided me across the yard toward the inn. Mr. Shenanigans and Mr. Kerfuffle walked in first and I heard greetings being shouted across the tavern, and some good-natured banter; those two were clearly well known in the establishment. Then the occupants noticed Jamie and me and a hush fell over the room. I kept my head down, but I quickly realized it wasn't me who was the problem.

"Guardian," a voice said, and I raised my head a little to look out from under my shroud of a hood. The demon behind the bar was the size of a grizzly bear, with a head that resembled a large boar. Tusks curled out from below either side of his upper lip and the whole of his

head was covered in coarse auburn hair. The rest of his body was that
of a large man, although when he placed his hands down on the bar I
could see he had only two wide, trotter-like fingers on each.

"We want no trouble here," he said to Jamie.

"You'll have none from me," he replied.

The demon visibly relaxed and his customers began to chatter among
themselves once again, filling the room with laughter and affable conversation. We followed the demons across the bar to an empty table in
the corner, and as soon as Jamie and I were seated, Mr. Kerfuffle walked
to the other side of the tavern while Mr. Shenanigans stood scanning
the other customers before sitting down beside us.

"What'll you be having?" asked the waitress—although looking
at the way she was dressed, I did wonder if she would technically be
called a serving wench. She was around five feet in height and her
ample bosom was in real danger of overspilling her white cotton
blouse.

"A jug of ale and four tankards, please, Leila," Mr. Shenanigans said.

She looked at him from below long purple lashes and flicked her lush
lilac curls away from her brow, then gave him a slow smile. "I haven't
seen you in a while," she said, then ran her pointed tongue suggestively
across her top lip.

"I've been away on business," he said.

She glanced at Jamie, but barely spared me a moment's attention.
"Business with the Guardian," she said. "My, you have gone up in the
world."

He gave her a lopsided smile, and I was sure that if he could have
blushed he would have turned bright pink. He got to his feet and moved
her slightly away from the table before whispering something to her
that caused her to glance back at us with a frown. Then he whispered
something else and she batted her eyelids at him and turned away with
a swish of her skirt, sashaying across the tavern with a wanton sway of
her hips and leaving me in no doubt that if Mr. Shenanigans was up for
it, he could be having a very interesting night.

He watched her all the way back to the bar, then sat down with a
sigh.

"There'll be other nights," Jamie said to him.

"Leila seems very . . . nice," I said. It was the best word I could think of.

Mr. Kerfuffle arrived back at our table at the same time as the drinks. Leila plunked the tray on the table and bent—probably lower than she needed to—to pass the tankards to each of us. She certainly made sure we all had a good view of her very ample cleavage. Mr. Kerfuffle leered unashamedly, while Mr. Shenanigans tried to avert his gaze. Jamie's eyes sparkled and I could see he was trying very hard not to laugh at the demon's discomfiture.

"Did you find him?" Jamie asked Mr. Kerfuffle once the barmaid had gone, but he shook his head.

"No. Apparently he hasn't been around for some time, though there is another who might be worth a try."

"Like?"

The demon took a swig of his beer and mumbled something into his tankard.

Jamie narrowed his eyes. "Sorry? I didn't quite hear."

He mumbled again and Mr. Shenanigans shot him a look that wasn't entirely friendly. "Did you just say what I think you did?"

He slammed his tankard on the table and growled, "If you can do any better you're welcome to try."

Jamie leaned back in his chair, his eyes not leaving Mr. Kerfuffle. His expression was difficult to read, but if this had been a barroom scene in an old western movie I would have expected all three of them to be fingering their revolvers by now.

"What's wrong?" I asked, but no one answered me. Mr. Kerfuffle shifted in his chair and Mr. Shenanigans studied the contents of his tankard. Jamie crossed his arms, still watching Kerfuffle.

"Come on, what is it?" Still no one spoke. Frustrated, I decided to wait for them to come out with it and picked up my tankard instead. I sniffed the dark amber liquid. It smelled delicious; there was a dark, malty edge to it and a fruitiness that hinted at raspberries. I wasn't sure whether I should risk it or not: it might be nectar to demons, but I didn't know that it wouldn't kill me . . .

Once again Jamie could have been reading my mind. "It won't harm you," he said, but his stare was still fixed on the smaller demon.

I took a small sip of the drink and rolled the liquid around my tongue. It wasn't half bad. I took another mouthful and then looked at my three morose companions. They still hadn't spoken.

"So, is someone going to tell me what's going on?"

Jamie glanced at me, then gestured at Mr. Kerfuffle. "I'm beginning to wonder if Kerfuffle really is on your side."

The little demon jumped to his feet, knocking his chair back with a clatter, and if the table hadn't been between them I think he might have gone for Jamie's throat. His eyes looked dangerous, dark chips of anger, and his usually soft pink cheeks glowed crimson. "I'm more on Mistress Lucinda's side than you will ever be," he snarled. "It's *your* motives I would question. This is not Guardian business."

"It *is* my business," Jamie said, "and I hardly think a harbinger of death and destruction is a suitable addition to our number."

"I would have thought a creature who can bring a demon to his knees with a mere touch would be a *very* suitable addition."

Jamie studied Mr. Kerfuffle with a thoughtful frown. "Very well," he said at last, getting to his feet. "Let's go and find him."

Mr. Shenanigans threw some coins on the table as he got up to leave. They looked like gold to me, and if they were, by their size alone I would have thought them worth a small fortune.

As Mr. Kerfuffle stomped out of the inn ahead of us, muttering to himself as he went, I said to Jamie, "I think you've really upset him."

Jamie gave a snort. "I'll do more than upset him if this goes badly."

"What's the problem?" I asked.

"*Who* is the problem is more the question," Mr. Shenanigans said. It looked like even he wasn't happy with his small friend.

"Don't you start talking in riddles as well," I said. "It's bad enough Jamie can never give me a straight answer to a simple question."

Jamie stopped midstride. "You're about to meet one seriously dangerous individual. He's a bringer of death—literally. Where he walks, death and disaster follow." Mr. Shenanigans looked at me and nodded as Jamie continued, "When he traveled across Europe the Black Death was not far behind him; when he passed through the streets of London the Great Fire kindled; when he left the city of Pompeii it was consumed by molten rock. He doesn't often visit your world now as humankind is destroying itself quite nicely all on its own, but if the need arises it will be he who will proceed the next epidemic or cause the seas to rise up and consume whole populations."

"If you're telling me I'm about to meet a dude wearing a long black robe and carrying a scythe I think I'll pass," I said.

Jamie laughed, though it wasn't a happy sound. "No, he's not the Grim Reaper. The Reaper is another creature altogether." He started walking again and I watched him for a moment, not at all sure I wanted to follow.

Mr. Shenanigans hovered by my side. "The Guardian won't let any harm come to you. He is more than equal to the demon of death."

Pyrites padded to my side and stood there, paddling from foot to foot. I laid my hand on his flank. Even the dragon was unhappy at the prospect of meeting my fifth bodyguard. "It's all right, boy," I said, and bracing myself for what was to come, I followed Jamie, who had stopped at the corner to wait for me.

"It's best you stay close," he said to me. "Pyrites will be by your side. Shenanigans, you watch our backs."

The demon nodded. It looked like any previous animosity between him and Jamie when they'd found him at the cottage had been put to one side, if not forgotten. For which I was grateful, it may be that their cooperation would keep me alive.

When I reached Jamie he took hold of my hand and raised it to his lips, brushing them against my knuckles as he had done once before. "Your safety is my sole concern. If the death demon pledges an oath to protect you, we can rest easy in his company. If not, you'll do what I say without argument."

I frowned. "Why? What reason would he have to harm me?"

"The fact that he's here, right now, gives me cause for concern. It may be he has been sent to do another's bidding, though that isn't usually his way, but until we speak with him we won't know."

He tucked my arm under his and led me around the corner into a small yard lit by several brightly burning torches. Beer barrels were stacked in neat piles near a back entrance to the inn, together with crates of empty bottles. There were two wooden outhouses—I didn't need to guess what they were for; the smell as we passed by was quite enough. We walked through another doorway into a high-roofed barn, similar to the one where we had found Pyrites.

Mr. Kerfuffle was standing halfway down the barn. His face twisted into a scowl upon seeing us and he immediately turned his back and stomped toward the far end, which was distinctly dark and uninviting.

I heard Mr. Shenanigans sigh, and Pyrites nudged me with his snout; Jamie's grip on my arm tightened. All three were uneasy and I could feel my own anxiety levels soaring. If I wasn't safe with a demon, a dragon and an angel as my guards, would I ever be safe again?

It didn't help that there were no torches burning apart from those just inside the entrance—but then I realized that it would have been a little foolhardy to have a lot of open flame in a wooden barn filled with dry straw.

We passed several stalls blocked off by bolted gates, and although I couldn't see inside, I could hear sounds made by the sleeping creatures. I would have liked to have taken a look inside, to see what other beasts were used as steeds in this world, but that would have to wait; right now I was about to meet a demon who sounded quite strange enough.

Mr. Kerfuffle stopped by the main entrance. Despite his grumpy expression, he waited for us to join him.

"Is he here?" Jamie asked, and Mr. Kerfuffle scowled at him.

"Don't freak out," Mr. Shenanigans said. "It was a shock, that's all."

"After all these years? You at least should know to trust me," the little demon said, and when his friend nodded his agreement, he gave a sniff and his dour expression softened a little. "He may not come anyway." He gestured for us to follow, then stepped through another doorway and back outside.

There were lamps hanging around the space, but their flickering light hardly penetrated the darkness. I pushed back my hood, which kept flopping forward so I couldn't see and was irritating me beyond belief. Jamie didn't object, so I guessed now we were away from the inn it didn't matter.

Pyrites dropped back on his haunches while Jamie and the two demons scanned the courtyard.

"Well, hello," a voice drawled from somewhere in the shadows, and I looked toward the sound, but could see only darkness. I glanced at Jamie, who was also searching for the owner of the voice.

"It's been a very long time, brother," the voice said, and a figure peeled away from the gloom.

Just as Jamie was everything you might imagine an angel to be, this demon was the epitome of the Devil. At first his skin looked coal-black, but as the light from the lamps caught him in their glow I could see his face and bare chest were actually a shining dark maroon.

Short, sharp horns protruded from either side of his brow, and hair a few shades darker than his skin was swept back against his head—it wasn't until he turned slightly that I could see it was pulled into a tight braid that fell to just below his hips.

He was wearing black leather pants tucked into black leather boots, and had a tail that was long and thin with an arrow-point at the end that curled around past his thigh and waved back and forth as though on a gentle breeze.

His smile was dazzlingly white and his eyes crinkled with suppressed humor, his gold and green irises glowing brightly.

"So," he said, looking straight at me, "you're who all the fuss is about." Jamie moved, putting himself between me and the devil-demon. "Aren't you going to introduce us, brother?"

Pyrites got to his feet and moved closer to me, making a low rumbling sound in his chest, and the stranger threw back his head and laughed. "Oh dear, dear, dear! We are all mighty suspicious, aren't we?"

He took a step closer, and Jamie raised a hand. "Stay where you are, Jinx. Until I know your intentions I'm treating you as an unfriendly influence."

"James, my boy, if I wanted your lady-friend dead, it would be so. But as it happens, I'm thinking she's probably of far more interest to me alive." Then he turned to me and studied my face. "It's lucky that you hold no resemblance to Baltheza. I think I'd have been tempted to put you out of your misery for that alone if you had." He chuckled.

For a demon who apparently brought death and destruction everywhere he went he was pretty jolly—but then, I thought, why wouldn't he be? It wouldn't be him doing the dying, after all.

He took another step toward us and in a moment of panic, I remembered how Henri had gradually moved closer and closer until he was within pouncing distance. I shuddered.

Now fully illuminated beneath the lamps, Jinx's skin shimmered with a dark ruby glow and I realized I didn't think I'd ever seen anyone so stunning. I couldn't say beautiful, though like Kayla he *was* beautiful, in a terrifying way. The lamplight caressed his body, highlighting every toned muscle and every sculpted curve, dip and plateau. I could hardly drag my eyes away from him.

I think he realized the effect he was having upon me as his smile grew even broader, if that was possible. He swooped down into a low bow. "I'm Jinx," he said, "and you must be . . . ?"

"Lucky—" My voice came out as a low, husky whisper, which was entirely unintentional, and too sexy by far. I swallowed and tried again. "I'm Lucky de Salle."

"Lucky, Lucky, Lucky. And are you lucky, Lucky? Are you a lucky lady?"

"You haven't killed me yet," I said, and I felt Jamie's hand tighten around my arm; I was sure that if I'd managed to drag my eyes away from Jinx I would have seen his alarm for me written all over his face.

Jinx roared with laughter. "You make your own luck, lucky Lucky," he said. "James, my boy, isn't she grand? I can see why you've involved yourself in this merry game."

"It's not a game, Jinx," Jamie said.

"Ah, you take life too seriously."

"You take death too lightly."

The smile on the demon's face softened and though he still smiled, now it was tinged with an expression bordering on sadness, or maybe regret; I wasn't sure.

"That's where you're wrong, brother," Jinx said, "I take death very seriously indeed." His bright eyes slipped back to me. "Why have you brought her here?"

"The Lady Kayla wished it," Jamie replied.

"And what the Lady Kayla wants, the Lady Kayla gets?" Jinx said.

"In this case, yes. Lucky has already been visited by one of the court assassins—but I suppose you already know that."

The demon didn't answer; instead, he looked over my other companions, studying them one by one. "And how did you two get involved in all this?" he asked the two demons. "No offense, but neither of you are High Court."

"If you were Kayla, would you trust anyone from her father's court?" Jamie asked.

"We have, on occasion, been of service to Lady Kayla," said Mr. Kerfuffle, standing up straight, "particularly while she has been away these last few years, keeping her abreast of things at court and the like."

Jinx's brow creased as if he were in thought. He pursed his lips—then, with a flash of white, the smile was back.

"So, brother, you've pledged to serve this lucky, lucky lady?"

"I have."

"And you two?" Jinx said to Mr. Shenanigans and Mr. Kerfuffle.

"We have," they echoed.

"An impressive entourage," Jinx said, moving just that little bit closer.

"State your intent or stop right where you are," Jamie said, and Pyrites took a step forward and breathed out a puff of smoke—a very warm puff of smoke.

If Jinx was worried he didn't show it. "Easy now, fella; I'll not be hurting your mistress this day."

"This day? I rather hope you actually mean 'any day'?" I said, and once again I felt Jamie tense beside me. I hoped he didn't think I was trying to be brave. I was scared half to death, but I had this feeling that Jinx was somehow testing me, and if I was found wanting I might be a smoldering pile of ashes or a moldering corpse pretty soon. Neither option was particularly appealing, so if I had to play mind games with him to stay safe, I would. I just had to hope we were playing by the same rules.

Jinx grinned. "You know something, brother? I'm beginning to quite like her."

"State your intent," Jamie repeated.

"I caught a whisper on the wind of dark and dangerous aim. On this night there should be death and for one some meaningful gain."

Jamie pushed me behind him and as Mr. Shenanigans encircled me in his arms Jamie said, "You'll have to go through me first."

"He who whispered hid behind a cloak of shadows and mist. If you wish a person dead you should at least have the courage to let them know your name"—Jinx took another step toward us—"and I am not a hired assassin."

He dropped to one knee and reached out a hand. "Step aside, Guardian."

Jamie hesitated, then did as he said.

"My lucky lady," Jinx said, "I will join your guard and protect you from all harm as best I am able. This I swear."

Mr. Shenanigans opened his arms and nudged me forward and I gave the kneeling demon my hand. He brushed my fingers with his lips just as Jamie had done, then he jumped to his feet, took hold of my other hand and twirled me around and around before turning me and swinging me back toward him—then he lowered me down, his body sloping close against mine, in a movement any champion ballroom dancer would have been proud of, and pressed a kiss against my lips. It wasn't a soft, gentle kiss, but what my father—or the man I had always thought was my father—would have called a real smacker. It left my lips tingling and me gasping for breath.

Jinx grinned at my shell-shocked expression, pulled me back up and spun me around one last time before releasing me to stumble back into Jamie's arms. Jamie pulled me against his chest and I could feel the tension in him. Then he slowly exhaled and relaxed.

When I looked up at him he was staring at Jinx. I looked at the death demon, who wasn't actually laughing, but I could see he was close to it: his eyes glittered with suppressed mirth and his lips twitched upward at the corners.

"You've given your oath," Jamie said.

"Aye, I have," the demon replied.

"And your mark."

Jinx grinned.

"The Lady Kayla—"

"—will be very pleased," Jinx said.

"I somehow think not."

Jinx chuckled. "They do say to be careful of what you wish for."

I had no idea what was going on between the two of them—Jamie wasn't happy, though he'd relaxed. But I didn't bother to ask—I knew I would only get more riddles. Still, as far as I was concerned, I could only be grateful for having a death demon on side. I could work out the whys and wherefores later.

"What now?" I asked, hoping this at least was a safe question and wouldn't result in yet another ambiguous answer.

"Now, to court," Jinx said.

"I don't think she's ready," Jamie said.

The demon studied me as his thumb and forefinger caressed his chin. "You don't have time to teach her."

"Teach me what?" I asked, more than a little irritated at how they were both talking about me as though I wasn't present.

Jamie turned me to face him. He put his hands on my shoulders and looked down at me. I had found it hard to drag my eyes away from Jinx, but now I was facing Jamie I found it equally hard to look away. His dark blue eyes were mesmerizing, and his lips looked too soft and kissable by far.

"Remember what I told you before: you'll see and hear things at court no human should ever have to see or hear—but to look away, to show any expression of fear, revulsion or horror, will be seen as a weakness and used against you."

"He's right," Mr. Kerfuffle said, and I realized, looking around, that even Jinx had lost his smile.

"I don't think this is something you can ever teach me, Jamie."

"No," he said, his expression suddenly bleak. "No, sadly I think you are right."

Ten

There was some argument as to whether I should be found some suitable clothes for my introduction to the court of Lord Baltheza rather than wait until later. In the end they decided that my clothing was the least of my worries. This small piece of information did nothing to lift my flagging spirits, which were rapidly sinking right down into the region of my boots.

Mr. Kerfuffle took one of the torches from the wall and led us to a small covered cart at the far side of the courtyard. He started pulling out bundles, which he handed to us—so obviously some preparations had been made for our arrival.

To my surprise both Jamie and Jinx wrapped themselves in hooded cloaks similar to mine. I could see why I should disguise myself, but they were both of this world.

Mr. Shenanigans must have noticed my puzzled expression for he leaned down close to me and whispered, "A Guardian and a Death-bringer entering court together could cause difficulties if their presence isn't immediately understood."

Mr. Kerfuffle gave a snort. "'Difficulties'? What he means is 'mayhem.' Until they announce themselves as part of your guard,

Lord Baltheza might believe his court is under attack, and react accordingly."

"But why?" I asked.

"The Guardian and the Deathbringer are two of the most powerful demons in our world, and only they have the right to dabble in the lives of humans."

"I thought there were other Guardians."

"Not like him," he said, jerking his head at Jamie, then he lapsed into silence as Jamie and Jinx joined us. The little demon pushed back the cart's cover and hopped inside. "Here," he said, handing Jamie something long and thin and suspiciously sword-shaped wrapped in rags. He rummaged around a bit and handed another to Mr. Shenanigans and then, reluctantly, offered a third package to Jinx.

"No thanks. I've come with my own weaponry," he said.

"Suit yourself."

"*Weaponry?*" I asked in alarm, but I was ignored as they unwrapped their packages. I saw metal glint in the lamplight. "Oh my God," I said as Jamie pulled a sword almost as tall as Mr. Kerfuffle from a dark leather scabbard and weighed it in his hand.

"Not a word I would use around here," Jinx said.

"What?"

"The G word," Jinx said. "It makes some of us a mite uncomfortable."

"It makes Baltheza apoplectic with rage," Mr. Kerfuffle added with a grin.

"Why?" I asked.

All of them stopped what they were doing and looked at me, even Pyrites. Their expressions ranged from anxious to incredulous. Jamie looked patient and Jinx looked amused. Pyrites just purred at me.

"She does know where we are, right? And where we're going?" Jinx asked with a chuckle.

"Religion down here is something best not talked about," Jamie said.

"Why?" I asked again.

Jinx laughed out loud. "I'll give you a clue," he said, and then stood beside Jamie and pulled back his cloak. Jamie glanced at him and with a shrug, did likewise.

"What do you see?" Jinx asked.

I studied them both. What I actually saw, truth be told, was two incredibly sexy men, but I didn't think that was what Jinx was getting at.

"Well," I said, trying to choose my words very carefully, "Jamie looks like what we—as in *we humans*—would call an angel."

Jinx opened his cloak a little wider, allowing his tail to curl around from behind him and wiggle at me.

"And you look like"—and I was really trying hard to be diplomatic— "you look like what we—we humans, that is—would call a, um, a . . ." Jinx waved his hand in a rolling motion as if to say: get on with it. *Screw it*, I thought. "You look like the Devil."

As I whispered the last word Jinx threw back his head and laughed: a really deep, from-the-stomach belly laugh. "Oh, she is so sweet it isn't true," he said.

"That's another word I wouldn't use if I were you," Mr. Shenanigans said. "Not all of us have a sense of humor like him."

By the time Mr. Kerfuffle had finished unloading all the weapons I was surprised the four of them could walk under the weight of all that ironwork. Jinx had disappeared for a few minutes, then returned with a sword whose blade was as black as coal. It glowed in the darkness as though it had an inner light. He also had a dagger tied around his thigh and I thought I glimpsed another peeping up out of the side of his boot.

Jamie was just as laden: he had the sword Mr. Kerfuffle had given him hidden under his cloak, and as well as the dagger in a scabbard attached to his belt, a leather slingshot. Both demons had short daggers attached to their belts, and Mr. Shenanigans also had a fairly large ax strapped to his back.

At home arriving with so much weaponry at a royal court would probably cause a war, but as none of my guards were apparently bothered I decided against raising the point. They, I hoped, knew what they were doing.

Mr. Kerfuffle hopped down from the cart and handed Jamie a final small package, then jerked his head in my direction. Jamie frowned and the little demon shrugged and that brief exchange was enough to make the others stop what they were doing and look at me and then to Jamie and back again.

Jamie unwrapped the package and walked over to me. "This is for you," he said, holding out the object.

A short dagger in a jewel-encrusted scabbard lay on his palm. The precious stones glinted darkly in the lamplight. I stepped a little closer so I could take a better look, though I didn't take the proffered weapon. The scabbard was made of gold—I was sure of it—and engraved with a flowing, swirling pattern. Inlaid was a single ruby, surrounded by darker stones. If I had to guess, I'd have said they were sapphires. The hilt of the dagger was similarly decorated with smaller stones set flush with the metal, so one could get a comfortable grip.

"The Lady Kayla sent this for you," Mr. Kerfuffle said.

"I don't want it."

"You need to carry a weapon," Jamie said, stepping closer to me.

"No," I said, and backed away, still staring at the beautiful but deadly object on his outstretched palm. "I wouldn't even know what to do with it."

"You will if the time comes," Jamie replied.

"No." I knew I was being stubborn, but I really hated knives—I couldn't even watch a knife-fight in a film without hiding my face behind a cushion.

Jinx moved to Jamie's side. "It's a pretty little piece and a gift from your sister. So why not take it, if only to make her happy?"

"I couldn't . . . I just can't . . ."

Jinx took the dagger from Jamie's hand. "If it comes to it, you could and you would," he said, "but for now, just accept it as the gift it is and hope you will never need it." He reached out and took my hand in his, then pushed the dagger against my palm and wrapped my fingers around it. "It cannot hurt you, but it could save you."

When Mr. Kerfuffle produced a leather belt I allowed them to thread it around the waist of my jeans and attach the weapon.

Jinx nodded in approval and we left the courtyard.

★ ★ ★

We entered the castle through a side entrance next to the kitchens. I could feel the heat of the ovens through the open door as we
walked past, and the air was damp with steam and the smell of boiled
vegetables.

We had left Pyrites outside and although he had been mine for only
an hour or so, I found it very hard to leave him. I had petted his snout
and laid my head against his, whispering to him that I would be back
to collect him very, very soon, all the while hoping it wasn't a lie. He
had rubbed his head against my shoulder and purred.

"Never fear, mistress," Mr. Shenanigans told me. "If you call him
he will come, even if it is into the great hall itself. If you are in danger he will find you."

The dragon had obviously understood, because he dropped down
where we left him and rested his head between his claws, looking for
all the world like a faithful hound.

The demons led the way through the gray stone corridors, with
Jamie and me following and Jinx behind us, moving at a speed that had
me trotting along to keep up. I didn't argue this time—I was too scared
to argue. A lump the size of a golf ball had formed in my throat, and I
wasn't quite sure how I was remaining upright, let alone walking when
my legs felt like jelly.

We came out of the corridor and into a large room and immediately
I could hear the murmur of voices—many voices. I presumed we must
be in an anteroom, especially when I noticed two dragons hewn out
of glittering rock guarding a doorway with wide open iron-bound,
wooden doors. The burning torches clasped in each of their claws did
little to dispel the dark; the shadows closed in around us.

"This is it," Jamie said, giving my hand a squeeze. "Keep close to
me and stay quiet."

We walked through the entrance and across a flagstoned floor,
our footsteps echoing within the high, stone walls, and into what I
imagined was the great hall. For the first few yards it was pretty much
empty, as most of the people were standing at the other end. They were
in loosely formed groups, their backs a wall between us and—whatever
they were obscuring. Long wooden tables and benches lined either side

of the hall, all laid out with cutlery, plates, goblets and other dining ware, but no one was sitting.

Vast tapestries cloaked the walls, along with gruesome-looking weapons and swathes of brightly colored silks and velvets, the prevalent colors of which were scarlet, gold and green. If I had been anywhere else I would have thought the tapestries were depicting characters from fairy tales, but they were probably portraying individuals and events historical to this world. Beautiful snake-haired women, hideous demons with heads of lizards, boars, dragons and other beasts were stitched in vibrant and—I assumed—lifelike colors.

The high ceilings were full of shadows and smoke that drifted up from the burning torches below, but I was sure I could see movement up there in the dark. I looked away. If there was something lurking in the rafters, I preferred not to know what it was.

After a few further steps, all thoughts of my surroundings disappeared, for Kayla was nearby. I couldn't see her past the throng of people, but I knew she was there—I could feel her. I began to walk across the hall as though I was being pulled toward her. I could almost feel her heartbeat alongside my own. I felt Jamie take hold of my arm, but still I kept moving. I could hear people chattering, music playing, but it was like my ears were stuffed with cotton balls: it all seemed so far away.

"Lucky," I heard Jamie whisper from somewhere distant, "*Lucky*."

Then someone pinched my arm very hard and I was free. "Ouch," I said. "That hurt."

"Good," Jinx said and his smile had deserted him.

A couple of people glanced around for a quick look at the new arrivals, but no one was taking much notice of us. One of them was taller even than Mr. Shenanigans—and by a good three or four feet—and twice as broad. I only caught a quick glimpse of his face, but it had looked pretty normal, except for the extra eye just above the bridge of his nose. His hands hung like joints of ham by his side, almost to his knees and it was obvious he would have been able to crush a mere mortal like me with a single blow. The woman beside him was slim and shapely, with wave upon wave of auburn curls cascading down her back—but when she turned briefly toward us I caught a glimpse of the skeletal features of a long-dead corpse.

I took a deep breath. I had known I would see strange and possibly horrible creatures—there had been a few at the inn—but I still felt terribly unprepared. I wanted to turn and run.

Jamie must have sensed my urge to bolt, for he placed his arm around my waist and started to move me forward. I looked up into the rafters again and this time saw what was hiding there.

So, I could see the dead in this world too. Gray misty ghosts came floating down from the vaulted ceiling to mingle with the crowd who, blissfully unaware of their presence, continued to chat and gossip. They were the spirits of this world and therefore demonic in appearance—but why were there so many in this one place? This puzzled me, until I began to wonder, looking at their varying expressions of fear and anger, whether the hall was used for a purpose other than banqueting and entertaining.

I didn't have too much time to ponder on it, for Mr. Shenanigans was clearing a path for us through the crowd. Demons moved aside without complaint, several acknowledging him and Mr. Kerfuffle by name. We stopped a few rows from the front: close enough so that we could see, but still far enough away that we might not be noticed.

The first person I saw was Kayla, sitting on a large throne of gleaming, ornately carved chestnut-brown wood, complete with scrolled legs and armrests. Her terrible beauty struck me once more: she was magnificent, she was awesome—and I could absolutely see why Lord Daltas might want her for his own. She was dressed like a princess from a fairy tale in a long, flowing creation of gold and emerald silk with shimmering gold threads cuffing the sleeves and edging her low neckline.

She was scanning the crowd—I knew she had felt my presence as I had hers—and her eyes found mine almost immediately. Her lips curled into a small smile, then she made a motion with her hand as if to touch her hair and pinched her finger and thumb together, drawing them down over her forehead. She was telling me to pull my hood further over my face. I gave her a weak smile of my own and did as she had asked.

The man next to her spoke. "Daughter mine," he said, touching her sleeve to get her attention, and she swiveled her head to face him. Her smile turned up a notch, and although it wasn't my Kayla sitting there, the Kayla I knew and loved, I still knew a false smile upon her face when I saw it.

"Father," she said, and he murmured something in her ear that only she could hear. Her smile froze, her fingers tightened on the armrests of her chair, then she forced herself to relax. He patted her hand.

I studied the man—the demon—who was apparently my father. Even sitting, I could see he was tall—maybe not as tall as Mr. Shenanigans, but taller than Jamie and Jinx: probably six foot six or so. His chest was broad beneath a white silk shirt and scarlet velvet jerkin. Slim leather-clad legs stretched out before him, one ankle crossed over the other. Black leather boots adorned his feet. He had the same opalescent skin as Kayla, but that was where any resemblance ended. Now I understood Jinx's comment about putting me out of my misery: had I looked anything like Lord Baltheza, I think I might well have begged him to do it.

Baltheza's hair was a raven-black mass of curls that hung to his shoulders; it was the only attractive thing about him. His brow was divided into three by two thick ridges of puckered flesh running up from either side of the bridge of his nose and across the place his eyebrows should have been. These ridges ran up to his hairline and met where twisted horns curled into cornets like a ram's. His nose was aristocratically long and thin, and his lips were pious slithers of jade. His eyes were almond-shaped, a dark blaze of orange dissected by vertical slits of black. I couldn't believe my mother would have willingly succumbed to such a person, for he was as ugly as he was terrifying.

A creature the size of Mr. Kerfuffle hurried to his side and whispered something in his ear. Lord Baltheza tilted his head to listen, then stood and clapped his hands together. The crowd's chattering stuttered into silence.

He sank back down onto his seat as his eyes slid across the sea of faces, not really seeing any of them—the gesture and his arrogant smile were only for effect. Slowly and deliberately he tapped one long yellowed, talon like fingernail on the arm of his chair, the *click, click, click* echoing throughout the now silent hall.

"I understand we have guests joining us this night," Baltheza said.

For one terrible moment I thought he meant us, then the crowd began to shuffle back, taking us with it, until a semicircular space had formed in front of Kayla and her father and a narrow avenue had opened up through the center of the hall.

"Welcome, Lord Daltas," Baltheza said, gesturing to the back of the hall.

The crowd began to mutter, and there was a steady *slap, slap* of leather on stone as Daltas and his entourage made their way to the front. I stood up on tiptoe, trying to see over the heads blocking my view, but it was hopeless and I had to give up and wait like everyone else until he had arrived at the front.

He bowed low before Baltheza: a dramatic, over-the-top gesture which I would have found vaguely insulting, had I been Kayla's father. Baltheza just looked bored.

"My lord," Daltas said, then turned to Kayla, "my lady."

It was clear from the twist of her lips and arch of her eyebrow that Kayla's feelings toward Daltas were not entirely friendly.

I stood on tiptoe again, trying to get a better view past the shoulders and heads of the demons in front of me. I wanted a good look at this Lord Daltas, as it was down to him that Kayla and I were in this mess.

He was actually quite handsome, in an odd sort of way: his lavender hair hung long and straight to his waist, and when he turned to introduce the nobles in his entourage, I could see his eyes were the same color, just a shade darker. His skin was scaled, but not like a snake's: it was soft and a shiny dusky pink. He was tall and slim and dressed entirely in black except for his white shirt, which he wore open to below his navel, showing violet curls that scattered across his chest and ran down his stomach to disappear into his tight breeches.

His fingers were long and slender, and would have looked almost human had it not been for the long white talons sprouting from their tips. He too was wearing leather boots, so I couldn't tell if his feet were the same.

"Lord Baltheza," he said, "I come bearing gifts for both you and your most beautiful daughter."

Kayla raised her chin in a haughty gesture. "I have everything my heart could desire, Lord Daltas. I don't think there is a thing you could give me that I would possibly want."

I heard Jamie take a deep breath from beside me, and Jinx chuckled. To give him credit, Lord Daltas's smile didn't slip an inch. If anything, it grew a little brighter.

"Oh, I think you may like this little offering I have for you," he said, turning to look at the back of the hall. I couldn't see much from where I was, but I heard gasps and then laughter from some of the crowd.

"Oh shit," whispered Jamie.

"Someone you know?" asked Jinx.

Jamie ignored him and grabbed hold of my arm so tightly it hurt. "You remain silent," he whispered, "do you hear me? If you don't, I may never get you home."

I twisted in his grip to look up at his face. His skin was pale and his expression grim. He pulled my head against his chest and murmured into my hair, "Don't look. It's best you don't look."

I knew that he was telling me not to look for a reason, but I had to see; the fact that he was so scared for me meant I had to know what was happening. I twisted and struggled in his tight embrace and managed to turn myself so I could see the front of the hall.

Of course Jamie was right: I shouldn't have looked. I felt his lips against my head, but he didn't speak; he was just comforting me and I loved him for it. I needed him then, even if he couldn't make everything better.

Philip was naked except for a pair of torn and grubby boxer shorts: all that was left of the clothing he had been wearing when Lord Argon had taken him. Daltas held him on a silver chain attached to a wide leather collar wrapped tight around his neck. The skin at his throat had been rubbed raw and open wounds on his chest and legs were weeping blood. But the most terrible thing of all was his expression: total hopelessness. His eyes were glazed and his skin was sallow; his lips the lilac hue of death.

Daltas jerked the lead and Philip staggered and fell painfully to his knees. Jamie pulled me even closer as I looked at Kayla. Her face was a frozen mask of indifference.

"And why, exactly, would I want this pathetic creature?" she asked after several heartbeats.

Daltas laughed. He knew he had wrong-footed her.

But that was a bad move on his part; Kayla had never liked being laughed at. She got to her feet. "Be careful, Lord Daltas," she said, "for I might well ask how you came to possess this *human*—and what games you have been playing in the Overlands."

"Games? I've been playing no games."

She looked down her nose at him. "Well, someone has, and if not you then someone close to you."

"This is neither the time nor the place," Baltheza said.

She spun around to face him. "I have it on good authority that this human, or his master, summoned Lord Argon to take a woman from the Overlands and bring her here against her will. When she could not be taken, Lord Argon took this pathetic creature, as was his right. But how is the human now in the care of Lord Daltas? I wouldn't have thought that Lord Argon would give his prize so readily to another."

"My daughter, if this is true, then Argon was within his rights to take the servant of he who called him—and if he chose to give his captive to Lord Daltas, then that is his business. And does this not imply it was a human who sought to harm the woman, not someone from our world?"

"The woman had already been visited by one of his court," she said, pointing an accusatory finger at Daltas. "There is some intrigue at play that I don't like. It could be dangerous to me, the woman, and dare I say it, you," she said, turning to Lord Baltheza. Then, with a swirl of silk, she sat back down and her dark eyes met mine.

Baltheza gave a deep sigh and turned to Daltas. "How did you come about this man?"

"I exchanged him for what Argon considered a sweeter meat," the demon said, and there was a glint in his eye that made me shudder. "Lord Argon, bring forward your new pet."

Again the mass of people parted and Lord Argon walked to the front. I was watching Kayla's face and although she hid it well, I saw the flicker of emotion and the way her eyes instantly jerked my way—but she wasn't looking at me this time; she was looking at Jamie.

"Come on," he said. "We're getting out of here."

He turned and tried to pull me with him and when I glanced back at Kayla she gave a little nod, telling me to go with him. God help me, I almost went—but then I heard a voice cry out, "Daddy, Daddy, help me! Please help me—"

"No!" Philip shouted. "*No!*"

I wrenched myself out of Jamie's arms, dodged Jinx as he made a grab for me and pushed my way forward through the crowd.

Philip had one hand on his collar and was trying to hold it away from his neck as he strained against the chain. His other hand was stretched out toward Lord Argon, who was holding a similar chain, on the end of which a young fair-haired girl was struggling to get to Philip.

Argon yanked on the chain and the girl fell backward onto her butt. The demon laughed and picked her up, making a great show of sniffing her hair and stroking her face. I was frozen in midstep for only a moment, but it was long enough for Jamie and Jinx to grab hold of me.

"Such a pretty dear—a virgin too," Argon said. "When she reaches womanhood she will be an interesting distraction through the long, dark nights."

Although Argon was at least wearing breeches this time, I remembered the awful thing that hung between his legs—and I wasn't the only one. Philip began to struggle and scream and I felt like screaming too, but I knew it wouldn't help the girl.

"We must do something," I whispered to Jamie.

He shook his head, but it was Jinx who answered. "A virgin is most highly prized. I suspect Daltas orchestrated this as a punishment for her father."

"A virgin?"

"I doubt Argon could be persuaded to trade the girl for anything less."

"She's a child," I said.

"She should be safe until she reaches womanhood, but after her first menses he will take her."

"So he'll have to be patient," I said.

"Not one of Argon's strong points," Jinx said.

"But we have time to try and think of a way to save her?"

"Do you think anyone will take him to task if he doesn't wait?" Jinx said.

"I can't let this happen," I said, and started toward the front. She was a little girl. I had to do something.

"What are you doing?" Jamie asked, trying to pull me back.

"I'm a virgin," I said.

"Don't be stupid," he said.

"I'm a virgin," I repeated.

"I'll knock you out rather than . . ."

"Hold fire, brother," Jinx said.

"What?"

"She bears my mark."

"I can't stand this," I said. Philip's pleading was painful to hear: the man was on his knees, begging for someone to help his daughter—anyone at all, but most of the crowd were just laughing and jeering at him.

"Do it," Jinx said.

"What?" I asked.

"If you want to save a girl you don't even know—"

"—the daughter of the man who betrayed you," Jamie piped in.

"Then do it."

Mr. Shenanigans looked like he was about to add his two pennies' worth, but Jinx raised a hand to stop him. The demon didn't look happy, but he remained silent. Something was going on, but I couldn't think straight. The girl let out a strangled scream and I turned to see Lord Argon dangling her by the lead, her toes scrambling to touch the floor, her face turning red as the collar cut into her throat.

I pushed my way through the crowd and shouted, "Stop it! Stop it, you damn *pervert*!"

The court fell silent. Argon could see me, but he chose instead to look over the top of my head and glance around the room as though I wasn't there.

"Did someone speak?" he asked, and the whole room erupted into laughter.

Kayla wasn't the only one who didn't like being laughed at. I shrugged back my hood and stalked forward so I was standing beneath him.

"I damn well did," I said and, because he was still looking around the room as though he couldn't see me, I stamped down hard on his scaly claw. I doubt it hurt him much, but it did get his attention.

He let go of the lead and the girl fell to the floor in a sobbing heap. As he bent down to look at me his expression was puzzled. "What are you doing here?"

Before I could reply, Kayla was by my side. She grabbed hold of my arm and pulled me away from Argon.

"What are you doing?" she asked, her voice strained.

"She's a little girl, Kayla."

"It's too late for her," Kayla said. "He won't give her up."

"Can't you make him?" She shook her head. "Then I'll have to." I tried to shake myself free of her grasp, but she wasn't about to let go. "Lord Argon," I shouted up to him, "the girl for me."

"Lucky!" Kayla cried.

The demon laughed out loud. "Why would I want you when I have this piece of very fresh meat?"

"Because you'll have to wait for her."

"She is pure: a virgin, a sweet little morsel—perhaps worth waiting for."

"So am I," I said. "A virgin, that is."

The laughter from around the hall petered out and the demon bent to my level, so his eyes looked into mine.

"You speak truly?"

"I do."

He thought for a moment, then leaned forward a bit more and sniffed me. A slow smile crept across his face.

"You let her go and I'll take her place."

"Lucky, no," Kayla said. "You don't know what you're doing."

"It's a deal," Argon said.

Out of the corner of my eye I saw Jamie rush over to the child, pick her up and hand her to Mr. Shenanigans, who hurried away through the crowd with Mr. Kerfuffle in his wake.

"Well. It looks as if my nights are going to be warmer sooner than later," Argon said, reaching for me.

My hand went to the dagger under my cloak. I wasn't sure whether one could kill a demon with such a small weapon—especially as Jamie *had* said they were immortal—but maybe if I stuck the dagger in hard, right where it hurt, I could delay the inevitable? I wasn't sure what kind of justice system they had in this world, but I was pretty sure I was in big trouble whichever way it went.

"I'm afraid, Lord Argon, we have a problem here," I heard Jinx call out and he stepped forward and pushed back his hood. Several of the courtiers moaned, and those standing closest to him shrank away.

Argon pulled himself up to his full height, his smile sliding from his face to be replaced by a worried frown.

"This woman carries my mark and I am not about to release her."

"Nor am I," said Jamie, throwing back his own hood.

Argon's eyes bulged and he paused for several seconds before he could find his voice. "She carries *both* your marks?"

They both smiled those dangerous smiles they were so good at.

"My, my. You have been a busy girl," Kayla murmured under her breath.

"I don't know what they're talking about," I whispered back.

The look she gave me wasn't friendly. "I don't understand what is happening here, but be grateful for it—they've probably just saved your life."

"I'm well aware of that," I said.

"I want the girl back," Argon said with a pout.

"Sorry," Jinx said, "a deal's a deal. When we've finished with this one you can have her, but until then"—he shrugged—"she's unavailable."

"You've tricked me," Argon said, and turned to Baltheza. "They've tricked me and I demand recompense."

"Lord Argon, unless you wish to take issue with the Deathbringer and Guardian, I suggest you hold your tongue and be grateful *I* don't take issue with you for having lascivious intentions toward my daughter."

"D-Daughter?" the demon stammered. "I would never even contemplate the Lady Kayla with anything but the most honorable intentions."

"I don't mean Kayla, you idiot," Baltheza said. He didn't bother to explain further but got up out of his chair and clapped his hands again. "Let us eat."

The ladies and gentlemen of the court converged on the long tables, which were now laden with steaming dishes, bowls of fruit and flagons of wine and ale, while Baltheza walked over to Kayla and me. "I suggest you take her somewhere quiet and out of the way and"—he stared pointedly at Jamie and Jinx—"take them with you."

"Yes, Father," Kayla said.

"And Kayla?"

"Yes, Father?"

"Make sure you're back to the table before your soup grows cold. I will speak to you and to them"—he nodded toward Jamie, Jinx and me—"later."

She dropped into a low curtsey. With a glare in our direction, Baltheza turned and strode away.

"Come on," she said, grabbing my hand and pulling me along after her. "I'd better get you out of the way before he changes his mind and lets Argon have his way with you."

"Lady Kayla," Jinx said, "with all due respect, even your father is not above the law."

She ignored him as she hurried us to a door set behind the two thrones and led us through a series of long stone corridors, some lined with wooden doors, some leading onto stairs. She was moving so fast my feet were barely touching the ground. What was it with demons? They were immortal, so why were they always in such a damned hurry?

Eleven

Kayla half-dragged me up a winding flight of stairs, flung open a door at the top and almost threw me inside.

"Careful," I said, only just remaining on my feet, "there's no need to be so rough."

"No need?" she said. "*No need?* What in the name of Hades were you thinking? And you," she said, turning on Jamie as he followed us though the door, "how *could* you? How could you let her risk herself like that? And how could you let *him*"—she pointed at Jinx—"mark her?"

"Same old Kayla," Jinx said. "If things don't go exactly as you want you throw a tantrum."

"I am not throwing a tantrum."

Jinx and Jamie exchanged a smile.

"I'm not throwing a tantrum," she said, stamping her foot.

"Kayla," I interrupted, "actually, you are."

She turned on me and I took an involuntary step back. He eyes glittered and her color was high. Anger—no, not anger, *rage*—pulsed out of her and enveloped me and I began to feel as if I was being crushed. The air was forced out of my lungs and I couldn't draw breath.

"Kayla, stop it," Jinx said.

She glared at him.

"I said *stop it*!"

I was gasping for breath, seeing stars—then the air grew warm, there was crack like thunder and Kayla flew through the air and landed on her backside in a pool of silk.

I remained doubled up, my hand on my chest, sucking in lungfuls of air: air that tasted and smelled a little strange but was somehow familiar. *Sulfur*, I remembered as my head began to clear: it smelled of sulfur.

Jinx strode over to Kayla, took her by the arm and pulled her to her feet. "She bears my mark," he told her, "and it would be best you remembered it."

Jamie came to my side. "Are you all right?" he asked and I nodded, still gulping in air. He rounded on Kayla. "What's going on? You're the one who wanted her here and yet now you don't appear to be in the least bit pleased to see her."

Kayla's anger evaporated as quickly as it had begun. "I'm sorry," she said, walking over to me and hugging me to her. "You really scared me," she said, and I could hear the tremor in her voice. "Lord Argon isn't the sharpest knife in the drawer—his brain is located mainly between his legs," she said, "but once his mind is fixated on things of a carnal nature all sense of reason deserts him. The knowledge that he was offending my father or me would've been of no consequence until after the event, when it would've been too late."

"Philip's daughter is a little girl, Kayla."

"I know, and had I known what Daltas had planned, I would have tried to stop him. This is all such a damn mess . . ."

"Can you do anything for Philip?" I asked.

"You cannot possibly be serious! He *betrayed* you—"

"He was trying to get his daughter back."

"You don't know that."

"It seems fairly obvious," I said.

Kayla tapped a finger against her lips. "Just because something seems obvious doesn't mean it actually is."

"Daltas offered you Philip as a gift. Can't you accept?" I asked.

"No," she said, "that's out of the question."

"Why not? Hasn't he suffered enough?"

"You explain to her," she said to Jamie. "I have to get back."

"Kayla, please."

She shook her head and started toward the door. "I can't keep our father waiting," she said, "and if I'm to keep you safe, I have a lot of work to do."

With that she swept out of the room, leaving me staring at the open door. Jinx closed it behind her and turned to me. "Well, that went better than expected," he said.

"You think?" I said, wanting to either smash something or smack someone. "I hate this place."

"Oh, it's not bad once you get used to it," Jinx said.

I sat down on Kayla's huge bed. It was scattered with velvet cushions and silky pillows, and piles of furs. When I looked around the room, it occurred to me it was more a chamber for entertaining than sleeping.

"Why won't Kayla help Philip?"

"Putting aside the fact he's a back-stabbing shit," Jamie said, "if she accepted him as a gift from Daltas she would be more or less indicating her assent to let Daltas call upon her."

"Oh," I said with a frown. "Couldn't she just dump him after a couple of dates?"

Jinx chuckled. Apparently he'd regained his sense of humor. "Daltas is going to be persistent enough without her giving him any sign of encouragement."

I sighed and massaged my temples with my fingertips. I was getting a stinking headache. Jamie climbed up onto the bed behind me and began to massage my shoulders. It felt really good and I relaxed back against him, my eyes closing.

"Does that feel better?" he asked.

"Mmm," I murmured. A sudden thought occurred to me and my eyes snapped open. "What was all this about you having marked me?"

Jamie's fingers hesitated for a moment, then he began to rub my shoulders again. "Nothing for you to worry about," he said.

"*Jamie?*"

He moved around so he was sitting next to me. Jinx strolled over and plunked himself down on the dressing table stool so he was facing us. "This I've *got* to hear," he said.

Jamie glared at him and when Jinx flashed him a grin he growled, "Everything is so damn amusing to you."

"Not really," Jinx said, "but you have to admit this has a funny side to it."

"You think?"

Jinx's smile grew broader and he turned to me. "If I'd known you were already marked I wouldn't have marked you too. But James here is a lot more subtle than I am—I didn't sense his mark upon you."

"Mark, what damn mark?" I got up and marched across to the dressing table, then leaned past Jinx to look in the mirror. "I can't see any mark."

"It's not visible to the eye," Jinx said, "but as soon as another touches you they will know you are . . ."

"I am . . . ?"

Jinx glanced down at the floor and suddenly looked rather bashful. "I am *what*, Jinx?"

"They will know you are mine," he said, still not looking at me.

"Yours? What do you mean 'yours'?" I asked.

"Now, now," Jamie said, "there's no need to get upset."

"Upset? Why should I be upset? I've just found out I've been marked by a death demon and I now belong to him, so why should I be upset?"

Jinx gave me what I suspected was meant to be a winsome smile. On another occasion it probably would have worked, but I was steaming.

"And you?" I said, turning on Jamie, "you marked me too?"

"I'm afraid my mark is nowhere near as powerful as his," Jamie said, "but while you carry our marks—of one or both of us—you can't be touched by another from this world without them having to face dire consequences."

"Dire as in, I can demand their head on a spike if someone should harm you," Jinx explained.

"But they can still do me harm?" I said, my temper abating a little. It was beginning to look like they had only been trying to protect me.

But somehow I had a feeling they still weren't telling me everything. As usual.

"They could, but they would have to be prepared to take on not only a Guardian but also a Deathbringer."

"Is that your title?" I asked. "Because if it is I think I'd change it."

Jinx laughed his deep, throaty laugh. "I have many names, but I prefer Jinx."

"But other demons fear you?"

"Even immortals fear death."

"Hmm," I said, then went back to my first question. "So why was Kayla so angry if a mark means you have offered me your protection?" I looked from one to the other, but it looked like they had both discovered their footwear to be very interesting.

Before I had a chance to inquire further there was a knock on the door, Mr. Kerfuffle's marshmallow head popped around the edge and he walked in, closely followed by Mr. Shenanigans.

"What did you do with the girl?" Jamie asked.

"Leila at the inn is taking care of her until we can return her to her world," Mr. Shenanigans said.

"Is she all right? She must be terrified," I said.

"Leila has a younger sister. We left them getting to know each other," he said.

I glanced at Jamie; the thought of a terrified child being left in the company of a small demon wasn't particularly comforting, but he gave a smile as if to say it would be all right; I guessed I'd have to trust their judgment.

Mr. Shenanigans went over to the window and opened the curtains. "With your leave, I'll call Pyrites. He's pining outside on his own."

"He'll never fit through the window," I said, "and if he did, there wouldn't be much room left in here."

"He's a drakon," he said, as if that explained everything.

When I looked at him, Jinx added, "What he means is, Pyrites is a very flexible little creature."

"I would call Pyrites many things, but little wouldn't be one of them—he's the size of two very large elephants."

They all smiled. "You'll see," said Jamie.

"What do I know about anything?" I said grumpily. "Call him, then."

With some trouble the demon pushed his head out of the window and gave a long, low whistle. If he had difficulty fitting his head through the narrow opening I didn't see how on earth a dragon was going to get inside without causing major damage to either itself or the masonry.

Mr. Shenanigans pulled his head back inside and stepped away from the window as a dark shadow passed by. There was the sound of wings beating, then something strange happened: the sound didn't exactly grow quieter, it just became softer until it was almost a flutter.

I took a step toward the window just as Pyrites's head popped through the gap and he hopped inside.

"Pyrites?" I said, shocked.

The creature was now no bigger than a Yorkshire Terrier. He scampered across the floor to me and rubbed his snout against my calves. When I crouched down to pet him, he rewarded me with a puff of smoke and a purr from deep inside his throat.

"But—" I started, looking up at my smiling bodyguards, "how can this be?"

"Drakons are magical creatures: they can change their size at will. His true size is as you saw him earlier, and that's when he's at his most comfortable and safest from predators. When he's in friendly company he's equally happy to be the size of a small dog—or even smaller if needs must," Jamie explained.

"Go on boy, show her what you can do," Mr. Shenanigans said.

Pyrites sat up on his haunches and started to grow. When he reached the size of a small donkey he stopped and looked at me with those wonderful multicolored eyes.

"What a clever boy you are," I said, scratching him under the chin. "Can he stay like this for as long as he wants?"

"Pretty much," said Jamie, "though if he needs to feed he'll have to return to his normal size and go hunting. But apart from the odd titbit, drakons only need to eat every few days or so."

"So I don't have to go down the store and get dragon food?" I said. They all laughed and Pyrites blew a cloud of steam through his nose.

"No, Pyrites is more or less self-sufficient. You don't even need a litter tray."

"What is a litter tray?" Mr. Shenanigans asked. Mr. Kerfuffle tugged on his sleeve and the large demon bent right down so his friend could whisper in his ear. "Oh," he said, with a perplexed frown, "I'm not sure we could find a receptacle big enough."

"So why didn't he come inside with us earlier?"

"We were incognito," Jamie said. "Only royalty would have a jeweled drakon as a companion."

I sat back down on the bed, Pyrites shrank to the size of a large cat and hopped up next to me to settle down with his head in my lap. As I petted him, I pondered on my present predicament. Jamie and Jinx were being very defensive and I was sure they were keeping something from me. Kayla was clearly unhappy with them both—in fact, she'd been more than a little unhappy with me too, and yet I hadn't done anything wrong.

"I'm hungry," Mr. Shenanigans said suddenly. "Is anyone else hungry?"

"I'm starved," Jinx said, getting to his feet and stretching. "I could probably eat a small drakon."

Pyrites quivered under my hand and let out a small puff of smoke. "Not funny, Jinx," I said.

"Only joking," he told Pyrites with a grin. "Drakons, I'm assured, taste like shit."

Pyrites tossed his head with what I imagined was a disgusted grunt and then curled into a ball with his back to Jinx.

"Shows what he thinks of you," Jamie said.

"I'll go and get us something to eat," Mr. Shenanigans said.

Mr. Kerfuffle decided to go with him, and I found it comforting that they were both happy to leave me alone with Jamie and Jinx—apart from anything else, it would give me the opportunity to try and get a straight answer about these "marks."

"Now," I said, once Mr. Kerfuffle and Mr. Shenanigans had left the room, "I need you to explain fully what you mean when you say you've marked me."

"It's for your own good," Jinx said.

"Then why so defensive, gentlemen? And why was Kayla so angry if my protection is all there is to it?"

"To carry the mark of the Deathbringer isn't exactly a good thing," Jamie said.

"And carrying the mark of a Guardian is?" Jinx asked, and although he was still smiling, his tone had become terse.

"All right, all right: Jinx is a death demon—I get it. Where he goes, death follows."

"More or less," Jinx replied.

"So, Jamie what does a Guardian do? You said something about border patrol."

"He's like a gunslinger," Jinx said. "If someone starts causing trouble up top he goes and puts it right."

"Gunslinger?"

"Not a good analogy," Jamie said with a frown at Jinx, "but yes, I suppose you could say I uphold the law relating to the interaction between our world and yours."

"So," I said, "going back to these marks, what does my having one mean to me?" They again exchanged an uncomfortable look.

"If you won't explain I'll just ask Mr. Shenanigans when he gets back."

"Probably best you didn't," Jamie said. "He and Kerfuffle would probably be just as angry as Kayla is."

They looked at one another and then, rather reluctantly, Jinx turned to me. "First, I'd like to point out this is a highly unusual situation."

Jamie nodded in agreement.

"Never before have I heard of a mortal being marked by two different beings."

"Nor I," added Jamie. "I didn't think it possible."

"Are you sure you marked her?" Jinx asked. "If you did, I should have felt it—in fact, I shouldn't have been able to leave my mark."

"I have no explanation. I preformed the ritual immediately before we crossed over."

Jinx frowned for a moment and then his face lit up with a smile of understanding. "You marked the Overlander—I marked the Underlander."

"Ah! Yes, that could explain it."

"Oh goody," I said, my voice heavy with sarcasm. "I'm so glad you two have worked it out."

They exchanged another glance, but Jamie's expression was troubled; he knew I wasn't going to like what they had to tell me. Jinx's expression, on the other hand, was harder to read. He was smiling, but it was a cunning smile—no, not cunning—more calculating.

"I guess you could say it was like we were engaged," Jamie said in a tentative voice.

"Like we were *what*?"

"Engaged."

For a moment I was speechless, then Jinx started to laugh, a deep, rumbling, very sexy laugh. "You must have a very warped view of marriage," he said to Jamie.

"Jinx?" I said.

"Our Guardian is trying to make it sound acceptable, but basically, it means you belong to us. You should belong to either him or me, but somehow it's *us*."

"And when you say belong . . . ?"

"As in: you are ours to do with as we please: our servant, slave, sex toy—whatever."

I stared at the two of them. At least Jinx was being honest, but *sex toy*?

I shifted Pyrites off my lap and onto the bed and stood up. "Okay, boys, so this is the way it's going to be: I don't give a rat's ass whether you've 'marked' me in some way." I did the quotation mark thing with my fingers to make sure I had their full attention. I could feel red-hot anger gathering up inside me and I started to tremble. "But we are *not* engaged." I took a step toward them and glared at Jamie. "I am *not* your servant, or slave, and"—I poked my finger into the middle of Jinx's chest—"I am most certainly not your *sex toy*. Have we got that clear?"

I stood there, glaring into Jinx's eyes. He was still smiling, but there was something else there—I wasn't sure, but it might have been respect.

He leaned forward so his lips were brushing my ear. "We'll see," he whispered, and my treacherous body gave a little lurch deep down in my stomach.

He stepped back and his glittering eyes met mine once again: eyes full of a dark knowledge that left me in no doubt that it wasn't just my life I was in danger of losing in the Underlands.

Even if I had managed to find the words, I didn't have time to say them because the door behind me swung open and the demons were preceded into the room by the smell of roast meat.

All the anger drained out of me, to be replaced by cotton-ball-headed weariness. I sank back down on the bed as Jinx sauntered past me to see what the boys had pilfered for our dinner. When I glanced at Jamie, I saw he was watching Jinx. There was a coldness in his expression that made me shiver and for a moment, if I had been asked which of the two men was the death demon, I'm not sure I'd have been able to decide.

He must have felt my eyes on him for he glanced my way, and he did so without his usual gentle smile. He knew something had happened between Jinx and me, though he clearly wasn't sure exactly what.

Which made two of us.

I patted the bed beside me and he moved closer. "What's wrong?" I asked, my voice low so the others wouldn't hear.

His eyes flicked to Jinx and back to me. "I don't trust him with you."

My expression must have shown my alarm because he gave me a tight smile. "No, I don't mean I think he might hurt you. He has sworn to protect you and it means he will. No, I mean . . ." He sighed. "Are you really a virgin?"

"What kind of question is that?"

"Lucky?"

I lowered my eyes and started petting Pyrites's ears. The little dragon was asleep but even so, he shuffled a little closer and rested his head against my thigh.

"I thought you said you'd had boyfriends."

I kept my eyes on Pyrites. "And I told you they never lasted long."

"I thought they'd been serious, though."

"Serious enough that it hurt when they left me."

"But not serious enough for you to—you know?"

"Oh yeah," I said, "they were serious enough for that." My voice sounded bitter and I tried to lighten it, though I'm pretty sure I failed. "But it's a bit of a passion-killer when you never know when your best friend—whom your boyfriend can't see—is going to come strolling into the room."

"So you never?"

"Almost—but there's only so many times you can push a guy away without him either calling you a tease or thinking you're crazy."

"Does Kayla know?"

"She said it was for the best."

He took hold of my free hand. "Maybe she was right."

"I guess," I said, still not meeting his gaze. "Anyway, what is it with you and Jinx?"

"What do you mean?"

"Come on, Jamie, I don't have to be psychic to tell there's history between you."

He gave a wry smile. "Oh, I guess you could say sometimes we find ourselves at odds with each other."

"How come?"

"I'm a Guardian; I ensure that subjects from this world don't cause harm to those in yours, and vice versa. Jinx is tasked with the destruction of humans—the very thing I try to stop."

"But it's his job."

"Yes, it is," Jamie said, "but it doesn't mean I have to like it."

"Why the serious faces?" Jinx asked, as he plunked himself down opposite us. He had a roast leg of something in one hand and a goblet in the other. "Try the food. It's good." He then proceeded to gnaw heartily on the joint.

"I'll get you something," Jamie said, and left me to watch Jinx devour his meal.

Pyrites's nose began to twitch and he lifted his head, his eyes still closed, and sniffed the air. Then he opened one eye and looked across at Jinx. Dragons might well only need to eat every few days or so, but Pyrites was clearly more than a little interested in the meat in Jinx's hand. His ears pricked up, his other eye snapped open and he scrambled up into sitting position.

Jinx put his goblet down on the dressing table and tore a bit of meat off the bone. "Here," he said, throwing the piece up in the air.

With a flap of wings Pyrites shot up from the bed and caught the meat before it had even begun to fall to the ground. Then he floated down and sat on the floor by my feet to chew the morsel.

Jamie handed me a plate of food and a knife and fork, placed a goblet on the floor between us, then went off to get some food for himself. Like Jinx, he had a leg of something or other. When I looked around I could see I was the only one honored with cutlery and a plate, which was piled with slices of various different meats. Had I been at home I would have assumed I was smelling chicken, pork and lamb, but now I thought it better I didn't ask. What I didn't know wouldn't hurt me—and I was so hungry.

There were vegetables too: some things that looked like roast potatoes, which had a similar texture when in the mouth, though they tasted sweeter, and a green boiled plant which looked like spinach but tasted like nothing I had ever eaten before. It was good, though, and the meat was heavenly. It melted in the mouth and tasted just like meat should, only somehow *better*, probably more like meat tasted years ago when animals were all free range and not pumped full of chemicals.

"Well, milady, you certainly have a fine appetite," Jinx said as I finished the last scrap.

"That was wonderful," I said, and the demons both gave me sunny smiles. Food in the belly certainly improved everyone's humor—although it could have been the ale too, which was flowing freely—no sooner had anyone drained their goblet than Mr. Kerfuffle was hurrying over to refill it. He topped mine up each time he passed as well, and at first I'd started to wonder if he had a hidden agenda for giving me so much, but when I checked, the others had their goblets topped up just as often.

Once we'd finished eating, the weariness I had felt earlier returned in full. My eyes kept flickering shut and I was having trouble keeping up with the light-hearted conversation. Though I tucked my legs underneath me, despite wriggling around a bit, I couldn't get comfortable.

"Why don't you lie down?" Jamie said.

My eyes were drooping shut and I was too weary to reply. I dragged myself up the bed and flopped down with my head on a pillow. I could still hear them talking as I drifted off into sleep.

I woke up feeling all warm and cozy, then realized with a start that my face was pressed against bare skin. My eyes flew open—and yes, I was lying in bed with my head resting on a naked chest. Jamie was asleep, his eyes closed and his long, dark lashes feathering his rosy cheeks. He really did look angelic with his perfect lips curled into a gentle smile—if he was dreaming, they were happy dreams. I tried to move without waking him, but something was resting against my back, and it was then that I noticed a slim maroon arm trailing across my waist.

My fully-clothed waist.

I gave a sigh of relief, unable to stop the words "sex toy" from floating through my head.

Someone was snoring, but if it wasn't Jamie and it wasn't Jinx—? I tilted my head upward. Pyrites was curled up on the pillow just above me and small clouds of smoke came puffing out of his nostrils with each breath. I hoped dragons didn't have nightmares. If they did, Jamie was going to end up with more than just singed wings. I was just grateful the other demons hadn't joined us on the giant bed.

I removed Jinx's arm from across my waist as carefully as I could and eased myself into a sitting position. Now I was awake I needed the bathroom, and God alone knew what that would be like—if indeed they even had bathrooms . . .

Once I was properly sitting up I could see I'd been wrong: Mr. Shenanigans was sprawled facedown across the end of the bed, with Mr. Kerfuffle curled in a little ball by his side. It was fortunate the bed was so huge.

But Kayla was conspicuous by her absence, though it was probably just as well—the bed was quite crowded enough already and I didn't like to think what she would say if she came across me like this. Somehow I doubted she'd be impressed . . . then again, maybe being all curled up together in a pile was a demon thing.

I really didn't want to wake anyone, although I was beginning to think I'd have little choice, not just because I needed to get out of the bed, but because I needed to know if there was a bathroom, because I really did need to pee.

Jamie looked too sweet to wake and I doubted Pyrites would be of much help. Mr. Shenanigans was dead to the world, and Mr. Kerfuffle had just started to snore big time. I twisted around to take a look at Jinx, only to discover that asleep, he looked almost as angelic as Jamie. True, he was dark maroon, had horns and a pointed tail, but he was smiling in his sleep, and he looked completely guileless. Then I remembered what he had whispered in my ear and once again my stomach gave that funny little lurch that wasn't actually at all unpleasant. Unfortunately, it didn't help my need to pee.

I looked around me, trying to figure out what to do: whichever way I moved, I'd wake someone—

Something nudged me in the back and when I turned, Pyrites was scampering down the bed. He turned, gave a little puff of smoke, flew up past my head and hovered in front of me. Then he began to grow, and when he was the size of a small pony, he dropped down and reached out his front claws. I hesitated; did he want me to take them? He waited, claws outstretched, so I took one in each hand and he slowly ascended into the air, lifting me until I was standing on the bed, then he rose up a bit further, still carrying me with him until I was dangling midair.

Then he flapped his wings a little harder, causing a gentle draft, and carried me away from the bed until he could lower me to the ground.

"Thank you, boy," I whispered and he dropped down on his haunches in front of me with a soft purr. "You are a very good boy—I don't suppose you know where the bathroom is?"

Pyrites cocked his head to one side as if considering my question, then stood and trotted across the room. He stopped by a long black velvet curtain speckled with gold and silver dust so it glittered like the night sky, extended a claw and dragged it aside to reveal a door.

"You are such a clever boy," I said, giving him a scratch on the head.

The velvet curtain was soft against my fingers, like a kitten's fur— even the glittering threads were downy to the touch, not scratchy or coarse as I had expected. I drew it back, opened the door and stepped inside.

The large room was dominated by a huge black stone bath quite big enough to accommodate my five bodyguards and me with no trouble at all. Like the bedroom, I had the distinct impression this was more a room for entertaining. It was lit by twenty or more candles; all white, all different sizes, some in lamps on the wall, others were in candlesticks placed about the room. Some floated in small dishes of water, scenting the room with a beautiful but unfamiliar perfume— something close to spring flowers after April rain would've been my best guess. But my urge was almost overwhelming now; I'd have time to examine the room after I'd found the toilet, which was not immediately in view.

There was a wooden screen fashioned out of some highly polished dark red wood across the far corner of the room, portioning it off, and behind was the toilet, carved out of the same polished black stone as the bath. Beside it was a hand-pump, together with a large gold jug: so apparently it had to be flushed manually. I didn't care; I counted myself lucky that the thing at least had a waste pipe, though the pressure on my bladder was such I would have gone in the jug if I'd had to.

I had thought the stone would be cold and uncomfortable, but it was actually warm to the touch. While I relieved myself, I studied the screen, which was decorated with a Chinese dragon painted in gold. His long, squirming body stretched across the whole expanse, with his head in the top left corner and the tip of his tail in the bottom right.

When I'd finished I spent some time admiring the room, which wouldn't have looked out of place in one of those magazines showing the houses of the rich and famous. The bath was carved out of some shiny black stone—onyx, maybe, or something similar—which glinted and gleamed in the torchlight. When I stepped closer, I could see it was flecked with tiny specks of gold and silver. Like the velvet curtain it mimicked the sky at night. There was a plug and plughole in the base, so I knew they had at least basic plumbing, even though there were no taps—but there was another hand-pump, also fashioned from a metal that looked a lot like gold, standing at the other end of the bath. I assumed the ore that was so precious in my world must be commonplace here.

Along one wall there was a bench made of the same highly polished reddish wood as the screen, upon which rested a deep round bowl carved out of the same stone as the bath. This had a hand-pump too, slightly smaller than the one for the bath.

I closed the door quietly, but no one had stirred; my men were still where I had left them. Even Pyrites was back on the pillow, eyes closed and little puffs of smoke emanating from his nostrils. Jamie had rolled over onto his side so he was facing Jinx and looking at them both like that they were almost mirror images of each other: one good, one bad—or no, not bad. I didn't think Jinx was bad, despite the horns and tail and whole Deathbringer thing—but seeing them lying there together made me think they were the two sides of a coin: opposites, though somehow the same.

Jinx's tail quivered and then lifted up from behind him and wrapped itself over his thigh and down under his knee. His nose twitched and his eyelids fluttered as if he was about to wake—but no; he bowed his head down a little further so his chin was almost touching his chest. His forehead was now only inches from Jamie's—if he shifted his head forward he would be in danger of impaling Jamie on his horns. But once again it was as if Jamie could read my thoughts, even while asleep, because he rolled onto his back and then twisted onto his other side so he was facing away from the death demon.

I sat down on a large overstuffed chair by the window and curled up with my legs beneath me. I wondered where Kayla was, what she was doing. Then I glanced over at the bed. It wasn't lost on me that at home she had sat on a similar chair watching me sleep. The thought brought a lump to my throat. I closed my eyes and wanted to cry, but tears wouldn't help me, not here. Tears were a sign of weakness, and Jamie had warned me I mustn't show any emotion, as it would be used against me. Was standing up to Argon and stamping on his claw showing weakness? I hoped not, otherwise I'd blown it already, and big time.

I was wide awake now, and very agitated. Where was Kayla? I had no idea how long I had been asleep. I got up and went to the window, but it was still dark outside, although the two moons were lower in the sky now. I went back to the chair and made myself comfortable again. I would just have to bide my time until she returned and hope I hadn't caused her too much trouble with her father—*our* father. How could that creature be my father? It was impossible, surely—though my bodyguards all appeared to believe it was so, and even Baltheza had said I was his daughter. What had my mother been thinking? Maybe he had made himself look human, as my demons had at the golf club?

I sank back into the cushions, closed my eyes and hoped I would sleep.

Twelve

"Lucky, Lucky, wake up," a voice whispered, then someone lost patience, grasped me by the shoulder and shook me none too gently. "Lucky."

I opened one eye. Kayla backed away and glared at me, one hand on hip, the other clasped in a fist against her chest.

"Kayla?" I said.

"Shush." She cast a quick look across the room at the sleeping men. "We need to talk—alone."

"Now you want to talk; I think we've passed the talking stage, don't you?" I didn't mean to be grumpy, but she had woken me from a deep sleep and I wasn't yet firing on all cylinders.

She ignored me and grabbed me by the forearm, pulled me up from the chair and half dragged me across the room to the bathroom. She all but pushed me inside, then she closed the door as quietly as she could, leaned back against it and let out a long breath.

"Where's the child?" she asked.

"Somewhere safe."

She studied my face while I studied hers. Her cheeks were flushed and her eyes glittered. The little snakes in her hair wove around her ears

and forehead showing small, sharp teeth and giving sibilant hisses of
discontent. She was unhappy, so I guessed they were too.

"You sure?"

"Mr. Shenanigans says so."

"At least something good has come out of this whole sorry mess,"
she said.

"What about Philip?"

"What about him?"

"Is he still with Daltas?"

She shook her head. "Daltas offered him to Argon in recompense
for the girl."

"No!" I gasped, but Kayla laughed unhappily.

"It's all right, but you owe me big time." She crossed the room and sat
on the side of the bath. When she looked up at me her lips had curled into a
small smile, but her shoulders sagged and the snakes had retreated in among
her hair. She patted the side of the bath next to her.

Even with the snakes hiding I was wary of sitting too close to her,
but I didn't want to hurt her feelings. I sat close enough that our thighs
were almost touching and hoped with all my heart that she would
remain calm so the serpents would too.

"I accepted Philip as a gift from Daltas, as he knew I would, rather
than see him fall into Argon's hands. He always has been and always will
be a manipulative shit."

"So you're officially dating him?"

"I've permitted him to call on me, but that's all."

"He's not bad looking," I said, trying to lighten the mood. "Well,
for a demon."

She gave a nonchalant shrug.

"You like him, don't you?" I got up from the bath to look down at
my friend. "That's it, isn't it? You actually like him, even though he *is*
a manipulative shit."

She crossed her arms, hugging herself. "I *loathe* him," she said, "but
once . . . There's something about him, when he's near me—it makes
me want him to take me in his arms and kiss me."

I stared at her for a moment. "Wow," I said, and sat back down next to her.

"Yes, wow," she said, sounding thoroughly miserable.

"So this isn't a good thing?"

"No, most definitely not. If I married Daltas it would be like putting a target on my father's forehead."

"Daltas would kill your father for the throne?"

"Essentially, yes: if he didn't order my father assassinated himself, his followers would."

"But if he was married to you, surely he wouldn't want to hurt you?"

Kayla laughed out loud. "Lucky, we're demon royalty: once married I'll be of use to him for one thing only."

"Which is?" Even as I said the words I knew what she was talking about and shuddered.

"Bearing him offspring, and once that's done and they're grown I'll become excess to requirements."

I suddenly felt very cold. "He'd have you killed?"

She gave a small nod, and I took hold of her hand. I had been wrong: she might not look like my Kayla anymore, but she was still her, and the thought of anyone hurting her or taking her away from me scared me to death.

She looked up and smiled at me: a real smile for the first time in such a long while. "Don't you worry about me," she said. "I can look after myself, and Lord Daltas isn't about to have everything his own way."

"No?"

"No way. He thinks he's so clever, but he's never lived in the Overlands. He hasn't watched human TV and knows nothing of *Dirty Harry*, *The A Team*, James Bond or *Eastenders*. I have more than enough knowledge of both worlds to lead him a merry dance."

This was more like it. I grinned at her. "I'm almost beginning to feel sorry for him."

"Don't," she said, "he doesn't deserve any sympathy, particularly not from you. It was he who sent Argon to steal you from the Overlands. I can't prove it, but I'm sure it was so."

"Philip was being blackmailed, I think."

"I wouldn't feel too sorry for him either. He allowed himself to be drawn into all this by his hunger for power. He was targeted by Daltas's pet human, offered more wealth and power than he could ever imagine and then, when he was in too deep to get out, they stole his daughter to keep him in line."

"He said they killed his wife."

"I think he wanted you to feel sorry for him."

I frowned. "They didn't kill her?"

"Oh yes, they did, but—and again, I can't yet prove this—I think he offered her up to save himself."

"Dear God—"

"Please don't say that word here," Kayla said. "It doesn't bother me, but Father always throws himself into a complete royal rage at His mention."

"Why?"

She laughed. "Why do you think? He's jealous."

"*Jealous?*"

She looked at me curiously. "Wouldn't you be? Our father is one of the most powerful creatures in existence, and yet, does anyone in the Overlands worship Lord Baltheza? No. Has anyone on Earth even heard of Lord Baltheza? No. They have wars in the name of their gods—thousands upon thousands die every year in their names alone; the name of the so-called righteous—but not one of those names is Lord Baltheza. Ironic, don't you think? All those people tortured and killed in the name of righteous human gods, and yet not one killed in the name of the Lord of all Daemonkind."

Maybe to a demented sociopath this would make some kind of sick logic—but then, I was pretty sure Kayla's father fell into that very category. I still couldn't think of him as being related to me in any way, shape or form; I guessed that was something I'd have to get used to.

"Now, enough about me," Kayla said. "How in all of Hades have you managed to get marked by not one but two demons?"

I frowned at her. "Jamie isn't a demon."

Kayla gave a sniff. "Lucky, we are all demons here."

I wasn't about to argue the point with her. After all, what did I know? "I have no idea, although Jamie and Jinx seem to have worked it out."

"You do understand what it means?" she asked, cradling my hand in both of hers and gripping it a little bit tighter. Her expression was deadly serious. Suddenly it wasn't Kayla I feared for.

"Jamie said it was like we were engaged?" I said.

Kayla gave an exasperated snort. "He would. And Jinx?"

"He was a little more blunt."

"And?"

"He said I belonged to them and if they wanted I would be their slave and . . ." I bit my lip and looked down at her hands gripping mine, ". . . and I was their . . . their sex toy."

Kayla's hands went rigid around mine and I didn't dare look at her face. She exhaled slowly and I risked a quick glance up at her. She was staring at the door and from the twist of her lips I was pretty sure she was thinking of the various terrible injuries she wanted to inflict on Jinx's anatomy.

She exhaled again. "Well," she said, "I suppose he was at least honest."

"He was telling the truth?"

She gave a slow nod. "You belong to both of them, but the very fact you do keeps you safe from others such as Argon—that you are marked by two such powerful demons keeps you safer than I ever could . . . but to be marked by Jinx"—her breath came out as a soft sigh—"that makes me fear for you in other ways."

"Why? Mr. Kerfuffle seemed to think I'd be safe with him as one of my guards."

"As a guard? Yes. You do realize what Jinx is?"

"A death demon?"

She pursed her lips. "The most powerful of death demons."

And all of a sudden I remembered the other members of the court shrinking away from him, the gasps of horror when they saw him within their midst.

"He's not Death, is he?" I whispered.

Kayla drew my hands to her lips and kissed them. "As good as to humankind, though he's not the Reaper. Did he give his oath to keep you safe?"

I nodded. Once again words failed me.

"Kerfuffle and Shenanigans are good servants and they wouldn't have asked for his help if they didn't think it was for the best."

"Mr. Shenanigans and Jamie weren't happy about it."

Kayla's lips twitched a little and her eyes sparkled. "I think that might be for reasons other than just your safety."

"What do you mean?"

She laughed, a real laugh. "I think maybe Shenanigans—and certainly the Guardian—feel like they have a little competition."

"Competition?"

"Don't you think Jinx is good looking?"

I kept my expression neutral and waited a few seconds before replying, as though considering her question. Kayla was my best friend, but color me suspicious: I wasn't at all sure of her motives yet, and alarm bells were ringing in my head.

"Both Jinx and Jamie are easy on the eye," I said slowly, "but why should it matter to me?"

Kayla gave me a smug look. "No reason."

That was enough to let me know there was a very good reason for her asking. The question was: should I rise to the bait or let it go? I could see her watching me from under lowered lashes, and then I could see the glint of several pairs of eyes peeping out from within her hair and that brought a smile to my face. The tiny snakes mirrored her emotions. If I couldn't read her expression I would look to the snakes and they might give her away.

"What?" she asked, her smile replaced by a puzzled pout.

"Oh, nothing," I said. "I was just thinking how good it is to see you again."

Her smile returned. "I have missed you," she said.

"And I you." And that was the truth; I had missed her very much indeed.

"Come on," she said, getting up from the side of the bath, "we'd better get some sleep. It's going to be a long day tomorrow."

She slung an arm across my shoulders and guided me back into the bedroom.

"Chance would be a fine thing," I said, gesturing toward the bed.

Mr. Shenanigans had rolled over and was lying spreadeagled over the whole of the bottom half of the bed, with Mr. Kerfuffle huddled beneath his right arm. Jamie was curled up on one side along the top of the bed, with his head pressed against the headboard, and Jinx was at a similar angle with his back to him, with Pyrites nestled behind the back of his neck.

Kayla stood watching them all sleep, her forefinger tapping her bottom lip, before stalking over to the bed and kneeling on the end next to Mr. Kerfuffle. She reached over Mr. Shenanigans, grabbed hold of his left arm and started pulling on it until he gave a little start and then rolled over onto his side. She got down and made her way to where Jinx was sleeping, leaned over him and blew into his ear. He lifted a hand and batted at it as if to brush off an annoying insect, and she did it again; this time he shifted his head. And again, and he murmured, "Damn drakon," and shifted away from Pyrites until he was lying along the edge of the bed.

"There," she said, "room enough?"

I frowned at the space that had been left on the bed. "How about you?"

"I have relocated to the chamber next door."

"Can't I go with you?"

"No," she said, her expression wistful, "I have seven guards in my bed and if they were joined by one marked by the death demon, it would—well, let's say it would *unsettle* them."

"This is usual then?" I said, indicating the sleeping men.

"They are your guard: it is their job to protect your body and they need sleep as you do, so what better way than to sleep with you?"

"Couldn't they take shifts or something?"

"Believe me, Lucky, if danger stalked this room all five would be awake in an instant and between you and it." She must have seen that I was unconvinced. "Watch," she said.

She lifted her skirt and pulled a dagger—the twin of mine—from beneath it, then pointed it at me.

One hand gripped my wrist and another took hold of my shoulder, pulling me backward. Bodies appeared all around me as the room reverberated with the sound of beating wings and fists started hammering on the door.

Kayla laughed. "You see?"

My bodyguards had surrounded me and I couldn't even see Kayla as Jamie had me wrapped within his wings.

"It's okay, boys," Kayla said. "It was just a test."

"Mistress!" I heard a voice cry, and the door burst open.

"Stand down," I heard Kayla order. "No one is at risk of harm here."

It went quiet for a moment, although the atmosphere in the room bristled with tension. Then, slowly, Jamie's wings lowered so I could see, although he still didn't withdraw them completely.

It was like I'd always imagined being in the middle of a Mexican standoff must feel. Kayla stood facing me with her seven guards around her. Mr. Shenanigans, Mr. Kerfuffle and Jinx stood in front of Jamie and me, their weapons in hand. A breeze tugged at my hair and when I pushed my head back against Jamie's chest so I could look up I saw Pyrites hovering above us, puffing black smoke.

"Easy, Pyrites," I said. I didn't want him crisping anyone by accident.

The dragon hovered there a few seconds more, then with a flick of his tail, he floated down beside us.

"See," Kayla said.

Her guards were glaring at my guards, and mine were no doubt glaring back. It was all far too macho for my liking.

"Milady?" a tall demon said, taking hold of Kayla's hand. He was a few inches taller than her and his skin—not scales, I noticed—was a beautiful jade green. His hair flowed like a glossy emerald waterfall down his back to his waist. One short horn of twisted ivory parted his glorious locks in the center, just above the hairline. His eyes, a pale liquid green, looked at odds with the stern set of his jaw and unhappy curve of his lips.

He was barefoot and wearing little more than something similar to boxers, which did nothing to hide his muscular torso and legs to match. He held a sword in his right hand.

"Lucky, I would like you to meet Vaybian, captain of my guard."

I shrugged my way out of Jamie's wings and smiled at the demon. "Hi," I said.

He frowned at me.

"That is a form of greeting in the Overlands," Kayla explained to him.

He gave a little bow in my direction. "I am most pleased to meet you at last," he said, but the narrowing of his eyes told another story.

Even more interesting was Kayla's expression and the way she was gripping his hand. It was clear to me that Lord Daltas had a rival.

Kayla didn't bother to introduce any of her other guards, and I could see what Jamie meant about them being chosen more for their looks than professional ability. Although clearly demons, they were all muscular and good looking, in their demon way. They were also wearing very little: it looked like Kayla's bodyguards actually undressed for bed.

"We'll see you in the morning," Kayla said with a smile, and I smiled back and watched her leave still holding her captain's hand. The other guards followed after casting a few more distrustful looks in our direction.

When the door finally closed behind them Jinx began to laugh. "Oh, what fun this is going to be."

"I think I misjudged her guard," Jamie said. "They might look very pretty, but Vaybian for one is not someone with whom I'd want to cross swords."

Mr. Shenanigans and Mr. Kerfuffle murmured in agreement, but I said quickly, "But they're Kayla's guard, and Kayla is my sister, so there's no problem." I looked at the solemn faces of my men. Only Jinx was smiling. "Right?"

"Not necessarily," Jinx said.

"Then elaborate, why don't you?"

Jinx gestured to Jamie. "You explain," he said. "Court politics is more your cup of tea."

Again there was an obvious tension between the two men, but even so, Jinx was obviously finding it all incredibly amusing.

"Lucky," Jamie began, and paused. After a moment, he went on, "What you must understand is that although Kayla is your sister and your friend, she's also your rival—or at least, you are hers."

"But I don't want to be queen. I just want to go home."

"What *you* want has nothing to do with it. Daltas was conniving enough to get you here, so now he has another string to his bow: if Kayla won't marry him freely, then he'll try to force you to be his bride so he still has a shot at being the next ruler."

"Baltheza wouldn't choose me over Kayla," I said. "He doesn't even know me."

Jamie looked troubled. "Jinx, you explain. You're much better at giving bad news than I am."

Jinx took hold of my hand, led me to the bed and gestured for me to sit before taking the dressing table stool opposite me. He leaned forward, put his elbows on his knees and clasped his hands together to support his chin. "Lucky, it has nothing to do with you or Kayla, other than that either of you could become queen. You're just the vehicles for others' ambitions."

"Charming," I said, "but that still doesn't explain why we should have a problem with Kayla's guards other than all the usual macho shit."

Jamie and Jinx exchanged a glance and Mr. Kerfuffle snorted.

"What?"

"Vaybian," Mr. Kerfuffle said succinctly, and the other three nodded.

Every time I asked a question I received an answer that left me none the wiser—it was like pulling teeth. "So what about Vaybian?"

Five sets of eyes were suddenly on me; even Pyrites looked astounded by my ignorance.

"Captain Vaybian is ambitious, and he has always been favored by Lady Kayla," Mr. Kerfuffle said. "He didn't appear at all happy to meet you, and the taking of her hand was more than the protective gesture of a guard to his mistress."

This time even the dragon nodded in agreement.

"You think Captain Vaybian is Kayla's lover?" I asked.

Jamie looked to the heavens and Jinx laughed. "I thought women were meant to be good at this sort of thing?"

I glared at them all. "I thought as much myself! But I think the reason he's not so happy with me is that Kayla accepted Philip as a gift from Daltas—no doubt he blames me for that."

"Not good, not good," Mr. Kerfuffle said.

"Oh, I don't know," said Jinx. "It may focus the good captain's attentions on the Lady Kayla and keeping her happy rather than that Lucky herself is a potential threat to his ambition."

"Would Baltheza ever entertain him as a successor?" Jamie asked.

Jinx shook his head. "Baltheza doesn't entertain *anyone* as his successor. He plans to rule forever."

"And will he?" I asked.

Jinx's expression became grim and he glanced at Jamie. Those two might have appeared to be enemies but they certainly had an affinity with each other. Sometimes I could have sworn they'd had a whole conversation without saying a word out loud, a bit like Mr. Kerfuffle and Mr. Shenanigans, now I thought about it. Right now they both looked deep in thought, but there was something else going on; I was sure of it.

"I wouldn't be surprised if there wasn't an immediate assassination attempt on Baltheza once word of your identity gets out," Jamie said at last.

"Death is not waiting at his elbow," Jinx said, "so he is a long way off a natural demise, but then, he is an immortal."

"Kayla thinks Daltas or one of his supporters will make an attempt," I said.

Jinx snorted. "Is that what she told you?"

"Yes."

Jinx shot Jamie a look and my angel frowned unhappily. "I think she's probably right. The question is: will Vaybian try first? Or even— dare I say it?—Kayla?"

I stared at him. "No," I said shaking my head, "no, Kayla's not like that. Kayla wouldn't hurt anyone, and certainly not her own father."

I waited for someone to agree with me, but it looked as if I would be in for a long wait. No one would meet my eye.

"She wouldn't," I repeated, "I know she wouldn't." This time even I could hear the desperation in my voice.

"Lucky," Jamie said, "it's different here: people do awful things just to survive, and Kayla's chances of survival would probably double with Baltheza and Daltas out of the way."

"No," I told him. "Kayla is like me: neither of us would ever want to kill anyone." Then a vision of Henri smelling my hair and licking my face flashed into my head and I began to wonder whether I *did* want to kill someone; if I did he and Lord Argon would certainly be distinct possibilities.

"You seem unsure, princess," Mr. Shenanigans said.

"Henri le Dent," I admitted. "He could possibly change my mind."

"Ha!" Jinx said. "So you have met Monsieur le Dent, Daltas's assassin of choice?"

"I won't say it was a pleasure."

"It was why I went to her," Jamie said. "I had a suspicion that Daltas was interfering in the Overlands—not that he'd admit to it."

"Well, if Daltas is here, Henri will be too. Just keep as far away from him as possible," Mr. Kerfuffle said.

He didn't need to state the obvious. The moment I saw Henri coming for me I'd be putting all five of my guards in between us. Strangely, although he was the most human to look at, out of all the demons I had seen so far he scared me the most. He oozed malevolence and evil intent, and I didn't think I'd ever be able to smell Parma violets again without also feeling a surge of fear.

"I think our little princess is well aware of how dangerous Henri can be," Jinx said, and he wasn't smiling, which made me wonder whether there was some history between him and the terrible Henri. Then he did flash a smile in my direction. "Come on, let's get some sleep. I have a feeling tomorrow is going to be a long day for some of us."

"*All* of us," Mr. Shenanigans corrected.

Jinx gestured for me to climb onto the bed, then added, "Don't you think you might be a little bit more comfortable wearing something else?"

I gave him a look through narrowed eyes. "And what might you suggest?"

He straightened up and practically danced across the room to draw back another black velvet starlight curtain. He opened the door behind it. "I suspect you might find something to your liking in here."

I crossed the room and peeped through the door. It was a walk-in wardrobe and it was filled with rail upon rail of clothes in every color, fabric and style I could ever have imagined: sapphire silks, emerald velvets, gold and silver lace; long-sleeved dresses, short-sleeved dresses, gowns with tiny spaghetti straps; long leather coats lined with fur and short leather coats decorated with feathers . . . There were racks of shoes and boots lining the walls under the hanging clothes. The strong scent of leather perfumed the whole room, although there was an underlying aroma, perhaps of cedarwood.

"If these are Kayla's they'll be too big for me," I said with regret as I ran a finger across the soft pile of a most beautiful dark blue gown.

Jinx stepped into the wardrobe behind me. "Didn't she tell you? These are now your chambers, and these are your clothes."

I swung around to face him. "Really?"

He grinned. "Really. But I suggest you hurry up and choose something to wear, otherwise there will be no room left for us on the bed." He squeezed past me and walked to the end of the wardrobe. "How about this?" he asked, holding up a dusky pink satin nightgown.

"It's beautiful," I said, walking over to him and taking the material between my fingertips. "Are you sure no one will mind?"

"They are yours to do with as you please," he said, "but I would suggest you wear them rather than burn them on the fire or throw them out with the trash." He turned and walked outside, closing the door.

I rubbed the luxurious material against my cheek. The gown was long enough to brush my toes and high enough that it didn't expose any cleavage. I turned it around, holding it up high. There were no slits at the sides or back, so I didn't think it was too provocative. Call me old-fashioned, but if you're intending to sleep in the same bed as four men and a dragon, in my opinion it's best to dress discreetly. I was vain enough that I didn't want to look frumpy—though looking at the selection of clothes around me I doubted that would be possible—but sexy was another matter altogether.

With a smile I quickly stripped off all of my clothes except my underwear and slipped the nightdress over my head. The satin slithered down my body, the material cool against my skin. I turned to admire myself in the large mirror covering the far end of the wardrobe, but upon seeing my reflection the smile slipped from my face. I shivered, suddenly cold and very scared. I walked toward the mirror, staring at the woman walking toward me. It was me—it had to be me—but she didn't look like me, not really.

She was frowning, as I guess I was. She looked me up and down, as I did her. Our eyes met and my hand flew to my mouth to stop myself from crying out. Hers did too. I reached out and touched the mirror. Our fingers met.

"Oh, dear God," I whispered, and her mouth moved in time with my own. I dropped down to my knees, my fingertips sliding down the glass and she followed me. I reached out to touch her face, my fingers hovering above the mirror's surface; she did the same.

Her opalescent skin wasn't the same white as Kayla's; it was a living shimmering pink. Her hair was longer than mine, although just as straight, but where my locks were dark chestnut brown, hers were a glistening curtain of mahogany and eggplant. When I stared into the mirror, eyes of violet and garnet stared back.

I lifted my hands and looked at them. I found ordinary skin; ordinary pink, blunt nails. But in the mirror, she looked upon long, slender, shimmering fingers with pointed maroon nails.

The door must have opened behind me, although I hadn't heard it, nor did I see them walk up behind me. It was only when I felt strong fingers grip one shoulder and a palm rest on my other that I looked up at the images of Jamie and Jinx standing on either side of me.

"Is this how you see me?" I asked.

Jamie crouched down beside me and put his arm around my shoulders. "Not yet, but if you stay you'll become your true self."

"What if I go back?" I said.

"You'll be able to cover yourself with the human veneer you've been wearing since moments after you were born. It's second nature to you; this is why you're still hiding from yourself."

I stared at my reflection. "No, this is me," I said, gesturing down at myself. "This is the *real* me. Not her in the mirror."

Jamie kissed my head. "Don't you think she's beautiful?"

He was right; she was beautiful. "But she looks so scared."

"No, Lucky, it's you who's scared. But not for much longer. Come on," he said, drawing me up from the floor, "come to bed and dream sweet dreams."

Jinx put his arm around my waist while Jamie kept his across my shoulders, and together they led me from the room.

As we walked out of the wardrobe I glanced back. She gave me a sad smile as the door closed behind us.

Thirteen

I didn't think I would—or could—sleep, but exhaustion took over as soon as I closed my eyes, though my slumber was far from restful. I struggled to wake as I tumbled from one frightening dream to another, trying to stop my endless flight through dark scenes of pain and fear, each episode worse than the previous. Every time I escaped one peril I was thrust straight into something even more dreadful, and the last nightmare was so terrible I could hear my screams echoing around and around my head so loudly that I thought my skull would split open.

"Hush, hush, little one," a gentle voice said, and a cool palm rested against my forehead. "Hush, and dream of moonbeams, stardust and light."

Then there was blessed peace, and I was staring up at the night sky, following the paths of shooting stars that filled the heavens with bright swathes of light and sparkles. I could hear a child giggling in delight and realized it was me: *I* was the child laughing at the stars and pretending they were fairies flying through the skies.

The stars faded and the sky grew brighter. Dawn was coming, and with it came a dreamless sleep. No more fear, no more tears, just oblivion.

I woke up to the sound of male singing, the smell of freshly baked bread and a waft of warm air tousling my hair. I opened one eye. There was no bare chest beneath my cheek this time, just an excited dragon kneading my pillow. He gave another little puff of smoke and then flicked a long forked tongue across the side of my cheek. His breath smelled sweet, not bad at all—almost like barley sugar with a hint of licorice.

"Hello, boy," I said, and he kneaded the pillow some more, then nudged my shoulder with his snout, three times. He dropped back on his haunches and looked at me, his head cocked to one side as though expecting something from me. "What is it, boy?"

"He's telling you that if you don't get up now, there'll be no break-fast left," Jinx called through a mouthful of something.

I struggled into a sitting position and saw the four demons were sitting on the floor around a low table, scoffing from plates loaded with what looked like bread and butter, cheese, sausages and various sliced meats. Obviously demons didn't suffer from high cholesterol.

I clambered off the bed and made for the bathroom. "A bath's been run if you have a care for it," Mr. Kerfuffle called after me.

I gave him a wave of thanks and shut the door behind me. There was no lock, so I could only hope bathing together didn't follow on from sharing a bed. Looking at the size of the bath I had my suspicions it probably did, but right now my guards were more interested in filling their stomachs, so I hoped I would be uninterrupted. I used the toilet as quickly as I could and hurried out from behind the wooden screen.

The bath was filled with steaming water to within ten inches of the top, filling the air with clouds of pale purple mist that smelled of lily of the valley with a hint of freesia. When I dipped three fingers into the foaming water I found it hot, but not too hot.

I pulled off the nightgown and my underwear, sat on the edge of the bath and lowered myself into the bubbles. I stayed under for the count of five, then burst up through the surface, sending waves of water cascading over the bath's edge and across the flagstone floor. I worried for a second, then thought *what the hell*; if it needed to be cleaned up, no

doubt someone would do it. I leaned back and closed my eyes, luxuriat-
ing in the hot suds. Heaven.

There was a knock on the door and it opened a crack. "Are you
decent?" Jinx called.

"No," I said.

"Good," he said, and came in, shutting the door behind him.

I opened my eyes and looked up at him as he sat down on the edge
of the bath. "Can't a girl have any privacy?"

"Nope. At least one guard with you at all times, preferably more."

"I suppose I should be glad you gave me a few minutes."

Jinx trailed his fingers through the bubbles and smiled. "That was
Jamie's doing. He said Overlanders have strange hang-ups about nudity
and bodily functions."

"Well, he'd be right," I said, closing my eyes again.

"Can't understand it myself."

"I thought you'd been to my world?"

"All work and no play," he said, but there was a note in his voice that
made me open my eyes. I was just in time to see him disappear under
my bubbles.

"Jinx! Get out—get out, now!"

There was no sign of the Deathbringer, and I already knew that
the water was as clear as clear could be beneath the bubbles on the
surface. I was tempted to get straight out, but I hesitated. Would
Jamie have allowed him into the room if he thought he might hurt
me?

Hell, what was I thinking? Of course he didn't mean to hurt me—
hurting me was probably the furthest thing from his mind. If he truly
considered me a sex toy it was more than likely he'd come to play. I
snorted. If that was the case he was going to get more than he bar-
gained for.

He rose slowly out of the water right in front of me, eyes closed,
head thrown back, and reached up and swiped the water away from
his face before he opened his eyes. He smiled, a slow, dark smile,
and rose up on his knees. The water was high enough to leave what
was below his waist to my imagination and I felt a small hiccough

of disappointment—and I could tell by his growing smile that he knew it.

"You'd better get out now," I said, but my voice came out low and sexy, half an octave lower than it should have—and sexy definitely wasn't the impression I wanted to give. It was actually quite the opposite: I was beyond scared. I didn't want to have to fight a death demon for my honor. In fact, I wasn't sure whether I wanted to fight Jinx at all, as all my bravado was melting away with the gradually disappearing bubbles.

"Jinx," I said, "this isn't funny."

"It's not meant to be." His twinkling eyes belied his words and there was a huskiness in his voice that promised whatever he intended would be fun.

I sank further under the water so my chin was skimming the surface. "Jinx, please get out, I don't want to fall out with you."

"Nor I, you," he said, moving on his knees toward me.

"Jinx, stop tormenting her and get out of the bath," Kayla said from the doorway. I could see Jamie beside her and his expression was murderous, although, somewhat to my surprise, Kayla looked only irritated.

"Killjoy," he said, pulling himself up onto the side of the bath. I was all set to clench my eyes shut when I realized he was still wearing his pants.

Kayla gestured with her thumb for him to get out and he gave us both a grin and me a wink and left, taking Jamie with him. No sooner had the door closed than I could hear raised voices outside.

"He was just teasing," she said with a sigh. "If he'd meant business we wouldn't have been able to get through the door."

"Great," I said, "now I feel so much better."

"Don't be sarcastic."

"So glad you're in a good mood this morning."

"I didn't come here to argue."

"Good."

She wandered around the bathroom picking up candles, moving baskets of towels, fussing with bits and pieces.

"Kayla, what's the matter?"

She leaned back against the sink, her hands grasping the edge of the bench. "You told me not so long ago that whatever I'd done, or whoever I was, I'd always be your friend. Is it still true?"

"Kayla, you know it is."

"Even though I'm demon?"

"It seems all my best friends are."

"Don't be flippant."

"I'm not," I said. "Think about it—what friends do I have?"

Her forehead wrinkled. "Rita and what's-his-name, at the pub?"

"Roger," I supplied, "and they're not real friends—I doubt they'd even miss me now you've got rid of Balmy Bill."

"How about Mrs. What's-her-face? You know, the one with the cat?"

"Kayla, she's been dead for two years. The only reason she waves to me is that I'm the only one who ever waves back."

"That's true."

"So the only friends I've got are you and possibly four more demons and a dragon."

"Demons and a drakon."

"Whatever."

"If you're going to stay, you might as well get the language right."

"I'm not staying," I said.

"Don't be too sure."

"Okay, what's going on?"

"Father has agreed to meet you."

"Well, that's just dandy. What if I don't want to meet him?"

"That isn't an option."

"He hasn't been interested before so why the interest now?"

"You weren't here before and now you are."

"Kayla, I just want to go home."

"This'll soon be your home."

I crossed my arms and glared at her.

"You said yourself this is where all your friends are," she said, with a bitchy little smile.

Trouble was, she was right. I sighed. "All right. If it makes life easier for you I'll meet him—but you'll have to promise me you won't let him do anything terrible to me."

She laughed. "It is rare for demon royalty to kill their daughters. If you were a son it would be a different matter. No, it's not our father you need to fear—at least, you don't need to fear that he might kill you. Lord Daltas is another matter, though."

"Goody, I feel so safe and secure. Though I'd have thought Daltas would want me around as his alternative option, just in case you decide to marry your handsome green captain." Kayla wasn't the only one who could be bitchy.

Her head snapped up. "What did you say?" She strode across the room toward me.

"You heard," I said, sinking back down into the bath. Just what protection I thought some fast-vanishing bubbles would be I had no idea.

"Who told you about Vaybian?"

"You did, Kayla."

"I never did—I've had no time."

"Kayla, the way he took your hand last night? And the way you held onto it and didn't let go? It was pretty obvious to all of us."

"All of you?"

"Good God, Kayla, even Pyrites knew!"

"I told you not to use that word," she snapped, and she marched to the door in a flurry of gold silk. "Be ready at dusk. Make yourself as beautiful as you can manage. I would suggest the emerald velvet with the three-quarter-length sleeves. We'll be dining in the great hall."

"Can the others come with me?"

She tapped a finger against her lips, as if in thought. "They're your guard, and your body will need more guarding than it did in this bath, that's for sure. So yes." She opened the door to leave and then turned back. "And Lucky . . . ?"

"Yes?"

"Don't be a martyr. Whatever pain you have seen poured upon another can just as easily be poured upon you. You were lucky with

Argon; he is just a walking penis and our father despises him. Speak out of turn to another and I mayn't be able to save you."

She turned her back on me. As she went to walk through the door I called after her, "I thought that was what my bodyguards were for."

She hesitated for a moment, not long, but long enough for a bevy of serpents to appear out of her hair and hiss their disapproval. Then she walked out of the room, pulling the door shut behind her. Not for the first time I wondered if Kayla was truly the best friend I had always thought her to be.

Any pleasure I'd had in the bath was gone. Kayla had been about to tell me something, I was sure of it: something she thought might come between us. Now I was worried about what it might be. Was she going to risk an assassination attempt on her father? I really hoped not, but if she did, I was selfish enough to wish it wouldn't be while I was present.

I climbed out of the bath, slopping more water over the floor as I did so, wrapped a large fluffy towel around me and another smaller one around my head in a turban. At home I might have gone and lain down on my bed for a while, maybe dozed for a while, but I didn't think that would be a good idea here. I didn't know if demons were into group sex or not, but judging by Kayla's guards' attire—or lack of it—it wouldn't have surprised me.

Once dry, I slid the nightdress back over my head and walked into the bedroom. Mr. Kerfuffle and Mr. Shenanigans were still breakfasting, but there was a definite atmosphere between my other two guards: Jamie, sitting on the bed, was glaring at Jinx, who was leaning against the wall by the hallway door and smiling back. Jinx saw me first; when he jerked his head in my direction Jamie forced his lips into a stiff smile.

"Apparently, I'm to be presented to Baltheza this evening," I told them.

The demons, no daemons—*I must get it right*—both stopped eating. "Will you be dining with him?" Mr. Kerfuffle asked.

"In the great hall, Kayla said. At dusk."

"I'd have preferred your first meeting to be private," Jamie said.

Jinx pushed himself away from the wall and walked over to join me. "You look troubled," he said, a frown clouding his face. "Did Kayla say something to upset you?"

"You getting into the bath probably upset her," Jamie said.

Jinx's lips twitched into a smile and his eyes twinkled. "I don't think so."

Jamie looked even angrier. "You think you're so great, don't you?" He jumped to his feet.

Jinx gave him a dark smile. "Just stating a fact."

"I should . . ." He took a step toward Jinx.

"Should what?" Jinx said, squaring up to him.

I stepped in between them. "What are you doing?" I asked, laying a palm on each of their chests. "Don't I have enough problems without you two taking a pop at each other?"

Jinx was still smiling, but both men had clenched fists hanging by their sides. Then Jamie's shoulders relaxed and he admitted, "You're right."

"And you," I said, poking Jinx in the chest with my forefinger, "*never* do that again. In fact, I don't want any of you entering the bathroom without invitation while I'm in there. Are we clear?"

There were a couple of "yes, mistresses," but Jinx leaned close to me and whispered, "I'll look forward to being invited."

I tried to glare at him, but he winked at me and I couldn't help but laugh. "You are what we at home call a bad boy."

He grinned and his tail curled around in front of him to wiggle at me. "Of course I am. They don't come any badder."

"Oh, please," Jamie muttered under his breath.

I turned to my pouting angel. "Jamie, I need you all to get along, particularly if you think Kayla and her entourage are going to be a problem."

He stood up very straight. "Your safety is, and always will be, my first priority."

"As it is mine," Jinx said quickly.

"Good," I said, but the atmosphere was still crackling with animosity. I wasn't sure what had changed, but something had sure cranked up the tension between them.

The morning seemed to drag on forever. All four men refused point-blank to let me explore, even in their company.

"There'll be enough time for that after you have been welcomed into the court by Lord Baltheza," Jamie had said.

After lunch the four hours before dusk sped by, and my anxiety levels increased with each passing minute. By the time Jamie finally announced I should start getting changed for dinner, I was sick with nerves, and the prospect of food didn't help any.

"Which gown do you want to wear?" asked Jamie as we walked between the rails of dresses in the wardrobe.

Jinx followed along behind as I ran my fingers along the various different dresses. Now and then Jamie would make a suggestion, but I was finding it hard to concentrate.

"Come on, Lucky," Jamie said at last. "There must be one dress out of all these that you like."

"I like them all," I said.

"Why not start by picking a color?" Jinx said.

"Kayla said to wear the emerald-green velvet," I remembered.

"There are several that match that description," Jamie said.

I looked along the avenue of dresses, trying to remember exactly what she had said. "It had three-quarter-length sleeves, I think."

Jinx and Jamie both turned and studied me, calculating expressions upon their faces. I found their scrutiny rather disconcerting, particularly as they'd started examining every inch of me from head to toe.

"Come on, boys," I said at last, "you're making me feel very uncomfortable."

"I don't see her in green," Jinx said, ignoring me.

"She looks good in green," Jamie said. "She has this little silk blouse that makes her look great."

I frowned. He made it sound like the shirt had made a silk purse out of a sow's ear. "I think I'll wear blue," I said. "The velvet one I was looking at this morning. It's a kind of French navy."

"The blue?" It was Jamie's turn to frown. "Are you sure? The court is a colorful place."

"There seemed an awful lot of monochrome too," I said. I did remember all of those beautiful scarlets, golds and greens, but I didn't want to admit it; I was feeling stubborn. And besides I didn't want to draw more attention to myself than necessary.

"That's the men," Jamie said. "The women tend to dress like peacocks."

"Well, I'm going to dress like a peahen."

Jinx studied me a moment and then turned and rummaged through the dresses until he found the gown I'd been fondling earlier. It was long, elegant and fit closely on the top half, but flowed outward from my waist to the ground. It was strapless and showed just about the right amount of cleavage to be a little sexy but not slutty.

"Off you go," I said, gesturing for them to leave me.

As soon as they had gone I stripped off and stepped into the dress. The material was soft and slinky and wonderful to touch. The hem pooled on the floor: I would need heels to do the dress justice.

I studied the rows of footwear. There were boots aplenty—short ones, long ones, buckled ones, buttoned ones—but not a lot in the way of actual shoes. I was beginning to think I'd have to change the dress when I spotted a pair of gold sandals. They were perfect: high, spiky heels with thin gold straps around the ankle and across the toes. I tried them on and walked back and forth. They were comfortable enough, although a mile-long hike would be out of the question.

I turned toward the mirror then hesitated before I faced it. Did I dare look at myself again? Would I see me, or that other woman—the woman Jamie and Jinx said was the real me? I took a deep breath, turned and looked.

The dress suited her better than it did me, I was quite sure. The color of the dress really set off the pinkish-red tones of her skin and hair. I smiled at her and she smiled back, showing perfect white teeth with slightly longer canines than my own. Now that I had got over the shock of seeing my alter ego, I found that I could study her objectively.

Although clearly not of my world, she wasn't as demonic as Kayla, nor quite as human as Henri. It was the iridescent skin that set her apart; without it, she *could* have passed as human, albeit one with expensive contact lenses and strange taste in hair color. She was my height, not tall like Kayla, and her body shape was the same as mine. I turned to one side and then the other, but my first impression had been right: even her bust size was the same as mine. Fortunately, there were no reptiles weaving in and out of her locks—although I wasn't particularly scared of snakes, I'd still rather not have them living in my hair.

I turned away abruptly, shocked by the thought that I was beginning to accept that maybe—just *maybe*—Jinx and Jamie were telling the truth.

All five of my guards were sitting on the bed waiting for me when I came out of the wardrobe. Pyrites hopped down and scampered across the floor to rub himself around my ankles.

"Well?"

Jinx grinned and Jamie looked me up and down. "You were right about the blue," he said.

"Mr. Shenanigans? Mr. Kerfuffle?" I needed all the validation I could get.

"You look lovely, mistress," Mr. Shenanigans said, and Mr. Kerfuffle nodded enthusiastically in agreement.

I sat down at the dressing table to brush my hair, a little surprised to see my own reflection looking back at me, though I was grateful for that. I rummaged around in the dressing table drawer to see if there was anything vaguely resembling makeup for me to use—even the ancient Egyptians used makeup, so I was hoping there might be at least be some mascara.

"How long have we got?" I asked the men, over my shoulder.

"About twenty minutes before we need to leave; it's considered rude to arrive later than the monarch, unless you're a visiting dignitary," Jamie said.

I wondered why Mr. Kerfuffle had jumped down from the bed and trotted across the room, but before I could ask he was answering a knock on the door.

"Milady," he said, and I saw Kayla in the mirror as she swept in. I turned to greet her. Kayla had always been breathtakingly lovely in my world, but each time I saw her here she was even more beautiful. Maybe I was getting accustomed to this world, or maybe it was as my guard had suggested: that I was becoming my true self.

She was dressed in burgundy silk, cut low enough at the front to show the tops of her breasts, though not so low she was in danger of overspilling. A gold-mounted ruby hung from a gold chain around her neck and nestled between her breasts.

She looked me up and down. "You decided against the green?" My fingers caressed the velvet, but before I could answer, she admitted, "It suits you." She sniffed and added, "Though it would be more appropriate in the Overlands."

"It was in the wardrobe," I pointed out.

"I suppose it was."

"Do you have such a thing as makeup?" I asked.

"We don't have any need for it in this world," she said. "Natural beauty is enough."

I bit back a bitchy response and asked, "Did you want something?"

She closed her eyes and hung her head for a moment. "I'm sorry," she said, and gestured for me to move along the stool to make room for her, then searched through the open drawer. "Here," she said, taking out a pot. She unscrewed the top and dabbed a finger inside. "Close your eyes," she ordered.

I felt her rub her fingertip across my eyelids once, and then again; then after another rummage around in the drawer I felt something gently tugging at my eyelashes.

"There," she said.

I opened my eyes and looked into the mirror. She had smeared gold dust across my eyelids and had darkened my lashes. She handed me another little pot filled with a rose-colored cream.

"For your lips," she said. "Your cheeks are fine as they are."

I dabbed a little of the cream across my lips and then blended it in. It smelled faintly of rose petals and I wondered if she'd had it specially made for me, if makeup wasn't generally used in this world.

"Dinner is going to be a fairly intimate occasion, after all," she told me. "Our father has invited Lord Daltas and Lord Oberon to join us, and not wishing to offend the Guardian and Deathbringer, he's invited them to dine with us as well. You'll not need any other guard to attend you."

"Lucky is entitled to have five guards with her," Jamie pointed out.

"Each of us is to be attended by only two guards this evening, Lord Baltheza included."

"How about the drakon?" Jamie asked.

Kayla tapped a finger against ruby lips. "If he can sit upon her shoulder or nestle at her feet, he may come. The others may have their pets by their side so I see no reason why Lucky shouldn't."

Jamie looked at the other demons, who didn't appear to be very happy, but after a moment they nodded in agreement.

"Come," she said, "we'll go down together."

We got to our feet and I followed Kayla to the door. Something touched my shoulder and when I turned my head, I found myself nose to snout with Pyrites, who had shrunk to the size of a small parrot. He rubbed his head against my cheek and then settled down on his haunches.

"Good boy," I whispered, and he answered me with a soft purr.

Fourteen

The great hall was empty compared with the previous evening. Lord Daltas was at the far end, already waiting, goblet in hand, together with another demon. I hadn't seen him before but I assumed he was Lord Oberon. Both bowed low as we approached.

Four others loitered near them, obviously their guard: close enough to their masters to protect them, but far enough away to make it obvious they felt secure.

Henri was leaning with one shoulder against the wall, ankles crossed, cane in hand. His lips curled into an insolent smile upon seeing me. I looked away. I didn't need him to make me any more uncomfortable than I already was and I didn't think I'd be able to speak with him there without my teeth chattering.

Lord Oberon was short and portly, a caricature of a Dickensian dandy, and his attire—an unnecessarily tight bottle-green velvet jacket over a silk waistcoat of gold and silver and a cravat of gold silk—was a couple of hundred years out of date too. His bloated rosy cheeks, lumpy port-wine nose, puffy jowls and dark pink decadent lips made him the very picture of debauchery. Piggy eyes peeped out from beneath heavy lids and followed us as we approached.

"Lady Kayla," he lisped, and gave a bow that displayed the ridge of spines that ran from forehead to neck and parted his hair. "You grow more beautiful every day."

"Lord Oberon," she said. "I would like to introduce you to Lucky de Salle, a very good friend of mine."

He didn't seem at all phased by the fact I was human, so I was pretty sure he'd been forewarned. He gave another little bow. "Charmed," he said.

I smiled but kept quiet, as I had no idea what I should say. Kayla laid a hand on my arm and pressed it lightly as she turned to Lord Daltas. "Lucky, this is Lord Daltas."

He took my hand and bowed and as he brushed his lips across my knuckles his eyes flew instantly to my face and then to the two men behind me.

"So, it is true," he said, his lips twisting into a distasteful sneer. "You've both marked the wench."

Kayla stamped her foot, and before anyone could reply she had turned on him. "Watch it, Lord Daltas. The blood of my father runs through her veins and I will not have her spoken of as if she's a court trollop."

He bowed again, first to me and then to Kayla. "Forgive me," he said.

Kayla sniffed and turned away from him with a swish of her skirt. She had definitely developed the knack of making her clothing speak for her.

Her guard hadn't come down to the great hall with us. Which surprised me a little, especially when I remembered their distrust of me and my entourage, but the sudden upward turn of Kayla's lips told me that her green captain had just arrived. I swung around, and sure enough, Vaybian and another demon were marching across the hall to meet us.

"Lucky, you have met Captain Vaybian," she said.

"Hi . . . Hello again," I managed to murmur.

"And this is Diargo," she said, gesturing toward the other guard.

Diargo might be the shortest guard in the room, but what he lacked in height he more than made up for in muscle. His skin was a shiny third-degree-burn-red, but as he didn't appear to be in any pain, I assumed that was his natural tone. Two small horns peeped out of his silken curls of scarlet which flowed down to his waist, and when he bowed to Kayla I spotted small bat-wings sprouting out of his shoulders and poking through his mane. Except for the beautiful hair he looked just like your traditional demon.

They didn't join the other guards at the end of the room but hovered within touching distance of Kayla, making it obvious they weren't very comfortable with Jamie and Jinx being anywhere near their mistress. As for my two, they treated Vaybian and Diargo with studied indifference.

If Kayla noticed any of this she didn't let it bother her. She smiled at Vaybian. "Could you get Lucky and me a drink?"

"Lady," he said. As he strode off to do her biding I noticed the little gesture that resulted in Diargo moving a step or two closer to his mistress. I wasn't sure whether it was my guard or me who worried them the most. I assumed Jinx was responsible for most of it, but I got the impression they weren't overly fond of Jamie either.

Vaybian returned and handed Kayla a goblet, then passed another to me. A deep golden frothy liquid almost overflowed the brim. Kayla and Vaybian exchanged a glance and she gave him a tight little smile: she was nervous, and that made me doubly so.

Jamie appeared at my elbow. "Here," he said, taking the goblet from my hand and exchanging it for a glass. "I believe Lady Lucinda would prefer the wine."

Kayla arched an eyebrow in Jamie's direction, her serpents hissed and their little black eyes sparkled like jet beads. "Give that to me," she said, reaching out for the goblet.

Jamie studied her for a moment, then did as she asked. Then, looking Vaybian in the eyes, she chugged back half of the contents and handed the goblet to him, and he promptly downed the rest.

"See?" she said, and turned to me with a smile.

"A very pretty trick," Jinx said, appearing beside Jamie, "but you're immortal. A sip of poison that could kill Lucky in an instant would merely give you and your man bellyache for a few hours."

"Not if she's demon."

"But possibly if she's half human."

Kayla glared at him. "I would *never* harm Lucky."

Jinx made a disbelieving sound. "But you may well murder your sister, albeit by another's hand."

Vaybian stepped between Kayla and Jinx, one hand upon the pommel of the sword hanging from his belt. "Be careful, Deathbringer. You are speaking to our princess."

Jinx, very slowly and deliberately, let his eyes wander up and down the guard, his lips curled in an arrogant sneer. "It is you who should be careful, Captain. Draw that sword against me and I'll see you a rotting corpse."

Kayla rested her hand on Vaybian's wrist. "Not here, not now," she said. "This night we honor my sister's homecoming. I want nothing to spoil it."

Someone gave a snort of laughter and Kayla swung around. "You have something to say?" she asked Lord Daltas.

"No, my dear," he said, but he was still laughing, and I couldn't help but think he was deliberately trying to annoy her.

Kayla's eyes glittered and her lips tightened into an angry line. The serpents within her hair writhed and hissed. She was working herself up into a real royal tantrum.

"Kayla," I whispered, "he's trying to pull your chain. Don't let him."

She froze for a second, then her features relaxed into a slow feline smile. She took hold of my hand and drew me away from the others. "You've only been in the court a few minutes and you've already learned how to play our games," she said.

"No, I know nothing about court, but I do know about people. Daltas isn't stupid; he knows he's got a rival."

"No—"

"Kayla," I murmured, "listen to me. The way you and Vaybian look at each other is a dead giveaway. If he's the one you want, why not lay your cards on the table?"

Kayla led me further across the room, out of earshot of the others. I glanced over my shoulder to see all eyes were upon us, but the men's expressions varied from speculative to concerned. And there were a couple that were unreadable, at least to me.

"It isn't as easy as that," she said. "To save your damn human I've had to agree that Daltas can call on me. I can't openly court another until I've at least spent a few evenings in his company."

"Where is Philip, by the way?"

"Entertaining my guard, I would imagine," she said with a sniff.

"What do you mean?" I asked in alarm, a multitude of awful visions immediately popping into my head.

She must have guessed from my horrified expression what I was thinking as she began to giggle. "Oh, don't worry. They'll not harm him—they'll just tease him a bit. He is quite funny, actually."

"Kayla, don't be so cruel."

"Lucky, harden your heart. If you're going to survive this place you mustn't appear weak—to care so much is a definite weakness."

"If to care is considered weak, then weak is what I am," I said, shrugging her hand from my arm. "I'll not become heartless, not for you or anyone."

"If not heartless, then at least try not to let your emotions show so much. Your face is an open book."

"Only because you know me."

"No, Lucky, because you're a good and kind person who can't hide it when you're shocked, outraged or upset. You cry watching films, even when they have a happy ending."

"So do you," I said.

"Name one film," she said, with a smirk.

When I thought about it, I actually couldn't: I'd seen her almost crying with laughter, but never weeping over a sad film—and if I were honest, I would have to admit that her merriment was usually because of my tears.

I steeled myself and changed the subject. "Kayla, Jamie and Jinx think you mean me harm." As she pulled in a deep breath and tilted her chin, a haughty motion, I said quickly, "Just stop it why don't you? It's me, Lucky, your friend—your *best* friend."

Her head dipped down and she bit her lip. "Lucky, I—"

"Kayla, if I'd drunk from that goblet, would I be dead now?" I had to ask. My chest felt tight, and I knew I would want to curl up and die if she gave the wrong answer. Then again, if she gave the right answer, could I believe her?

She looked at me long and hard, then she raised a slender finger and tapped a pointed red nail against her lips. "No," she said, "if you died of a poisoned brew passed to you by the Captain of my guard in full view of witnesses, his life would be forfeit. I wouldn't so risk him."

I had to swallow twice before I could speak, for I had felt something wither inside me. "So it wouldn't be the loss of my life you'd mourn, but your lover's?"

She rested her fingers on my sleeve. "Whatever I tell you, whatever I say, you won't believe it, but at least listen to me. I love you, Lucky. You're my friend and you're my sister, and if I'd wanted you dead I'd have arranged an accident long since. I want you here with me and I want you safe. Please believe that."

"Then why are Jamie and Jinx so nervous about your intentions?"

She took another deep breath and glanced toward my two guards. "Jamie is a Guardian so he's suspicious of everyone. As for Jinx—well, Jinx is Jinx. He's a Deathbringer. He doesn't trust anyone either. He has been called upon to bring death to others too many times to let him trust anyone's intentions."

"I didn't think he was an assassin."

"He isn't, but there are those who think he is because of the death that follows in his wake. There are many who will call his name and expect his deadly hand to strike, but it doesn't work that way. Jinx is the bringer of death: it follows him; he doesn't smite an individual unless it is their time, or"—a smile tugged at her lips—"or they truly piss him off."

"Kayla, if you love me so much, please tell me—am I safe with you and yours? If not, at least give me the heads up."

Her eyes met mine. "There are those among my guard who would see you dead to protect me. They can't understand why I don't see you as a threat. Truth be told, I'd rather it was you who became queen."

"Why?"

"Think about it," she said, "I know you'd never attempt to assassinate me. If you were queen I could live my life in safety and do as I pleased. If I become queen, the chances are I'll be tied to a man I despise and who'd be rid of me as soon as conveniently possible."

"How about Vaybian? Would he not want to be king to your queen?"

"Ruler," she said. "We don't call them king in this world."

"Kayla?"

"Vaybian isn't a political animal. He's a warrior—or at least he was once."

"So he doesn't see me as a danger to his ambitions, just to you?"

"He is ambitious, but—" She stopped and turned toward the door at the back of the hall. Lord Baltheza had arrived.

Kayla grabbed my arm and dropped into a low curtsey, pulling me with her. "Lower your eyes to the floor," she whispered.

I could hear his footsteps as he walked across the flagstones, stopping now and then, welcoming the Lords Daltas and Oberon, and then Jamie and Jinx. If it hadn't been for Kayla gripping my arm I think my legs would have given way beneath me: I'd not had any practice at curtseying and I discovered it was an uncomfortable position to hold for any length of time.

Finally a pair of black leather boots appeared in front of us. "Rise up, my daughters," Baltheza said.

Kayla rose, bringing me with her. She stepped forward and dropped a light kiss upon her father's cheek. "Father," she murmured, and linked an arm through his.

He turned to me. "So, this must be Lucinda," he said.

"She prefers Lucky," Kayla said.

"Lucky," he said, extending a hand.

My eyes flicked to Kayla; I didn't know what I was supposed to do. She mouthed the words "take it." I reached out and took his hand and his lips curled into a smile which didn't reach his eyes. He raised my fingers to his lips and grazed my knuckles against them. His eyes widened slightly and I guessed that like Daltas, he had felt both marks upon me.

He lowered my hand but continued to hold it as he studied my face. "She doesn't look as if she is of this world," he said to Kayla.

"She's been this way for so long; it'll take time for her to revert to her true self."

"You think?"

Kayla nodded.

"She does bear some resemblance to her mother, even in human form," he admitted.

I frowned, wondering what he meant—my mother was human, wasn't she? Kayla, seeing my expression, quickly moved to stand slightly between us.

"Let's get to table," she said, "I'm starving."

Baltheza laughed. "Always hungry. Does your sister have a similar appetite?"

"No, Lucky is restrained in most things."

"Yet she bears the marks of the Guardian and Deathbringer—or was this your doing?"

"Oh no," Kayla said with a tight smile. "She managed this achievement all on her own."

"How about the drakon?" he said, gesturing toward the small creature perched on my shoulder.

"Again, not my doing."

"Remarkable: to tame a jeweled drakon. Who would have thought it?"

He looked me up and down again and this time his smile brightened. He gave my fingers a gentle squeeze before letting them go. "I am looking forward to getting to know you, Lucky. Kayla has told me so much about you, but I never for one moment imagined you would be so alluring that both a Guardian and the Deathbringer would fall under your spell. As for a jeweled drakon—well," he said, "I am seriously impressed."

I had no idea what to say; I was completely out of my depth and desperate not do something incredibly stupid or, even worse, dangerous. All I could do now was to follow Kayla and her father across the room toward the long dining table. Jinx and Jamie appeared on either side of me.

"Speak only when spoken to," Jamie whispered in my ear, "it's safer that way."

That suited me fine. I was going to have enough trouble swallowing, let alone speaking.

Vaybian and Diargo followed behind, together with two other demons I assumed were Baltheza's bodyguards. Unlike Kayla's guard, they'd not been chosen for their looks. They were both huge, with fists the size of small barrels. One was green, scaly and covered with knobbly warts; the other was dark gray with the wrinkly hide of a rhinoceros—he even had ivory tusks on his brow and snout, very much like Mr. Shenanigans, except he exuded menace, which was something Mr. Shenanigans didn't do unless threatened.

To my surprise, Lord Baltheza led Kayla and the rest of us past the table and through another door: it appeared we were to eat in more intimate surroundings than the great hall.

A large circular table dominated the next chamber and as we took our seats various servants laden down with huge covered platters and steaming bowls of vegetables began to appear.

I was seated opposite Baltheza, with Jamie to my right and Jinx to my left. Kayla sat on her father's right with Lord Daltas next to her. Oberon sat on her father's left.

"You may leave us," Baltheza said to Vaybian and the other guards, and as Vaybian's eyes flicked to Kayla, "Captain Vaybian, you would do well to remember that it is I who rule here, not my daughter. Leave us now."

Vaybian bowed to Lord Baltheza, then to Kayla, and withdrew, taking Diargo with him.

"You too," Baltheza said, gesturing to Henri and the others.

Daltas didn't look happy, but he was wise enough to keep his displeasure to himself. Oberon didn't appear bothered one way or the other; his attention had been captured by a buxom serving wench whose three enormous breasts were barely constrained by her low white blouse. They wobbled and jiggled alarmingly by his right shoulder as she served thick slabs of meat. His eyes followed her around the table and when she had finished dishing up and had left the room, he gave an undisguised sigh of disappointment.

I waited to see what the etiquette was when dining with the royal family, but it was pretty simple: as soon as Lord Baltheza speared a slice of meat with his knife everyone began to eat. The use of cutlery was apparently optional, for Oberon didn't bother even cutting the meat, just shoved it into his mouth with his fingers. Kayla had a leg of something and was eating it off the bone, but at least she held it within a napkin and dabbed at her lips with a lace handkerchief between bites.

Lord Daltas had moved his chair so his shoulder was almost touching Kayla's and I could see him whispering in her ear at almost every opportunity. Her eyes sparkled, her cheeks were flushed and, despite what she had said about him, his attentions didn't appear entirely unwelcome.

Somehow I managed a mouthful or two, but although it smelled good, I was feeling nauseous, and my mouth was so dry the food could have been ashes for all I knew. I took a sip of the wine, hoping it would help me swallow, but nearly choked instead.

"Are you all right?" Jamie asked. I nodded as I dabbed at my mouth.

"You don't look it," Jinx said.

I took another sip of wine. "I'll be fine," I managed to whisper.

"Lucky," Lord Baltheza said from across the table, "how does our world compare to the Overlands?"

I gulped and tried to clear my throat. "It's . . . different," I managed to say.

"Very different," Kayla said.

"You must have liked it," Daltas said to Kayla, "for you stayed there long enough."

"Too long," said Baltheza. "You stayed away too long."

"I stayed away as long as I thought necessary," Kayla said. "To have returned sooner would have been a mistake."

"For whom?" Daltas asked.

Kayla dropped the leg of meat back onto her plate and turned to face Daltas. "For Lucky," she said, "and I think that has been proven."

"How so?" Baltheza said. "She is here, she is well, and there have been no attempts upon her life, or has something happened of which I'm not aware?"

"She was visited by Lord Daltas's pet assassin and Lord Argon attempted to abduct her."

Baltheza waved away her protests. "That was there—and anyway, it was I who sanctioned the visitation from the assassin. He didn't hurt her, did he? He just delivered a message."

Kayla sat very still, her expression revealing nothing, but the snakes peeped out of her hair, their tongues flicking. Her father didn't appear to notice.

"He was actually quite taken with Lucky," Daltas said. "It's a shame she saw fit to consort instead with a Guardian and the Deathbringer."

Jamie had been reaching for his goblet, but he hesitated for a second and when he held the stem his knuckles were bone-white, so hard was he gripping it. I knew how he felt. I was getting mightily fed up of being referred to in the third person, and my nausea was fast being replaced by irritation.

Kayla's eyes flicked to Jamie and then to me, probably warning us both to keep quiet, but then Jinx began to laugh.

"Something amuses you?" Daltas asked, his lips twisted in arrogant distaste.

"You, brother, you amuse me," Jinx said.

Daltas's lilac skin flushed violet. "Watch it, Deathbringer."

Jinx was leaning back in his chair, goblet in hand, his smile playing on his lips, but it was a dangerous smile: a smile I wouldn't wish him to bestow upon me, because I was pretty sure it was the sort of smile that preceded violence.

"Come, come," Oberon said, "we're all friends here."

"Are we?" Daltas said. "I think not. In fact, I wonder at the prudence of breaking bread with two demons such as these."

"Lord Daltas, are you deliberately trying to alienate every single one of us at this table?" Baltheza asked.

"My Lord," Daltas said, scrambling to his feet, "forgive me, I meant no disrespect."

Baltheza waved his apology aside. "Sit down, sit down. This is meant to be a celebration. Not only has my beautiful daughter returned to us, but she has brought her sister to sit by her side. Let's finish this feast and then return to court for some fun."

"Fun!" Oberon said, clapping his hands together. "What sort of fun?"

Baltheza grinned. "The fun I like best."

"Good-o," Oberon said, with a malicious smile.

Baltheza took hold of Kayla's hand and planted a kiss on her fingers. "I suspect you will have missed the kind of entertainment we enjoy at court."

Kayla cast a worried glance in my direction. "I think your kind of fun might be a little too extreme for Lucky's taste—she is newly arrived in our world, after all."

"She's a princess and she must learn to act like one. The sooner she embraces our customs the better. Who knows, it may help her on her way to becoming her true self instead of this pale imitation."

That was it; I'd had enough. "Excuse me?" I said. Two hands gripped my knees; Jamie's from the right and Jinx's from the left. "First, I am actually here in this room, and second, I'm not 'a pale imitation.' I'm me—period."

Everyone stared at me. Kayla's expression was one of horror, Oberon's jowls quivered with suppressed merriment and Daltas's nostrils flared as he looked down his nose at me. Baltheza's expression was unreadable.

"Father . . ." Kayla began, but he raised a hand to silence her.

Baltheza continued to stare at me and, since there wasn't much else I could do, I stared right back and hoped my expression wasn't something similar to a mouse about to be pounced upon by a snake.

"Well, my dear," Baltheza said eventually, patting Kayla's hand, "had I any doubts at all that Lucky was your sister she has laid them to rest. She may not be the absolute image of her mother, but she is certainly her mother's daughter." He grinned at me. "I think you and I are going to get along very well together, and if we don't, I'm sure we'll have fun trying."

Fun—that word again. It was a word that should mean laughter and happiness, but somehow every time Baltheza uttered it I found myself growing more fearful and anxious.

He stood, pushing his chair back with a loud screech of wood against stone. "Come, let's have some sport."

We all stood, and he swept out of the room with Kayla's hand on his arm and Daltas and Oberon following close behind. Jamie let out a deep breath and Jinx chuckled.

"That went better than expected," Jinx said.

Jamie grunted. "But now it's fun and games time, and for us I doubt it'll be either." He put his hands on my shoulders. "Lucky, the time has come for you keep your mouth firmly shut and not let that expressive face of yours show any emotion. When Baltheza has fun it means things are going to get very bloody. It's unlikely it will be any of us, but you can never be too sure, so just keep quiet and hope he forgets you're even here."

"That won't happen," Jinx said. "I have a feeling whatever he's got planned is entirely for Lucky's benefit."

"I so hope you're wrong," Jamie said.

"So do I, but I wouldn't bet on it."

Fifteen

While we had been eating, the great hall had been transformed into an arena; the chairs and benches laid out along three sides were now heaving with spectators. They all stood while Baltheza and Kayla made themselves comfortable upon the thrones set up on a large wooden dais erected at the top end of the hall. There were other chairs beside their thrones, and as soon as they were seated, Daltas and Oberon joined them. Jamie and Jinx led me to the remaining chair and stood behind me. Once we were settled, the audience sat with a scraping clatter of chairs and began to chatter among themselves.

I noticed the other bodyguards were now on the dais, standing behind their respective masters, and although Henri and I were separated by Baltheza and Kayla and their guards, he was still too close for comfort. I tried not to look at him but I couldn't stop myself, and every time I glanced in his direction he was smirking at me.

Pyrites could feel my growing anxiety because he kept nuzzling my neck and kneading my shoulder like a cat. I tickled his chin and he settled down with a small puff of steam.

After a few minutes, Lord Baltheza stood and clapped his hands three times. The crowd quieted, giving way to an expectant hush across the hall.

"My lords, ladies and gentleman of the court, I welcome you to the great hall for an evening of entertainment to celebrate the return of my beautiful daughter, Kayla. And to add to my joy, she has brought another with her, one whom I had thought lost to us: her sister, Lucinda." Baltheza took my hand in his and bent down to press a kiss upon my cheek and I tried to stop myself from shuddering inwardly; somehow I managed not to recoil as his lips brushed my skin.

There were gasps from the crowd, and surprised murmuring, and several people stood to get a better look at me. I felt my face flush pink under such tremendous scrutiny. I realized then that no matter what was going to happen in the arena tonight, my reaction to it was going to be the sideshow. I forced my lips into a smile and hoped I'd be able to blot out any unpleasantness.

"Tonight I welcome a demon who needs no introduction at this court: Yarla Sal will be the Master of Ceremonies for this evening." As Baltheza gestured, a tall demon dressed in scarlet and gold entered the arena to thunderous applause. He walked to the front of the dais, bowed low to the royal family and then turned and bowed to the enthusiastically clapping audience.

"Thank you, my Lord Baltheza," he started. "Thank you, ladies and gentlemen of the court. For your entertainment this evening, a convicted felon will take his chances against Zarzar Tang, our own Court Champion."

Loud cheers and roars of approval rang from the crowd until Yarla Sal raised a hand to silence them.

"Four disobedient slaves will run the race of life."

More cheering and chanting and stomping of feet.

"Three criminals will have their sentences carried out for all to see."

The crowd clapped and shouted.

"And for those who like to have a little wager, there will be several exciting contests between court slaves and wild beasts from the Marshes of Zool."

The spectators cheered and shouted some more. My ears were ringing and the entertainment hadn't even started yet. I wasn't sure I could call it "entertainment"; it all sounded terrible to me. I wondered whether there was any possible way I could return to my room, but somehow doubted pleading a headache would be a good enough excuse.

"My lords, ladies and gentlemen of the court, to get things under-way, may I introduce to you the person responsible for making these evenings the spectacular events they are? Let's give it up for the one who is responsible for the pursuit and punishment of criminals, our very own High Court Enforcer and Corrector: Amaliel Cheriour."

The crowd fell into an uncomfortable silence as the huge doors opened and a figure draped in a long black hooded robe entered. Although his face was in shadows, burning eyes of fire glowed from within the folds of his cowl. I shivered, and I didn't think I was the only one. The audience members closest to the demon edged away from him as he passed them. He stopped a few yards from the dais, looked up at Baltheza and gave a brief bow. Then he turned toward me and for a moment my heart stopped still. He gave another bow.

"Brother," Jinx said, and I let out the breath I hadn't realized I'd been holding. It was Jinx whom he had acknowledged, not me.

The demon turned away and held out a jaundiced, almost skeletal hand toward the door. A creature resembling an ox, although twice as big with double the usual number of horns, lumbered in pulling a wooden cart laden with a cage roughly forged out of some dark metal. Inside were the three poor wretches who I assumed were the criminals about to have their sentences carried out in front of the crowd. Alarm-ingly, two other soldiers wheeled in what looked like it could be a gib-bet and I didn't have to guess what that was for.

The cart was flanked on either side by three guards, all dressed up for the occasion. Highly polished armor gleamed in the torchlight and their swords and other weaponry shone brightly, which made the creatures in the cage look even more pathetic. The rags they were wearing were filthy, and all three had manacles around wrists and ankles. They hud-dled together in the middle of the cage, and although there were few human features about any of them, I still recognized the fear on their faces. Whether demon or man, fear is fear and it turned my stomach.

Yarla Sal gestured for someone to open the cage and as he did so the three demons edged into the furthest corner. The guard reached in and grabbed the smallest by the wrist and dragged him out. He was thin and wiry, with skin the color and texture of walnuts and a bloated, undernourished belly peeping out through the rips in his shirt. Even so, he fought hard to break free and a second guard had to take hold of his other arm to restrain him.

I glanced across at Kayla and was shocked to see her lips were curled into a small smile and her eyes gleamed. Her father's expression was even more enthusiastic, and Oberon was practically drooling. This was too terrible for words and I wished Jamie or Jinx was sitting next to me; I wanted someone to hold my hand. I wanted someone to hold me.

Pyrites nuzzled my neck and hopped down onto my lap and I felt a hand rest on my right shoulder and another on my left, one pale, one maroon. I let out a shuddering breath in relief. I had my wish.

The two guards dragged the struggling demon to the middle of the arena, where Yarla Sal waited for him, and threw him to the ground. He scrambled up onto his knees, his eyes darting back and forth between Yarla and the High Court Enforcer and Corrector.

"My lords, ladies and gentlemen," Yarla announced, "*this* is Dumah Dask. His crime is treason."

The crowd gasped and the little demon started crying out, "No, no, I have done nothing! *Nothing*—"

"Did you not incite others against our beloved Lord Baltheza?"

"No, no I did not—"

"But a judge and jury thought otherwise."

"They were told lies," the creature whined.

"He has been judged and sentenced. Get on with it," Baltheza said.

The guards pulled the demon to his feet and he began to struggle and kick with renewed vigor until a third guard stepped in and hit the creature on the head with the pommel of his sword, knocking him back onto his knees. Before he could right himself, a noose was slipped over his head and he was dragged by the neck over to the wooden gibbet which had been erected in the center of the arena.

Despite myself, I was puzzled: the creature wasn't very tall, probably five foot eight or so, but neither was the gibbet: even hanging from the shortest length of rope, his toes would touch the ground. The guards strung him up and sure enough, his toes rested comfortably upon the flagstones.

The creature was weeping now, and although no tears came from his eyes, snot hung in strings from his huge nostrils. He had given up struggling; he knew all chance of escape or mercy was gone. Instead, he began to mutter to himself between hiccoughing sobs. I found it distressing to watch, but the crowd were obviously enjoying themselves. Amaliel Cheriour stepped toward the hanging demon, withdrawing a dagger from his sleeve, and the crowd went silent with anticipation.

"Quick or slow?" Yarla Sal shouted to the audience.

"Slow, slow, slow," they chanted.

Dumah began to struggle again.

"Slow, slow, slow."

Amaliel sliced down what was left of the creature's shirt and pulled it wide open, then did the same to the daemon's breeches, which slipped down his legs and sagged around his ankles: the final humiliation before dying.

"Slow, slow, slow."

He turned to the crowd and held the dagger up high so they could all see its vicious curved blade.

"Slow, slow, slow."

The demon tried to cover his bare chest and belly with his manacled arms until the Corrector gestured to the guards and one held the demon tight while the other undid the chains and then relocked them so his arms were now fastened behind his back.

Still the audience chanted, "Slow, slow, slow."

The demon suddenly leaped into the air and let his body drop so his neck took his full weight. The rope pulled taut and the gibbet shuddered.

The crowd roared its disapproval, then cheered when the dazed demon staggered back to his feet. He did it again and again, but his neck was too sinewy, too tough. The Corrector stood to one side, letting him do it until he hung limp and exhausted, from the rope.

"After attempting to spoil our fun, we want more than slow, ladies and gentlemen, we want *painful*, don't we?" Yarla Sal yelled to the crowd. "We want agony—*excruciating* agony!"

"Pain, pain, pain," they chanted.

"I can't stand this," I whispered to no one in particular, and fingers squeezed my shoulders. "Really," I said.

The fingers gripped so hard they were almost painful. I frowned at the crowd; I frowned at the pathetic, sobbing creature attached to the gibbet and I glared at the fiery-eyed Corrector.

"This is just sick," I said.

Amaliel Cheriour looked straight at me as if he had heard my words and I looked straight back. I suspect he was smiling. He floated toward Dumah Dask, dagger in hand and lifted it dramatically so the torchlight reflected off of it and onto his victim's face, casting a swath of light across his wide, desperately scared eyes.

He reached out and pressed the knife's point against Dumah's chest, just below the breastbone. A teardrop of blood the color of jade erupted from his skin and trickled down his body. All the while, the Corrector's eyes were locked on mine.

I went rigid with horror as he drew the knife down Dumah's chest and stopped just above the bulge of his belly. Blood flowed down his body in a stream.

I looked across at the people lining the hall. As my eyes swept across them their faces were alight with some kind of emotion I found hard to comprehend, and I knew for certain that none of them mirrored what I was feeling. I could see their mouths moving and I knew they were shouting, chanting, stamping their feet, though all I could hear was a roaring in my ears.

When I looked back Amaliel Cheriour bowed his head to me and turned to his victim. The knife must have been razor-sharp because it slid effortlessly through the creature's fat and muscle. Dumah screamed and more blood spurted from the wound, followed by a swell of something white that pushed through the gash in his gut. The flesh gave way, splitting wide open, and Dumah screamed again as his entrails flopped out and fell down to his knees, reminding me for some reason of pasta being poured from a colander. Spaghetti was, or had been, one of the few dishes I could cook well, but I wasn't sure I'd ever want to eat it again, then I caught a whiff of rotten eggs, and something worse. No—spaghetti, in fact, pasta of any kind, was definitely off the menu.

Dumah looked down and screamed again and again and again until my head felt like it would split open.

Amaliel gestured, beckoning toward the side of the arena, and two more guards entered carrying a large copper cauldron between them. Both wore thick leather gauntlets and the contents of the cauldron were smoking. As they got closer I could see its base was glowing red.

"Shit," I heard Jamie whisper.

They put the cauldron down in front of the dying demon and the Corrector leaned in close to whisper in Dumah's ear. His eyes bulged and his screams turned to moans as he started repeating, "No, no, no, please, no—"

The crowd shouted, "Yes, yes, yes!," stomping their feet and clapping in time to their cries.

A guard proffered a gauntlet and Amaliel pulled it on theatrically, then reached into the smoke and pulled out a glowing poker. I felt bile rise up into my throat. I couldn't watch this. I lifted my eyes so they were fixed on a point across the other side of the hall and clenched my teeth together, hoping my expression wasn't giving away my true feelings.

The demon screamed again, and this time his cry tailed off into a wet gurgle, followed by the crackle and smell of sizzling bacon. Another smell, or rather, a mixture of smells filled the air: shit, piss and vomit. My fingers were gripping the arms of my chair so hard my knuckles hurt.

There was a disappointed sigh from the audience: so it was over, at least for Dumah.

As they dragged the body away I heard Baltheza calling for wine and ale.

Sucking in a breath, I lowered my eyes to look across the hall. Dumah Dask was standing by the gibbet, watching as the soldiers hauled his body out of the hall. His arms were wrapped around his chest, his shoulders heaving. Even though he was now free from pain he was visibly distressed, and it was terrible to see. I was about to rise to go to him when other spirits floated down to join him from above and within moments he was surrounded by them, all gray shadows of their former selves, welcoming him into their world. A small spirit, not much bigger than a child, took Dumah by the hand and started to lead him across the hall, followed by the others, some of which were already beginning to slowly rise up and disappear among the dark shadows above us.

I reached up and laid my hands upon those resting on my shoulders. Fingers squeezed in response.

Jinx leaned forward and whispered into my ear, "I'd be lying if I told you there wasn't worse to come."

I'd guessed as much: Dumah was just the warm-up act. My dinner was only staying down by pure willpower and I realized I wasn't going to get through the rest of the evening without disgracing myself.

"I know," I said, my eyes returning to the retreating apparitions. The small spirit glanced back over his shoulder and his eyes roved across the crowd until they alighted upon me. A strange expression passed over his face and he stopped and faced me. His lips were moving and although I couldn't hear the words, I could read what he was saying.

"Milady," he said, and Jinx's fingers tightened on my shoulder.

"Lucky, are you all right?" I heard Kayla ask and as I turned to face her the weak smile I had forced onto my face slipped away. Her smile was one of bitchy satisfaction.

A little voice in my head, sounding remarkably like Jamie's, whispered for me to keep quiet. I bit my tongue and turned away before I let my anger show.

"We have to get her out of here," I heard Jinx whisper to Jamie.

"We can't just—"

"Brother, listen to me, *we have to get her out of here now*."

"Jinx?"

"*I morti*," he whispered.

I glanced at him, wondering what he was talking about, then a cold breeze caressed my skin and when I looked up it was into a sea of gray faces: a host of ghostly figures had drifted across the hall toward me, the small spirit at the front hand in hand with Dumah. They knew I could see them. Some lifted their hands toward me, as though welcoming me.

"Lucky, can you pretend to faint or something?" Jinx asked.

"Why?"

"You can't see them?"

"Of course I can," I said, looking up at him. His expression was unexpectedly grim, and when I peered over my shoulder at Jamie, who was scanning the room himself, he looked equally grave. "What's wrong?"

"No time," Jinx said, and when I looked back into the hall the demon ghosts were almost upon us.

"They can't hurt me," I said.

"No, they can't, but Baltheza most certainly will if he realizes you can see the demon dead."

I didn't ask why—that could wait. Jinx wasn't the nervous type and if he was telling me we had to go, we had to go.

"Okay," I said. I took a deep breath and let all the horror and disgust I had been feeling well up inside me and turn into a wave of anger, making me brave—though some might say foolhardy. I swung around in my seat to look at the woman I'd once believed I knew better than anyone else in the whole world. "Actually, Kayla, since you ask, I'm not fucking all right."

Her smile disappeared as she turned away from her father to face me. Clearly this wasn't the reaction she had expected—or wanted. Fingers dug into my shoulders; I didn't think it was the reaction they had wanted either, but I wasn't going to damn well pretend to faint. I shrugged them away and stood, displacing the little drakon who flapped his way back onto my shoulder in a flurry of wings.

"I am going to my room to throw up," I said, "and not only because of the disgusting display I've just witnessed, but because I've only just discovered that the person I thought was my best friend is in fact a monster." I turned to Jamie and Jinx. "We're going."

They looked from me to Kayla to Baltheza and back to me.

"As my lady wishes," Jinx said.

I had the wherewithal to drop a small curtsey to Baltheza before leaving, then with a flick and swish of my long skirt Kayla would have been proud of, I turned and stalked off the dais, out of the hall and back toward my room.

No one tried to stop me, which was just as well. Kayla wasn't the only one who could work herself into a real old tantrum. Pyrites hopped off my shoulder and flew ahead, probably because I was walking too fast for him to keep his balance. I didn't look back to see if Jamie and Jinx were following, I just assumed they were—I really hoped they were.

I flung open the door to my room and marched in. Mr. Kerfuffle and Mr. Shenanigans both jumped to their feet, hands to weapons, but visibly relaxed when they saw it was me. I heard the door close behind me.

"What exactly did you not understand about keeping your feelings to yourself?" Jamie asked. He didn't sound angry, just weary.

It didn't matter; *I* was angry and I wanted to take it out on somebody. "You said I had to leave, so I left."

"Couldn't you have pretended to faint or something?"

"What? And give Kayla and the whole court the satisfaction of seeing you two carry me out of there?" Now I was on a roll and I couldn't stop. "Apart from anything else, I meant what I said: you may be able to stand and watch such atrocious cruelty and keep your dinner down, but I can't. If I'd stayed any longer I was going to throw up, and that would have shown quite spectacularly how I was feeling, I'd have thought."

Jinx laughed and I turned on him, shouting, "What the hell do you think is so funny?"

He grabbed me by the hand, swung me around and plunked a kiss on my lips, then laughed at my expression, which I had no doubt was one of utter shock.

"I'm proud of you," he said. "It might not've been the most sensible thing you could've done, but I think Baltheza will respect you for it. And you certainly made an impression on Amaliel Cheriour."

"How do you know?"

Jinx chuckled. "You met him eye to eye and showed him your displeasure. He's not used to that."

"A friend of yours, is he?" I asked.

Jinx gave me a wry smile. "No, quite the opposite actually."

"All that aside, why did you need me to leave? What difference does it make if I see spirits here? I've always seen the dead."

"You have no idea," Jamie started, and Mr. Shenanigans looked at me, distinctly worried.

"Mistress Lucky sees the dead of our world?"

"What is it now?" I asked, exasperated.

Jamie sat down on the bed. "In the human world your gift is considered at best an oddity, at worst a sickness of the mind. In our world, it is something else altogether."

I sank down on the bed next to him.

"It's a power that makes you dangerous," Jinx explained. "The dead traditionally tell no tales, and there are those who would very much prefer it remained that way. And a large percentage of those are in this very court."

Suddenly, I understood. Given the sort of world this was, there were probably a lot of demons who had secrets that had been laid to rest with the death of another. "So if they knew I could commune with the dead, it would make them pretty . . . unhappy."

"Unhappy?" Jamie said with an exasperated snort. "*Unhappy?* More like desperate."

"To commune with the demon dead," Mr. Shenanigans said, sucking in breath through his tombstone teeth, "is—"

"—is something best kept to ourselves," Jinx interrupted.

The huge daemon's lips curled down into such a despondent expression it was almost comical, though no one else was laughing. My ability to see the dead in this world was obviously a very big deal. "So why has no one mentioned this before? You must have realized there was a high possibility I could see your dead too . . ."

"Never crossed my mind," Jinx said, a little too quickly for my liking.

"Why would it?" I asked. "You didn't even know I could see the dead in my world."

"Exactly," he said, and gave me one of his winsome smiles.

I ignored it. "Jamie?"

"I suspected you might, but I really hoped you wouldn't. You were so scared of coming to our world in the first place that I didn't want to put another impediment in your way."

"So you didn't warn me. Well, thanks for that," I said, getting to my feet and beginning to pace.

"Ah, come on, my lucky Lucinda," Jinx said. "What are a few dead demons between friends?"

"You see them too," I said, "so why doesn't that worry anyone?"

His smile became sad. "I'm the Deathbringer, Lucky. I see the dead and they see and fear me, but I don't commune with them, nor they with me. It's an unwritten law."

"Look," Jamie said, "we could talk about this all night, but right now we have more pressing matters to worry about."

"Like?" I asked.

"Like insulting Kayla and then Baltheza by walking out in the middle of tonight's entertainment."

"He probably thought it highly amusing," Jinx said.

"Yes, and consequently he'll find even more awful things with which to torment Lucky."

"Maybe," Jinx acknowledged, "and maybe not, but tell me, brother, don't you respect her all the more for speaking out?"

Jamie looked up at me, his expression open and honest, and gave a sad smile. "Yes, but I also fear for her."

"She bears our marks."

Jamie took a deep breath. "Let's hope that's enough. I fear Baltheza won't be so easily deflected."

"You undervalue yourself, brother, and you undervalue me."

"How about Kayla?"

"Ah yes, the lovely Kayla," Jinx said. "I suspect we'll be receiving a visitation from her very shortly—in fact, more than likely within the next ten minutes or so, before the next bit of 'entertainment' begins."

"If she does come, you can tell her I don't want to see her," I said. "I'm going to take a bath and then go to bed."

"I think you should speak to her," Jamie said.

"Not tonight. She knew I'd be upset and she *reveled* in it. I don't think I can bear to be in the same room as her at the moment."

"I'll run the bath," Mr. Kerfuffle said, and trotted off to the bathroom.

Mr. Shenanigans looked from one to the other of us then followed his friend, Pyrites flew up off the bed and landed on his shoulder.

"You shouldn't be too hard on Kayla," Jamie said, as soon as the huge demon had closed the bathroom door behind the three of them.

"Jamie, she watched that creature being tortured to death and *enjoyed* it." Jamie and Jinx exchanged a glance. "Please don't tell me you both enjoyed it, too," I said, getting angry all over again.

"Jinx may be a Deathbringer, but it's not his way," Jamie said, "and as for me, I'm more about preserving life than destroying it."

"I don't understand how they can enjoy watching such cruelty? Is it a demon thing?" I asked.

"Were the ancient Romans demon?" Jinx asked.

"Pardon me?"

"Their idea of a good time was throwing Christians to the lions and watching men fight each other to the death," Jinx said, and now there was a hint of anger in his voice. "Then of course there was crucifixion, though it was rather long and drawn-out for a really good spectator sport."

"Jinx," Jamie warned.

But Jinx was only just getting started. "Hangings were great—everyone enjoyed a good hanging, or even better: seeing someone royal getting his or her head chopped off."

"I think you've made your point," Jamie said, with a glare in his direction. Then he said to me, "Lucky, not all demons enjoy cruelty, just as not all humans do."

He and Jinx were right, of course: human history was full of accounts of man's inhumanity to man—but that still didn't make me feel any better. I sank down onto the dressing table stool.

"I felt so helpless," I whispered. "I wanted to stop it, but I couldn't—I knew I couldn't, and I was scared that if I tried I'd make it worse . . . I hate it here. I want to go home."

Jamie sank down beside me and put his arm around me while Jinx took hold of my hand.

"It will be all right," Jinx said. "We'll make sure you'll be all right."

But the look he and Jamie exchanged said something very different.

Jinx was right: within minutes of entering the bathroom I heard Kayla's voice in the room next door. I stopped getting undressed and waited: if she was going to burst in on me, which was more than likely, I would have preferred to be fully clothed.

Her voice grew louder until she was shouting, but I wasn't sure whether it was at Jamie or Jinx; the voice responding to her was too low for me to tell. The door slammed and after a moment or so there was a gentle rap on the bathroom door.

"Are you decent?"

"Come in," I said, sitting down on the edge of the bath.

Jamie popped his head around the door, and seeing that I was indeed fully dressed, he came in, followed by Jinx.

"She's gone," Jamie said, "but she wasn't happy."

"Too bad," Jinx said, leaning against the wall.

"She said she'll see you tomorrow."

"Not if I see her first."

"She was very upset that you were angry with her," Jamie said.

Jinx grunted. "She was upset because she wasn't getting her own way for once."

"True," Jamie conceded.

"She won't be coming back?" I asked.

"No," Jinx said, "not tonight, at least. We made it quite clear you should have a bit of space."

"In that case, I'll take my bath."

"Don't let us stop you," Jinx said, with a grin.

"Out," I said, hiking my thumb toward the door, but I couldn't help but smile.

Jamie opened the door and ushered Jinx outside, then paused in the doorway. "Lucky, don't be too hard on Kayla. I don't know if she has an agenda, and I'm not sure if she means you harm, but you know the old saying . . ."

I gave a small shake of my head.

". . . keep your friends close, but your enemies closer. Until we know which she is, I recommend you show her a friendly face."

He was right. If there was one person to whom I mustn't show my true emotions—at least for the foreseeable future—it was Kayla. And that was going to be difficult when she was the one person who knew me better than anyone else.

Sixteen

I had thought I would have nightmares after all that had happened, but I didn't; I slept well. Maybe the long soak in the bath helped, or maybe being surrounded by four demon bodyguards and a drakon made me feel safe.

"I think this morning would be as good a time as any for you to have a riding lesson," Jamie said as we tucked into our breakfast.

"It would also keep you out of Kayla's way," Jinx added.

"When you say riding lesson"—I glanced at Pyrites—"what exactly do you mean?"

"Pyrites can take you for a spin," Jamie suggested.

Upon hearing his name, the drakon trotted over to me and flopped down with his chin resting on my feet.

"I don't know," I said. "Will he mind?"

Jinx laughed. "Of course not; drakons like nothing better than to fly, and if he can take you with him he'll be happy."

"Fly?" I said, my voice coming out an octave higher than normal. "I'm not sure I want to fly."

"It'll be fun," Jinx said.

"Fun has a different meaning here . . ."

Jamie gave me a sympathetic smile. "No, just Baltheza's idea of fun."

"I didn't see anyone else in the court complaining about his entertainment."

"Do you think they'd dare? Besides, the ladies and gentlemen of the court aren't necessarily indicative of the others of this world."

"In other words, the court has become as depraved as Baltheza," Jinx said.

"Shush," Mr. Kerfuffle said, putting his finger to his lips. "He has ears everywhere."

"I don't fear Baltheza," Jinx said.

"I'm with the little guy on this one," said Jamie. "He might not hit out at you or me, but he could make us pay through our friends."

"On that happy note, let's get out of here and have some fresh air," Jinx said. "Whether she wants to or not, Lucky needs to be able to ride the drakon."

"I am here, you know. Why is it that everyone talks about me as though I'm invisible?"

"Did someone speak?" Jinx said with a frown, looking straight past me.

I thumped him on the shoulder, hard enough for him to wince, but it brought a wide grin to his face.

There wasn't anything I thought appropriate for a riding lesson among the racks of clothes hanging in the wardrobe so I dressed in my jeans, shoved on a loose white top and chose a short black leather jacket and a pair of flat black lace-up boots. Even though most of it had clearly been made in the Underlands, it would have passed as human fashion back in my world. I certainly received approving glances from Jamie and Jinx, though I had avoided looking in the mirror as I was scared of what I might see. I was more determined than ever not to become part of this terrible place.

I was nervous when we left the room. The thud of our boots upon flagstones echoed downstairs and through the empty corridors, announcing our passing to all and sundry. By the time we reached the kitchens, the staff were already well into their working day, bustling here and there to the crash of pots and pans and calls for assistance. They were all too busy to pay us much heed as we crept past the door and out into the courtyard. Mr. Kerfuffle led the way, and as soon as we were outside the castle I realized just how alien this world was to my own.

When I had arrived, it had been dark; other than the two moons shining down upon us, the landscape and sky hadn't appeared very different from my own. In daylight it was a different matter. I had assumed it was the orange glow of the moons that had colored the surrounding fields and grass, but this wasn't the case: they really were a rusty red, and two blue suns shone in a deep purple sky.

When we reached the fort's outer wall, rather than walk for ages and in the wrong direction to find the gateway out, Jamie flew me across while Pyrites very graciously carried the other three. Apparently a drakon normally only carries their master or mistress, and they declared themselves "honored." According to Jamie, Pyrites was more amenable than most; it was why he had been considered as my possible steed in the first place.

Once outside the fort, Mr. Shenanigans strode off in his usual way with us trotting behind, trying to keep up. He led us up a hill and down the other side into a deep valley, where we were out of sight of the castle.

"This looks as good a place as any," Jinx said, flopping down on the grass.

Pyrites lay down beside him and stretched out, head between claws. It was hard to believe that the huge creature spread out across the grass had managed to shrink so much he could sit on my shoulder.

"Just supposing I even managed to climb on his back, how would I hold on?" I asked, looking at his shiny scales. "One quick dip and I'd slide right off."

"You'll be fine," Jinx said.

"You sit in the curve of his neck, just in front of his wings," Mr. Shenanigans explained. "He has a gap between his spines where you'll fit. You hold on to one of the spines; they're soft enough to fit to the grip of your hand."

"Won't I hurt him?" I said.

Pyrites lifted his head and gave an indignant puff of dark smoke.

"Sorry, boy," I said, patting his flank, and he gave a little purr from the back of his throat and laid his head back down between his forelegs.

Jinx jumped to his feet. "Come on," he said, "let's get you on him."

"If you're sure . . ." I certainly wasn't, and I was really hoping they weren't suggesting something that might end up killing me.

"Here," Mr. Shenanigans said, entwining his fingers and bending to give me a leg up.

I put one hand on his shoulder and the other on Pyrites's flank, put my foot in his hands and next thing I knew I was sitting in the crook of the drakon's neck. I reached out and took hold of a spine, and it was just as Mr. Shenanigans had said: it fitted into my fist a bit like a joystick might.

"Grip lightly with your knees, as if you're riding a horse," Jinx said.

"I keep telling you, I've never ridden a horse."

Jinx laughed. "This could be interesting, brother," he said to Jamie, and slapped Pyrites on the shoulder.

The drakon gave a big puff of gray smoke, jumped up onto his feet and then we were airborne. I screamed, gripped tight with both hands and closed my eyes. The wind whistled past my ears and through my hair.

"Open your eyes," Jamie shouted from somewhere beside me. "It's fun!"

I opened my eyes, saw the landscape coming up fast in front of me, and promptly shut them again.

"Come on, Lucky, if I can do it so can you," I heard Jinx say.

Jinx? Jinx couldn't fly; he didn't have wings, did he?

I gritted my teeth and reopened my eyes. We were moving alarmingly fast and I gripped Pyrites's flanks so hard that my thighs ached. By the evening I'd be walking like a cowboy.

After the initial few seconds my nerves began to settle and I risked a glance around. Jamie was to my left, gliding gracefully along beside us, then slowly rising up—maybe he'd caught a thermal. Jinx was to my right, but he was not alone: his steed was a winged horse, but the creature was as far from the gentle, noble Pegasus of mythology as any animal could be. I couldn't help but think that Amaliel Cheriour would have been at home on the beast, which was so black it could have been carved out of obsidian. There was no shimmer of blue or silver, just black, even when the light reflected off its body. Its eyes were the only hint of color: they glowed red with a burning infernal fire. Its wings weren't feathered but leathery, and stretched taut over a strong frame of bone. It snorted breath out through flared nostrils in puffs of steam and its muscular flanks glistened with sweat.

Jinx held onto its mane with one hand, his head thrown back in joyous laughter as the creature pounded through the air. Compared to them, Jamie and Pyrites were practically silent as they flew.

Gradually, I began to relax and enjoy the sensation and the view. We flew over vast forests of huge trees that were similar to pines— except their foliage was rusty-red—as well as sparkling lavender lakes and long, snaking rivers. Now and then I could see small groups of cottages, some with smoke spiraling up from their chimneys. In the far distance there was a fort and castle, smaller than Baltheza's, but no less impressive.

"Daltas's home," Jamie shouted over to me.

By the time we returned to the valley I was actually enjoying myself, and sorry when Pyrites swooped down to land beside Mr. Shenanigans and Mr. Kerfuffle, who had been patiently waiting for us.

Mr. Shenanigans was immediately on his feet to help me down. "Did you enjoy your flight, mistress?" he asked, as he swung me off the drakon.

"Yes—better than I would've ever had imagined." I patted Pyrites on the head and said, "Thank you." He purred at me and flopped down with a contented sigh.

Jamie glided down beside us, followed by Jinx and his beast. The creature stomped the ground with its massive hooves, snorting and snuffling, and steam rose off of its coat. Jinx jumped down and ruffled his mane.

"Good boy," he said, and the creature whinnied and then, with a flap of wings, flew up into the skies: a black stain among the pink clouds.

"Where did he come from?" I asked.

"He's an old friend," Jinx said. "He comes when I have a need for him."

"Has he a name?"

"Bob." Jinx laughed.

"*Bob!*" I was astounded. "How can such a creature be called Bob?"

"It was the best I could come up with at the time."

"Black Bob," Jamie said with a grin. "It does have a certain ring to it."

I looked around at the smiling men and for the first time since I'd arrived in this strange world, felt like I might just be happy.

Then Jamie said, "We'd better get back," bringing my spirits crashing down.

"Do we have to?" I asked. "Can't we just go off somewhere else?"

"Wherever we went Baltheza would find us, and believe me, it's better we're staying at the castle of our own free will rather than at his pleasure."

The smiles slipped from the daemons' faces. "You wouldn't wish to visit the Chambers of Rectification," Mr. Kerfuffle said.

"What goes on down there makes last night's entertainment look quite tame," Jamie added.

"Dear God," I said to him, "does none of this shock you?"

Jamie gave a snort. "Lucky, I've lived here nearly all of my life. I might not like what goes on, but I know it happens. What excuse has your kind for the cruelty they heap upon each other?"

"What you saw last night was a method of execution used by your forebears several hundred years or so ago," Jinx added. "And the Inquisition did far, far worse."

"There are some now doing far worse, only behind closed doors," Jamie added.

"We could take you to see for yourself if you so wish," Jinx offered.

They were right: humans weren't so very different. They just weren't as open about it.

★ ★ ★

We took the same route back into the fort, but when we reached the door by the kitchens a tall green figure was waiting for us. Captain Vaybian was leaning back against the wall; when he saw us he straightened to his full height and his hand moved to rest on the pommel of his sword.

"Where have you been?" His tone was far from friendly.

Mr. Kerfuffle and Mr. Shenanigans were suddenly between him and me. "It's none of your business," Mr. Kerfuffle said.

"I'm making it my business," Vaybian said, leaning forward so he overshadowed the small demon.

But Mr. Kerfuffle wasn't so easily intimidated. He put his hands on his hips and tilted his head back so he was looking up into Vaybian's eyes. "Well, you can go and shovel shit as far as I'm concerned."

The captain's sneer grew angry and he took a step forward—then Jinx stepped between them and put his palm flat against Vaybian's chest. The green demon jerked away from him, almost stumbling in his haste to put some space between them.

"Easy, brother," Jinx said. "We're all friends here."

Vaybian glared at him. "I think not, Deathbringer."

Jinx shrugged. "As you wish, but I'm not here to bring you or yours harm. I'm here to protect Lucky."

The captain's lips twisted with disdain. "Since when did you start protecting life rather than taking it?"

"Since your *mistress* saw fit to have Lucky come to court." It was pretty obvious by the way Jinx stressed the word "mistress" just what he was implying.

Vaybian had his sword halfway out of its scabbard before he hesitated.

"Think long and hard before you do something we might all regret," Jinx said.

Vaybian didn't stop glaring at him, but he let the sword slip back into its sheath and withdrew his hand from the pommel. "Lord Baltheza is asking for her," he said, jerking his head in my direction.

The three demons standing in front of me all shifted slightly, their bodies tensing, but I couldn't tell whether that was because of Vaybian's discourtesy, or the fact that Baltheza wanted to see me. Personally, I didn't give a crap whether Vaybian was rude to me or not, but Lord Baltheza wanting to see me turned my legs to jelly.

"Where's Kayla?" Jamie asked.

"*Princess* Kayla is with her father."

Jinx turned to me. "Looks like it's time for you to have a chat with Daddy."

"I'm going to be sick," I whispered.

He grinned. "You'll be fine."

"Are you coming with me?" I knew I sounded desperate, but that was because I was scared shitless.

His grin broadened. "I wouldn't miss it for the world."

I glanced at Jamie. Lines creased his forehead and his lips were curved into a tight downward arc. I might not have been happy, but neither was he.

"This isn't a game," he hissed at Jinx.

Jinx's grin softened to a smile. "I think you'll find it is, brother. One big game."

Jamie's frown deepened. "Right," he said. "Let's get this over with."

Vaybian opened the back door and gestured for us to go through, but Mr. Kerfuffle and Mr. Shenanigans both crossed their arms and didn't budge. Vaybian scowled and, realizing the two demons wouldn't be shifted, stomped into the corridor and strode off without waiting to see if we were following or not.

"Nice one," Jinx said to the pair.

"Damn upstart," Mr. Kerfuffle grumbled.

The two demons went first, followed by me, with Pyrites on my shoulder, ears pricked and alert. Jamie and Jinx were very slightly behind me so I was guarded from all sides. They were suddenly taking their duties very seriously, and that realization made my anxiety levels shoot up several notches. If they were nervous, I was doubly so.

Vaybian led us in a different direction and within minutes I was completely lost. I wouldn't have been able to find my way back to the outer door, let alone my chambers.

"Where are we going?" I whispered.

"To Baltheza's private chambers by the looks of it," Jamie replied, his voice tight.

I glanced back at him. "Is there a problem?"

He let out a shuddery breath. "I hope not, Princess. I truly hope not."

Princess? Jamie had never called me "princess" before, though Mr. Kerfuffle and Mr. Shenanigans had. What was going on?

Baltheza's chambers were very similar to mine, but larger and divided in two by a latticed partition. The outer section was the sitting area, but through the latticed screen I could see a huge bed scattered with black silk covers and velvet pillows. If I wasn't mistaken, there were bodies lying beneath the sheets.

Baltheza sat in a large leather armchair which would have been at home in Philip's golf club, and for a split-second I wondered where he was. Baltheza cradled a goblet of something in his right hand while his left played idly with the hair of a young woman curled up at his feet. She could have been human, except for the single horn protruding from her forehead and her skin being the color of duck eggs. She was naked other than a leather collar around her neck, which was attached to a chain looped around Baltheza's wrist.

Kayla reclined on a sofa opposite him, though I could see her back was pushed into the corner, so she wasn't quite as at ease as she looked. She acknowledged me with a tight smile. The snakes peeped out of her hair, tiny eyes darting from me to Baltheza and back again, forked tongues flicking in and out. She was anxious; that made two of us.

Vaybian stood behind her, one hand resting on the back of her seat, the other on the pommel of his sword. He was the only member of her guard present. It looked like Baltheza didn't feel the need for protection at all, as there were no guards standing at his back.

He smiled at me in welcome, though his expression hardened when he greeted my men. I didn't curtsey—it would have looked ridiculous while wearing jeans. Instead, I gave a small bow and kept my eyes lowered, hoping I was doing the right thing.

"Come here, my dear," he said, beckoning to me. "We don't worry about ceremony here in my chambers."

As I took a few steps forward he handed his goblet to the girl at his feet and rose to greet me. He put a hand on each of my shoulders and kissed me on both cheeks.

"Sit," he said, indicating the sofa and I took the other end to Kayla, perching on the edge. "You can leave us," he said to my men.

Mr. Kerfuffle and Mr. Shenanigans exchanged glances, as if they didn't know what to do. I understood their dilemma: they might be sworn to protect me, but to refuse an order from their ruler could mean a trip to the dreaded Chambers of Rectification.

Jinx sauntered past them, murmuring something to them as he passed, and the two bowed and with a final apologetic glance at me they scuttled out.

Jinx smiled at Baltheza, but it was that smile again: the dangerous one. "I'm thinking that you weren't directing that order to me and my brother."

Baltheza smiled an equally dangerous smile. "I would speak to my daughters alone."

Jinx's gaze wandered around the room to Vaybian and then back to the girl at Baltheza's feet. "Hardly alone."

Baltheza jerked his head in Vaybian's direction and gestured toward the door and the captain glared at Jinx, but then went to leave with a bow.

"Wait," Kayla said. Vaybian stopped midstride and turned to her with a surprised and somewhat anxious frown. "Father, the Guardian and Deathbringer won't leave her side, and if that is so, I petition for the Captain of my guard to remain with me."

"By Beelzebub's balls, Kayla, I will say who leaves or remains in my own chambers."

Kayla rose to her feet. "If Vaybian leaves, then so shall I."

"Be careful, daughter mine. You are not above spending time in Amaliel Cheriour's company."

The snakes weaved in and out of her hair, hissing and spitting. "Will you leave?" she said to Jinx.

"Not on your life," he replied with a grin.

"See," she said to her father.

"You are not above the law either, Deathbringer," Baltheza said. "I am ruler here, and if I say you are to leave, then you shall."

"I'll not leave Lucky in this room with you when one she fears lingers on the other side of that partition," he said, gesturing toward the bedroom.

Jamie stepped to Jinx's side, his eyes straining to see through the latticework. He frowned and turned to glare at Baltheza.

A curtain at one end of the partition drew back and Henri wandered in, his lips curled in a condescending smile. He held his cane in his right hand and a chain-lead in the left. He smiled at me, flashing his teeth, then gave the lead a vicious tug and Philip came tumbling into the room, his hands grasping his throat. He fell to his knees and stayed there, his arms across his chest, his hands stuffed under his armpits and his head bowed.

He looked terrible. Last time I had seen him he had been in a bad enough state, but now his skin was the color of rancid milk—at least the flesh that wasn't bloodied or bruised.

I jumped to my feet and turned on Kayla. "What's Henri doing with him? I thought Daltas had given him to you; I thought you were protecting him."

She pouted. "I said I'd accepted him as a gift from Daltas. What more did you want?"

"Look at him, Kayla. He's half-dead."

"Not my doing," she said.

"Oh, so it's all right then?"

"Lucky," Jamie murmured in warning.

I was too angry to care. "Don't," I said, "just *don't*. And you"—I pointed a finger at Henri—"you only pick on the defenseless. You're nothing but a damn bully."

Henri's lip curled and he gave the chain another jerk, pulling Philip close enough to touch. He ran a fingernail down Philip's cheek, drawing blood, then grasped the lead tighter and hauled Philip to his feet. Philip strained against it, trying to keep away from the demon, but Henri obviously had other ideas. He pulled Philip's face close to his and very slowly ran the pointed tip of his tongue along the fresh wound. Philip moaned.

Henri grinned at me.

"Stop it," I said.

"Make me."

I took a step toward Henri and Jinx stepped between us. "Not your battle," he said.

"But—"

"Lucky, this is of his own making. Be satisfied you saved his daughter."

"Enough," Baltheza said, slumping back in his chair. He flapped a hand at Kayla. "Take the human."

Henri's grin wilted and with an audible sniff he strutted across the room, dragging Philip behind him, and threw the lead in her lap. She picked it up between finger and thumb and dropped it on the couch beside her.

"Get out," Baltheza said to Henri.

"My lord"—Henri glanced toward Jamie and Jinx—"do you not think it better I stay?"

"By Titan's testicles, I will be *obeyed*!"

Henri flinched. "My lord." He swept down into a low and graceful bow and backed out of the room, closing the door behind him with barely a sound.

"Sit down," Baltheza said to me.

I returned to the sofa and did as he said. Jamie took up position by the door and Jinx leaned against the wall by the entrance to the bedroom. No one was coming in and no one was going out without passing one of them.

Vaybian hesitated, then returned to Kayla's side, his hand still resting on his sword.

Baltheza's eyes flicked to each of the three men. He ignored Philip. "I suppose it's all right with you gentlemen if I at least speak with my daughters?"

"Be our guest," Jinx said, not in the least concerned by Baltheza's obvious irritation.

Baltheza sat up in his chair and leaned forward as if to snap a retort, but stopped. His eyes narrowed as he contemplated the death demon. "What are your intentions toward my daughter?" he asked suddenly.

For once Jinx was speechless. He straightened up from the wall, his eyes wide as he looked from Baltheza to me, then he glanced at Jamie.

"You ask as if I were a prospective groom."

Baltheza's lips curled into a crafty smile. "She has your mark upon her."

"She has his mark also," Jinx said, pointing at Jamie.

"Then I will ask the Guardian the same question." He turned to Jamie. "What are your intentions toward her?"

"Are you going to ask the same of Captain Vaybian, or has that question already been answered?"

Kayla gave a small gasp as Baltheza's scrutiny swung to her. "Is that a question I should be asking, daughter mine?"

Kayla licked her lips and the serpents in her hair hissed at Jamie, their tiny black eyes glittering with the evil intent she was no doubt feeling.

"Vaybian is the Captain of my guard," she said, "and his place is by my side."

"To protect your body and maybe satisfy its needs, but is there more to it than that?"

Vaybian's hand slid from the back of the chair onto her shoulder.

Kayla hesitated, then she rested her hand on his.

Baltheza picked up his goblet and rolled the stem between his fingers, his eyes not leaving the pair. "You've been back but a moment and already you fill my court with intrigue," he said at last.

"It was not my intention," Kayla said.

"What about Daltas?"

"What about him?" she said.

"He wants the throne."

"He'll not get it through me."

He studied her for a moment longer, then returned his attention to me. "And what about you?" he asked. "Which of these two fine stallions are you rutting with? Or is it both?"

It took me a second to work out what he was implying. "Both?"

"In the Overlands it is frowned upon to take more than one lover to your bed at the same time," Kayla said.

"Really? Then all the more reason you should stay in our world," he said with a deep chuckle, "for you can sleep with your whole damn guard and no one would think badly of you—although fucking a drakon would be seen as a little perverse."

A single puff of smoke by my ear reminded me that Pyrites was still balanced on my shoulder. With a flap of wings he floated down to my feet and as soon as he touched the ground started to grow until he'd reached the size of a very large dog. He sat down and rested his head across my knees with a rumble from deep in his chest. He clearly felt that either I or he—or maybe both of us—had been insulted.

"Lucky isn't bedding either of them," Kayla said, and couldn't quite keep the smirk from her lips.

"They all share the same bed," Baltheza said.

"To sleep," she said, with a confident but bitchy smile. "Only to sleep."

"She truly is a virgin?"

"Probably 'til the day she dies."

"Will you stop it," I said. "I am right here." They both grinned, and suddenly I could see the likeness between them. I knew I was frowning and hoped I wasn't pouting; only Kayla could pull that off without looking like a big kid.

"You wanted to speak to me," I said to Baltheza.

His expression grew gentle, but I didn't trust it. I didn't trust him or Kayla, and that realization had me fighting back tears. I took a deep breath. I would not break down.

Pyrites's head shifted up onto my thigh. Looking at me with his beautiful multi-colored eyes, he gave a little purr, almost as if he was saying to me "I still love you." I stroked his head and he gave a contented puff.

"I was hoping to convince you that you belong in my court," Baltheza said.

"I sort of got the impression I didn't have any choice in the matter," I said. I didn't dare look at Jamie, as I was pretty sure he would be gesturing for me to shut up.

"Of course I want you to stay—I want to get to know you. I want you to become your true self and not hide behind this"—he gestured toward me—"façade."

"This is me," I said. "What you see is what you get."

He and Kayla exchanged a glance.

"What?" I asked.

"You've got to tell her," Kayla said.

Baltheza took a sip of his drink then put the goblet down on the floor beside him. "Lucky, my dearest child, it seems you are under the impression that you are at least part mortal."

"What are you talking about?" I asked, but I suddenly felt very cold inside, and a small butterfly of fear fluttered deep in my chest.

"Don't," I heard Jamie mutter from what sounded like a million miles away.

"Apparently you've been led to believe that you're the creation of a union between me and a mortal lover," he said. His smile grew: the smile before delivering the killer punch-line. It was the smile of someone who knew something you didn't and was going to thoroughly enjoy the denouement. It was the smile of someone holding all the cards.

My hands began to shake and I tried to hold them as still as possible.

"It's true that you're the product of my loins, but—" He stopped and gave Kayla an affectionate smile

No! I thought, *it can't be.* The room seemed to shift slightly.

"Your mother was Kayla's aunt."

The world stopped spinning. Although I should have been horrified, I was deeply relieved: I wasn't the child of an incestuous relationship between father and daughter. I almost smiled, but then the lightbulb came on with an almighty flash. Kayla's mother was undoubtedly a demon, so it stood to reason that so was her sister. And that meant . . .

I looked down at my hand lying on Pyrites's head. It was a shimmering rose-pink.

I jumped to my feet. "You're lying," I said. "I've seen pictures of my mother. She was beautiful—and very, *very* human."

"Now, now, daughter mine," Baltheza said, "no need to distress yourself."

I glared at him. "You are not my father and you"—I pointed at Kayla—"are neither my friend, nor my sister. You're a lying, two-faced, bitch."

"You said nothing would ever come between us."

"So that allows you to behave however you like? I don't think so."

"Sit down," Baltheza's tone was such that it didn't brook any argument. "Sit down, and let's discuss this like reasonable adults."

I sat on the sofa, fists clenched into tight balls, and took a deep breath in an effort to calm my pounding heart. I couldn't bring myself to look at Kayla, but as I could hear the low hiss of serpents I guessed she wasn't happy either.

"Ours was a clandestine liaison obviously, and I had no idea Veronica was with child. When she disappeared from court I thought nothing of it."

"So you didn't care for her?"

"Care for her?" He sounded bemused. "Why would I care for her?"

I winced inwardly. This was getting better and better. "Go on."

"Then there was a disturbance in the Overlands: a child was born into the human world, one who didn't belong. That child was you." He bent down to retrieve the goblet, took a mouthful and sat contemplating me over the rim. "When your mother returned to our world, she eventually confessed where she'd been and what she'd been doing. She told me the human who believed he was your father was a man of some substance who could adequately provide for you. And that would have been that." He glanced at Kayla. "However, my daughter had other ideas."

"She needed protection," Kayla said.

"From what?"

I looked at her and she bit her lip.

"I knew when she came of a marriageable age there were those of our world who would try and use her—and I've been proven right."

"If you'd not left us for the human world they'd have been none the wiser."

"Her presence was felt everywhere," Kayla said.

"Only for a short time."

"Because I shielded her—if I hadn't gone to her, who knows what would have happened."

"The Guardian would have happened," Baltheza said, turning to Jamie. "Is it not your responsibility to deal with breaches between our worlds?"

"A Guardian was sent, but it was too late; Lucky had been hidden from us," Jamie said, giving Kayla a pointed frown.

She sniffed and looked away.

"What happened to my mother?" I asked.

Both Baltheza and Kayla went very still. Even the little serpents stopped their weaving within her hair and fixed their tiny black eyes on me. A maroon hand rested on my shoulder and Jamie came to stand by my side. I had obviously asked a question I shouldn't have.

Baltheza took another mouthful of wine, savoring it before swallowing, giving himself time to consider his answer. Kayla watched his face, and Vaybian's hand dropped from her shoulder to the pommel of his sword.

"She died," Baltheza said at last.

I tried to swallow, but couldn't; something hard had stuck in my throat. She might have abandoned me, she might have never loved me—she might have even been a demon, for Heaven's sake—but this was the woman who had brought me into the world. The woman who had broken my father's heart, and mine.

"How?" I asked when I eventually managed to speak. I looked him straight in the eyes. I didn't need a mirror to know my expression: I was angry and it showed.

Baltheza handed his goblet to the girl sitting at his feet and gestured to the decanter sitting by his elbow. She unraveled her legs from beneath her and rose up in a sinuous movement. Part of me wondered how she could bear to be on the end of that chain, and how she could tolerate being so close to a creature who oozed such cruelty?

He took the refilled goblet from her and she sank back down to the floor, her head resting against his thigh. He took a strand of her hair and idly twisted it as he contemplated me.

"Killed by a jealous lover is what I heard," Kayla said when the silence in the room was beginning to weigh heavy on all of us. It felt like the moment before a storm breaks.

Baltheza continued to match my stare, his lips curled into a reflective smile. "She was very beautiful—even more so than her sister, Kayla's mother." Kayla's glared at him. "She was also headstrong; a trait you seem to have inherited." He gave me a benign smile. "It was probably that trait that got her killed."

The message wasn't lost on me, but even so, the question hovered on my lips: *Did you kill my mother?* Jinx's fingers tightened on my shoulder and I clamped my mouth shut so tight my teeth hurt. I didn't have to ask. If he hadn't killed my mother himself she had died on his orders. Which set me to wondering: *Why?*

When we got back to my chamber I went to the dressing table and sank down onto the stool. I didn't dare look in the mirror; I had to build up to that one. My clenched fists lay on my thighs, but they were no longer shimmering rose-pink, they were just normal. Had I imagined it? I hoped so, but if what Baltheza had said was true? I breathed in and out, hesitated, then looked up into the mirror.

My eyes were wide, my cheeks pale, my hair was a tousled mess from my drakon ride, but it was me, not the woman I had seen looking back at me from the wardrobe mirror.

"Did I change?" I asked, still staring at myself in the mirror. The reflections of Jamie and Jinx appeared behind me.

"What do you mean?" Jamie asked, though his tone was guarded.

"In Baltheza's chamber I thought . . . I thought I changed. My hand . . ." I looked down, but it was still my hand, "I thought it had changed." I looked up just in time to catch Jamie and Jinx exchange a glance.

"It's this place," Jamie said after a pause. "It can make your mind play strange tricks on you."

Jinx raised an eyebrow at him, but didn't comment. "Where are Shenanigans and Kerfuffle?" he asked, changing the subject.

"I doubt they'll be gone long. Shenanigans is very protective of our little princess."

"Don't call me that," I said. "I'm not a princess."

"Baltheza seems to think you are," Jinx said. "I'm actually surprised he admitted to you being his daughter."

"If it's true," I said.

"Why would he have said it if it wasn't so?" Jamie said.

"To mess with her head," Jinx suggested, staring at my reflection in the mirror.

Jamie sighed. "A pretty thought, but would either of us be here if it were the case?"

"I admit to being puzzled by your involvement."

"There was so much demon activity in the Overlands, and it was all concentrated in one area. I had to find out what was going on. It all led to Lucky."

"Did Baltheza send you?"

Jamie's expression turned to frost. "No, I'm not Lord Baltheza's puppet."

"No offense, brother."

"Why do you think he killed my mother?" I asked.

Both men turned to me, their expressions guarded. "Who says he did?"

"Come on, boys, he practically admitted it—and there was a pretty big hint that if I didn't stop asking awkward questions the same would happen to me."

"It's not something we should talk about here," Jamie said.

"For goodness' sake, Jamie," I said, "it's not as though he's had the room bugged. You told me yourself you don't have modern technology here."

"I'm with the Guardian on this one," Jinx said, "Baltheza has ears everywhere."

I was about to argue when the door opened behind us and they both turned away from the mirror, their hands on the swords hanging at their waists. I swung around on my seat.

"Oh, it's you two," Jinx said. "Where have you been?"

"Checking on the human child," Mr. Shenanigans told him.

"More likely checking on the innkeeper's lovely daughter," Jamie said with a laugh, but when he turned to me he put a finger to his lips. He was right; our friends didn't need to hear what I thought Baltheza had done to my mother. It could put them in terrible danger.

Mr. Kerfuffle smirked up at his huge friend who bowed his head and shifted from foot to foot.

Jinx slapped him on the shoulder. "Go for it, why don't you?"

"I have promised to serve Mistress Lucky, and it is a promise I intend to keep."

"That doesn't stop you from stepping out with the luscious Leila," Jinx said.

"You know her?" Jamie asked.

"I have supped an ale or three at the Drakon's Rest Inn."

"I'm surprised they serve you," Mr. Kerfuffle said.

Jinx grinned. "Of course they serve me—and it usually comes on the house."

"Who in his right mind is going to turn away a thirsty Death-bringer?" Jamie said.

"Or Guardian," Jinx added.

"I can't recall ever getting my ale for free," Jamie said.

Jinx looked him up and down. "That, brother, is because you don't appear threatening."

Jamie frowned. "I'm not . . . unless the need arises."

"Nor am I, yet people fear me," Jinx said with a smile, and for once it didn't make the skin around his eyes crinkle.

I watched him from the corner of my eye, not wanting him to see I was studying him. It was only the second time I had ever glimpsed any vulnerability in him. I had thought there was a hard core of steel beneath his jovial exterior, but I was obviously at least partly wrong.

"How did it go with Lord Baltheza?" Mr. Kerfuffle asked.

Jamie made a face.

"So not well?" Mr. Shenanigans said.

Jinx chuckled. "As well as could be expected. Lucky lost her temper and spoke her mind. Neither Baltheza nor Kayla were expecting it."

"Is there cause for concern?" Mr. Shenanigans looked grim.

"I doubt it. Baltheza may be unstable, but he likes people around the court who either amuse or surprise him and I think Lucky probably does both."

"Thanks," I said. "Nice to know I'm at least amusing."

"Don't sulk, it doesn't suit you," Jinx said with a grin. "Now, I think it's time for some lunch. How about we go to the Drakon's Rest? It'll give the big fella a chance to woo the lovely Leila."

Mr. Shenanigans suddenly found his boots very interesting, and after some more banter in a similar vein it was agreed we would go to the inn. He even took the trouble to change his jerkin, although he did take some ribbing for that.

Jamie and Jinx were bare-chested, as usual. I could understand why it was difficult for Jamie, having wings and all, but I figured Jinx just liked showing off his toned muscles. If he had a problem with clothing, it would be with his pants, though I could see they were specially made to accommodate his tail, which was probably almost as expressive as Kayla's snakes.

"How's Philip's daughter?" I asked as we left the castle.

"Fine," Mr. Kerfuffle said. "She's made friends with Leila's youngest sister."

"I hope she has more luck with her than I did with Kayla."

"Oh, come on girl," Jinx said, "you and Kayla were the best of friends until this happened."

"She wasn't the person I thought she was." Even I could hear the bitterness in my voice.

Jamie caught me by the arm and drew me around to face him. "I'm not Kayla's hugest fan, but think on this: she changed for you. She tried to act in a fashion acceptable to you, and she chose to live a spirit-like existence so she could be with you. She's different here because she has to be." He paused and ran a hand through his blond curls. "She gave up a lot to be with you—you don't think her relationship with Vaybian is a new thing? I bet she and he were together before she left this world."

I bit my lip and lowered my eyes from his. I had nowhere near for-given her, but Jamie was right. Maybe I was being too hard on her. At least he had given me something to think upon.

Even before we reached the inn I could tell it was busy. Laughter and the hum of voices spilled out into the yard, along with the smell of beer and cooking meats. We had to push our way through a wall of people to get inside, but as soon as the first demon turned and saw Jinx and Jamie the voices around us quieted and a corridor formed between the bod-ies. Jamie led the way through the crowd to the table where we had sat before. It was occupied by a party of demons, but a green demon with tusks looked up, no doubt wondering why it had suddenly grown so quiet, and when he saw us approaching he gave a sharp gesture to his colleagues. Though none of them looked happy to see us, they got up and moved pretty damn quickly.

"You guys can be quite handy to have around," I remarked.

"Barron, the landlord, won't be too pleased," Mr. Kerfuffle said. "Most of his customers will drift away once they've finished their drinks. Drinking with a Deathbringer is seen as a mite unlucky."

"Ridiculous, really," Jinx said. "I don't bring death to this world."

"Just mine," I said.

He smiled. "As I told you, not so much now."

"So why was it you used to do it?"

"If humankind had been left to their own devices they would have soon swamped the Overlands. My job was to make sure they didn't."

"But our population is growing."

"It's balanced out by your inability to produce enough food for everyone and your ability to make war on a pretty regular basis. Throw in other manmade disasters and my job is pretty much done for me these days."

"So you're out of work?" I said.

He grinned. "No; I just had a change of job description, like the boy here," he said, gesturing to Jamie.

We were interrupted by Leila sauntering up to our table. Her fine attributes were even less restricted than before and Mr. Kerfuffle's eyes were almost bulging out of their sockets. Jamie and Jinx kept theirs averted, though I think that was more for my benefit—or maybe even for our lovelorn friend's. Leila certainly made sure Mr. Shenanigans had a good look; as she leaned down beside him to wipe the table, her breasts brushed his shoulder and forearm. His face glowed and he seemed to be having trouble swallowing.

Both Jinx and Jamie were trying hard not to laugh and I had to look away; if I started to giggle I wouldn't be able to stop.

Then Jinx gave a snort, which he turned into a cough. "Leila, I think I need a beer," he managed to gasp.

"I'll be right back," she said, and sauntered away with a wanton swing of her ample hips. Halfway across the room she glanced back over her shoulder to make sure the men were watching and gave Mr. Shenanigans an exaggerated wink.

As soon as she disappeared Jinx began to laugh, and Jamie soon joined him. "Lordy," Jinx said to Mr. Shenanigans, "she looks like she wants to eat you alive."

"That's what he's afraid of," said Mr. Kerfuffle with a smirk.

I was about to laugh too, then I frowned; the image of a female spider eating her mate floated through my head. "She wouldn't really, would she?"

They all looked at me as though I was completely insane, then everyone, even Mr. Shenanigans, burst into hysterical laughter.

"What?" I said.

"It was a *joke*," said Jamie.

I was too relieved to be angry—besides, it was good to laugh. I hadn't done a lot of that lately.

Leila returned with a tray of tankards and a couple of flagons. She obviously thought we looked a thirsty bunch. Our food orders boiled down to various meats, on or off the bone.

"After we've eaten I'll take you to see the human child, if you want to meet her," Mr. Shenanigans said to me.

"I'd like to know she's all right."

"We're going to have to work out how to get her back," Jamie said.

"She may not want to go," Jinx said.

"Don't be stupid. Why would she want to stay here?" Jamie asked.

"What has she to go home to? Her mother's dead and her father's Kayla's pet."

"Can't we help him escape?" I asked.

For the second time that evening they all looked at me as though I was crazy, but this time it wasn't followed by laughter.

"Well, he can't stay here," I said crossing my arms.

Jamie and Jinx exchanged one of those glances I now recognized as a "do you think we ought to tell her or let her find out on her own?" look.

"Come on, out with it," I said.

Jinx drained his tankard and refilled it.

"Jinx?"

He took another swig and white froth covered his lip. He wiped it away with the back of his hand and gave a small belch, then leaned back in his seat and stared at a point midtable for a few seconds before raising his eyes to meet mine.

"Lucky, I'm afraid your friend is lost to your world forever. He can't return."

"Why?" I asked. "If his daughter can go back, then so can he."

"His daughter has spent most of her time here in relative safety. She hasn't been marked by this world."

"What do you mean?"

"Lucky, you saw him," Jamie said. "You saw the state of him."

"He looked terrible," I agreed, "but if we got him home—if we took him somewhere where he could be nursed back to health—it wouldn't take long. He's only been here a matter of days."

"I think I'll go and see where our meal is." Mr. Shenanigans stood.

"Good idea," his small friend said, getting to his feet and following behind.

I watched them push their way across the room. They knew I was about to be told something I didn't want to hear. My attention turned back to Jamie and Jinx.

"Lucky, I wouldn't be surprised if Philip hadn't lost his mind by now," Jamie said gently.

"You don't know that. If we managed to get him home he could get better."

Jinx reached across the table and took my hand in his. I tried to snatch it away, but he held onto it fast. "Listen to me," he said. "Argon was sent to the Overlands to collect *you*. He failed, so he took Philip. Argon doesn't like to fail, and he would have let his displeasure fall on the person who caused that failure. Then Philip was handed over to Daltas, whom he had also failed: he had promised to give you to him on a plate and he didn't. Daltas would have made him pay for that. What you saw happen to Dumah yesterday might have been horrible, but there are worse things that can be done to a being while they still live."

"We must be able to do something—"

"I would suggest putting him out of his misery, but I doubt you would welcome that as an idea," Jinx said.

"You mean kill him?" This time I did yank my hand out of his and pull it back across the table.

"I mean put him to sleep, never to awaken," Jinx said.

I shook my head back and forth. "No, no, you can't. It's murder."

"It's the end of pain; it's the end of torture."

I continued to shake my head. Maybe it wasn't just Philip who had lost his mind. I took another deep breath. "There must be something we can do."

"I gave you my opinion," Jinx said.

I glared at him. "Murdering him is not an option."

"It wouldn't be murder. I told you: he'd just go to sleep and never wake up."

"You can do that, can you?" I asked, not sure that I wanted to hear the answer.

Jinx just stared at me.

"He is a Deathbringer," Jamie pointed out.

"So if you decided you'd had enough of someone—me for instance—I could just go to sleep one night and not wake up?"

Jinx regarded me over the rim of his tankard. "Pretty much," he said eventually.

"It doesn't work quite like that," Jamie said, casting an anxious look at Jinx.

I looked from one to the other. "Well," I said, "I'm going to give you two options. You either help me get Philip back to my world, or you don't; either way I'm going to try."

"Lucky, the bastard set you up!" Jamie sounded exasperated. "It should have been *you* dangling on the end of Daltas's lead. Why in the name of Beelzebub would you want to help him?"

"Because I want to sleep at night. Sometimes you have to at least try to do what's right, whatever the consequences."

Jinx turned to Jamie and grinned. "I really do like her, you know."

"What?" I asked.

"We sort of guessed you'd want to try and free him," Jamie said with a smile. "It just proves you really are the good—although quite insane—person we thought you were."

My cheeks suddenly felt very warm and it was my turn to study the inside of my tankard. They added to my discomfort by laughing out loud.

"Oh, isn't she sweet?" Jinx said, and I thought my face might very well melt as it flamed up a few notches.

"Adorable," Jamie confirmed.

"Stop it. I am neither sweet nor adorable."

They exchanged a glance and laughed even louder.

I was saved from making myself look any more foolish by the return of the other two demons and the arrival of our food. Leila made quite a production of serving the four men, but plunked my plate on the table almost as an afterthought.

"We don't serve drakons," she said as Pyrites's head popped up from where he had been laying on the floor beside me. "If he wants something to eat he'll have to have it outside."

"He won't be any trouble," Mr. Shenanigans promised.

Leila sniffed. "The last drakon we had in here almost burned the place down. He destroyed a table and two chairs before we put the fire out."

"Pyrites doesn't mind his meat oven-cooked, as long as it's hot," Jinx said.

She gave another sniff. "So *you* say, but I have no reason whatsoever to believe one word that comes out of your mouth."

"That's hardly fair," Jinx said, adding, "I'm deeply hurt," but the crinkling of the corners of his eyes said otherwise.

"I seem to remember it was you who said Cedric was okay for a giant—just before he ate Tasker and then wrecked the place."

Jinx shrugged. "True."

"And wasn't it you who said that Caspian could hold his drink one minute before he threw up all over the floor and passed out cold?"

"Guilty as charged."

"And wasn't it you who told me I was the love of your life and you would never look at another, only for me to find you outside with Caroline the kitchen maid?"

Jinx didn't even have the good grace to look sheepish. "Ah, sweet Caroline—whatever happened to her?"

"She married the blacksmith," Leila said. "I heard she had to—but that would come as no surprise to anyone, least of all you!" And with that she stomped off, taking all thought of Mr. Shenanigans's seduction with her.

The huge demon gave a sigh.

"Sorry, brother," Jinx said, topping up his tankard, and then almost as an afterthought, his own.

"Give her half an hour," Mr. Kerfuffle said though a mouthful of roasted leg of something. "She'll be back."

"You think?"

He nodded, his mouth too full to reply.

"I'd bet on it," said Jamie.

"Did you really tell her she was the love of your life?" Mr. Shenanigans asked.

Jinx stopped chewing and put on a thoughtful expression. "I don't remember using *exactly* those words, but I do remember waking up with an aching head the following morning."

"Was that from the beer, or courtesy of Leila?"

"She was angry," Jinx reminisced, "but not that angry."

"For a death demon everyone seems to fear, you sure have had your fair share of lady friends," I said.

He grinned. "All the girls love a bad boy," he said, then launched into a long story about another drunken escapade.

I jabbed a knife into the piece of meat on my plate, not really listening to the conversation going on around me. My thoughts returned to Philip and how I could get him out of the castle. I had to get him back to my world, but despite my brave words, I knew I didn't have a hope in Hell without their help. I didn't even know how to get home myself.

Jamie hadn't liked Philip from the start, and Jinx didn't have any reason at all to help him. As for Mr. Shenanigans and Mr. Kerfuffle, I didn't want to get them in trouble, particularly not if it might mean a trip to the Chambers of Rectification where the awful Amaliel Cheriour plied his trade. Even the thought of that loathsome creature and his glowing red eyes made me shudder.

"Someone walk over your grave?" Jamie asked.

"Sorry?"

"You shivered."

"What are you talking about?" Mr. Shenanigans asked.

"It's an expression in the Overlands," Jinx explained. "For when you inexplicably shiver."

"Oh," the demon said, looking none the wiser.

"As it happens, you were closer than you can imagine. I was thinking about Jinx's friend, Amaliel Cheriour."

"I told you, he is no friend of mine."

"He acknowledged you," I said, although I knew I was baiting him. "All right."

I frowned at him. "All right what? All right he's your friend?"

"No, all right as in: I'll help you get the mortal back to the Overlands."

Mr. Kerfuffle paused his chewing. "Is that a good idea?"

"If it stops her from being cranky," Jinx replied.

He pursed his rosebud lips in thought, head tilted to one side. "I see your point."

Jamie leaned back in his chair. "It won't be easy," he said to Jinx.

"Nothing ever is."

"I suppose."

"What's your plan?" asked Mr. Shenanigans.

"Damned if I know."

"Me neither," Jamie said.

"If he belongs to Princess Kayla, can't we just take him?" Mr. Shenanigans said.

"Like she's going to give him to us," Mr. Kerfuffle said with a snort.

"Why wouldn't she? After all, she didn't really want him. She only accepted him as a gift to please Mistress Lucky."

Jamie and Jinx both frowned, and then began to laugh. Jinx slapped his palm against his forehead. "He's right. We'll just ask her for him."

"I doubt she'll say no. She doesn't want Lord Daltas, so she'll hardly care if she offends him," Mr. Shenanigans added.

"Sometimes brother, I think you're more brains than brawn."

The huge demon looked bashful. "Just practical, I suppose."

"When can we do it?" I asked. If they had said right then, I would have been up and out of my chair like a shot, though that seemed a little unlikely as Jinx was busy refilling all our tankards.

"I think, just to make it more fun, we should steal him from her," Jinx suggested.

Jamie looked surprised. "Why go to all that trouble, not to mention risk, when we can simply ask her for him?"

"So she can deny all knowledge should we get caught taking him back to the Overlands," Jinx said.

"Caught by whom?" I asked.

"Daltas."

"Hmm." Jamie looked at me. "There you may have a point."

"Surely we have a better chance of getting him if I ask Kayla nicely," I said, crossing my arms.

"After calling her a backstabbing bitch you're going to have to do a lot more than ask nicely, methinks," Jinx pointed out.

"Did you really call her that?" Mr. Shenanigans looked wide-eyed with amazement.

Mr. Kerfuffle gave a little snort of laughter. "You'd think the Lady Kayla would be used to being called names like that by now."

I frowned at him.

"I'm only telling it as it is."

"I thought you were her friends?" I said.

"Employees," Mr. Kerfuffle said, "not friends."

"Kayla is a user," Jinx said, and there was something in his tone that made me sit up and take notice. He was studying the bottom of his tankard as he swirled the beer around and around, a small frown wrinkling the middle of his forehead.

"Did you and Kayla have some sort of relationship?" I asked.

Three pairs of demon eyes swung his way, and even Pyrites sat up and laid his head on the table, his eyes fixed on Jinx.

His frown intensified. "No, we did not," he said, a little too emphatically.

"Then what?"

His frown turned to a scowl that was bordering on sullen.

"Jinx?"

His expression softened into a rueful smile. "We *almost* had a relationship—almost, but not quite. I saw her for what she truly was before it was too late."

"So she was the one," Jamie said.

"The one what?"

"The one who broke your heart."

Jinx began to laugh. "Nooo, my heart is just fine, thank you very much. It was my balls that were nearly broken."

"So you and Kayla never . . . ?"

Jinx raised an eyebrow at me. "No, never."

I tried to keep the relief from showing on my face, though I don't think I succeeded as Jinx's smile grew broader and Jamie's smile all but disappeared. This made me wonder, and not for the first time, whether *guarding* my body was the only thing on their minds.

Seventeen

When we had finished eating, Mr. Shenanigans went to pay Leila, and after a few whispered words, beckoned for us to follow him across the room and through a door behind the bar. The door led into a small passageway to a flight of rickety wooden stairs.

I was grateful we were following the huge demon: it stood to reason that if they could withstand the weight of his giant frame, I wasn't in any danger of falling through the creaking wood.

I could hear children giggling as we came to the top and stopped outside a door. With a smile, Mr. Shenanigans put a talon to his lips.

"Snap!" a voice cried, and then there was more giggling.

Then we heard, "You cheated!"

And "Did not!"

He pushed the door open. "Can we come in?"

"Mr. Shenanigans!" several voices cried out as he stepped into the room.

Mr. Kerfuffle gestured for me to enter next. I wasn't sure what to expect, but what I did see proved to me that beauty was certainly in the eye of the beholder. Four children were clustered around Mr. Shenanigans hugging him around the waist. Two looked human and I recognized Philip's daughter right away. The other was a younger boy of about five or six with jet-black curly hair and dark blue eyes. The other two were definitely demons: one was a mini version of the landlord, except he had yet to grow his tusks, and the other was a willowy creature of about ten or eleven with heather-colored hair tied in a thick braid that hung to her ankles. Her almond-shaped eyes were a liquid grass-green; luminous skin the color of moonstones made it look like she was glowing.

"I've brought someone to see you," he said to the children and they all stepped back, but Philip's daughter clung to Mr. Shenanigans's hand, her eyes wide and frightened. Then she saw me and the fear on her face fell away, to be replaced with a shy smile.

"This is Mistress Lucky," he told them, then to me, "Mistress, this is Angela."

"Hello, Angela," I started, "how are you doing today?"

"Good," she said, and flushed pink.

"This is Petunia, Leila's sister," he said, gesturing to the willowy creature, who dropped a little curtsey.

"Hello, Petunia."

"This is Odin, Leila's brother." He rested his claw on the head of the boy demon and when I said hello he gave me a shy little wave.

"And last, but by no means least, this is Teasel."

When I greeted Teasel the boy looked up at me with huge eyes, stuffed a thumb in his mouth and slowly raised his other hand to grab hold of Mr. Shenanigans's huge claw.

"Teasel is sort of adopted," Mr. Kerfuffle whispered to me.

"What do you mean?" I asked.

"He was left on the doorstep of the inn as a baby and Leila's parents took him in. No one claimed him, so he just sort of stayed."

"But he's human," I said.

Mr. Kerfuffle smiled at the child. "He may look it, but demon blood runs through his veins."

"Turn around, boy," Mr. Shenanigans said.

Teasel kept hold of his hand, but turned slightly so I could see his back: a long tail curled from a strategically placed hole in his breeches and hung down past his knees. It gave a little twitch and waggled as though he was waving at me.

"Is that the only sign?" I asked.

Mr. Kerfuffle nodded. "He's a good boy. Very quiet—too quiet really, it gets him bullied sometimes."

"By whom?"

"The other boys," Petunia broke in. "If it wasn't for Oddy he'd always be in fights—but not many of the others will take on Oddy." Her brother smiled and puffed out his chest.

"Odin may not be big, but he's good in a scrap," Mr. Shenanigans said.

"So you look after Teasel," I said to him.

"He's my kin now. We look after each other," Odin said.

Mr. Shenanigans gestured to the kids to go back to their play and they all drifted away to the other side of the room except for Angela.

He led her a little closer to me and Jamie crouched down so he was eye level with her. "Are they looking after you here?" he asked.

She gave him a hesitant smile. "Are you an angel?" she asked.

He smiled back. "I'm not good enough to be an angel."

"You look like one."

"I'm demon, like all your friends."

A small frown creased her brow. "Are you here to take me home?" she asked.

"Not yet," Jamie said, "but soon."

She bit her lip. "I really like it here," she said.

"Do you?" I asked.

"Everyone's so nice to me."

"Don't you want to go home?" I said, aghast. How could a young girl want to remain in such a terrible, scary place?

She shrugged her small shoulders. "Mommy's gone. Daddy is . . ." Her bottom lip began to tremble. "Daddy isn't Daddy anymore. I hate school. They all pick on me." A single tear slid down her cheek. "Here no one cares whether I'm rich or poor. No one cares what I wear and if it's in fashion. No one judges me."

My own eyes started to tear up. I knew exactly what she meant—and she was just an ordinary little girl. Maybe my childhood hadn't been so unusual after all.

"She can stay here as long as she wants to," a voice said from behind me. Leila was standing in the doorway, leaning against the doorframe.

"Won't your mom and dad mind?"

"We're lucky here: business is good so there's plenty of food, and the kids all look out for each other. If she stays she can go to school with them."

"Won't she get picked on because she's human?" I asked.

"Not if I have anything to do with it," Odin piped up from across the room.

Leila gave him an indulgent smile then turned her attention back to me. "Maybe for the first couple of days the other children will take a little bit more interest in her, but only because she's new, that's all. They only pick on Teasel because he's shy. I think Angela will be able to look after herself."

"Everyone here looks different from everyone else," Jamie said, "but in this world it doesn't matter."

"We'd better get back," Jinx whispered in my ear.

I smiled at Angela. "I'll come to see you again soon."

"I'd like that," she said, and then, after a brief glance up at Mr. Shenanigans, who gave her hand a gentle squeeze, she skipped off across the room to join her friends. As the door closed behind us they were already giggling again.

"She's happy enough," Jamie said once we were outside the inn and negotiating the labyrinth of narrow alleyways.

"She is, isn't she?"

"Why make her go home if she doesn't want to?" Jinx said.

"She doesn't belong here," I said. "It's a cruel and violent place."

Jinx gave a snort. "And the Overlands isn't?"

"What about that disgusting display the other night?"

"Lucky, do you know when there was last a war in the Underlands?" Jinx asked.

"Of course I don't," I said.

"Before I was a twinkle in my father's eye—and I was old by human standards when the pyramids were under construction," Jinx said.

"We don't have much crime," Mr. Shenanigans said.

"I'm not surprised, judging by your justice system," I said.

"Come on, Lucky! There are countries in your world where they still stone people to death—and for pathetic reasons, fornication being one of them," Jinx said.

"I doubt there'd be many left in this world if that were the case here," Mr. Kerfuffle mumbled.

Jinx ignored him. "There are governments in your world—and I'm not just talking about tin-pot regimes in Third World countries—who think nothing of using torture to get information behind closed doors."

He was right—I knew he was right. I'm not a conspiracy theorist, but I'm not naïve either.

"Okay," I said. "Let's try and get Philip back and then see if she wants to return. If she knows he'll be there she might change her mind."

"You heard her, Lucky. She doesn't think her daddy is her daddy anymore. He'd changed before he even came here: he let his wife die and his daughter be kidnapped to further his own ambitions and, sad to say, I think she knows it."

I sighed. Jinx had a point.

"And that's another reason why you should probably leave Philip to rot in Kayla's tender care," Jamie said. "The man is a complete and utter bastard."

"I know," I said, "but can't you at least try to understand? I'm not like Philip, and the moment I start to behave anywhere near as badly as him you have my permission to put me to sleep, never to wake."

"Don't say that," Jinx murmured. "Never say that again." And his expression was so troubled I was sorry I had.

"Jinx?"

"Life is such a fragile thing—you shouldn't chance your luck."

"You're immortal so it's hardly fragile for you."

"I'm not worried about me. I can look after myself."

"So can I."

He raised dark eyes to mine and studied my face for so long I could feel my color rising. "I would rather you let us do that for you," he said at last.

"Yes," Jamie murmured, and once again I wondered if there was something going on of which I was completely unaware.

I didn't get the chance to ask the question. We weren't far from the castle when Mr. Shenanigans and Mr. Kerfuffle, who were walking slightly ahead of us, came to such an abrupt stop I walked straight into the huge daemon's back. I was about to apologize when he gave a sort of grunt and dropped down onto his knees.

"Mr. Shenanigans?" I reached out to touch his shoulder but my fingers barely skimmed his jerkin before he pitched forward. A hand grabbed my arm before I could move, holding me back.

"Stay still," Jamie hissed in my ear.

My eyes jerked up to see three figures swathed in black filling the alley. All three held swords at the ready, and the weapon of the figure in the center dripped with green gore. His face was hidden within the shadow of his cowl, but I recognized his glowing eyes. Amaliel Cheriour.

Mr. Kerfuffle crouched down by his fallen friend and laid a hand on his back. He looked up at the Court Corrector. "Why?"

"Get out of my way, little man," the demon to Amaliel's right said.

Mr. Kerfuffle leaped to his feet and drew his sword. "Go screw yourself—"

"Drop your weapons!" a voice shouted from behind us and when I turned around I could see three more figures behind us. I glared at Amaliel. "Who the hell do you think you are?" I said, shrugging off the hand gripping my arm.

"Lucky, for once in your life, *shut up*," Jamie whispered.

"James, my boy she's made a very good point. Who exactly does he think he is?" Jinx said and I didn't need to look his way to know he was as angry as I.

I wasn't finished. "Mr. Shenanigans is my friend," I said, "and"—I pointed at Amaliel—"you're a psychopathic bastard who needs a taste of your own warped medicine."

The creature laughed—at least I think the gurgling gasp was supposed to be a laugh. "And who's going to give it to me, little girl? You?"

My cheeks flamed and my heart was pounding, but my fear for Mr. Shenanigans outweighed the many other emotions running through my head. My big strong guard was lying flat on his face in the dirt and he didn't deserve it. He was truly a gentle giant: the children loved him and so did I, I suddenly realized. What I had said was true; Mr. Shenanigans was my friend.

"I thought you were the scourge of this world: the most feared creature to walk the court of Lord Baltheza, and yet it takes you and five others to do his dirty work," I said.

"Lucky," Jamie cautioned, but it was no good; I was past reason.

"If Mr. Shenanigans doesn't recover, I will—"

"You will what?" Amaliel said, taking a step closer.

My heart was pumping so hard I could feel the pulse in my temple and throat. I was trembling, but it wasn't only fear, it was also outrage.

"Get her out of here," I heard Jinx say. "Get her away from here, *now!*"

I felt hot tears on my face.

"How sweet," Amaliel said. "She weeps for the oaf." Then he laughed again.

I felt someone move up behind me and grab me around the waist. "No," I shouted, "*no!*" I tried to pull away from the arm locked around me.

"Pyrites," I heard Jamie say over my shoulder.

"Jamie, let me go," I said. "Let me go this instant."

The drakon suddenly filled the space between Amaliel and me and I was manhandled onto his back. Before I had a chance to scramble down he'd flapped his wings and we were off up into the skies, with me hanging on for grim death. We had barely left the ground when the clash of swords filled the alleyway.

"No, Pyrites. *Take me back!* I have to go back—"

He snorted and spurted out a jet of flame—the first I had seen from him. I sensed he was angry too, but he was being a good bodyguard:

his job was to get me out of harm's way and he wasn't going to fail his companions or me. He didn't take me back to the castle, but flew into the countryside instead.

Through my tears of fear and frustration, I could see fields of rust, copper and bronze flashing below me, then tall forests of scarlet and burgundy pines, but still we flew on.

I soon realized Pyrites was avoiding the villages, flying around them rather than over them, and keeping well away from roads. We flew until the light was fading from the sky and my eyes were drooping shut, then we crossed the brow of a hill and I saw mountains stretching out before us. Lush rust-red foliage evaporated into gray rock and then into shimmering streaks of white crystal. I assumed this was one more barrier Pyrites was going to put between us and any would-be pursuers, but as we approached the mountain range he swooped low, hovered and then touched down on a wide ledge just above the tree line.

He shrank to the size of a pony almost immediately, with me still sitting in the crook of his neck.

I wondered if I should get off, but when I asked, he shook his head and began to pick his way up the mountain slope. I pushed myself back so I was sitting cross-legged between his wings, which I hoped would be a bit more comfortable for him, although I wasn't quite so secure. I hoped we didn't have much further to go.

I was pretty sure only mountain goats would have been able to follow the route Pyrites took, for there were no discernible paths. He took us higher until the trees tops were way below us, then just when I thought our journey was never going to end he stopped abruptly, turned his head and made a little rumbling sound.

"You want me to get off?" I asked, and when he gave his little purr I slid from his back and he shrank some more until he was the size of a mastiff. With another gesture he led me along the ledge and disappeared into a narrow fissure in the rock face. The tunnel-like crack lasted only for a foot or so before the rock on either side of me disappeared and I stood in pitch-black emptiness. I stopped dead.

"Pyrites?" I whispered.

There was a flash of flame and the aroma of sulfur and a small fire burst into life: Pyrites was padding around the cave sending jets of flame toward torches attached randomly around the walls.

"This is—nice," I said, looking around the small cavern.

It was probably the size of the ground floor of my cottage, although the ceiling was twice as high. It was bone-dry, and now Pyrites had lit the fire, growing warm as well.

The drakon trotted across to the far end of the cavern, dropped onto his haunches and turned to me. When I didn't immediately follow he stood, scratched at the wall beside him then sat again, his head cocked to one side.

"You want to show me something?"

He gave a snort, which, judging by the fact he also rolled his eyes, meant something close to an exasperated "at last."

I wondered if the cavern was a prearranged bolt-hole; it was certainly beginning to have that feel. Next to where Pyrites was sitting there was a large slab of rock leaning up against the wall. Pyrites helped me to shift it, revealing a deep hollow. I dropped down onto my knees and peered inside, but it was too dark to see much. With a certain amount of trepidation I reached out a hand, and although I knew it offered me no protection at all I closed my eyes. I really hoped I was not about to encounter anything large and hairy with eight or more legs. My fingers stretched out, finding nothing, so I moved closer to the wall and pushed my shoulder up hard against it, stretching my arm out as far as it would go, and this time my fingers brushed across something. I recoiled for a second but it hadn't felt scary, whatever it was, so I reached out again and touched something rough and slightly hairy. As I ran my fingertips over it I realized it felt like a loop of rope. I repositioned myself and stuck my head inside the hole; I still couldn't see a thing, but now I was in far enough that I could manage to grab hold of the rope. When I gave it a pull something large and heavy slid toward me, grating on the rock.

I kept pulling and when I heaved it out of the hole it turned out to be a wooden chest with rope handles. I dragged it across the floor until I was kneeling above it.

"Who left this here?" I asked.

Pyrites's expression said very clearly, "Who cares?" but I persisted, "Pyrites, you knew about this place. Was it Jamie?" The drakon gave a small puff of smoke then stalked back to the fire and flopped down, head between his forelegs.

I knelt down next to the chest. When I pulled on the clasp it opened with a solid click to reveal blankets and pillows. So I was right: someone had prepared this place as a hideout. I pulled out a blanket and laid my cheek against the rough brown material. It was a little scratchy, but it didn't smell musty and would keep me warm enough.

Beneath the bedding I found a round brown paper package tied up with cord and a bottle of something; wine, maybe, or beer; both would keep better than water, which would go stale after a few days. There was also a jar of some kind of pickled vegetables.

I shut the chest and placed the round package on top. It was with some trepidation that I cut the cord with my dagger, but when I pulled the paper back and spread it flat I found a shiny black globe inside. I studied it with a frown, then I placed a fingertip on the surface. It felt a little waxy and I smiled despite myself. It was a wax-covered ball of cheese, I was sure.

"Cheese?" I asked Pyrites.

He lifted his head, sniffed the air with flared nostrils and tilted his head to one side. He sat up and peered at the globe, then gave a little nod.

My stomach rumbled its approval and I realized though I hadn't given it a thought before, I was actually quite hungry. It was hours since we had eaten lunch—and the memory brought me up short: we had been laughing and joking and teasing poor Mr. Shenanigans, and now he was . . . I gave a shuddery sigh. I mustn't think it; they were daemons—immortals—and they kept telling me they didn't die as easily as humans. They had told me so, again and again.

But they can die, said a little voice in my head. I decided I wasn't going to listen to it. Jinx was a Deathbringer, Jamie was a Guardian. *And Amaliel Cheriour is the High Court Enforcer and Corrector.*

"Pyrites, they will be all right, won't they?"

The drakon came and sat next to me and laid his chin on my thigh. I stroked his head and he gave a little purr, but it wasn't a happy one; I thought he was as worried about our friends as I was. That put an end to any pangs of hunger I may have had.

Instead, I snuggled down in front of the fire, Pyrites by my side, and tried to sleep. The drakon was soon snoring, but for me, sleep was elusive. Every time I started to get that warm, fuzzy feeling you get just before sleep carries you off, the image of Mr. Shenanigans keeling over in front of me would suddenly appear in my head, together with a tall, black figure with blazing eyes: Amaliel Cheriour. I swore to myself that if anything bad had happened to my friends, if Mr. Shenanigans didn't recover, I would do everything in my power to make him pay. Eventually, sheer exhaustion won the battle against my overactive imagination and I slept.

When I woke the fire had almost burned out, leaving just a few glowing embers. The torches in their brackets still filled the cave with their yellow glow, but it wasn't as bright and comforting as before. I had lost all track of time; for all I knew I could have slept for an hour or a day. But Pyrites was still asleep, so I snuggled back down and dozed until a loud roar and a flash of flame awakened me with a start.

"Pyrites, you silly fool, it's us!" I heard, and I looked up to see Pyrites was standing over me like a mother protecting her infant. A low rumble burbled in his chest.

"Pyrites?" That was Jamie's voice.

The drakon carefully stepped over me and moved toward the entrance, where he dropped to his haunches, tail wagging.

"Stupid creature," Jinx said affectionately. "We were almost roasted."

Pyrites purred at him and, with a flick of his tail, shrank back down to dog size, making a bit of room in the cave for Jinx to enter, closely followed by Jamie.

I jumped to my feet and ran to them. "Mr. Shenanigans—is he all right?"

"Fret not," Jinx said, "Shenanigans is being cared for by the laudable Leila and her siblings. Kerfuffle too."

"Is Mr. Kerfuffle hurt?" I asked in alarm.

Jinx laughed. "Only his pride, dear girl. Only his pride."

"Jinx saved him from a skewering," Jamie said, "but he's fine."

"Is Mr. Shenanigans badly hurt?"

"Nothing that won't heal," Jamie said.

"But what about us?" Jinx said. "She is all anxious tears and trembling lips for our fine friends, but asks not a thing about our own well-being or lack of it."

I looked from one to the other. "I thought you were uninjured?"

"Mostly," Jamie agreed.

"Mostly?"

Jinx reached out, took hold of the edge of Jamie's right wing and pulled it open. A large patch of russet stained his snowy feathers.

"Jamie, you're hurt," I said, taking a step toward him.

"It's nothing," he said, shaking Jinx's hand away.

"He's being brave," Jinx said, giving me a nudge. Jamie frowned at him and Jinx grinned. "Just telling it as I see it."

"Well, don't."

Jinx wandered over to the chest. "Good, she left us some." He frowned. "In fact, she hasn't touched a thing."

"I was too worried about you all to eat," I said.

Jinx grinned and pulled out a dagger from the side of his boot, wiped it on his pants and proceeded to slice the cheese into chunks. "Make yourself useful and open the beer, brother. I have a fierce thirst upon me."

"I hope it isn't too fierce," I said, "There's only one bottle."

"Pyrites, be a good boy and pop in there and bring out another couple of brews," Jinx said.

The drakon hopped to his feet and shrank to the size of terrier and then bounded into the hole in the wall. He returned with one bottle and then scurried back for another.

"There's enough in our cupboard to last a day or two, but I think we'll have to be moving on before then," Jinx said, flopping on the floor.

Jamie dropped down and sat beside him and they shared out cheese and ale. I accepted a proffered bottle and a hunk of cheese.

"Did you find out why Amaliel was there to meet us?" I asked.

Jamie and Jinx exchanged one of their looks, then Jinx said, "Kayla and Vaybian have been arrested for suspected treason." He lifted the bottle and swallowed, wiped his mouth with the back of his hand and continued, "Fortunately for Kayla she is under house arrest, so she is merely confined to her chambers. Captain Vaybian isn't so blessed; he's languishing in the Chambers of Rectification."

I shuddered; it had been obvious Vaybian didn't like me one little bit, but even so, I wouldn't wish his present predicament upon anybody. "But why does that mean Amaliel Cheriour would come looking for us?"

They exchanged another glance and Jinx gestured for Jamie to tell me the good news.

"Lord Baltheza has issued orders for your arrest too. It appears you are also charged and are to be tried in your absence for treason."

"Treason? What am I supposed to have done?"

"He believes you've conspired with Kayla and her lover to assassinate him and, in his current state of outraged fury, he doesn't much care if you're brought back alive or dead, as long as you're found," Jinx told me.

"But why should he believe that?" I asked, perplexed.

Jinx looked at Jamie and Jamie frowned at Jinx. In the end Jinx lost the stare-out. He gave me one of his most winsome, heart-stopping smiles. "I suppose because, from the evidence, it would appear to be true."

This wasn't the first time in my life I had been accused of something I hadn't done, but never before had the possible consequences been so dire. Dumah Dask had been horribly executed for uttering a few words of dissention—if he'd even done that; I'd not been convinced of his guilt at the time. I suspected the penalty for plotting the monarch's death would be far worse. My imagination started going into overdrive.

I put the bottle down and forced myself to swallow the last bite of my bread and cheese. "What evidence can they possibly have against me? I haven't done *anything*. What aren't you telling me?" I began to wonder just how far I could trust these two men if they were never going to tell me things straight.

Once again Jamie knew the way my mind was going. "Lucky, if no one else, you can trust us," he said.

Jinx frowned at him. "Of course she can trust us."

"She's thinking maybe not."

"How do you do that?" I said. "How do you *always* know what I'm thinking? Can you read my mind?"

Jamie chuckled. "Kayla's snakes give her real feelings away, but you're no better," he said. "When you're irritated you tap your middle fingernail against your thumb and if you're sitting you judder your right leg. When you don't trust someone your face closes down—it just goes blank."

I glared at him.

"Sorry," he said. "I've spent a long time studying human behavior."

Jinx laughed out loud. "So, brother, what's her tell-tale sign that she wants you in her bed?"

It was Jamie's turn to glare. "I don't know," he muttered.

"Yet," Jinx murmured, so softly I wasn't sure whether I'd actually heard it or not.

An unreadable expression passed across Jamie's face; it might not have been pain or sorrow but it was certainly not happy.

"I don't know about you," Jinx said with a yawn, "but I need a nap; we've had a long day."

"Me too," Jamie agreed.

Pyrites lay down on his side and stretched out so the two demons could use his belly like a pillow.

"Come on," Jinx said, scooting over a bit so there was room for me to snuggle up between them.

I bit my lip. Did I really trust them?

"I told you," Jamie said, "we both swore to protect you, and protect you we will."

I couldn't really argue with that, so I settled down between them and let them pull the blanket up over us. Pyrites curled his head and tail around us so that we were surrounded by his body, and within minutes all three of them were snoring.

I was too uptight to sleep; my mind was a whirl of anxiety. Kayla was under house arrest—but how much danger did that really put her in? Was there a real chance she or Vaybian would become the source of the court's entertainment at the hands of Amaliel Cheriour? Was this to be my fate too? And what about Philip—what had become of him? All these questions were whirling around in my head while my protectors were snoring away as if they didn't have a care in the world.

That was a point: if I was accused of treason, what of them? They had been my constant companions since my arrival in this world. And another terrible thought crossed my mind: Mr. Shenanigans and Mr. Kerfuffle were still within the fortress walls—were they really safe at the inn? What if they were captured by Amaliel?

As each moment passed I got more and more worried until I could barely stay still. In the end I couldn't stand it any longer.

"Jamie," I whispered, giving him a nudge. He gave a little snort and rolled over away from me. "Jamie!" This time I tapped him on the arm.

He shivered and pulled the blanket up higher.

I shuffled over a bit so I was almost lying against his wings. "Jamie," I whispered into his ear.

"Hmm."

"Jamie, are you awake?"

"He isn't, but I am," Jinx said from behind me.

I rolled over to face him and found him so close our noses were almost touching. He grinned at me.

"As he's asleep, is there anything I can do for you?"

"You can answer some questions."

He gave an exaggerated sigh. "And there was I thinking you were lusting after my fine, feathered friend's body."

"Jinx, you are incorrigible—"

He kissed me on the tip of the nose before I could pull away. "And you're adorable."

"Jinx, I'm not in the mood."

He grinned. "For what?"

"Playing your word-games."

"There are other games we could play." He chuckled.

I tried to ignore the glint in his eye; it was hard though—but it would have been a lot harder if I hadn't been so scared I felt like throwing up. I made a mental note to myself: if I managed to survive another day, I should keep my distance from him, at least when we slept.

"Jinx, is Kayla safe? I mean, is Baltheza likely to do anything horrible to her?"

"Baltheza, for all his faults, has rather a soft spot for his daughter. If he hadn't he would already have made her watch while he had Vaybian tortured to death."

"He could be doing that now."

"No." He pulled me closer protectively. "He's going to save that fate for you."

"Thanks," I said, as my heart plummeted down to my toes. "I feel so much better for that."

"Don't worry. He'll calm down over the next day or so and when he starts thinking rationally he will realize he's being manipulated."

"By who?"

"Who was it who sent the message for Kayla to come back?"

"Baltheza said he did."

Jinx grunted. "But whose idea was it? Whose assassin delivered the message?"

"Daltas?"

Jinx nodded, his horns brushing my hair.

"But why is he doing all this?"

"Why does anyone do anything?"

"Jinx, please don't talk in riddles. I'm so scared I can hardly think, let alone try to decipher your cryptic clues." He must have heard the tremble in my voice as his face softened and he reached up to smooth the hair from my face.

"Don't be scared," he whispered. "You bear my mark and you are the first for such a considerable time—I wouldn't let any harm come to you. If Baltheza was thinking straight, he would know it."

"You would take on Baltheza?"

He snorted. "I already have: by taking arms against Amaliel Cheriour, James and I have shown where our loyalties lie, and they're not with Baltheza."

"So now you're both in danger?" I asked. Unbidden, I felt a tear run down my cheek.

Jinx wiped it away with the tip of his finger. "Oh, sweet Lucinda," he murmured and cupped the back of my head in his palm, pulling me to him so my still damp cheek rested against his chest.

I closed my eyes and snuggled closer. I could hear his heart beating, feel his chest rising and falling. My own heart thudded in time with his.

I knew it was dangerous to let myself be so close, but I felt so safe in his arms. Safe, warm and comfortable. I had so many other questions I wanted to ask, but I didn't want to draw away from him. I wanted him to wrap himself around me. I wanted . . . oh, I so wanted him.

I froze. My eyes snapped open. What was I thinking?

"Hush," he murmured, his voice dark and husky like honeyed chocolate. "Sleep, sweet Lucinda, sleep."

Sleep? My head filled with cotton-ball clouds; yes, I needed to sleep. I relaxed against him again. He hugged me and my head began to spin, slowly at first, then faster and faster and then—nothing.

"Hush, you'll wake her," Jinx said.

"One of us will have to release her, you know," Jamie said.

"Why?"

"Because she can't belong to both of us." Jamie sounded exasperated and I knew I should let them know I was awake, but this I wanted to hear.

"Why not?"

"You'd share?" Jamie asked.

I felt Jinx shrug.

"Human's aren't into polygamy," Jamie said

"I think you'll find they are, brother. They just pretend they aren't."

"She may choose one of us over the other."

"It is she who bears our marks, not us hers."

"She's very independent."

"I like that about her."

"So do I."

"Well then, that's settled," Jinx said.

It was difficult trying to pretend to be asleep when I actually wanted to kick both of them. I was no one's slave. *How about sex toy?* that little voice in my head said.

My eyes snapped open and Jinx grinned at me. "I told you she'd wake up."

I could feel Jamie's laughter as a rumble against my back, so close was he pressed to me.

I frowned at Jinx. "Was that all for my benefit?"

His smile widened and he flashed those impossibly white teeth. "You decide," he said, then kissed me on the forehead and in one fluid movement jumped onto his feet. "Come," he reached out a hand to help me stand, "we need to move on."

Jamie's lips brushed the back of my head and he too leapt up. He also reached out his hand. I looked from one outstretched palm to the other. Was it some sort of test? I reached out, took both and let them pull me to my feet.

Both were smiling and it occurred to me that maybe belonging to two such handsome men—well, all right, *demons*—wasn't such a bad thing. As long as they realized who really was the boss we would get along just fine.

I looked up and they were both studying my face. "What?"

They exchanged one of those glances I was getting so used to. "She's smiling like the cat who's got the cream," Jamie said, looking puzzled.

"Or the *Mona Lisa*," Jinx added quizzically.

Their expressions made my smile grow even wider as I bent down to pick up the blanket. Yes, as long as they realized who was the boss, the three of us would get along just fine.

"Where's Pyrites?" I asked, as I was packing up the last few bits and pieces onto the chest.

"He's gone hunting," Jamie said. "He had a long flight yesterday and will have another today so he needs to feed."

"Where are we going?"

"To the next range of mountains: the further we are away from Baltheza's court, the better."

"Will Amaliel Cheriour come after us?"

Jinx laughed out loud. "He and his men are probably still licking their wounds."

"You beat them?"

"Of course," Jinx said, as though the answer was obvious.

"I don't think they were expecting us to join in the fight," Jamie said. "If they had, they wouldn't have made such an obvious attack."

"They thought you would stand back and let them take me?"

"They must have known we wouldn't," Jamie said, a frown clouding his features. "You bear our marks."

Jinx's smile was thoughtful. "I think we might have been played."

"What do you mean?" I asked.

"Baltheza is insane, so there is no rhyme or reason to anything that he does. Amaliel, however, knows the law," Jamie said. "He would know that he would have to parley with us to discuss terms."

"Not if she had committed treason," Jinx said.

"He didn't read us the charges; he just attacked."

Jinx stared at him for a moment. The torches' flickering flames reflected in his eyes making them burn with gold and green fire. His tail curled around and gave a little twitch, then quivered before waving back and forth as if on a current of air.

I was about to ask what he was thinking about when there was a thump against the outside of the cavern that causes pieces of rock to clatter to the floor and plumes of dust to fill the air. Pyrites staggered into the cavern, shaking his head from side to side.

"Stupid creature," Jinx said. "He must have come in too quickly and hit the side of the mountain."

Pyrites gave another shake of the head and then began to transfer his weight from foot to foot. Jamie and Jinx looked at each other again.

"What is it, boy?" Jinx asked, laying his hand on the drakon's snout.

Pyrites gave a rumble deep in his chest and a puff of gray smoke erupted from his nostrils.

"Someone's coming," Jamie said.

"Friend or foe?" Jinx asked.

The drakon dipped his head and purred.

Both demons let out deep sighs. "Friend," Jinx said to me.

"Who?" I asked.

Jinx frowned. "Mr. Kerfuffle?" he asked the drakon.

Pyrites nodded.

"Go guide him and Bob in," Jamie said, and with a flick of the tail Pyrites was gone.

"Didn't you fly in on Bob?" I asked Jinx.

"I sent him back, just in case—looks like it was probably as well."

"This certainly isn't good," Jamie said. "Something's wrong."

Jinx's head dipped again and his eyes flicked to me.

"It's too soon," Jamie said. "She's not ready."

"Ready for what?" I asked, looking from one to the other. Jamie's expression was worried, while Jinx had a strange contemplative curl to his lips and his eyes were gleaming.

"We'll see," he said.

Mr. Kerfuffle entered the cavern first with Pyrites close behind him. "Shenanigans has been arrested," he said without any preamble. "He's to be executed tonight."

"What about Leila?" Jamie asked.

"It was a close thing but in the end they believed her when she told them she had no idea he was a fugitive." The small demon gave a miserable sigh. "I should have been there—I should have been with him, but he told me to go."

"If you hadn't, then there would be two of you awaiting Amaliel Cheriour's attentions and only two of us to protect our princess," Jinx said.

Pyrites gave a disgruntled snort and puffed black smoke.

"Sorry, boy: *three* of us to protect Lucky," he amended.

Pyrites padded over to stand by my side and pushed his head up beneath my hand. "Good boy," I said, absently stroking his head though I felt sick with worry for Mr. Shenanigans. "So what do we do now? How do we rescue him?"

"The sensible thing would be for us to keep to the original plan and put as much distance between us and the court as possible," Jamie started, but I interrupted him.

"What about Mr. Shenanigans?" I repeated as the image of Dumah Dask's last moments floated through my head; suddenly I could hear his last terrible screams. "No," I said, "we must go back for him."

Four sets of eyes swung to me. "He'll be imprisoned in the depths of the castle," Jamie said. "We'd never get to him."

Mr. Kerfuffle shook his big head, his chubby cheeks quivering with emotion. "And anyway, we'll be too late. They put him to trial right away so they could execute him at once. He's to be tonight's entertainment."

"Hell's bells and buckets of piss," Jinx said.

"If we leave now, can we make it?" I asked. My heart stopped as I waited for their reply.

Jamie and Jinx looked at each other, then Jinx said, "You might on Pyrites—he's a nimble little bastard when he puts his mind to it. Jamie's quick, but not that quick, and Bob will be carrying two."

"Then I'll have to hope I can hold things up until you get there," I said.

"Lucky, you might save Shenanigans, but if you do, Baltheza will execute you in his place."

"Then you'll just have to make sure you get there in time to save me," I said. "Come on, Pyrites, we're going."

"Lucky, wait," Jamie said, blocking my way. "You don't know what you're risking."

I looked up into his blue eyes and couldn't help but smile, even though I didn't think I'd ever see my new friends again. I would never get to find out whether Jinx would live up to all those smoldering promises his eyes conveyed; I would never know if Jamie really was an angel or whether the way he could make my toes curl with anticipation meant he'd be a devil in bed. I was going to die horribly—and even worse, a virgin. I knew exactly what I was risking.

"I'm sort of guessing that Dumah had it easy compared to whatever Amaliel will have dreamed up for me . . ."

All three avoided my eyes. It was what I'd expected, but I felt cold with fear.

"Is it better that I don't know?"

"He'll want your heart," Jamie said. "He'll want it torn from your chest so he can see it lying beating on the palm of his hand."

The cavern shifted under me and I closed my eyes. When I opened them again everything was where it should be.

"Okay," I said. "I'll see you at the castle."

I turned to walk away and a hand grabbed my wrist, whirled me around and pulled me into a tight embrace. "You are mine, Lucky de Salle, and just you remember it," Jinx whispered against my hair. And then he kissed me: not a smacker like before, but a long, deep kiss that lasted a lifetime. I think I would have fallen when he released me, had another pair of hands not caught me.

"Lucky," Jamie said, turning me to face him and hugging me against his chest, "don't worry. You will have that special moment," he whispered softly into my ear. "You and I, we will share it together." And he also kissed me: a soft, gentle kiss; a kiss full of promise that seemed never to stop. I could almost see us lying naked together under a tangle of sheets, both still glowing with passion.

I took hold of his hand and reached for Jinx's. "I'll see you both soon," I said, giving them each one final squeeze, then I turned and walked out of the cavern with Pyrites following behind me.

Eighteen

I clung to Pyrites with all my strength as he flew faster than I could have imagined. Even so, I wasn't sure we would make it to the castle in time, and I didn't dare look over my shoulder to see how far behind Jamie and Jinx were. Without them I would be at the mercy of Baltheza, and he was highly likely to execute Mr. Shenanigans first and then me. I hoped with all my heart that I wasn't about to get myself killed for no good reason, but I knew I had to try and save Mr. Shenanigans—I just had to.

Pyrites kept low, skimming the tops of trees and dropping below the skyline whenever he could. I had to trust his instincts—he knew the urgency of our mission.

The suns sank in the empurpling sky, the shadows lengthened, stars began to twinkle above us and the two moons rose, glowing red. Pyrites powered on, but with every mile my heart sank lower. We weren't going to make it; I was going to be too late to save my friend. I began to pray, though to whom, I wasn't sure: *Please let me get there in time. Please, even if it means my own death. He doesn't deserve to die—he's kind and gentle and the children love him.*

Then up ahead pinpricks started to appear in the dark: the lights of the castle. We were almost there.

Pyrites circled the keep and then flew over the wall, dropped down and landed as close to the kitchen door as he could manage. As soon as his claws hit the ground and I'd jumped off his back, he shrank and hopped up onto my shoulder. I didn't stop to let myself think; I just took off and ran, past the kitchen and through the maze of corridors, all the while hearing the sound of voices, shouting and cheering, and getting louder as I grew closer.

Please, God—!

I ran into the entrance hall, where the chanting was almost deafening, and through the huge ornate doors into the great hall.

As before, the hall was lined with benches full of people. I had to push my way through those standing at the back by the doors, and I could hear Yarla Sal shouting to make himself heard above the hubbub.

"Ladies and gentlemen, your attention please!" he was crying.

I pushed my way toward the front and stopped behind the first row, where I was still hidden from view. Baltheza was sitting on his throne with Kayla sandwiched between him and Daltas. Three guards stood within touching distance, all weaponed up and in full armor.

I had been so angry with Kayla when I left, and I thought I still was—until I saw the lost expression on her face and my anger drained away. There was a violet smudge across her right cheek and circles of purple around her wrists as though she had been recently tied. I couldn't see any snakes in her hair; they must've been hiding, in fear of their mistress' life and therefore their own.

In the center of the makeshift arena I could see Mr. Shenanigans and Captain Vaybian on their knees, facing the royal party. Each had been stripped down to underclothes, and both had bloody scars across their shoulders and backs. Even so, they knelt upright: they were warriors, and as such were determined to die with as much dignity as they could. That Baltheza had tried to strip them of that dignity along with their clothes made me hate him all the more. He would *never* be my father.

Daltas had a supercilious smirk on his face. He sneered at the two demons, then leaned in close to Kayla. He whispered something to her, and though her expression didn't change, I could see her fingers tightening on the arm of her chair; that told the story: whatever he had said to her was cruel—I didn't need to hear the words, I could feel her pain from across the room.

"Ladies and gentleman of the court," Yarla Sal said, "silence please!"

At last the yelling and chanting quieted to a low murmur and the Master of Ceremonies beamed his approval. "We have come to the final entertainments of the evening!" he cried, which elicited some groans of displeasure, even a couple of boos. He raised his hand, asking once again for silence. "But fear not, for this will be a real highlight."

He moved across the arena to where the two demons knelt. "These two who kneel before you are traitors," he roared, and the crowd roared back.

"Yes, ladies and gentlemen, these are traitors who have conspired against our great Lord Baltheza—"

There were more roars of disapproval from the crowd.

"—and these traitors," he said, "were offered the chance of freedom if they would just give up the whereabouts of their coconspirators, but—they would not." The Master of Ceremonies moved around them and walked up to the front of the dais. "Our great lord offered them freedom, despite their crimes against him. How magnanimous is that?"

The crowd grumbled.

"And what did they do, ladies and gentlemen?" He paused for effect then, shook his head in mock amazement. "They threw it back in his face!"

His expression became solemn. "Even so, our great lord was willing to give them one last chance. He offered them death by mortal combat; one against the other, and . . . *they refused.*" He sounded astonished.

The crowd wailed with disappointment.

"I know, ladies and gentlemen: it was a great opportunity, an act of kindness, and yet they would not fight."

Kayla's eyes were on Vaybian, and although she was trying very hard to hide it, I could see her despair shining through. She really did love him—and by getting him executed, and presumably me too, at some point sooner rather than later, Daltas would get his way: he would marry Kayla and become de facto heir to the throne.

"Don't get mad, Kayla, get even," I murmured.

I peered around me, but there was no Jinx and no Jamie—I knew they couldn't possibly have got there yet, so I really was on my own. I turned back just in time to see Yarla Sal raise his hand for quiet.

"And now, without further ado, let's hear it for the demon we've all be waiting for, the demon who makes these evenings so special, our very own High Court Enforcer and Corrector—the great Amaliel Cheriour."

The spectators fell into an uneasy silence as Amaliel Cheriour emerged through the door at the other side of the arena. There were some half-hearted cheers, though it was clear that he was certainly not the most popular person in the room.

Kayla reached out and touched Baltheza's sleeve. Her lips moved. I couldn't hear her words, but I could see what she said—I had learned to read the lips of the dead at a very young age, so words from the lips of one I knew so well were as clear as day.

"Father, I beg of you," she said.

"Give me your whore of a sister and they will go free," he said with a malicious grin, and then rose to his feet. "My people," he said, with a sweep of his arm in Kayla's direction, "my daughter has asked that I spare these two criminals, and I would gladly do so—except for one thing: she will not tell me the whereabouts of the instigator of this treason." He moved to the front of the dais. "Know this, Captain Vaybian: you are to die because my daughter will not give up her harlot of a sister. A woman who this very day, in her absence, was convicted of crimes against me and my kingdom." He turned to Daltas and gestured that he join him at the front of the stage. "Know also that before your body has even grown cold, my daughter will wed Lord Daltas."

"No," Vaybian cried and struggled to stand, but the guard behind him stepped forward and gave him a brutal swipe across the head with his armored fist. Vaybian fell back to his knees.

"Lord Cheriour, you may begin. Start with this one if you will," he said, gesturing at Vaybian, and returning to his seat.

"Pyrites," I whispered to the drakon still perched on my shoulder, "if it all goes wrong you must save them if you can." He nuzzled my chin. "I know," I said, stroking his snout, "but I have to do this. Hide in the crowd, and if you have to roast all of them to get Mr. Shenanigans and Captain Vaybian to safety, do it. Understand?"

He purred again, his huge eyes staring into mine as if trying to make sense of it all. I could feel tears building up, but I couldn't afford to look weak; I had to be strong.

"Go now," I said, and kissed him on the snout.

He puffed a little smoke, then he flew up into the rafters and lost himself among the shades of the long dead.

Amaliel Cheriour was making a great show of considering the two demons before him. He gestured to one of his robed henchmen, who hurried to his side and handed him a viciously serrated blade.

He took a step toward Vaybian and I stepped out of the crowd. "Get away from him!" I cried.

"Lucky?" I heard Kayla murmur.

I turned to Baltheza. "You asked that Kayla turn me in: well, here I am."

"Traitor," Amaliel Cheriour hissed.

I gave him what I hoped was a haughty glare. "So I'm told, although I have not the faintest idea what I am supposed to have done to deserve such an accusation."

Baltheza pulled himself up out of his chair and walked to the front of the dais to stare down at me. "You conspired to murder me, then steal my throne."

I laughed. "I don't even like this place!" I gestured around the court with an exaggerated wave. If Amaliel could play to the crowd, so could I—and I had one advantage: the crowd didn't hate me. "I didn't ask to come here, and I'd very much like to go home."

"So you say," said Amaliel.

I gave him another look. "This is nothing to do with you so go back to whatever stone you crawled out from under and stay there."

The crowd gasped, and a murmur of what could have been reluctant approval rippled around the hall.

I turned back to Baltheza, ignoring the Corrector and hoping he wasn't about to take the law into his own hands and stab me between the shoulder blades. "I have come here to hand myself in, at my sister's request. My understanding is that these two will now be released." I pointed to Mr. Shenanigans and Captain Vaybian.

Daltas sidled up to his ruler. "They've been found guilty of treason. They must both die."

"I think Lord Baltheza knows the laws of his own court," I said. "And where's your evidence?"

"We have evidence in the form of witness testimonies and letters—as you would know if you had attended your court summons!"

That stumped me for a moment. How could they have found something that did not exist? Of course, I wouldn't have put it past Daltas to plant "evidence." I snorted. "I did not receive a court summons. And I think, with the exception of Kayla's father, we all know I'm not the one plotting against him."

He licked his lips. "She's trying to trick you," he whispered to Baltheza.

"No, not me. I'm not the one into trickery—Lord Baltheza," I called, "I believe you are a man of your word." Actually, I didn't believe that for one minute, but I hoped he wouldn't want to look bad in front of his people. "Will you release your prisoners in exchange for me?"

Baltheza frowned and I held my breath. "It is true that I promised my daughter their lives if she gave you up to me."

"Well then, here I am. Let them go and I'll come peaceably."

"You are in his court, surrounded by his guards—you will be taken, peaceably or not," Daltas said.

I managed to summon up one of my bitchiest smiles. I had learned it from Kayla. "What's the matter, Daltas? Things suddenly not going the way you planned?"

A murmur ran through the crowd. Baltheza's frown grew deeper; his face was clouded with confusion. He thought for a few moments then, with a grunt, waved a dismissive hand in the direction of the kneeling demons. "Release them," he said and turned to me. "You're under arrest."

"No, mistress," Mr. Shenanigans shouted as he struggled to his feet, "you can't do this."

"It's all right," I called, "I do understand what I'm doing."

He would have argued more, but two guards grabbed him and frog-marched him out of the hall, Captain Vaybian following behind. All I could do was hope that Baltheza would keep his word.

"Well, well, well, Lucky de Salle," a voice said from behind me, "I always knew I'd get a taste of you one day."

I froze. I hadn't planned on Henri being here—idiot that I was, I hadn't given him a thought. I swallowed hard and turned to him, hoping that my expression didn't give away my fear and revulsion. "Henri, how very unpleasant to see you again."

He smiled, his pointed teeth prominent in his otherwise human face. "I've been so looking forward to us meeting like this." He raised his eyes to Baltheza. "May I?"

Baltheza smiled and gave a brusque nod.

"But, my liege," Amaliel said, "surely it is my duty to—"

Baltheza waved his arguments aside. "It was he who brought Lord Daltas proof of the plot against me; I think it only fair that he should have the honor of finishing it."

Henri stroked my hair and lifted a handful to his face, sniffing it. He ran his fingers across my cheek and I tried not to flinch, but failed, making him chuckle to himself.

Then he stopped, his eyes narrowed and his brow furrowed. His eyes shot up to his master. "It is true," he said. "She bears the mark of both the Guardian and the Deathbringer."

Daltas smirked at him. "Why, my good fellow, I could almost believe you're afraid."

Henri's nostrils flared and he glanced back at me. "She's also pure," he snapped.

"I thought that was the way you liked them," Daltas said, sitting back down and arranging his jacket around him.

Henri glared at his master with open animosity, but he held his tongue.

Amaliel sniggered. "Still want her, boy?" he said. "Still think you're demon enough?"

It was very odd to see Henri so suddenly unsure of himself. "Lord Daltas?"

"You wanted her," Daltas said with a sneer, "and now you have her. Don't tell me you're afraid of those two relics?"

"I fear no one," he announced loudly, "least of all them."

"Then don't keep us waiting: finish her."

"Don't you see what he's doing?" I said to Henri. "He's used you, and now he's throwing you to the wolves. If you kill me, the Guardian and Deathbringer will demand retribution."

"I doubt they even care," Daltas said, looking around theatrically. "If they did they'd be here—and if they really did care, I think you would have lost your virtue long since."

"Father, please," Kayla said, "don't let him hurt her. She has done nothing—*nothing*."

"She has plotted against me," he said, sitting down and folding his arms across his chest. "She wanted me dead so you and Vaybian could rule." He turned his attention to Daltas. "Tell your man I want her heart, and if he doesn't have the stomach for it, maybe Amaliel can see to it that he has no stomach at all."

Henri's eyes widened and then he turned on me with a snarl.

"No!" Kayla screamed.

Before I could react, he flung me across the arena and I hit a pillar on one side of the dais, smacking my head hard enough against the stone for me to see stars. Then he was upon me, grabbing my wrists in one hand and forcing them up above my head, pinning me against stone. I struggled against him, but he was so strong; he lifted me with no effort at all, so my feet were dangling uselessly, then as he smiled his razor-toothed smile and pushed his face closer to mine the sweet scent of Parma violets washed over me.

I tried not to scream, but when I saw those pointed teeth glistening with drool I couldn't help myself, and that made him laugh, whatever initial worries he'd had apparently long forgotten. His tongue slithered out and across my face. Although I tried to pull away from him, I was trapped; whichever way I turned his tongue was there, licking me, *tasting* me.

"Stop him!" I heard Kayla scream. "I'll do anything you want, but stop him."

"Too late," Baltheza said. "Not so long ago you told me she loved you with all her heart. Now she's going to prove it."

I heard Kayla scream "No!" as Henri tore open the front of my shirt. Leering at me he snagged a claw under the front of my bra and tugged until the material gave way with an elastic twang. He ran a claw down my left breast, scratching, but not cutting.

Now I really was struggling with all my might, pushing my feet back against the pillar and trying to propel myself forward. But nothing I tried was doing any good; it was only because Henri was prolonging my terror that I wasn't yet dead.

I could hear Kayla screaming and crying in the background, then a sibilant whisper of voices groaning, "No, nooo!" made me open my eyes to see the little spirit I had seen leading Dumah toward the rest of the dead. It was followed by a host of others, drifting across the hall toward us, their faces contorted in despair.

"Say goodbye, Lucky," Henri told me, dragging my eyes back to him.

"Don't do this. Please, don't do this," I whispered, and once again I heard the ghostly figures moan.

Then there was a roar from behind him and a blast of burning-hot air. Henri let go of my wrists and swung around, holding me in front of him, as Pyrites, now the size of a baby elephant, gave another roar and stomped toward us. Henri's grip around my throat had loosened, but he had pulled me tight up against him with his other arm pressed beneath my breasts.

"Stupid creature," he called. "You roast me and you roast your mistress."

Pyrites puffed more steam and then sat back on his haunches.

"Kill me and he'll see you burn," I managed to gasp as I began to struggle again.

"Not if the guards kill him first," he said.

I jerked my head around to look at him and he gave me a supercilious smile before beckoning to Baltheza's guard.

"Pyrites, go!" I shouted, "get out of here—"

Then there was a shout from the back of the hall and the rapid shuffling of many feet on flagstones as the crowd opened up to reveal Jamie and Jinx pushing their way through to the front, swords drawn and looking as though they were prepared to use them.

Jinx drew alongside Pyrites and rested one hand on his flank, holding his sword in the other as if daring the guards to come closer. Jamie stood on the other side, sword extended.

One of the guards who was braver than the rest—or maybe more foolhardy?—came at Jamie, sword raised, but before he could strike, Pyrites snorted out a blast of flame, turning the blade a glowing red, and the demon dropped it with a shriek, waving his already blistering claw in the air to try and cool it. The other guards backed away: an angry drakon was bad enough, but adding a Guardian and a Death-bringer into the equation? That was apparently too much for them and they weren't about to risk themselves, and certainly not on Henri's say so.

Henri pulled me tight to him again, and this time I could have sworn I felt him trembling. Jamie and Jinx moved a little away from Pyrites and stepped just in front of him, then they advanced.

"Let go of her, Henri," Jamie said, but the demon began to edge away, dragging me with him. Though I fought him every inch of the way, it was no good; I just wasn't strong enough to make him drop me. I realized he was pulling me toward the door that led into Baltheza's private dining room—if he got me in there and managed to lock the doors, I was done for.

"If you don't let her go there will be nowhere in this world or the next where you will be able to hide," Jinx said. "I will find you and I will kill you, and if you think Amaliel is creative with his methods, you have no idea how much more imaginative I can be."

Henri's hand clutched my throat and he began to squeeze. "Come one step closer," he told my advancing guard, "and I will rip out her throat. She will be dead before she hits the ground."

"And your screams will echo around these halls for eternity," Jinx said.

"Lord Baltheza," Henri said, "tell them I am carrying out your bidding."

I glanced toward the man who said he was my father. "She has committed and been found guilty of treason. The law says—"

"Baltheza," Jinx said, and even in my state of panic I could hear the menace in each syllable, "believe me when I tell you that if you allow the *murder* of this woman—because that's what it would be—no law here, or in the Overlands, will save you from my wrath."

"Even you have to obey the law, Deathbringer," Daltas said, "so save the dramatics."

Jinx glared at him and Daltas suddenly found his shirt cuffs very interesting.

Henri's fingers tightened even further around my throat and I threw myself from side to side in a desperate effort to make him loosen his grip, but to no avail; I was fast beginning to see stars.

Henri gave a cry of triumph: he had reached the door. I couldn't scream, I could barely breathe, and darkness was closing in all around me. I couldn't fight him anymore.

Someone called my name—was it Jamie, or was it Jinx? My eyes flickered shut, and all of a sudden recent images of my life flashed through my mind: I saw Jamie unfurling his wings for the first time; Jamie dressed in a suit looking nothing like the Jamie who had arrived on my doorstep in jeans and a hoodie. I saw Pyrites, lying there in the stable the first time I saw him, so big he could have eaten me with one snap of his jaws. Then Jinx, my sexy bad boy, dancing me across the courtyard; Jinx rising up out of the bath, eyes closed, swiping the water from his face; Jinx taking my hand and folding the jeweled dagger within my fingers.

The dagger.

My hands were hanging by my sides like lead weights, but I forced them to move. I dragged my fingers up my hips and felt for my waistband and the belt. At last I felt cold metal beneath my fingertips. *Come on, Lucky, come on . . .* My fingers curled around the dagger's handle.

I heard something—something important? Was it a door opening? It didn't matter; nothing mattered besides the dagger. I pulled it from the scabbard and hoped I could hold onto it.

"Say goodbye, Lucky," Henri said, loosening his grip on my throat, and as I desperately sucked in air, the darkness that had been enveloping me began to recede a little. The dagger felt solid in my hand and the fear chilling my heart was replaced by a baser emotion: an overwhelming desire to survive. My fingers tightened around the dagger's jeweled handle, I raised my right foot and with as much strength as I could I stamped down upon the daemon's instep, then I brought my left elbow back into his gut, just as hard. Henri gave a yelp, his hand slipped from around my throat and I spun around, swiping out with the dagger and praying I wouldn't strike thin air.

A terrible screech went up, and although I didn't feel the dagger connect with anything solid, it must have done as my ice-cold fingers were instantly wet and warm. My vision still hadn't completely returned, but I could see well enough to make out a figure staggering away from me.

I stumbled toward it, the dagger raised, but before I could strike again I was gathered up into a tight embrace and the dagger taken from me; there was a bright flash, a terrible scream and the smell of burning pork.

"Good boy," I heard Jinx say. Then there was a soft kiss on my temple and another on my lips.

Then I began to shudder.

Jamie and Pyrites closed in on us from either side while Jinx held me as I trembled, but we were not out of the woods yet for the palace guards were advancing toward us, albeit reluctantly.

"You will release the woman into the care of Amaliel," Baltheza said, and gestured with his head toward his Chief Enforcer. The creature glided toward, but as he did so, several of his ghostly victims floated past him to stand between us, their hate for him twisting their features into masks of distaste and anger.

"The law is quite clear," Jinx said.

"A subject bearing the mark of a higher demon cannot be harmed or assaulted by another without consent," Jamie continued.

"She has been found guilty of treason," Amaliel said and laughed: a horrible sound that was like a death rattle. He reached out to grab my arm. "Even those so marked must pay the penalty for such a crime."

His fingers grazed my wrist, but with a sharp intake of breath he flinched away as Jinx pushed me behind him. Glowing eyes peered at me from within the folds of his cowl and Amaliel hissed something and turned to Jinx with a muttered gasp.

"What did he say?" I whispered to Jamie. "Did he say Soul Seer?"

"We have to get her out of here," Jinx said urgently to Jamie.

"Arrest her, you idiots," Amaliel said, gesturing to the guards who were still hanging back, no doubt preferring that the High Court Enforcer and Corrector deal with us rather than risk being roasted themselves.

"You'll have to get past us first," Jinx said, raising his sword.

"You are not above the law," Amaliel snarled once again, "and to attack the palace guard would be a severe contravention of that law, Deathbringer."

"It's true," Jamie said, in a low voice. "We can't break the law."

"Even to save Lucky?" Jinx said, but I could tell from his tone he knew Jamie was right.

Pyrites puffed steam and Jamie laid a hand on his flank. "No, boy, they'd hunt you down and kill you."

The palace guards, realizing our dilemma, began to move toward us again, this time with more confidence.

"There must be a way," Jinx muttered, then his lips curled into a triumphant smile and he stepped forward, causing Amaliel to lurch backward rather than be touched by him.

Jinx sheathed his sword. "Keep hold of her hand and rest your other upon the drakon," he said to Jamie as he grabbed hold of mine. He took another step forward, threw back his head and with arms outstretched cried, "*Omnes dormieris.*" His voice went ringing throughout the hall.

The echo of his words still hung on the air as the light drained from the chamber and it fell into shadow. The temperature grew frigid and a cold breeze caressed our skins. Within moments our breath had turned into small clouds of smoke.

I looked around in confusion. Although the ghostly figures of the dead were still milling around the hall it looked like everyone else was frozen in time: the guards had halted midstep, and even Amaliel was unmoving, locked in position staggering away from Jinx's advance. Only his robes stirred slowly, caught in the icy draft invading the hall.

"Come on," Jinx said, his voice sounding overloud in the eerie silence.

Jamie still holding my hand strode toward the entrance, with Pyrites padding along beside us, his head swaying from side to side as he looked out for danger.

Jinx hurried across to Kayla and touched her forehead with his finger. Her eyes blinked and she glanced around in bewilderment. "What . . . ?"

"No time," Jinx said, grabbing her by the hand and pulling her up from her seat. "Come on." She didn't argue but hurried along by his side.

When we hit the entrance hall we began to run. I clutched at the front of my shirt, trying to hold it closed and preserve at least a modicum of modesty, while Kayla hitched up her long skirt and hung it over her arm to free her legs from the heavy material.

Pyrites shrank to the size of a large bird and flew ahead of us, still puffing steam and scanning the corridors for potential trouble, though every person we came across had been afflicted by the same condition as those in the great hall. Maids carrying trays were as still as statues and guards marching through corridors were all halted midstride. Everywhere was silent, fractured only by the sound of our footsteps as we ran, until we reached the kitchen. As we passed the door I could hear the rattle of lids upon pots as their contents bubbled and spat and wisps of smoke and steam escaped from the crack beneath the door, tainting the air with the aroma of something boiling over and burning on the stove. I had a feeling there would be a few burned saucepans to be accounted for by the end of the day.

Nineteen

We didn't stop running until we reached one of the outer walls, and it was there Kayla decided we needed to split up. She wanted to find Vaybian and the rest of her guards—I could understand that, but she was my best friend and I didn't want us to part like that, not when there was still so much bad feeling between us.

"I know you have to find them," I said, "but there's so much we need to talk about—"

"We will talk, soon," she promised, hugging me, "I promise—but right now I have to get Vaybian out of here."

"What will you do?"

"We'll have to hide out somewhere for a while until Father gets over his tantrum and begins to see sense. Vaybian's family has a villa in the mountains. We should be safe there—for a while, at least."

Kayla turned to Jamie. "You will look after her?"

"You know it," Jamie said.

"Make sure you do."

"I'll see you soon," she said, and kissed me on the cheek.

We watched her hurry away into the shadows. She looked back once, raising a hand in farewell. The snakes weaving in and out of her hair became motionless for a moment, their little black eyes fixed on me. I waved back then turned away; we had to get out of there too and find somewhere safe to regroup, but I swear I could feel those beady eyes following me even when Kayla must have been long gone.

Jamie and Jinx took us straight to the Drakon's Rest, where we would meet Mr. Kerfuffle and, I hoped, find Mr. Shenanigans.

Leila led us to a hidden back room where we would be safe for long enough to work out what to do. Mr. Shenanigans and Mr. Kerfuffle were already there with a flagon of wine; the huge demon was in a far better state than I had expected after his ordeal, but we were all still anxious. Who knew what would happen when Baltheza woke up—and how long would they stay frozen anyway? Though Jinx assured us we had some time.

While Mr. Shenanigans and Mr. Kerfuffle went to gather some provisions together I started asking questions.

"What did you do to the court, Jinx?" I asked, pouring myself some of the wine.

He looked at me. "Sleep and unconsciousness are only varying levels of death, and as neither Jamie nor I could strike out at the palace guard within the palace walls without breaking the law, I did the only thing I could think of that would allow us to escape while causing no one any harm. I put them to sleep—or more accurately, into suspended animation."

"Why didn't you do that before? The day Amaliel and his men attacked us?"

"Even I'm governed by the laws of life and death and each act outside those laws has a consequence. When I call upon my skills to bring a layer of death to our world anyone nearby who is close to death could bear the brunt. I didn't dare risk Shenanigans."

I lifted my goblet to my lips, then paused, remembering something Amaliel had said to Jinx. "He called you a Soul Seer. What's a Soul Seer?"

"Soulseer," Jamie said, pronouncing it like sightseer.

"He wasn't talking to me," Jinx said. "A Soulseer is nothing like a Deathbringer; it's a completely different demon altogether."

They both looked at me as if they were waiting for something.

I thought about it for a moment, and then it dawned on me. "He was talking about me," I said. "*I'm* the Soulseer." I'd always known Jamie and Jinx had been keeping a lot from me, but this?

Jamie said reluctantly, "A Soulseer is one who can see the souls of the dead. They're very rare. The last one was millennia ago."

"Hang fire," I said, "Kayla could see the dead in my world and Henri could see the twins at the school and you most definitely saw Balmy Bill at the pub."

"That's different. We were like the spirits—not of your world. So we could see them as they could see us. Here it's different. I can't see the dead of this world and neither can Kayla."

I glared from Jinx to Jamie and back again.

"Look, it's no big deal," Jamie tried. "You were unusual in the Overlands—turns out you're just as unusual down here."

Put like that, I supposed he was right. "So, that's it? I'm a misfit in both worlds?"

"Other than the added danger being one here brings, it makes no difference."

They both gave me guileless, sunny smiles, but color me suspicious: I wasn't buying it. I couldn't get anything more out of them, though, and that was what settled it: I had to go back to my world, for at least a few days—or maybe even more permanently. I needed some space to think.

Jamie was not at all happy about taking me back home and in the end it was Jinx who convinced him, although he wasn't any happier about my decision, just more pragmatic. I told them I needed at least a week, maybe even as long as month, but at the end of that time I would give them my decision, one way or the other. It might be that I would never return to the Underlands for longer than a few days. I didn't want to leave them—of course I didn't—but their world wasn't my world. And anyway, they were still keeping secrets from me—or at least being very selective with the truth—and I was getting fed up with it.

Twenty

It was dark outside when I arrived back at the cottage. Jamie stayed long enough to make sure I hadn't been robbed or acquired squatters and went to great lengths to reiterate all the arguments he, Jinx and the others had used to try and make me stay in the Underlands. The one that had me almost changing my mind was when Jinx pointed out that if anyone in the Underlands really wanted to make an unsanctioned visit to my world and come after me they could. They would just have to be patient. Eventually some stupid person would dabble in something they shouldn't, like the girls at the school or Kayla's Satanists. Of course if Baltheza decided to send an assassin I was fucked. Jamie's parting shot was, "You won't last five minutes here all alone."

I was being unreasonably stubborn and I knew it, but it didn't take me very long to realize I probably *had* made a mistake. My cottage was tiny, but it felt like I was living in a vast, empty mansion. Every unexplained sound had me grabbing for my dagger or the hundred and one knives, hammers and other dangerous objects I'd stashed around every room.

Then I opened the fridge, and surprise, surprise, there was nothing edible there, leaving me with no choice but to force myself to drive the car to the supermarket to stock up. Wandering through the store all by myself set me thinking of Jamie and Kayla and our shopping trip together, and that made me even lonelier.

By the evening of the fifth day my nerves were a jangling mess and I was missing them all so much I felt like I was going crazy. I made myself a coffee—if I started drinking alcohol I might not stop, a dangerous thing to do in my present predicament—but I'd already run out of milk, so I had to take it black. The novelty wore off halfway down the mug and the rest ended up down the sink.

I opened the fridge again. An unopened bottle of Muscadet beckoned to me, but I slammed the door shut before it could seduce me. Later, maybe, but not at one o'clock in the afternoon . . .

My biggest problem—apart from being a wanted woman who was likely to be arrested for treason the moment I set foot back in the Underlands—was that I wanted to be with my friends. But I knew, despite their denials, that they were keeping something from me, and I didn't know how far to trust them because of it.

Of course, that meant I had even more questions—but now there was no one to answer them for me, no matter how evasive the answers might be.

Then I began to worry they might all decide they were better off without me: after all, it was because of me that Mr. Shenanigans had almost been killed, and he and Mr. Kerfuffle were probably still wanted men despite Baltheza's promise of a pardon—and as for Jamie and Jinx; they were likely to be in all sorts of trouble for helping me.

I started to pace: to the living room, then the hall, back upstairs to my bedroom, sit down on the bed, stand up. Use the bathroom; back to sit on the bed. Get up and go into the office to check my nonexistent emails—much to my chagrin no one appeared to have even noticed I'd been gone, though it proved Jamie right—and back to my bedroom. Sit down at the dressing table; pick up my hair brush, turn to the mirror . . . very, *very* slowly put the brush back down.

"Hello," I said, and her lips said it back to me.

I swallowed, and I saw her do the same. I took a sharp breath; so did she.

"You can't be here," I said. "This isn't your world."

And it was then that I realized it wasn't mine either, not anymore.

I looked down at my hands. They glowed pink. I lifted a strand of silken hair. It was eggplant.

"Oh my, Lucky de Salle, now you really do have something to worry about," I said to my reflection, and she smiled.

I ran my hands down my body, but I felt the same. I supposed I should be grateful that I hadn't grown a third boob or sprouted horns— small mercies. With this thought in mind, I ran my hands over my forehead, just to be certain.

I stomped downstairs: the siren call of Muscadet was growing stronger by the minute. I caught a glimpse of myself in the hallway mirror as I passed and did a double-take, then I stopped and peered properly at my reflection: my human reflection.

I felt a disconcerting glimmer of disappointment. "Lucky, you're losing the damn plot," I told my image.

"They do say talking to oneself is the first sign of madness," a voice said from the kitchen.

I jerked around.

"Jamie!" I cried, and took a step toward him, but he crossed his arms and gave me a look.

"Okay, okay, you were right," I admitted, "I've felt lost, scared and lonely without you, Jinx and the others around me."

His stern expression creased into a smile and he grinned at me. "Come here," he said, opening his arms.

I walked across the hall and leaned against his chest, wrapping my arms around him. He cupped my head in his hand and I could feel his lips against my hair.

"Do you think Jinx or I would let you leave us so easily? We've missed you."

"I've only been gone a few days."

"A few days too long. Pyrites is already pining for his mistress."

"Really?"

"He's given himself to you; without you he's incomplete."

Poor Pyrites; if only he could exist in my world. Then I frowned as a thought crossed my mind. I pulled away from him. "You wouldn't be trying to make me feel guilty, would you?"

Jamie's eyes opened a shade wider. "Pardon me?"

"You know exactly what I mean: Pyrites will pine away if I don't return to the Underlands? I'm surprised you haven't mentioned Jinx— and what about Mr. Kerfuffle and Mr. Shenanigans? I suppose they'll both be joining the demon equivalent of a monastery?"

Jamie cracked a smile. "Mr. Shenanigans has taken to staying at the inn of late, and as for Mr. Kerfuffle, he is seeing rather a lot of a kitchen maid at that same public hostelry."

"Good! I'm glad to hear their love lives are improving."

"Of course, there's also Philip. If you're to return him to your world—"

"Poor Philip," I said automatically, although I wouldn't ever forget what he had tried to do to me. "Where is he now?"

"I don't know and I don't actually care." I was about to argue then realized I couldn't. Philip had brought all his misfortunes down upon himself.

"Am I still wanted for treason?"

"I'm afraid so, and that's one of the reasons you should return; to clear your name."

"Or I could stay here."

"You could, but you're a wanted woman whether you're here or in the Underlands. Daltas or Baltheza might decide to try and get you back again to face the charges. Then of course there's Henri. You and Pyrites left him in a pretty bad way; how long do you think it'll be before he comes back to the Overlands seeking revenge? At least in the Underlands you have five guards to protect you."

Sadly he was right. I wondered whether I'd ever feel safe anywhere again. I certainly hadn't felt safe for the past five days.

"Of course, there is another reason why you should return." His expression grew serious as he pulled me back into his arms and his lips brushed against my cheek: a gentle kiss.

"And what would that be?"

"I made you a promise," he said, and for once he appeared a little unsure of himself.

"You did?" I said, thinking hard. He'd promised to protect me, and he had tried, despite my best efforts to wreck his attempts. "I don't . . ." Then I remembered another soft, gentle kiss, and a heartfelt whisper: "You will have that special moment. You and I, we'll share it together." And the image of Jamie and me lying naked under a tangle of sheets floated through my head, closely followed by another: and this time there were three of us curled up together and I was sandwiched between my beautiful angel and my sexy, irreverent demon.

I smiled up at Jamie and he smiled back: a knowing smile; a smile full of the promise of pleasures to come; a smile that left me in no doubt that he too had shared my vision.

His world was a strange and frightening place, but mine wasn't much better. In his world I had enemies, dangerous enemies, but I also had friends—good friends—friends who would die for me. I couldn't say the same in my world.

Maybe it was enough to know that.

I rested my cheek against his bare chest. "If I come back with you where will we go? What will we do? Won't you and Jinx be criminals too?"

"I never said it would be easy, but even though Baltheza is bordering on bonkers he's not totally stupid—and he'd have to be if he seriously thought he could charge Jinx and I with treason."

"I don't really have much choice, have I?"

"No," he agreed and gestured toward the front door.

When I turned around, I started: there was a blank void where the door used to be and the perfect black nothingness looked as scary as Hell.

"There's nothing to fear," he said. "Just close your eyes and hold on tight."

I did as he said, wrapping my arms around him. He lifted me up, took two steps forward and almost immediately we were falling. Wind whistled past my ears until his wings unfurled and we glided for a few moments before alighting on the ground.

I stood there enveloped in his arms, feeling safe and strangely calm, and finally I opened my eyes and looked around me. We were standing in the middle of a field with the light of the two red moons shining down upon us: an alien landscape, but no longer alien to me.

"Welcome home," Jamie said, hugging me to him.

There was a shout somewhere in the distance and two dark shapes started hurtling through the night sky.

Jamie raised a hand in greeting as Bob pounded toward us, Jinx astride his back, while Pyrites darted ahead, a plume of fire preceding him.

"See: you have been missed," Jamie said, releasing me and throwing his arm across my shoulders as we stood waiting for our friends to join us. "Have you missed us?"

I smiled up at him. I'd missed them more than he would ever know. Or maybe he did; after all, he appeared to know exactly what I was thinking most of the time. If he did know, he'd be happy. This world wasn't my home yet, but I had a feeling it could be. The last time I had been in the Underlands I had spent most of the time yearning for the safety of my little cottage, and yet when I had returned to it, I'd found there was nothing for me there.

Perhaps there was here.

As Pyrites came into land, he shrank and scampered over to me to rub his snout against my knees, while Jinx leaped from his black steed and ran toward us with a huge smile and his arms flung wide. A feeling of contentment swept over me, along with a sense of belonging—and I realized that it was the first time in my life I had ever felt like this. So perhaps Jamie was right: maybe this was now my home.

I was sure of one thing: despite the dangers, unless I gave it a chance, I would never find out.

Acknowledgments

To my dad, Jack, who inspired me to write, my mom, Ruby, who read every word I put to paper and would have been so thrilled to see me in print. Thanks to Howard for the kick up the backside that made me get started and actually do it, even though I probably scowled at him at the time.

Also thank you to Liz Bahs—you taught me a lot—and Toni, Curly Sue and Kate for your encouragement and support.

Last but by no means least I would like to take this opportunity to thank Nicola and Jo for having faith in me and being so very, very patient. Thanks, guys.

Turn over for your bonus content!

Interview

"Mr. Sal, Mr. Sal!" the court reporter shouted as he ran down the corridor after the court's Master of Ceremonies. "Mr. Sal—a moment of your time, just a moment."

"Get lost you little scumbag," one of Yarla Sal's bodyguards snarled over his shoulder.

"Mr. Sal, all I want is a brief interview for the palace news sheets."

"Shall I give him a thrashing?" asked another of the guards.

Yarla Sal gave an affected sigh, slowed down and then stopped. After a moment's hesitation, as if debating what he should do, he turned to the reporter. He flicked his straw-blond fringe back from his brow with long, lilac hued fingers and asked, "what do you want?"

"Just a few words about what happened this evening. I'm sure our readers would love to hear your take on it."

"I doubt half the riff-raff can actually read," he drawled. In slow, deliberate movements, he straightened the cuffs of his shirt beneath his scarlet and gold jacket.

"If they know it's an interview with you they'll get someone to read it to them," the reporter said. "After all, you're the great Yarla Sal, they all love you."

A smile tugged at the Master of Ceremonies's lips. "Yes, they do, don't they."

One of the guards raised an eyebrow, while one of the other two pretended to stick two fingers down his throat.

The reporter quickly looked away from the guards with a suppressed smile and pulled a small wad of parchment from his breast pocket, and a quill from the bag hanging from his belt. "Obviously you were there and saw it all?"

"The whole terrible travesty." Yarla Sal answered.

"Travesty?"

"Henri attempting an execution. It was preposterous, darling; I could have done better myself."

"Except you don't like getting your fingers dirty," one of the guards muttered.

If Yarla Sal heard the comment, he ignored it. "And letting two convicted felons go—what was that all about? I mean, treason is treason."

"Goes without saying," the reporter agreed, but there was a hungry look in his eyes. "So, you think the execution of the two daemons"— he flipped through his small book of parchment until he found what he wanted—"Vaybian and Shenanigans should have gone ahead?"

"If you try a person for treason and they're found guilty, what other choice do you have? By pardoning them you are either admitting they were scrap to catch a drakon, or, even worse, admitting they were innocent."

"And what do you think should have happened?" the reporter asked.

"I'm not paid to think, darling," Yarla said with a sniff, "if I were, I'd give Amaliel Cheriour some kind of makeover: the audience hates him; he needs to give them something a bit more than red glary eyes and bloodthirsty executions."

"You think they hate Amaliel?" the reporter sounded astounded and gave Yarla a wide-eyed look of surprise, but inside he was grinning. This was getting better and better.

"Have you not attended an execution? Have you not seen the way the crowd edges away when he enters?"

"Well I—" but Yarla was on a roll.

"If it wasn't for me, these events would be total disasters darling. Total. Disasters." He sneered. "*I* keep the audience on a high, despite Amaliel's best efforts."

"So, are you saying Amaliel Cheriour should be sidelined?"

"Not sidelined." Yarla wasn't quite that stupid. "He should just keep doing what he does best: tracking and catching miscreants, obtaining confessions and then leaving the final executions to fully trained professionals who have an aptitude for show business."

"Like . . ." the reporter hesitated, "*you?*"

Yarla's nose wrinkled in distaste. "Don't be ridiculous."

The guard who had muttered the earlier insult nudged the guard next to him and mouthed the word, "see?"

"So, who would deal with the executions?"

"The Royal Guard, of course," Yarla said, as though he found the question idiotic. "I'm sure they'd love the chance to do something useful—"

"Unlike guarding puffed up imbeciles," a guard muttered behind his hand.

"—and they'd step up to the challenge with alacrity—"

"If *he* was the first victim, I'd enjoy it even more" the guard's friend whispered back, gesturing toward Yarla. The guards were looking rather disgruntled.

Yarla Sal was oblivious to the negative reactions of his bodyguards. "Amaliel could maybe make an appearance and then leave, but to be quite frank he brings the proceedings down, so maybe he should just get a mention at the beginning and leave it at that."

The reporter's quill raced across the page, scribbling down every word. *When Amaliel sees this he's going to bust a gut—and probably not his own!* But Yarla Sal was only just getting started. "Maybe we should even take the whole execution thing to the masses."

"What do you mean?" the reporter asked, glancing up with pen poised.

"Well, if the populous actually saw the executions . . . for one"—he counted off, striking the forefinger of his left hand with the long curved talon from his right—"they would see what happens if one disobeys the law and two: they would have a really good time."

"You think?"

The guards were all wrinkling their snouts with distaste. "Perhaps they could place bets," one said with a disgusted grimace.

"What a good idea," Yarla said, clearly not sensing the mood. "I'll put it to Lord Baltheza. It would be a good way of raising revenue."

The guard who'd made the suggestion threw up his claws in disgust.

"Mr. Sal, we really should be going. Lord Baltheza is waiting," another of the guards said.

"Yes, yes, of course, of course," he said with an irritable wave of his fingers. "Have you enough?" he asked the reporter.

"Oh yes," the demon said, pocketing his wad of parchment. "More than enough."

"Make sure you send me a copy," Yarla Sal said over his shoulder as the guards hurried him away.

The reporter grinned after him. Oh yes, he would send him a copy all right—and another to Amaliel Cheriour. He was sure the Chief Executioner would just *love* to hear the Master of Ceremonies's ideas for a new format. It was only as the reporter walked away that he realized Yarla Sal had not given him any information on what had gone so terribly wrong at that evening's execution.

He pulled out his parchment and flicked through the pages. No matter, this was great stuff and if it didn't add fuel to the already growing animosity between Amaliel and Yarla, he'd eat his reporting parchment, quill and all. He could interview someone else for the real news story—this was the better piece.

Oh yes, after this went out on the streets he could see the desire for news from the court heating up quite a bit. He strode back down the corridor, whistling. He just *loved* celebrity interviews and the resultant fallout. They made his job worth doing.

Read All About It!

"Oyez, oyez, oyez. Read all about it! Read all about it!"

Shenanigans woke to a hubbub of noise from the street below and Leila shrieking out through the window: "Keep the damn noise down will yer; some of us are trying to sleep."

"What's going on?"

"They're pinning up news reports about something or other. No doubt your recent *companions* and your close escape will be mentioned in it somewhere," she said.

He shuffled up the bed to lean against the headboard. "If it wasn't for Mistress Lucky I wouldn't be here now. I'd be another of Amaliel Cheriour's victims."

"If it wasn't for *Mistress Lucky*, you wouldn't have found yourself arrested in the first place."

"Ah, calm down," he said, and patted the empty space next to him. "Come back to bed."

"Not 'til I've found out what all the excitement is about," she said, then stalked out of the room.

As she stomped down the stairs, Shenanigans wondered whether he might as well get up. He had a feeling that once she'd read the news, she wouldn't be in as exuberant a mood as she had been the night before, after he had quite literally been plucked from the jaws of death.

The clomp of her feet on the way back up the stairs was even more disheartening; her steps were slow and heavy. Then there was a snort and she started to laugh, which made him smile; maybe his luck was in after all. Her footsteps sped up and then Leila came through the door in a rush, kicked it shut behind her and bounced up onto the bed beside him. She thrust a piece of parchment under his nose.

"You've got to see this," she said, but before he could take it she snatched it back and began to read.

"'The court of Lord Baltheza was in disarray last night after two convicted felons were given pardons for their crimes and another escaped justice.'"

"Felons?" Shenanigans said with a wrinkled brow. "It makes me and Captain Vaybian sound like a common thieves."

Leila continued reading. "'Yesterday morning, a plot to murder our great lord was uncovered by Henri le Dent, servant of Lord Daltas. It was alleged that the instigator of this terrible conspiracy was none other than Lady Lucinda, the—until recently—estranged daughter of our great lord. The aforementioned lady was immediately put to trial in her absence and found overwhelmingly guilty of treason.'"

"By 'overwhelmingly' they mean Henri *fucking* le Dent stood up and said 'I believe Lucky de Salle has hatched a plot to assassinate Lord Baltheza and put her sister and lover on the throne'; then Baltheza asked 'is this true?' and Henri said 'yes' and that was it."

"There must have been more to it than that?"

"Not much. Only Daltas whispering his lies to Baltheza. By the time he'd finished doing so, Baltheza was so het up I doubt he much cared who'd done what. He probably only knew that someone should be made an example of."

"Yes: you and Captain Vaybian."

"She saved us, Leila. She gave herself up for us and she needn't have."

"She probably didn't think Baltheza would order her to be executed instead," Leila said with a haughty sniff.

"She did. Ask Kerfuffle; he was there when the Guardian and Death-bringer told her Amaliel would want her heart."

Leila turned her attention back to the parchment. "'Captain Vay-bian, of Princess Kayla's guard, and Mr. Shenanigans, of Lady Lucin-da's, were both sentenced to death as coconspirators in the plot, but were offered pardons if either they or the Lady Kayla would tell the court the whereabouts of Lady Lucinda. All three refused, saying they had no inkling as to where the lady might be, but just as the sentence was about to be carried out, the lady in question gave herself up. Our great lord honored his promise of pardon to the two demons Vaybian and Shenanigans and commanded that the Lady Lucinda be executed in their stead.'"

"This is as dull as ditchwater," Shenanigans interrupted, "what was it that made you laugh?"

"The palace correspondent interviewed Clarice and Gordo. You know Gordo, the giant with the extra eye."

"I know him, not sure about Clarice."

"Long auburn hair, very bad complexion."

"Ah, I know who you mean. What did they say?"

Leila sat up straight and fluttered her eyelashes. "'Ohh it was so awful,'" she said in a high-pitched falsetto.

"Gordo doesn't talk like that."

Leila gave Shenanigans a nudge in the ribs. "'Ohh it was awful,' *Miss Clarice Valdemion* told our reporter, 'Henri le Dent was about to tear out the woman's heart right before our eyes when the Guardian and the Deathbringer turned up. Then there was a total brawl. Everyone was threatening everyone else and meanwhile, Henri was choking the life out of the poor girl.'"

"Poor girl?" our reporter asked, "she was convicted of treason."

"Trumped up, I heard," Mr. Gordo Gavistump added.

"Miss Valdemion carried on, 'then when I thought the girl—'"

"Lucky de Salle?" our reporter confirmed.

"Yes, yes. Lucky de Salle. 'When I thought she was surely a goner, she stabbed the little shit—'"

"Henri le Dent?"

"Yes, Henri, 'she stabbed Henri and then her pet drakon gave him a good roasting and I must say it couldn't have happened to a finer fellow! Nasty little pile of dung.'"

Leila dropped the parchment on the bed and slipped under the covers beside Shenanigans. "No one likes Henri much, do they?" she said.

Shenanigans put his arm around her shoulders. "Can you blame them?"

"Well, by all accounts he's going to be out of commission for a while. It says here he was burned up good and proper."

"Good."

"That's not very charitable."

"More charitable than he deserves. It's a pity Pyrites didn't finish him off."

Leila slid down so her head was resting on the pillow and smiled up at him. "We've got half an hour before I have to be up and about," she said with twinkling eyes, as she twisted a strand of lilac hair around her forefinger.

Shenanigans shuffled down to join her. "Let's make the most of it while we can," he said, pulling her into her arms. At that precise moment the door flew open.

"Shenanigans!" Leila's younger brother and sister cried as they ran across the room and jumped onto the bed, followed by Angela and Teasel, their adopted siblings.

Leila and Shenanigans exchanged a look and Leila burst out laughing as the kids clambered over his huge bulk and snuggled down in between them.

"Shenanigans, tell us a story! Tell us a story about the Overlands!" Oddy, Leila's brother asked.

"Yes tell us a story. Please," the others cried.

Shenanigans sat up and pulled the pillow behind his back. "All right, all right," he said. "Let's see. Where shall I start?" He tapped a talon against his lips. "I know." He smiled down at the expectant faces. "Once upon a time, in a land far away, there lived a lucky, lucky lady . . ."